THE LION AND THE ROSE

THE LION

AND

THE ROSE

JANE OLIVER

G. P. Putnam's Sons   *New York*

© 1958 by Jane Oliver

FIRST AMERICAN EDITION 1959

Library of Congress Catalog
Card Number: 59-7848

For
PATIENCE ROSS
who made so much difference
to this story by believing
I could tell it

ACKNOWLEDGMENTS

MY MOST grateful thanks are due to Lord Elibank, C.M.G., D.S.O., for his inspiring interest and his kindness in reading the book in typescript; to Lt.-Col. H. A. B. Lawson, Rothesay Herald and Lyon Clerk, for his valuable assistance on points of heraldry; to Mr. Robin Laing for supplying me with data of exceptional interest on the Queen's ride from Jedburgh to Hermitage, which he had himself undertaken under conditions as near to those of the original expedition as the twentieth century could produce; to Dr. C. A. Malcolm of the Signet Library, Edinburgh, for answering an inordinate number of questions and lending me some important books; to Mr. Noel Poynter of the Wellcome Historical Medical Library for his expert guidance on the vexed topic of the illnesses of the Queen and Lord Darnley; also to Dr. H. P. Tait, Hon. Sec. of the Scottish Society of the History of Medicine; and Dr. M. H. Armstrong Davison, for letting me have a copy of the paper read on *The Maladies of Mary, Queen of Scots and her Husbands,* by the latter, before the Society.

I should also like to thank Miss Jean Mackenzie for the most helpful loan of lecture notes on Queen Mary, delivered by her sister, the late Dr. Agnes Mure Mackenzie; Miss Kathleen Burne for the loan of books; the authorities of the London Library for their usual unsurpassed service; and Mrs. E. D. Lukens for her illuminative criticism and arduous work on an almost illegible typescript.

CONTENTS

CHIEF CHARACTERS

[*as they appear, or are first mentioned*]

MARY, QUEEN OF SCOTS since the week of her birth, in December 1542. Her father, King James V, died soon after the Scottish defeat at Solway Moss, and his French Queen, Marie de Guise, sent her daughter to her kinsfolk in France for safety at the age of five, and acted as Regent of Scotland till her death in 1560. Mary, married to the Dauphin at sixteen, was Queen of France as well as Scotland for a few months in 1559, between the death of her father-in-law and that of her young husband. But afterwards the hostility of her mother-in-law, Catherine de Medici, became so distressing that Mary was glad to accede to the urgent petition of the Scottish leaders and return home, a widow of nineteen, two years later. In Scotland, Protestantism had been recognised as the national religion by Act of Parliament in 1560, but as the reformers were still numerically a minority, its future hung in the balance.

As the representative of the royal house of Stewart (which she had learnt to spell Stuart in France) Mary was sure of a tremendous welcome, but the task of ruling her divided country obviously demanded the utmost diplomacy. The country's Protestantism dismayed her less than its poverty, for she was both tolerant and compassionate. And at first she trusted her ambitious half-brother, Lord James who conducted a campaign against the Catholic house of Huntly, soon after her arrival, on a charge of high treason, and was rewarded with the Earldom of Moray. She had not yet been disillusioned in December, 1562, when Chapter I begins.

ANDREW MELVILLE, devoted Master of the Scottish Queen's Household at Fotheringhay at the time of her death. Sir Andrew's family of Scottish gentlefolk was typical of many whose traditional loyalty to the Crown had been set at odds with their sincerely Protestant convictions by the return of their Catholic Queen. His brother Robert tried to compromise, his third brother, James, soon turned against the Queen.

JAMES HEPBURN, 4TH EARL OF BOTHWELL, a staunch Protestant, yet an absolute loyalist to the Crown, even when worn by followers of the older faith. Held hereditary offices of Lord Admiral of Scotland, Sheriff of Lothian and Lieutenant of the Border. Served the Queen Regent, and afterwards Queen Mary, against the Anglophile party subsidised by Queen Elizabeth's astute Secretary of State, Sir William Cecil. Was twenty-seven in 1562.

LADY JANET HEPBURN, Bothwell's sister, married to LORD JOHN OF COLDINGHAM, the Queen's youngest half-brother and the most lovable of King James V's bastards. Lord John was thirty in 1562. Protestant.

ANNA THRONDSEN, daughter of a Danish admiral and former mistress of Bothwell.

ARCHIBALD CAMPBELL, 5TH EARL OF ARGYLL, Lord Justice of Scotland. One of leaders of Protestant party. His Countess, from whom he was estranged, was one of illegitimate daughters of James V. He would be thirty-three in 1562.

THOMAS RANDOLPH, English Ambassador to Court of Holyroodhouse.

LORD JAMES, Stewart by courtesy, and most ambitious of King James V's bastards. Sought to rule Scotland over his half-sister's shoulder. Thirty-three in 1562. Protestant.

JOHN MAITLAND, LAIRD OF LETHINGTON, Secretary of State at the Queen's return, and the most brilliant man in Scotland. In his thirties, he was at first delighted by the Queen, but when his vanity was wounded he turned against her, doing incalculable damage to her cause before returning, too late, to his allegiance. Protestant.

GEORGE GORDON, afterwards 5th Earl of Huntly, Protestant son of the " Cock of the North," leader of the Scottish Catholic party, who had been hounded to his death on a charge of treason soon after Mary's return.

MARY SETON   The Queen's devoted Maids of Honour, all of
MARY LIVINGSTONE   an age with herself, who went with her, at five
MARY FLEMING   years old, to France, and returned with her to
MARY BETON   Scotland, fourteen years later.

LADY DOUGLAS, former mistress of King James V, mother of the Earl of Moray, and widow of Sir Robert Douglas, Laird of Loch Leven.

JOHN KNOX, the fiery genius of the Scottish Reformation and leader of the Kirk party.

MATTHEW, 4TH EARL OF LENNOX, exiled for treason in her father's reign, and recalled from England by Mary. Catholic, with occasional expedient phases of Protestantism.

HENRY STEWART, LORD DARNLEY, his elder son, also oftener Catholic than not. Darnley's claim to the crown of England came through his mother, Margaret Douglas, who was the daughter of Margaret Tudor (sister of Henry VIII and widow of James IV of Scotland). Since he and Mary were both Tudor grandchildren, their marriage united their claims so that their son was Queen Elizabeth's most obvious heir. All Mary's diplomacy was vainly directed towards persuading Elizabeth to admit this.

JAMES, DUKE OF CHATELHERAULT, head of the house of Hamilton, and heir to the throne of Scotland (as great-grandson of James II, whose daughter, Mary, had married Lord Hamilton) until the birth of the Queen's son. Catholic, with Protestant expediencies. About fifty in 1562.

JAMES, EARL OF ARRAN, his son. About twenty-three in 1562, and already showing signs of the madness which was to eclipse his early promise. Protestant.

JOHN HAMILTON, Catholic Archbishop of St. Andrews.

JAMES DOUGLAS, 4TH EARL OF MORTON, head of the powerful and supremely ambitious house of Douglas, and therefore Darnley's kinsman on his mother's side. In his forties in 1562. Protestant.

DAVID RIZZIO, a middle-aged Piedmontese secretary who had come to Scotland in 1561 in the service of Count Moretta, Ambassador to the Duke of Savoy, and remained there, first to organise the music in the Queen's Chapel, and then to act as her confidential secretary in charge of her foreign correspondence. Catholic.

LORD ROBERT " Stewart," secular Abbot of Holyrood. Lazy and negligible. Another of James V's bastards. Protestant.

THE LADY OF MORHAM, Bothwell's widowed mother, and formerly Countess of Bothwell till his father, anxious to make a better match, " discovered " their marriage to have been within the prohibited degrees.

SIR ALEXANDER HEPBURN, Bothwell's kinsman and loyal supporter. Protestant.

JOHN, 4TH EARL OF ATHOL, leader, after Huntly's downfall and death, of the Scottish Catholics, who relied on France for support, as the Protestants turned to England.

LORDS SETON
       SEMPILL
       LIVINGSTONE   pro-Catholic supporters of the Queen.
       BORTHWICK

EARL OF RUTHVEN (married to a Douglas). Protestant. Hostile to the
       Queen.

EARL OF GLENCAIRN, Protestant, but at first a Queen's man.

EARL OF MAR, hereditary governor of Stirling Castle and guardian of
       the heir to the Scottish crown. At first neutral, later hostile to the
       Queen on account of his Lennox sympathies. His wife, Arabella
       Murray, and her brother, John Murray of Purdovis, were also Lennox
       supporters.

GEORGE DOUGLAS, called "the Bastard of Angus," an ex-priest and
       illegitimate brother of Darnley's mother, Lady Lennox. One of the
       vilest men in Scotland, though perhaps outclassed by

SIR JAMES BALFOUR, another ex-priest-cum-lawyer, the most nimble
       turncoat of the century, both in religion and politics.

JOHN LESLIE, Catholic Bishop of Ross. A Queen's man.

ADAM BOTHWELL, Protestant Bishop of Orkney. Unrelated to the Earl
       of Bothwell.

ALEXANDER GORDON, Protestant Bishop of Galloway.

LORD HOME, Scottish Warden of the Eastern Marches.

SIR JOHN FORSTER, English Warden of the Eastern Marches and deputy
       governor of Berwick.

LORD HERRIES, Scottish Warden of the Western Marches.

THE MASTER OF MAXWELL, his son. Both Catholic.

LORD DRUMMOND, the Queen's host at his castle near Perth, where the
       tragic love story of James IV and Margaret Drummond began.

GEORGE BUCHANAN, Latin scholar and former priest turned Protestant.
       Queen's tutor in her classical studies, at first lyrical in her praise and
       afterwards venomous (and quite inaccurate) in her defamation.

ARCHBISHOP OF GLASGOW, Scottish Ambassador in Paris. Catholic.

M. DU CROC, French Ambassador in Scotland. Worked strenuously for
       reconciliation between the Queen and Darnley, and between the
       Queen and the rebellious nobles. Catholic.

COUNT MORETTA, Catholic Ambassador of Savoy, one of the European
       powers pledged to advance the Counter-Reformation and extirpate
       heresy by all available means.

SIR WILLIAM KIRKCALDY OF GRANGE, a professional soldier. He sided against the Queen after her marriage with Bothwell but returned to his allegiance, though too late, in disgust at the excesses of the Confederate Lords. Was hanged after the capture of Edinburgh Castle, in which he held out for Queen Mary after she had taken refuge in England. Protestant.

WILLIE DOUGLAS, the boy who contrived the Queen's escape from Lochleven Castle.

LORD CLAUD HAMILTON, the over-confident young leader of the rescue party who afterwards led the Queen's army into the fatal ambush at Langside.

PREFACE

THOUGH the dust of almost four centuries lies thick about them, the sorrows of Mary, Queen of Scots, still haunt her people. Every now and then someone is driven to protest at the accusations made against her, as if, to the listening ear, the truth still cried from the ground.

As far back as I can remember, the accepted version of the Mary Stuart story never rang true. The theory imposed on the people of sixteenth-century Scotland by means of an insidious and anonymous smear-campaign which decorated the public buildings of Edinburgh with defamatory posters, was that Bothwell, with the consenting knowledge of the Queen, was responsible for the explosion which caused the death of her husband, Lord Darnley, at Kirk o' Field, during the small hours of the night of Sunday, 9th February, 1567.

I have never believed it. Nor, it seems, did many people in Scotland until the slanderous campaign conducted by the Queen's enemies had done its work. But how Darnley's body, reputedly blown out of the Provost's House and half across the garden by the violence of the explosion, was subsequently discovered without a mark on it, the story does not attempt to explain. It was not until I had read Mr. Gore-Brown's book, *Lord Bothwell,* however, that I realized how flimsy the case against him looks, in the light of our bitter modern knowledge of brain-washing. For it was built up on the statements wrung from his tortured servants, who were not only unable to read the statements they were alleged to have made against their master, but were afterwards executed immediately they had made their mark on them, for fear, presumably, of subsequent recantation of the stories which, incidentally, contradict each other at almost every point.

The whole tragedy, in fact, begins to look remarkably like a frame-up, devised by people who, for various reasons, urgently desired the Queen's ruin and used the vainglorious Bothwell to procure it. I do not deny that Bothwell could probably have saved Darnley's life that Sunday night, when a hint reached Stewart of Traquair, Captain of the Queen's Guard at Holyroodhouse, of a plot to blow up the Queen and all the members of her Council who were later to have escorted her back to Kirk o' Field on Darnley's earnest entreaty. Since the Queen and her husband were known to have been on the worst of terms for some time, such an idea did not seem unlikely, and her officers persuaded the Queen to remain at Holyroodhouse with Traquair to guard her, while Bothwell took a party to search the cellars at Kirk o' Field.

This search seems never to have been made. My theory is that, somewhere between Holyroodhouse and Kirk o' Field, someone gave Bothwell a broad hint that if he let matters take their course, the gunpowder would be put to better use than had originally been intended. Always appreciative of rough justice, Bothwell turned back, and when the explosion rocked the city he was found in his bed at Holyroodhouse, over a mile away. Could he, in the days before time-bombs, have contrived such an alibi and yet lit the fuse?

Even if he did, it does not seem possible that Darnley was killed by the explosion. His body was found in the garden, barefoot and in his night clothes only, unmarked by fire or violence, though his entire lodging had been reduced to rubble. His page, found dead beside him, had apparently taken time to grab a few clothes for his more terrified master before following him into the winter night. Evidence was later given by women living near that they had been roused by the arrival of armed men before the explosion, and heard Darnley cry aloud for mercy: "Have pity on me, kinsmen, for the sake of Him who had pity on us all!" It will be recalled that

Darnley's mother was a Douglas, also that the Douglas faction had never forgiven him for his desertion and betrayal of their part in Rizzio's murder. Darnley had more vindictive enemies in Scotland than the Earl of Bothwell, and suffocation can be a very quiet death.

But why, in the middle of a winter's night, did he leave the house at Kirk o' Field at all? No picture of him as the innocent victim of a plot fits into the pattern. If he anticipated violence from enemies outside the house, why did he not rouse his servants to barricade the doors and windows against them? On the other hand, if he had been roused by the smell of burning, and *knew* that gunpowder was lodged in the cellars, he might very well have left the house in such haste that he did not even stop for his shoes, though his page, lacking such terrifying knowledge, did. And if he knew, does it not make him look more like an accomplice than a victim?

Regarding the Casket Letters, as Sir Edward Parry says in his book, *The Persecution of Mary Stuart,* "The discovery and production of the Casket Letters, to use a phrase dear to the hearts of old lawyers, 'smells of fraud.' " And yet, having read them many times, I think the Queen's enemies probably had some material to work on. As the Scottish historian Patrick Fraser Tytler puts it, "the conduct of the Scottish Queen throughout the whole investigation was that of a person neither directly guilty nor yet wholly innocent."

This exactly expresses my own conviction, and I have sought to hold the balance of this astonishing story steadfast between those two extremes.

J.O.

PROLOGUE

January, 1587

PROLOGUE

K NOCK, knock, knock. . . .
The homely tang of hammer on nail, the snarl of saws
driven through timber, even an off-key whistle from one of the
men at work, were nightmarish as the painted smile of a child's
doll among the ruins of its home. The little group of exiles,
in their faded, shabby clothes, winced as if the hammer-blows
were falling on their flesh. Only the stout, middle-aged woman,
round whose high-backed chair their tragic glances eddied,
remained serene. Her little dog slept in her lap, flicking
an ear occasionally when the frayed edge of her black velvet
sleeve tickled him as her rheumatic fingers laboriously pushed
an embroidery needle in and out of the canvas stretched
across the frame before her. As the door opened, she slowly
raised her head and twenty cruel years fell from the heavy,
colourless face beneath the auburn wig as her shadowed eyes
smiled.

" Come in, dear Melville." Her welcoming gesture was
gracious as a falling leaf, though the rigours of imprisonment
had deformed the hand that made it. The singing voice was
hoarser nowadays. But it did not tremble. " Come and talk
to me. They are putting up my scaffold in the hall below.
The noise is—tedious."

" Madam . . ."

Sir Andrew Melville, Master of the Scottish Queen's
attenuated household at Fotheringhay, could say no more.
But the Queen patted the stool beside her chair as he stood
rigid. " This is no time for ceremony, Sir Andrew. We are all
friends here, and you look weary. Do you bring—news? "

Sir Andrew folded his long legs on to the square, four-legged
stool, topped with its exquisitely embroidered cushion. " No,

23

Madam," he said thankfully. A little sigh drifted towards them as the men and women in attendance ceased to hold their breath.

She turned the heavy frame towards him. " Then tell me what you think of my embroidery."

" Madam," said Sir Andrew awkwardly. " I fear I am but a poor judge of such things——"

" But this is a hunting scene, of which you should know more than I. Examine it carefully."

Sir Andrew leant forward to study the piece of tapestry before him. It showed a wounded deer which had shaken off the hounds from its torn throat, taking a prodigious leap from the edge of a ravine into the mist-hung distance, across which a rainbow arched.

" Are the colours true? " the Queen asked anxiously.

" Indeed, Madam, I believe they are," said Sir Andrew gently.

She nodded. " I am glad of that. But one corner is not quite finished. I have no more brown silk for the rocks."

" It might be that I could obtain some. Yet Sir Amyas is not——"

With a little grimace, she agreed. " It does not matter now. I have done so much embroidery since I left Scotland that my fingers are all corns. I shall be glad to rest them. The story of these eighteen years in England is stitched into the work, Melville. The bolster you are sitting on—no, do not move—I was making it when they brought me news that Edinburgh Castle had fallen to my enemies, with Lethington dead of poison and Kirkcaldy of Grange hanged at the Market Cross."

" Right ill was your Grace served by both," said Melville sadly.

" And yet they repented of it, and died for their allegiance at last," she said. " Strange that they should all have gone before me in the end. All the regents—Moray, Lennox, Morton and Mar—who ruled Scotland in my place. And all by violence, save the last. They are remembered in the cushion of the prie-dieu yonder, where I have so often prayed for grace to forgive my enemies. Ah, but there—" Her voice rose eagerly. "—is the footstool I was working when I had the first letter my son ever writ me by his own hand. It was a noble, loving letter, yet it is the postscript I remember, because it made me laugh." She was laughing again at the memory as she quoted carefully:

" 'I commend to you the fidelity of my little ape, who never stirs from me. I will often send you news of us.' He was thirteen, Melville. But afterwards his false advisers turned him against me——"

" I remember," Melville said heavily.

" I had no more such letters."

They sat for a while in silence. The Queen fondled the silky ears of the little dog asleep in her lap, her face suddenly taut, her eyes widening at the sight of the elaborate fire-screen on the far side of the hearth. Yes, she had been working on that design of Perseus rescuing Andromeda from the monster when they told her that James Hepburn had gone mad in his Danish prison. They said afterwards that he had made a full confession. But of what? She never knew. Nor what, once they had driven him out of his mind, they hoped to learn from it. It had been three more years before news came of his death.

For that deliverance she could still thank heaven, as the memory of his harsh voice broke over her, fierce and anxious, after more than twenty years. " *Madam, I have the uttermost horror of imprisonment.*" Ten years for James. Eighteen for her. Eighteen years of hope deferred, escapes thwarted, plots detected; years ghastly with the ashen faces of the men who had died for her. And dear Seton, she would have died too, broken by the years in those fetid prisons, had she herself not commanded her most devoted servant, on her allegiance, to return to France forthwith. And now, at last, it was her own turn to die.

" Sir Amyas took down my cloth of state when the news of the sentence came," she said tonelessly.

Sir Andrew Melville frowned, jerking back his head to stare at the wall behind her. She had hung her crucifix where her cloth of state had been. " As a dead woman, Sir Amyas explained, I had no right to the honours and dignity appropriate to a Queen. He tore the silk in his haste, which grieved me. I would have commanded my people to take it down rather than see him spoil it. It was my best work. Do you not think so, Melville? "

" Your Grace has made so many beautiful things," said Sir Andrew uncertainly. " It is hard to choose."

" I took special pains over my cloth of state," she said. " I hoped . . . it would serve my . . . son."

Her eyelids drooped on the last word. Sleep, which now eluded her aching limbs at night, often came on her unawares by day. The leaping deer in the embroidery frame seemed to swim before her into the torn achievement of the royal arms of Scotland in full heraldic colour, below which her own cryptic motto, in the French which still came to her more easily than her native tongue, streamed scarlet on its banner of gold.

" ' *In my End is my Beginning* . . .' " she murmured. Her chin fell forward, the loose flesh below it folding as her muscles relaxed. " *My Beginning* . . ."

Comforted by Andrew Melville's compassionate presence, her eyelids fluttered once or twice. She would have liked to discuss the old days with him. But she was so tired . . . so . . . tired. She sighed deeply. As she slept, the past like a great stone, was rolled away.

PART ONE

December, 1562—February, 1565

" Gules, on a chevron argent, two lions
pulling at a rose of the first."

*From the coat of arms of James
Hepburn, 4th Earl of Bothwell*

CHAPTER ONE

HOW suddenly darkness had fallen on the sear land. Almost, thought James Hepburn wryly, as if one of the giants of the old tales had snuffered the December sun with his helm. He paused in the lee of a great rock to strip off his crimson doublet and wring out the salt water with a couple of deft twists of strong, unexpectedly beautiful hands. Then he tugged it philosophically on again over his clammy shirt, hitched his sword-belt tighter to constrict his empty stomach, and set off along the beach. The pale frill of foam was barely visible as he trudged through the winter evening towards Scotland, moving with long, supple strides and whistling the tune of a bawdy French ballad through his teeth.

He was making for the one place where, without the price of a meal in his pouch, he could look for fire and food and laughter, and no inconvenient questions asked of a man who had broken ward. Admittedly, his recently married sister's new home was over ten miles up the coast from the anchorage where the storm-battered vessel in which he had hoped to reach France now lay. But this disconcerted him not at all. Born a Scottish Borderer, and fourth Earl of Bothwell since his father's early death, the contempt for physical hardship which his upbringing had given him had often proved useful during the varied adventures of twenty-seven years. It had given him, too, an almost catlike ability to find his way among hills, even across frontiers and past such fortifications as those of Berwick, in the dark. Moving like a shadow among shadows, James Hepburn at last stood outside the walls of the Priory of Coldingham, from which the Reformation had recently sent the monks packing, to the greater convenience of Lord John, the youngest of the late King James V's bastards, who was also James Hepburn's brother-in-law and very good friend.

There he paused for a while, humorously aware of weariness, but undisturbed by it as he looked up at the bright windows from which floated the medley of sounds proper to a household still celebrating the twelve days of Christmas in spite of anything Master Knox might say. Fiddles were sawing in the great hall, scullions singing raucously over the slosh and clatter of the washing-up in the vaulted kitchens below. But James was more interested in the oblongs of soft light from the second floor which indicated that the laird was using the smaller private rooms above. So John and Janet were not joining in the noisy gaiety? It was perhaps natural in a young couple who had not yet been married a twelvemonth. James fancied them holding hands in the candlelight as the year of their bridal swung towards its close, and grinned at the prospect of interrupting their sweethearting.

It would have been easy enough to hammer on the iron yett and order the shambling old porter to announce the arrival of a belated guest. But a man in Hepburn's uncertain position might do better to arrive unobserved. It amused him, too, to choose the more devious, somewhat melodramatic way of appearing, like a demon from one of the forbidden mystery plays, as if Hell had gaped to spew him forth.

Patiently, therefore, he waited for the moment when the old porter, troubled by the chill of the winter night, would shuffle from his gatehouse to relieve himself in the courtyard. Then, during the few minutes when the old man's attention was not on his duties, James slid past, taking the spiral staircase in great bounds, to reach the second floor almost without drawing breath. Softly he depressed the thumb-hold of the latch.

The chamber within was gloriously warmed by a great pyre of logs on the hearth. But beyond the firelight's range everything was shadowy. On a sideboard candles waited unlit in silver candelabra which had once beautified the Lady-chapel of the Priory. Three people, not two, were seated about the blaze. James Hepburn paused, the draught swept past him, and they shivered. Impulsive as ever, Lord John was at once on his feet.

"Heaven save us, does the old fool below suppose it to be midsummer?" he cried indignantly. "I'll have him——"

Then he caught sight of the silent figure in the doorway, and the sentence ended in the shriek of a drawn blade. James Hepburn raised open hands, laughing.

"Hold hard, John. Keep that skewer of yours for less friendly guts. Surely you know me?"

"James!"

Lady Janet's hand went to her mouth as the word left it. Like an apprehensive child, she turned in one curtseying movement of entreaty to the tall young woman in black velvet who had neither spoken nor moved, her slim fingers still shielding her pale face from the leaping flames. One woman's agitation, the other's stillness, told James Hepburn the truth. In the doorway he slowly knelt, his lips barely moving in a whisper of stupefaction.

"The Queen's Grace!"

Mary Stuart turned her head very slowly, as if she were giving herself time to consider how to deal with such an outrageous situation. She had been Queen of Scots from the first week of her life, early in that December which saw the linked tragedies of Scotland's needless defeat at Solway Moss and the heartbroken death of her father, the fifth King James. But she had only returned to Scotland from France, a widow of nineteen, little over a year since. And, in a few months, she had experienced rebellion, threats of violence, rivalry for her favour and threats against her person, so that in her bewilderment she had been thankful to delegate her authority to the most ambitious of her father's bastards, her half-brother James, giving him the Earldom of Moray which his ambition craved, in unwary gratitude for the elimination of the Catholic Earl of Huntly on an unproven charge of high treason. And

since the Earl of Moray had also imprisoned the young man
who now knelt before her, she surveyed him coldly.

"What does this mean?" Even in anger, her low voice
was beautiful.

"Madam, I ask your pardon——" Breathless with agitation, Lady Janet knelt at Mary's feet, "I beg you to believe
that neither my husband nor I knew of this——"

"Of what?" asked the Queen.

"Madam, it is my brother, James——"

"I know it. Have I not forbidden him my presence?
My lord of Moray found him guilty of treason——"

Lord John, his quick resentment boiling over, spoke from
the doorway. "Sweet sister, is it never possible for my lord
of Moray to be mistaken?"

"Surely," she flashed back at him, "this—this insolent
deception is unlikely to convince me of that? I came to your
house, brother, in the hope that you would offer me freedom
from all cares of state as you promised, here among my kinsfolk. Is it right that my confidence should be so abused? How
dared you bring a—a fugitive into my presence? Is this your
hospitality? Do you intend . . ."

Unconcerned, Lord John folded his arms and grinned.
Easy-going, pleasure-loving, unambitious, utterly unlike his
elder half-brother of Moray, he knew his royal half-sister's
fiery temperament too well to attempt excuses for his friend
till her quick anger should have spent itself. Though Mary
was incapable of bearing a grudge, she was also unable to
endure an affront. She had not been a Queen all her life for
nothing. Nor had her upbringing at the most gorgeous Court
in Europe tended to minimise her conception of the reverence
due to her crown. But when she paused for lack of breath, he
spoke quickly.

"Believe me, Madam, we were all taken equally unawares."
Lord John's sweeping gesture included his wife, his Queen and
his unexpected guest, who still knelt with bowed head, but
just noticeably shaken shoulders. Glancing questioningly at

him, Mary decided to assume that he had been chilled by the
night air. It was unthinkable that he should presume to be
amused.

"My lord of Bothwell," she said austerely, "you may
rise. But only in order to close the chamber door."

"I thank you, Madam," said James Hepburn humbly.
But there was little humility in the sweeping movement with
which he stepped across the threshold, closing the heavy
door behind him deftly, one hand at his back. And the wide-
set, blue-black eyes which questioned her were mocking.
He was bareheaded, not only out of reverence but because at
some point on his long slog across moor and moss his bonnet
had been clawed from his head by the branch of an unseen
tree, and he had not paused to grope for the elegant affair of
crimson velvet, sewn with silver thread, in which he had
somewhat fancied himself.

Queen Mary surveyed him disdainfully, and when she
spoke again it was in French. In times of stress the language
of her foster country still came to her more easily than that of
her own land.

"Explain yourself, my lord."

"Madam, what shall I say, save only that I offer my most
humble duty?"

Mary frowned, less at the meekness of the words than at the
pride with which he spoke them. She was still too angry to
notice either that James Hepburn had answered her in French,
or that he spoke it as well as she. She was more aware, now that
he knelt near her, of the splendid body outlined by the sodden
clothes that clung to it, mud-splattered and bramble-torn,
dark here and there with bloodstains, as if he had forced his
way through every obstacle that presented itself, disdaining
minor injuries as recklessly as he no doubt disdained all danger,
whether to body or soul.

"How is it that you, whom we had warded in the Castle of
Edinburgh, dare enter our presence here?"

"Madam," said James Hepburn simply, "I did not know

you were at Coldingham. I am an escaped prisoner, as your Grace has said, come to bid farewell to my kinsfolk before proceeding overseas. What knowledge could I have of the whereabouts of the Queen's Grace?"

"None," Mary admitted reluctantly, impelled by the love of justice which was to beset her all her life. She paused, frowning, checked in her rebuke. Then Lord John stepped forward, picked up one of her heavily ringed hands and laid his cheek against it.

"Sweet sister, if I now plead for my friend, will you listen? He was not alone in the project to surprise the young fool Arran in bed with his mistress with which the trouble began. Both D'Elboeuf and I were with him. And the brawl between Hepburns and Hamiltons in the High Street that followed was not of our seeking."

"That was but a prank," Mary admitted.

"Yet it angered Arran enough to make him accuse James of the crazy plan to kidnap you, his Queen, and bear you to Dumbarton. How could you believe it?"

"My lord of Moray believed," said Mary quickly.

Lord John snapped his fingers, laughing. "Believed that wild tale told by such a man as Arran who would say anything to slander a man who had made him ridiculous? Surely you would not condemn a dog on Arran's word? You know as well as I that he is now a raving lunatic, under his family's restraint."

"The evidence against my lord of Bothwell seemed good enough to those that tried his case," said Mary stubbornly.

"Yet I know my brother's loyalty to your Grace, Madam," pleaded Lady Janet, "too well to believe such a charge. Has he not been Lord Admiral of Scotland and Lieutenant of the Border since your lady mother's time? These are great honours, Madam. Why should he now seek to throw them away?"

"Why indeed?" asked Mary.

"Madam," begged Lady Janet, "will you not hear him

in his own defence? My brother may be the most perverse of
men. But at least he does not lie."

Mary inclined her head. For a moment she sat in silence,
her hands clasped almost as if in prayer. Then she looked
directly at the man before her. " My lord of Bothwell, you have
heard what has been said of you. Speak now for yourself.
Is the accusation of the plot by which you sought to kidnap
your Queen false or true? "

" False, Madam," said James Hepburn tersely.

" You swear it? "

" Madam, I swear it."

In the silence the click of falling embers, the flutter
of flames, seemed loud. Then Mary spoke, almost won-
deringly.

" I believe you, my lord."

Bothwell raised his head and looked directly at her, his
smile so changing his face that she seemed to be looking at
another creature, transfigured, like his own forlorn countryside,
by the coming of the sun.

" Yet I have still somewhat against you," Mary said, regal
again as she remembered her duty. " My lord of Bothwell,
you were sentenced to be warded in the Castle of Edinburgh
to await our royal justice. Why did you break ward and go as
lightheartedly about your business as if you were of right a
free man? "

" Madam——" Bothwell began. Then he checked the
impulse to excuse himself with an abrupt gesture.

" Speak on, my lord."

" I have the uttermost horror of imprisonment," said
Bothwell in his grating voice. " Freedom is more urgent for
me than food or sleep or firing. Without it I stifle."

" As a child it was always from dreams of chains and
dungeons that he woke screaming," said Lady Janet quickly,
while her brother bowed his head, as if he could not bear that
those about him should see one commonly accounted a brave
man so nakedly afraid.

" Do not send me back to ward," he muttered. " I would sooner wander the wide world."

" I will not send you back," she promised. " Yet I may not let you bide. It would be best for you to take up your journey again, none knowing you have been here."

" I thank your Grace." He was on his feet in an instant, ready to take his leave, it seemed, without rest or food or the chance of a change of clothes. Her raised hand checked him.

" We will forget for a little while that I am the Queen whose duty is to punish offenders. Here I am but a sister who seeks diversion among her kinsfolk. And—and also perhaps a woman who loves brave tales. They told me, my lord of Bothwell, that you loosened a stanchion from the window of your cell and climbed down the Castle rock in utter darkness. Can such a thing be done? "

" Aye, Madam, by those sufficiently set on the journey," said James Hepburn, grinning.

" You might have broken your neck——"

" Better to die than to rot." He clenched his fists. " Were I to be imprisoned beyond hope of escape, Madam, I—I should go mad——"

" Then tell me how you escaped." She indicated a stool, inviting him to draw it towards the fire. But though he obeyed, he did not at once begin his story.

" I am ever the defter at the doing of such things than at describing them afterwards," he said, running his fingers through the dark red hair which was beginning to crisp and brighten as it dried. " Yet I will adventure it, since it is your pleasure. My cell, by good fortune, looked not inwards on the courtyard of the Castle, but out over the sheer rock . . ."

Mary Stuart cupped chin on fists as she listened, quiet as a child, while he told of a stanchion prised from its place by the patient use of the dagger he had contrived to secrete about his person, till at last the bar was loose enough for him to lever it aside. But far below now cocks were calling, and the dawn threatened the night sky.

" You did not venture with so little darkness left? "

" No, Madam, I waited for the next night, fearful that though I crumbled bread and stuffed it in the socket, my guards would notice something amiss."

" They did not? "

" No."

Lord John, an elbow on the carved mantel, his handsome face in shadow, was hopefully watching his half-sister, on whom, by their father's untimely death, such a mortal burden had been laid. There were times, he thought, when it was an advantage to have been born out of wedlock. He had all he wanted, a position of some consequence, a lovely wife, and the comfortable certainty that nobody would ever call on him to rule Scotland. Why should anyone seek to be a King? Why did Moray, for instance, gloom and grab and grumble because of the bastardy that kept his head from a crown? Lord John, smiling down at his sister's intent face, fancied that he knew when he was well off.

Lady Janet, too, was watching the Queen. But her eyes were troubled. She knew James so well that she wished him a thousand miles away. At heart he was no ladies' man, to mince about in silk and satin and sigh love-ballads in the moonlight. He had always been happiest with his horses and hounds, toiling with the artificers over the mechanism of a refractory siege gun, or searching the mildewed tomes of ancient military history he had studied in Paris, for hints which would serve a soldier in sixteenth-century Scotland. Would women never realise how little they meant to him, and leave him alone?

Yet Mary was thinking less of Bothwell than of the tale he was telling. Her wide eyes, peat-brown as a Border burn, no longer saw the quiet room about her. She was aware of his deep voice, with its grating edge of mockery, disparaging his own achievement even while he described it, as his habit was. She could feel, as he spoke, the chill of the brief, moonless summer night, see the prisoner set his knee on the stone sill, heave himself up by the remaining stanchions, turn warily above the sheer drop, then lower himself to hang on his arms as he felt for the foothold that he could not see.

"And so I went down. When my foot found a ledge I would stand for a while to get breath and ease my arms. And then I lowered myself till my fingers gripped where my feet had been and I sought with my feet for a ledge below."

She could feel the harsh edge of the stone, imagine the cushions of moss, the frilling of lichen under his finger-nails. Nor did she pause to consider how strange it was that she, who had never climbed on rock, should know so surely what it felt like to hang over that fearsome gulf, muscles cramping with weariness, eyes smarting from the dust disturbed, breath aching in her chest.

"Once I dislodged a bird from its nest," said James Hepburn, "and its clamour was like to rouse the dead, let alone the men of the garrison——"

"Sweet saints," whispered Mary, "what came of it?"

"Nothing." He grinned. "I found another handhold and left the nest undisturbed."

"I am glad of that," she said.

He laughed harshly. "I left it less for kindness than because the mother bird was ready to peck out my eyes."

"While your hands grasped the rock you would have been defenceless," she agreed.

He nodded. "So I thought. But I came at last safe to the ground."

"And then?"

"I sought my mother's house at Morham."

"She sheltered you?"

"She scolded me."

"I am glad of that too," Mary said severely. But afterwards she smiled, looking about her like one waking from a dream. "I have been very well entertained, my lord," she admitted. "But we will speak no more of your adventures now. I bid you godspeed. We will remit the charge against you which you have denied, and as regards the matter of breaking ward, the Queen's Grace knows nothing. It is now my pleasure to retire. Lady Janet, your attendance will suffice till I have reached my chamber. Summon my women afterwards."

" I thank you, Madam," said Lady Janet gratefully. Sidelong she glanced at the brother whose secret the Queen was willing to keep. James was grave, but his eyes smiled as he and Lord John knelt to kiss the Queen's slim fingers, watched her pace deliberately from the room, her shadow falling across their faces as Lady Janet backed before her, holding an elaborately branching candlestick high, the flames of the hastily kindled candles streaming aslant as she went.

Left alone, the two men surveyed each other in silence. Then Lord John let out his breath in a long sigh of relief. " You were fortunate, James, that she did not order me to clap you in chains. She has an unpredictable temper. It was a crazy risk to take——"

" As heaven is my judge, I had no knowledge of her presence."

Lord John smiled. " I cannot believe, my friend, that you came here to bring us the season's greetings."

" I came to borrow money. From my sister," said James Hepburn curtly. " What I had went on my passage on that wretched hulk that is now never likely to sail again."

Lord John nodded. The explanation satisfied him. " Yet I had hoped the Queen might be moved to pardon your escape since it gave her such pleasure to hear of it."

Bothwell shrugged. " Not while my lord of Moray is her protector and guide. He will not rest content till he has brought about my death."

" I cannot understand," said Lord John, " what my most righteous brother of Moray has against you."

" Can you not? " James Hepburn grinned wryly. " If the Queen ventures to rely on any other but himself," he said with sudden bitterness, " it is enough to loosen his head

upon his shoulders. Why did he break Huntly? As much for
fear of his influence as for desire to annex the broad lands of
Moray!"

"Huntly was a Papist," said Lord John thoughtfully.
"Have you any fancy for the Roman obedience?"

"None."

"Then it could not be to strike another blow for the
new religion that he turned on you."

"Scarcely. He has done well enough on the spoils of
the old," said James. "I am for the Queen, as I was for her
mother, Queen Marie, poor soul. Yet I could never turn
Papist. I saw Master Wishart burn at St. Andrews when I was
a lad."

"How had you to do with that affair? Fife is not your
country."

"Master Wishart came to preach in Haddington. It was
my father who sent him to his death. May he burn in hell for
it," said James, rubbing the back of a hand across his eyes as if
to obliterate a persistent memory.

Lord John nodded. "I knew you were at odds with your
father. But not that Wishart the gospeller was the cause."

"There were other reasons."

"No doubt," said Lord John, who was not interested in
religious controversy. "Well, you must be famished. I will
find you something myself. Better the servants should not see
you here to-night."

But James scarcely heard him. He was standing before
the hearth, staring down at the flames, shoulders hunched and
thumbs thrust through his belt in a typical gesture. He was
seeing, not the neatly disposed logs on his brother-in-law's
hearth, but a more sinister conflagration, shaken again by a
small boy's sick horror at the slow, dreadful process of martyr-
dom, awed by a finer courage than any he had yet known.
For the gently-spoken preacher, who would have probably
shrunk from the swordplay in which young James already
delighted, had only smiled as they built the faggots about

him, speaking incomprehensibly of forgiveness for those who had brought about his death.

The sight had completed the alienation begun when his father divorced the mother James adored, using the belated discovery of kinship within the forbidden fourth degree. It was common practice of the time, yet to James, the falsity of it stank. He left home for France and did not return till, on his father's untimely death, he found himself, at twenty-one, fourth Earl of Bothwell, the possessor of a number of castles and lesser residences in the Borders and Lowlands of Scotland which were mostly in acute need of repair, besides a scallywag retinue of fanatically loyal vassals, a considerable area of unproductive land, and a depressing number of debts. Now, after six years of loyal service, as Lord Admiral of Scotland and Lieutenant of the Border, first to the Queen Mother and then to her daughter, his affairs were in a worse state than ever, thanks to Arran's demented malice and the chance it had given the Earl of Moray to ruin him.

"Indeed, James, if this is your idea of a seemly arrival, it is not mine!" said Lady Janet from the doorway. She thumped the candlestick she carried on to the sideboard. "Dredged out of the sea like a half-drowned whelp when we all thought you safe in France. What trouble are you in now?"

"Only the necessity of finding two thousand crowns," her brother said.

Janet gasped. "Heaven save us, man! What for?"

"My servants' wages in the first place. Since I was warded they have not had a bawbee between them."

"There's a likely tale!" she protested. "You want it for that Danish slut who followed you to Scotland."

"Anna Throndsen?" James shook his head ruefully. "She is no slut, more's the pity. Both rich and respectable, she is, I promise you. She wants to marry me."

"Respectable or not, what possessed you to let her come?"

"I did not." James grinned. "She came unasked. It is not me she fancies, but my office. Lord Admiral of Scotland:

the title rings sweetly in a pretty maiden's ears. It was not Anna I courted, that I swear. I courted her father's wealth and the Danish ships our Queen Mother sent me to Denmark to obtain. And then her death wasted all my pains."

" You must have encouraged the girl——" Janet persisted.

James shook his clenched fists above his head. " Heaven save me from all women. Civil I had to be, gallant even, no doubt. But never did I dream that she would follow me——"

Lord John, returning from the kitchen, laughed. " Did you promise to marry her? Many have heard her say so."

" I may have promised her the kingdom of heaven after a few measures of Danish schnapps," said James Hepburn angrily. " The stuff seethes a man's very brains. But I am prepared to wager you the two thousand crowns I hope to borrow that unless my fortunes mend she will seek to return home within a twelvemonth."

" Done, my friend," said Lord John, setting cold meat, bread and wine on the table. " I am prepared to wager not only that your fortunes mend, but that when they do, Mistress Anna Throndsen will be found seated at your prison door like a cat at a mousehole."

James grinned at him, his mouth full. " She will be wasting her time," he mumbled. " I am not one for wedding, as you well know."

Lord John chuckled. " Aye, James. Yet bedding, whiles, may be another matter. Do you mind the time——"

" That is enough," said Lady Janet, on whom the subject had, understandably, begun to pall. " Once you begin reminding each other of your adventures, you are like to continue half the night. And I'd have you know, James, that you had better not be found here by the Queen's Grace in the morning."

James Hepburn nodded, grave again, and when he spoke his voice was once more edged with bitterness. " I'll be off before day," he promised. " Give me but a few hours' sleep, no matter where, and have someone rouse me when the first cocks are crowing——"

" I'll see you have the money you wanted," said Lady Janet.

" I thank you, Jan," James said. " But I was forgetting. Find me a quill and parchment and I'll give you a receipt against its homecoming."

" Never mind that. I know you will pay when you can," Lady Janet said more gently.

" Things should be done decently and in good order, even between kinsfolk," said the Earl of Bothwell grandly. " Find me the writing things besides the money. And if you cannot contrive all of it at the one time, I'd sooner you paid the men than let me have it."

" I will do that," Lady Janet agreed.

James yawned. " And now, if I am to be off at cock-crow——"

His sister nodded. " You'd best be away to your bed." Then she smiled as she held out her hands. " Have a care of yourself, Jamie," she said. " You always contrive to wheedle me into helping your plans."

" You always did," said James.

Lady Janet laughed. " But you're to be away before the Queen's Grace stirs, mind. I'll call you myself to ensure it."

And so, in the goose-grey dawn, as the first threads of smoke were twisting up from newly kindled fires, James Hepburn vaulted across the horse his brother-in-law had lent him, pulling his borrowed bonnet slightly askew as he glanced up at the blank windows behind which the distinguished company still slept. Then, with a smile, and a shrug, and never a backward glance, he swung his beast round on its haunches and set off at a gallop towards the Border and the exile that lay beyond.

CHAPTER TWO

IN the forecourt of Holyroodhouse horses stamped and bridles chimed. Dull or clear, the sounds travelled far and wide in the icy air of early January. A few snowflakes, errant in an almost clear sky, drifted vaguely down on cloak or plume or velvet sleeve, and the small crowd of townsfolk who had gathered to see the Queen's Grace set out to ride to Castle Campbell for the wedding of the Earl of Argyll's sister, blew on their hands or shifted lead-cold feet. Huddled in their plaids, the goodwives whispered and nodded, the mop-headed apprentices gaped at the gorgeous trappings of the horses, pointed out to each other the horned bulk of the newfangled side-saddle on which the Queen's Grace preferred to ride, instead of sitting pillion behind one of the lords in attendance as the Scottish ladies did.

Within the Palace, the Queen was already dressed for her journey, smiling at the prospect of a mid-winter ride through the mountains, as she discussed it with those about her. Snug as a tawny squirrel she seemed in her rich, dark furs, the jewel-stitched black velvet of the mourning hood she still wore for her dead French husband framing her face like a star-spattered night sky, as she turned it back to receive the greeting of the English ambassador.

"Ah, Master Randolph, I take it kindly that you have come to bid us godspeed." Mary's smile almost concealed her dislike of the suave little man with the restless, close-set eyes. And the gesture with which she held out a small hand in a white buckskin glove, fringed with gold and stitched with rubies and pearls, was both friendly and regal, as her habit was.

" I do indeed wish you godspeed, Madam," said Randolph smoothly, bowing so low that Mary noticed with distaste the dandruff with which the shoulders of his elaborate doublet were dusted. " But I have also tidings which will send you on your journey, I believe, with a gladder heart."

" Yes, Master Randolph? " The soft voice was wary.

" Madam, your escaped prisoner, the Earl of Bothwell, has recently been captured by our peo} in Northumberland. He has been taken under guard to Berwick."

She looked at him in silence, her face blank, so that he wondered, as he watched her, if she had not been listening. As he afterwards wrote in his report to Sir William Cecil, he stood long in doubt as to whether the Queen owed him any thanks for his news. The dark eyes under the darker hood seemed to be looking beyond him, the stillness of her pale face concealed her thoughts too well. For she was listening indeed, but to the echo of another voice, a harsher, angrier voice which had said with sudden violence: " Madam, I have the uttermost horror of imprisonment . . ."

" Perhaps, Madam," Randolph ventured, " you would favour me with your instructions. What is to be done with the prisoner? Is it your Majesty's pleasure that we hold him fast, or that we deliver him to you again? "

She seemed to ponder still. Then, with a little sigh, almost like someone waking from a dream, she shook her head. " I am on the verge of departure now, Master Randolph, as you can see. I must have time to consult my Council. Ask me for an answer when I return."

The English ambassador bowed again as the Queen passed between the ranks of waiting noblemen into the courtyard and the lazily drifting snow.

" Think you," they heard her ask a gentleman in waiting, " that we shall be snowbound on the way to Castle Campbell? I have never ridden through a winter storm."

Apparently, Randolph thought, as he turned with a shrug to the Earl of Moray, who was preparing to follow his half-sister, she had quite forgotten his spectacular news. " And what do you make of that, my lord? " he demanded, blocking Moray's way.

Moray paused, a tall and sombre figure in his winter riding-cloak. " In my opinion," he said irritably, " the Queen is more favourably disposed towards my lord of Bothwell than she has cause to be."

" Indeed, my lord? " Excitement was incautiously evident in the Englishman's voice.

Moray nodded. " She is persuaded that whatever we say against him is rather because of our hatred than his deserts. I will speak more of this on our return," he promised. " We shall not be absent many days. Present yourself before the first Council her Grace holds afterwards."

" I will, my lord," said Master Randolph. As the cavalcade clattered out of the forecourt, thinly cheered by the half-frozen crowd, he made his way thankfully indoors, to scold his servants for letting the fire down and begin his despatch to Sir William Cecil, chief adviser of the Queen of England.

The wedding festivities went well, and the Queen returned without misadventure from Castle Campbell, to bring her usual determination to her less agreeable duties, such as the deliberations of her Council. Her ministers rose as she entered the chamber, followed by her ladies and a page bearing the embroidery with which she habitually occupied herself while listening to her Councillors. Embroidery frame and accessories were carefully disposed about the chair of state beneath the royal canopy, the solicitous flutter of her ladies subsided as they withdrew at her smiling nod, and the day's business of the Council began. Moray presided, assisted by Maitland of Lethington as Secretary of State, while the Earl of Morton, now Lord Chancellor in Huntly's place, brooded ponderously on the Queen's left hand, his small eyes, suspicious and sunken as a pig's, surveying the scene with avid attention to any possibility of personal advantage. It was not long before the English ambassador was announced. Persistent and precise,

he waited, his eyes inquisitive as they flickered from the Queen
to the Earl of Moray.

She was ready for him now. The stillness which was so
typical of her in moments of stress was once more evident
as she waited while he made his report of Bothwell's capture,
and the heads of her Councillors turned to each other as they
considered it. She let them speak, her attention courteously
given to each in turn. Then, with a little lift of her chin, she
indicated that, though it had been her duty to hear the views
of her Council, she now proposed to state her own.

" I take it in good part, Master Randolph," she said
politely, " that my good sister's officers, for their goodwill
towards me, have apprehended the lord Bothwell." She
paused for a moment, then went on in a soft rush of words.
" He has greatly displeased me. I pray you, therefore, write
to the Queen of England that I wish him to be sent back to
Scotland again."

" Madam," said Randolph, backing and bowing his way
towards the door, " I will write as you command this very
night."

But as the Queen turned to choose a fresh colour from the
bright medley of silks at her elbow, he raised an eyebrow,
caught the slight movement of a shaken head. He and Moray
understood each other, he fancied, pretty well. But to make
matters the more certain, Moray, too, wrote to Cecil that night.
It was not his habit to put his trust in any other creature, no
matter how nearly identical their interests might seem to be.
If action were needed, he preferred to depute it to others,
especially in enterprises of any danger. But when, as now, it
was a question of subtlety in understanding, he considered it
best that he should make the matter clear himself.

" In no way," he wrote to Cecil, in his crabbed, Gothic
script, " should the Earl of Bothwell return . . ." He paused,
considered the degree of ambiguity in various phrases, then
dipped his quill again, " but be disposed of as shall be thought
good by the Queen of England."

He sanded, sealed, and despatched his letter, smiling the
secret smile of a man well satisfied by the twist of fate which
seemed likely to have disposed of an enemy, and prepared
to possess himself in patience until he should hear further.
If the Queen of England were as well disposed towards
him as he hoped, it seemed likely that she would accept the
hint he had just given that in certain influential Scottish
quar⸱⸱rs a fatal accident to the lord Bothwell would not be
taken amiss.

It was not the fault of the Earl of Moray that Bothwell
had been handed over to Sir Henry Percy, who warded his
prisoner in his Castle of Tynemouth pending the decision of
the English Privy Council as to his fate. But it made a considerable difference to his prospects. As an English Borderer
who had often encountered James Hepburn, in his capacity
of Scottish Lieutenant, in battle or conference, Sir Henry
Percy was, technically, his enemy. But he was also a man of
knightly disposition, quick to appreciate valour in others.
And presently he too was writing to Sir William Cecil. " The
Earl of Bothwell is very wise, and not the man he was reported
to be." Perhaps, Sir Henry added, the Queen of England
might be interested to interview him in person.

It was February now, 1563, and with Candlemas more
than a week past, high time for the Earl of Moray to settle himself among his ledgers in the austere chamber at Holyroodhouse
in which he did his business, and set about adding up his rent
roll, a task which he never deputed. Owing to the irregularity
of his birth, Moray could only by courtesy call himself a
Stewart. But he had long since determined to obliterate the
bar sinister which he could not erase under every other distinction which he could acquire. Already, in his thirties,
among the richest and most powerful men in Scotland, he was
still not content, as he bent his sandy head over the great
ledger which might almost have been called his Bible. He
took after his mother, and the cold alien strain, less evident
in his looks than in his disposition, had dominated the quick-

tempered warmth of his father's heritage which was so notice-able in his younger half-brother, Lord John of Coldingham.

So, in spite of his pleasure at the tale told by the figures before him, he frowned. He had been disturbed by recent indications that the young Queen was developing a mind of her own. Her admiration and trust had been most gratifying when he had waited on her at the Court of France. But now . . . he was not so sure. And any deterioration in their relationship would be extremely inconvenient, thought the Earl of Moray, as he ran a thick forefinger down the list of his possessions.

It was a pleasantly long one. He had been given the wealthy Priory of St. Andrews by his father long since. For James V always provided for his bastards in the regal Stewart tradition. Pittenweem had been annexed from the Queen Mother, Buchan from its young Countess, whom he had betrothed for long enough to obtain—and keep—the custody of her lands. But he had done better from the dowry of the Lady Agnes, daughter of the Earl Marischal, whom he had actually married. And his latest prize, the rich earldom of Moray, was worth, he dared hope, more than all the rest. No, he had not done so badly, especially since Mary had made him Sheriff of Inverness, so that his writ ran throughout the whole of the far north. The Earl chuckled, hawked, and spat. He meant to do better yet.

But the nagging uneasiness persisted. Moray was not a sensitive man, but he had an uncanny flair for the detection of those who seemed to threaten his interests. Young lord Bothwell, that obstinately incorruptible Queen's man, had until recently, seemed likely to be dangerous. But surely he had now gotten his quietus? Queen Elizabeth was not com-monly patient with those who persistently refused her bribes. Then what of George Gordon, whom people were beginning to call the Earl of Huntly, in spite of his father's disgrace? Moray slammed his ledger shut, restored it to the coffer in which he kept it with his most cherished possessions, and carefully turned the key before setting off to have a word with his colleague, William Maitland of Lethington, in the quarters he occupied as Secretary of State, in another part of the Palace of Holyroodhouse.

Lethington was seated at a ponderous refectory table, wrapped in a cosily furred winter robe, with a large fire roaring half-way up the chimney at his back, writing verses in his elegant Italian hand, and laughing at the antics of the small capuchin monkey which squatted among the papers before him, scratching its back with one of its master's quill pens.

" Tch, tch," said the Earl of Moray, who was not fond of such eccentric pets.

Maitland of Lethington turned his slow, slightly over-sweet smile on his visitor. The contrast between the two men was evident. Necessity alone could make co-operation between such opposed natures possible. It pleased Lethington to defy convention. In a warlike country, he preferred silk and velvet to the commonplace of armour. And at a Court frequented by men who despised all culture as effeminate, it pleased him to write verses, speak French with the Queen and amuse himself by writing masques for the singing, dancing, play-acting household against which John Knox and his fellow ministers thundered. It also amused him to tease the Earl of Moray.

" My lord, you are most welcome," he drawled. " Forgive me if I do not rise to greet you, but my little friend here is so easily agitated by any sudden movement. I pray you to sit down in the great chair by the hearth."

Moray stumped crossly towards the fire, picking his way amongst a clutter of lutes and viols and half-scrawled scores, while the monkey leapt from a chair-back and ran along the carved stone mantel to chatter at him angrily, brandishing the flute it had snatched from the table in its tiny hands, as if proposing to beat him over the head with it. Lethington, hiding a smile behind his fingers, watched the small drama with interest, but made no attempt to interfere. At last the monkey, with a wild shriek, flung the flute far across the room and sprang for its master's shoulder, where it huddled, like a bright-eyed, furry necklet, muttering.

" That beast of yours makes my flesh creep," Moray protested. " For two crowns I would wring its neck."

" As it is very well aware, my lord of Moray."

" It's never a fit pet for a Christian man."

" It may be a better Christian than any of us, for all you know."

" You had better not let Master Knox hear you say so."

" Master Knox might guess—though I doubt it—that I am making game of you, my lord of Moray."

Moray glared. " Then have done. My time is precious."

" Each turn of the hour-glass worth its weight in gold? " murmured Lethington. " Then to what urgency do I owe the largesse of your visit, I wonder? "

Moray breathed heavily as he sought to keep his temper. Past experience had taught him that it was fatal to allow himself to be goaded when dealing with the Scottish Machiavelli, as Lethington had been called. " I came to seek your advice, my lord," he mumbled.

" Indeed? Well, such a gift costs nothing," said Lethington. He took a sweetmeat from his pouch and held it up to the little creature on his shoulder, whose avid hands, as they closed about it, were such absurdly faithful miniatures of his own. " Ask and it shall be given you."

" I am disturbed by the Queen's refusal to sign the death warrant of George Gordon. I had thought her fully aware of the need to obliterate the whole house of Huntly——"

" Yes, it was useful that the late Earl of Huntly had been so unwise as to complain to the Cardinal of Lorraine of the Queen's laxity in her religious duties, was it not? Otherwise I doubt if she would have been so easily convinced of his purpose of rebellion," said Maitland of Lethington pleasantly.

" I do not follow you, my lord." The Earl of Moray glared at the Secretary of State, whose monkey, now seated on its protector's head, glared punily back.

" Such a purpose of rebellion was nicely timed for discovery when you required the Earldom of Moray."

" Huntly was a Popish traitor who sought to use the Queen to win the country back for Rome," retorted Moray.

" No doubt," murmured Lethington. " But what a pity she fainted when the clumsy headsman bungled the execution of Lord John, yet recovered in time to forbid you to order young Adam to the block. After all, he was nearly seventeen."

" I am not concerned with the past, my lord, but with the future," rumbled the Earl of Moray. " The purge of that malignant family is incomplete while George Gordon still lies in the Castle of Dunbar, awaiting sentence of death."

" Since George Gordon was living quietly with his wife at Kinneil during the troubles, he could hardly have had art or part in Huntly's rebellion."

" No matter. He has been tried and condemned. Yet I cannot persuade the Queen to sign his death warrant."

Lethington offered his monkey another sweetmeat and deliberated whether to placate Moray or not. Presently he smiled. " But, my lord, it is the simplest thing in the world to bring about. You know how careless women can be when pleasure eclipses the consideration of business. Present the death warrant at the bottom of a pile of charters and such-like, ask for her signature at a time when she has some cherished amusement planned. By the time she reaches it she will be so impatient that she will not wait to read. She will sign all you put before her and toss the quill down."

Moray puffed out his cheeks in a blustering half-protest. But the advantages of the device were too obvious to be ignored. As he rose from the high-backed chair by the hearth and prepared to take his leave the monkey cut a caper. " I will think on it," he said grudgingly. " But I advise you to wring that creature's neck. It is a blasphemous mockery of all mankind."

" The Queen finds him charming," murmured Lethington.

" Bah! " exploded the Earl of Moray, as he stumped

towards the door. With his hand on the latch he paused, belatedly aware of his ungraciousness. " I am obliged to you for the suggestion," he admitted.

Lethington, negligently fanning himself with a rolled parchment, waved away the faint praise, while his monkey, swinging round his shoulder, let off a screech so shrill that the Earl of Moray almost leapt out of his shoes. Shaking his head as if to rid himself of the dirling in his ears, he let himself hastily out of the overheated, womanishly luxurious room. There were times when he heartily wished himself rid of Maitland of Lethington. But he had to admit that the Secretary had the nimblest wits in Scotland.

It was a raw, blustery morning when the Captain of the Castle of Dunbar received his instructions. These grieved him so deeply, honest man that he was, that for some time he could only stare at the warrant, muttering and shaking his head. Then he went slowly up the spiral stair to the turret chamber in which his prisoner, young George Gordon, who should by rights have now been the Earl of Huntly, was honourably confined, with freedom to come and go about the fortress, on parole to attempt no escape. Huntly was writing a letter to his wife when the Captain opened the door, sprawled across the heavy table with his elbows spread wide and the quill squeaking in his cramped fingers.

" Give me but leave to finish," he murmured. " For truly, once I take quill in hand, my thoughts elude me like a wisp of snipe."

" Take your time, lad. Take your time," said the Captain. He trudged across to the narrow window, to stand tugging at his grizzled moustache and watching the seagulls sweep past between the leaden sky and the green surge of sea which broke curd-white against the reddish rocks. The news he bore might surely wait till the letter was done. Was it not the last the poor lady could look to have?

" Now then, what's amiss? " demanded George Gordon at last, swinging round on his stool and grasping his right wrist. " How is it that I can wield sword or spear all day and none the worse, yet after writing a single letter I am half palsied? "

He broke off to stare at the silent man before him. " What is it? Speak out, man. If your news is already rank, keeping will not sweeten it."

" It is rank indeed," said the Captain heavily.

" Out with it, then. I am not squeamish——"

" I have here," said the Captain at last, " a warrant signed by the Queen's Grace, commanding me immediately to strike off the head of my prisoner, George Gordon, sometime known as Huntly——"

" Show it to me." The young man's face was dazed with unbelief. Snatching the parchment, he stared, his eyes slowly widening with dismay.

" It is her Grace's very hand," the Captain groaned. " I know the Italian script she uses. Few write so in Scotland."

" This is the malice of the Bastard! " cried young Gordon violently. " The Queen herself sent me assurance of her pity. I know, I am sure, it is not her intention to take my life."

" It would suit Moray well enough for her to do so," the Captain agreed. " Yet it is not his command. How dare I disobey? "

" Though it be the Queen's hand, I am certain it is not her desire," cried Gordon. " My friend, as a dying man I beg you to postpone the execution of this warrant till you have discovered that it is the Queen's will indeed."

The Captain hesitated. " To disobey is treason. If you are mistaken, it will be death for both of us. And yet——"

" I swear I am not mistaken," declared Gordon. He was on his feet now, roving to and fro between the table and the door. " I know it is much to ask. Yet if you succeed——"

" I will go," said the Captain curtly.

Young Gordon grasped his gaoler's hands, blinking sudden tears from his own eyes. " God bless you, my good friend," he said brokenly, " as we both shall, my sweet lady and I. Take to the Queen's Grace my most humble duty, and my oath to serve her to the utmost end of the life she has restored."

" I have not yet succeeded," the Captain warned him.

But George Gordon had swung too far towards hope even to glimpse the memory of despair. " You will succeed. But go, man, go! "

At Holyroodhouse the Queen had for once retired early. She had been troubled, recently, by the refusal of her musicians to play in her chapel for fear of the hostility of the people and the thunderings of Master Knox. Had it not been for the odd-looking Piedmontese who had recently come to Court in the retinue of the Duke of Savoy, she might have been without music even for the Easter Mass. And she could not rid herself of the nagging suspicion that her brother Moray was not doing all she could have wished to persuade her royal cousin Elizabeth to release the Earl of Bothwell. The thought annoyed her. If one of her subjects must be punished, she would prefer to do it herself.

So she was silent and thoughtful as her waiting women prepared her for bed. Sitting pensive before the fire in her bedchamber, she submitted to have her hair brushed and her nails tended, while distillations of choice herbs were brought for face and hands. Vainly her maids of honour chattered to distract her: saucy, indiscreet Beton, who had already caught the eye of Master Randolph, lovely Mary Fleming, whom even Lethington admired, and sweet-voiced Mary Livingstone, did everything they knew to make her smile. But plain, staunch Mary Seton, who knew her moods better than all the rest, hushed them with headshakings and admonitory finger to her lips. Inexorably she hastened the waiting women over their tasks, routed the Queen's little dogs from underneath the bed's valance, where, each night, they hopefully took refuge, and sent pages scuttling for fresh logs so that her mistress could enjoy the play of light on the carved and painted ceiling.

It was all quiet at last. The Queen fell asleep at once,

soothed and reassured by the loving service with which her adoring household surrounded her. She was not left alone nowadays, even at night. Since the outrageous occasion when the French poet Chastelard had concealed himself in her bedchamber, either Mary Seton or Mary Fleming shared the great, gorgeously hung bed with her. Her last conscious thought, as she drifted into a dream, was that she was glad it was kind Seton, though she did snore a little, rather than Mary Fleming, who slept quietly as a kitten, but liked to chatter half the night long.

She had no idea how long she slept, only that she woke to the sound of voices raised in altercation in the ante-room. With amazement she realised that an intruder must have contrived to make his way past the guard, into the royal apartments, and was now actually demanding an audience with his Queen in the middle of the night.

Always courageous, Mary was angry rather than afraid as she shook her bedfellow awake. " Seton! What is the matter? Rouse and listen. Something is going on out there . . ."

As Mary Seton bundled into her chamber-robe, a huddle of ladies-in-waiting appeared, wild-eyed and tousled, candles guttering in their hands.

" Madam, it is the Captain of Dunbar," said Mary Fleming, " on a matter of life and death which cannot wait even till morning."

The Queen was at once alert, though her heart was racing. " Light the candles. Prepare me to receive him. Bring me my comb, my looking-glass, and throw a furred robe round my shoulders. Now——"

" Shall I send for their lordships of the Council? " asked Mary Livingstone.

" Certainly not," the Queen said haughtily. " But let the guards wait in the ante-room."

They brought the Captain of Dunbar to her bedside, so weary that he reeled on his feet, while the ladies whispering

around the doorway drew their skirts aside with little cries of
dismay at the sight of his mud-plastered clothes. But he was
aware of nobody but the resolute young woman surveying
him from the centre of her great gold and crimson bed. Wasting
no time even in apologies, he crossed the royal bedchamber
in a dozen strides that left as many dark traces on the rich
carpet.

"Madam, I am here to report my obedience to your
command."

"What command have you had from me?"

"Madam, this morning I received your warrant, commanding me immediately to strike off George Gordon's head."

"Never in all this world!" cried Mary. "What treason
is this? Show me the warrant!"

"I have it here, Madam."

She read it in silence, the angry colour blazing into her
face, teeth catching her lower lip. There at the foot of the
warrant for the execution of the heir of Huntly, scrawled in
weary haste, stood her own name. She caught her breath, then
beat her hands together, dismayed beyond all discretion.

"Can this be my brother's subtlety?" she cried. "To
have contrived it, knowing that I was inattentive? Never
would I have believed it. Oh, sweet heaven, this man did me
no wrong. Yet he lies dead——"

"Comfort yourself, Madam," the Captain of Dunbar
made bold to say. "The young man's head is still safe upon
his shoulders. It seemed so strange an order that I ventured
to demand your Grace's pleasure from your own lips before
I carried it out."

"Oh, well done, my friend. Well done! I shall reward
your prudence!" Laughing and crying at once, the Queen
snatched the parchment, crushing it together because it was
too tough to tear. "Burn it, Seton! At once!" Then her
quick kindness made her aware of the man's utter exhaustion.
"My people shall see that you have rest and food. Come to me
in the morning . . ."

But she herself did not sleep again that night. Not even the hot posset which Seton brought could soothe her from the wakefulness which kept her tossing until dawn.

"Sweet Madam, can you not rest? Are you too hot? Or chilled?"

"Chilled to the heart, Seton, to think that my lord of Moray could use such a device against me. My own father's son, whom I trusted as myself . . ."

"It may be there is some explanation, Madam," said Seton. "Ask my lord of Moray to account for such a strange mischance in the morning."

But her mistress had not been schooled in vain by that most brilliant diplomat, the Cardinal of Lorraine. She laughed unexpectedly in the darkness.

"No, Seton, I shall say nothing," she murmured. "If he wishes to know why George Gordon still lives, he must ask me. I—do not think he will. And I shall sign nothing unread in future."

CHAPTER THREE

MAITLAND of Lethington was preparing to journey into England. The snug seclusion of his apartments was disturbed by draughts and sibilant with anxious whisperings as his servants hurried to and fro, stowing in coffers and saddlebags the astonishing assortment of possessions their master habitually required on his travels. In his bedchamber and adjacent wardrobe, furred robes, fine shirts, embroidered doublets, silken hose, gauntlets and shoes of tooled and scented leather, kerchiefs, close ruffs and jauntily plumed bonnets lay about in heaps, among Toledo-tempered swords and jewelled-hilted daggers, short capes of gold-stitched brocade, lined with contrasting satin, others of satin lined with contrasting velvet, sheets for his bed and unguents for his toilet. William Maitland did not care to endure the discomforts of other people's environment. He preferred instead, to carry his own environment with him. Only his monkey, in view of the rigours of a winter journey, was to be left behind. Uncannily aware of it, the little creature had abandoned its antics to sit sulkily searching itself for fleas in the chimney corner.

But while his servants scurried, Lethington himself remained unperturbed. It was his habit to let others agitate themselves on his behalf, and they knew well that he would visit any forgetfulness upon them in words which seared as shrewdly as a cruder man's blows. Anxiously, therefore, they folded and packed, while Lethington smiled thinly at the English ambassador who had sought a last minute interview in spite of the hubbub of departure.

" I trust, sir, that my presence does not inconvenience you? " said Master Randolph, who was, in fact, quite indifferent, as his host well knew.

" Not in the least degree," Lethington assured him. " I shall gladly hear all you can tell me regarding the mood of her Majesty of England, since I am to wait upon her by my Queen's command——"

" To treat of other matters besides the Scottish Queen's prospective marriage, I believe? " said Randolph delicately.

" Other topics, indeed, may arise," Lethington agreed blandly.

" Such as the succession to the throne of England? "

" Perhaps, Master Randolph."

The two diplomats surveyed each other between narrowed lids, their expression of wariness for an instant so identical that they might have been brothers. Both were subtle men, trained in the rapier thrust and parry of the international game, and to some extent in agreement, since each was pledged to the new creed at a time when the forces of the Counter-Reformation were preparing to do battle for the old. But there Randolph

was on surer ground, for Queen Elizabeth herself led the
Protestants of England, while Queen Mary was already perplexing Scotland by her determination to abide by the old faith.
Lethington's position, between old and new, was extremely
delicate. He changed the subject casually.

" There is also the matter of the Earl of Bothwell."

Randolph made a gesture as of flicking aside a fly. " That
vagrant? He is a very beggar, destitute enough to set at
nought——"

" Yet the Queen's Grace does not forget that he is a
Scottish subject." Lethington laid his hand on a document
which lay before him. " I have here her instructions that he is
to be returned to Scotland, where justice awaits him."

Randolph's thin lips curled slightly. " The Queen of Scots
is mindful of her royal duties. But I have heard that the Earl
of Bothwell has a way of exciting such concern. What was the
story of the lady from Denmark who followed him to Scotland
with high hopes? "

Lethington shrugged. " So you have heard the tale? "

" Who has not? "

" You will also have heard, no doubt, that she has now
abandoned him? "

" Indeed? I had not heard. Why so? "

Lethington shrugged, swinging round in his chair to snap
his fingers at his monkey, which turned its back on him
and continued to scratch. " It may be that she shares your
view of the gallant Earl's prospects. At all events, I have
here, among an intolerable mass of papers to be dealt with,
a petition from Mistress Anna Throndsen for a passport to
return home."

Randolph permitted himself to chuckle. " Mistress Throndsen shows her sense," he said. " The vainglorious fellow has
foundered himself now."

" I wonder? He has a way of finding friends where they
might be least expected," said Lethington.

" Sir Henry Percy was a blundering fool," said Randolph

sharply, " to intervene with her Majesty of England on his prisoner's behalf. Yet I predict Bothwell will not profit from his folly. My lord of Moray has written to Cecil on the subject, as I have done myself."

Lethington surveyed him thoughtfully. He was aware of Moray's hostility to Bothwell but not, so far, of its cause. On this depended his own choice of whether, should occasion offer, he himself would aid or hinder his countryman at the English Court.

" The beggarly fellow cannot even pay for a servant to attend him in his exile. Her Majesty of England would be prepared to be most generous——" grumbled Randolph.

" But the Earl of Bothwell is most inconveniently incorruptible——"

Randolph glanced sharply at the Scottish Secretary. He was inclined, not for the first time, to suspect that he was being mocked. But Lethington's hawk-like profile was composed. " Once Bothwell has been committed to the Tower, Mr. Secretary," Randolph retorted huffily, " I fancy we need trouble ourselves about him no more. It is not our Queen's habit to be lenient with those who refuse her kindness. And her Majesty's generosity extends, as is well known, to all those of her own faith whether in her realm . . . or beyond . . ."

Lethington was no longer listening. He was satisfied that he had turned the discussion away from the most delicate of the topics which he had been commanded to bring to the attention of the Queen of England during his forthcoming visit. He was prepared to let Randolph run on about anything rather than the Queen of England's attitude towards her successor, and his own hopes of persuading her to name the Queen of Scots.

But he was glad when the English ambassador at last took his leave, for he still had more than enough to do before his departure on the morrow. The Queen's absence at St. Andrews had added greatly to his labours, since he had already been obliged to follow her to Fife in order to receive her final instructions before setting out for the south. He knew that the question of the English succession was one on which Mary felt more strongly than any other aspect of her relationship with the Queen of England, and he dared not disregard her commands, however doubtful he might be of success. He was already aware that the Queen of Scots, at twenty, was showing signs of being as imperious as any of her forbears, who had personally ruled Scotland, for better or for worse, ever since her great ancestor, King Robert, had fought for and regained his country's independence against what seemed hopeless odds. A Queen who had served her apprenticeship in France, learning statecraft from such men as the Duke of Guise and the Cardinal of Lorraine, was unlikely to consent to be a mere figurehead.

The little house in South Street, St. Andrews, from which Lethington had recently returned, had been placed at the Queen's disposal by her brother of Moray, and was scarcely a stone's throw from the entrance to the Priory which Lady Moray, still newfangled with her great possessions, was transforming into a luxurious secular residence at considerable expense. Here it pleased Moray to keep the sort of state more suited to a King, served on bended knee, waited on with servility that soothed his chafing grievances like balm, followed when he rode abroad by a retinue which clattered behind him up the Pends, sending the echoes rolling and the rooks whirling up from the trees in the Dean's Court nearby.

The chime and clash of such comings and goings kept the Queen's Maries running to the casement from morning till night. For Mary Fleming was well aware that she had caught the eye of such a connoisseur as Maitland of Lethington, and Mary Beton was on the look-out for Master Randolph, who was paying her marked attention. But the others shook their heads at her.

" Have a care, Beton. Master Randolph has chosen you because your tongue runs fastest," Mary Seton warned.

" Master Randolph is a most discreet gentleman. I shall
model my talk on his," retorted Mary Beton, giggling at the
thought. She clasped her hands behind her back, folded in
the corners of her mouth and strode heavily across the room, to
pause before the Queen with a deep bow and a tilt of her head
which conveyed the impression of the English ambassador so
exactly that Queen Mary flung down the wooden spoon with
which she was playing at cookery, to clap delighted hands.
Safe in the seclusion of her own household, she had laid aside
the sombre richness of her royal mourning, girded her simple
white gown with a coarse linen apron borrowed from one of
the servants, and was making such comfits as they had enjoyed
in France. She now pushed back a strand of bright hair which
had escaped from the silk net into which she had bundled it
with a sugary hand, and shook a finger at her laughing
companions.

" Have a care, Livvy, for if you scorch the pan the flavour
will be ruined. Give me another spoon for the one I have
dropped in the ashes. I shall stir now."

" Oh, Madam, you will never endure the heat," gasped
Mary Livingstone, surrendering the spoon and the stool by
the hearth without reluctance.

" Am I a wax candle? " said the Queen gaily. Shielding
her face with one hand she began to stir the gently heaving
mixture wedged between three logs on the hearth of the little
parlour. Then, poising the spoon in mid-air, she flicked it with
a finger and put the finger to her mouth.

" How does it taste, Madam? "

" Does it need more spice? "

" Shall I add lemon juice? "

" Have we used enough butter? "

Queen Mary raised a flushed face. Sucking her finger, she
shook her head, looking happier, Mary Seton thought, than
she had ever been since they left France. Regality, with all
its anxieties, had fallen from her like her mourning robe.
She might almost have been the young merchant's wife she

wished to seem. Ah, if only such delights could endure beyond the few days of their reprieve from State affairs.

" Nothing more is needed. It is perfection," cried Queen Mary gaily. " Have you the greased trays ready? "

But next morning the messenger from France arrived. His appearance struck coldly at the little party's gaiety, for he was dressed in the deepest mourning, and both the ribbon and seal of the letter from the Duchess of Guise were black.

Queen Mary held out her hand for it. Still and silent, she was regal again at the hint of ill tidings. But the news she read hurt her more shrewdly than she had supposed, in her innocence, she could ever be hurt again. " Monsieur . . . my uncle . . . is dead. Ah, Jesu, Jesu! " The letter fell from her hands as she covered her face and wept. Anxiously the Maries clustered round her.

" The Grand Prior? It was to be looked for," sighed Mary Beton. " We knew he was sorely wounded when fighting against the Huguenots——"

" It is not the Grand Prior——" the Queen whispered.

" Who then? "

" The Duc de Guise has been assassinated," cried Mary Livingstone, who had snatched up the letter. " Oh, Madam . . ."

" My most splendid kinsman," faltered the Queen. " How is it possible . . . that he should die . . . while so many sorry villains live? When I remember . . . the golden days . . ."

They were all weeping now, not only for the great Duke who had been so much more glorious than the father Mary had never known, but for the wonderful life in France that his power and glory had epitomised. As she sobbed despairingly for the superb soldier who had been struck down unshriven, Mary wept also for Francis, the young husband who had adored her, the blissful days when they had been King and Queen together, the darlings and the wonder of all France. It was suddenly unbearable to be in Scotland, where the east wind swirled about the house, the grey sky shut out the sun, and the forlorn crying of the seagulls swept inland, emphasising her loneliness in a strange land.

It was all over now, her golden youth. Over, too, was the little interlude of play-acting. The comfits they had made so lightheartedly still stood in the greased dishes on the window-sill where they had been left to cool the night before. But the sight of them sent a wave of nausea through the girl who, a few hours since, had lightheartedly licked the sugar from her fingers. Soon she must emerge from her chamber, no longer the carefree merchant wife, but the Queen of Scots to whom her noblemen and the ambassadors of foreign powers must offer formal condolence for her uncle's death. She must summon her lifetime's training to help her to endure them royally, knowing that the sunshine of her childish memories would be dimmer for the loss of the terrifying soldier who had been gentle to her alone.

But she had not the heart to remain longer in St. Andrews, where memories of her happiness still mocked her. After she had attended the appropriate Masses for the welfare of the Duke's soul, given all the audiences requested, written all the letters the occasion demanded, she was thankful to accept Moray's suggestion of finishing her holiday elsewhere. In her grief and loneliness she had found herself forgetting her new mistrust of the man who had tried to trick her into ordering George Gordon's death and remembering only that he was also the elder brother she had loved and admired during the happy days in France.

"Your Grace must not allow your grief to affect your health," Moray said solicitously.

"No," she agreed.

"You are never well when you lack exercise," Moray went on candidly. "I advise you to take the chance of a few days' hunting, which always does you good. It is April now, with the winter behind us. Shall I make such arrangements as seem best?"

" As you will, brother," said Mary meekly. She knew that
Moray was right in believing that the exercise she loved would
offer the best cure. As she rode, with hawk on wrist, through
the glens where the first primroses had followed hard on the
last snows, Mary felt her courage revive. And with it revived
her hope and confidence. Her recent grief had cruelly emphasised the contrast between the universal devotion she had
known in France and the uncertain loyalty of her Scottish
subjects. It was her instinct, as it would have been that of her
greatest forbears, to attack her subjects' mistrust of her at its
source.

" I pray you, summon Master John Knox to wait on
me at the earliest possible moment," she told the Earl of
Moray when he came to bring her the latest report of her
Council's proceedings in her absence. " It may be we shall
fare better if he finds me in surroundings which do not
compel him to scold my poor ladies for their gaudy attire, and
it is my purpose to visit your kinsfolk at Lochleven this coming
week."

" I will see that Master Knox waits upon you there,"
Moray said. But he smiled privately to himself at her confidence in her ability to conciliate the great reformer.

For it would not be their first interview. Mary had
been exhorted, scolded, defied and exasperated by the leader
of the Reformed Church in Scotland ever since her return.
But this time she planned a new approach. Might not a personal
appeal succeed where royal authority had failed? Her auto-
cratic uncle of Guise would have disagreed. But he was dead
and her problems remained. It was so much simpler to command, where royalty commanded not only by divine right
but with sufficient strength to be obeyed. But when, as now,
division had weakened her authority, there might be something to be said for the viewpoint of the subtler Cardinal of
Lorraine. At the Council of Trent, she knew, he had strongly
recommended certain compromises as the only alternative to
the partition of Christendom, and though he had been over-

ruled by the zealots of the Counter Reformation, she was remembering his counsel now.

King James had married off his mistress to the Laird of Lochleven Castle, Sir Robert Douglas, before her son's birth, and Lady Douglas now received Mary with at least apparent homage. But her dark, fierce jealousy burned volcanically just below the surface, as she compared the position of King James's daughter with that of his son and hers. Mary had been delighted with the romantic situation of the Castle which Scottish Kings had long used as a hunting box when Moray had first taken her to visit Lochleven, and gladly returned to it now. It rose she fancied, like a fortress in a fairy tale from the opalescent waters of the loch as she was rowed towards the island through the early April evening appointed for her audience with John Knox.

She awaited him by the window of a chamber overlooking the loch to which the wild duck were now returning, the arrowy wake of disturbed water they left behind them tipped with streaks of gold and fire from the sunset's afterglow. According to Mary's standards, it was a simply furnished apartment, its walls hung with tapestry depicting hunting scenes, her chair surmounted by the canopy under which, as the royal custom was, she habitually sat to give audience. The floor was carpeted because rushes strewn on stone flags displeased her fastidious taste as a trap for dust and debris, and she and her ladies had themselves industriously worked on the rich tapestry with which the walls were hung. But to Knox the furnishings reeked of the privilege and luxury which he hated not only because his authentic spiritual genius compelled him to cry aloud in the wilderness of men's greed for great possessions, but also because any such display, especially in women, chafed the sense of inferiority which tormented him, less creditably, like an itch.

He strode into the Queen's presence in patriarchal Geneva gown and unwillingly removed his flat-topped cap before bowing a stiff greeting, his expression indicative of the same defiant, humourless hostility which had so antagonised her at their earlier meetings. But this time he also reminded her, unexpectedly, of one of the gaunt cormorants which had been pointed out to her as she crossed the loch, so that it was only after a violent struggle against laughter that she was able to speak.

" Be seated, Master Knox. Here is a stool beside my chair. I trust you find yourself well."

" As well, ·Madam, as God is pleased to permit," said Knox harshly, as he folded his gown about him and sat down. Mary frowned at the ripple of amusement among the ladies-in-waiting who should have been occupied with their embroidery at the far end of the room. They would have been out of earshot of discreet conversation, but a lifetime's preaching had given John Knox's voice a resonance which he found hard to subdue.

" And yet you will not suppose, Master Knox, that I asked you here to discuss your health."

" I do not, Madam. I would be glad to know for what purpose your Grace summoned me."

" I will not waste your time," Mary promised, smiling. She could be as direct as he. " I summoned you to seek your help."

John Knox bridled a little. He had no objection to assuming the gracious role of one whose assistance was sought by Queens. But he was wary. It was over fifteen years since the leaders of the old religion had sentenced him to the galleys for his part in the lynching of Cardinal Beaton. They had succeeded in breaking neither his body nor his spirit. But his ordeal had hardened his instinctive hostility against all those who professed the Roman obedience into an almost maniacal suspicion of even their fairest words.

" You shall have such help as I am able to give with a clear conscience, Madam," he said.

" I assure you I will ask nothing else, Master Knox," said Mary. " But since all Christians must revere the quality

of mercy, I beg that you will use your influence with the
gentlemen of the west who profess the new religion. I am
informed that they have captured some priests and propose to
put them to death."

"It is not in my power, Madam," said Knox, "to prevent
the laws against idolaters from taking their course."

Mary felt herself flush, but her voice was still steady as she
answered: "My Council has not ventured to enforce such a
law, Master Knox. They knew I must refuse to permit it.
It would therefore be treasonable for lesser men to take the
law into their own hands. But I so earnestly desire peace that
I am prepared to allow every man to act according to his own
conscience, provided I am allowed to act according to mine.
Will not that suffice?"

John Knox shook his head. "Madam, as the ruler of this
realm, it is incumbent upon you to punish all transgressors.
And the idolatries of the old faith have been forbidden by the
law of our land."

"It is not my pleasure," said Mary deliberately, "that
men should suffer the extreme penalty for their religion,
whether it be new or old. I have," she added, speaking more
to herself than to him, "seen too much cruelty shown for such
a cause elsewhere. For that reason I ask you to check the
people of your persuasion, when they seek to proceed to extremes
against those of mine."

The little group in the background sat idle, their needles
suspended among the gay silks, their frightened or indignant
eyes wide as the argument proceeded. Patiently, courteously,
Mary attempted to break down the hostility of the man before
her. But Knox's gaunt figure remained as immovable as if
carved out of oak, one powerful hand splayed out across each
knee, the craggy profile jutting forward, the fanatical eyes with
their distended pupils and yellowish whites fixed unblinkingly
on her.

"Madam, you may fail to carry out the laws against
idolaters," said Knox at last, "but there are some in Scot-

land who will not permit God's Majesty to be so manifestly defied."

Mary's quick temper, so far held in check, at last flared. " Will you allow that such men shall take my sword in their own hands? "

" Madam," Knox retorted promptly. " I know not how far you have had cause to search the Scriptures. You may remember, however, that the Prophet Samuel was required to slay Agag, the King. Perhaps you will also recall that Elijah was commanded by God to slay the false priests of Baal, and those others revered by the harlot Jezebel? "

Mary's education had not dealt in great detail with the utterances of the Old Testament Prophets. But she had heard enough of Jezebel to recognise the gross insult of the implied comparison. Here was crisis. She must either deal with it as such or pretend not to have understood the allusion. Always quick-witted, she weighed the alternatives and chose the second with scarcely a moment's hesitation. For it was the only possibility of avoiding an open and permanent breach with the leader of the powerful body of Protestant opinion which threatened her at every turn. She drew a little jewelled watch from the pocket at her waist where it hung on a slender chain.

" Seton," she said in a voice which shook with anger in spite of all she could do to steady it, " I see it is the hour for supper. Send a page to advise Sir William and his lady of our coming. Master Knox, you will join us, I hope? "

" No, Madam, I thank you," said Knox. He restrained an impulse to add a quotation about the leaven of the Pharisees, and discreetly took his leave. The result of his plain speaking did not displease him. He had said some of the things which crowded his mind, seething together like the lava which churns molten within the crater of a volcano, awaiting the opportunity of eruption. As the dedicated servant of God who would use him to chasten the ungodly, such opportunities were not for him to seek. But every now and then an opportunity, as now, arose. God at his own time and after his own fashion would no doubt continue to command his services.

His conviction made him quite fearless, dangerous as an eagle, and with an almost aquiline glitter in his hypnotic stare. As he made his way towards the landing-stage, where a boat waited to convey him to the mainland, his imperious strides kicked the folds of his black gown to and fro. From the doorway in which they had conferred for a few minutes after his audience with the Queen, Moray watched him go, wishing, not for the first time, that he knew whether John Knox were indeed the consecrated instrument of divine vengeance he apparently supposed himself to be, or the most plausible old hypocrite who ever took the name of God in vain.

CHAPTER FOUR

THE little dog ran round in circles, faster and faster, till the sunshine and green grass and sweet smells blurred about it and it flung itself panting on the ground.

" Let it rest, Beton, or it will do itself a mischief," said the Queen, who had been laughing at its antics, but now stooped over it anxiously, shaking her head at Mary Beton, who was trying to tempt it to further activity with a fluffy ball of many coloured wools. " It is but young yet, and knows not when to cry a halt." She glanced quickly about her, to make sure that, in the high-walled physic garden, they were indeed safe from observation, then, with a sigh of relief, flopped down on the grass beside it. The little dog thumped its plumy tail and laid a confident head on her knee, as the four Maries sank down about their mistress, their gowns belling out around them like flowers made brighter by contrast with the Queen's black velvet gown.

"Oh, Madam, this is the first summer day in Scotland as fair as any in France," sighed Mary Livingstone.

"And for a wonder, we are permitted an hour's leisure to enjoy it," said Mary Fleming. She pulled a daisy and began flicking off the petals, murmuring to herself: "*Il m'aime, un peu, beaucoup, passionement, pas du tout. . . . Un peu, beaucoup . . .*" Have you as yet any word of the return of the lord of Lethington, Madam?"

Her companions' laughter at her innocent tone made her pout and frown, as even the Queen, to whom Lethington's travels were no matter for amusement, smiled.

"Not yet, foolish one. It is known only that he has left the Court of England for that of France."

"Oh, Madam, is it intended that he shall journey also to Spain?" asked Mary Beton eagerly.

The Queen raised her delicately plucked eyebrows. "I know of no such plan. Why should he go so far afield?"

"Why, Madam, to treat of your forthcoming marriage," Mary Beton ventured.

The Queen frowned, her face hidden as she bent over the little dog, twisting the silky ears as it snuggled closer. "I have no mind to wed again, Beton, as you well know. See how red this little dog's tongue is? When we next embroider a hunting scene, I shall take a brighter silk for the tongues of hounds in full cry."

"But, Madam," persisted Mary Livingstone, "surely his Eminence your uncle of Lorraine has been in correspondence with the Emperor to obtain his consent for your betrothal to the Archduke Charles——"

"My uncle forgets that I am no longer a child," said the Queen sharply, "who must obey his bidding in a matter on which my preference should first have been ascertained."

"But Madam, his Eminence has no thought but for your welfare——"

"No doubt. But in such a matter my wishes are also of some significance," said the Queen.

" Madam," Mary Seton's voice was troubled, " you would never prefer Don Carlos to the Archduke? "

" To be Queen of Spain would be a great destiny," the Queen admitted thoughtfully. " For one who is already Queen of Scots and should be Queen of England hereafter . . ."

" They say Don Carlos is an idiot," Mary Beton blurted out. " He takes after his mother, poor Queen Joanna——"

" Hush," said Mary Seton. " Is there no man of Scottish blood your Grace could name? "

The Queen had taken a white ribbon from her dress to tie round the little dog's neck. " No doubt it will chew it to fragments," she said. " But it will serve till I can have a collar made. It shall carry a bell to warn us of its whereabouts."

" There is Lord Darnley," murmured Mary Beton, greatly daring. " I have heard that his claim to the English throne is second only to your own. Together——"

" I shall put the matter of the collar in your hands, Seton," said the Queen, smiling again. " You are less likely to forget it than these feather-headed folk who think of nothing but suitors, whether for others or themselves. I tell you again, all of you," she added, tweaking the little dog's ear, " that I have no mind to marry——"

" Oh, Madam . . ."

" Madam, unsay it . . ."

" Madam, you cannot mean . . ."

" Why not? " said the Queen, suddenly eloquent. " Am I to be treated like a bale of goods that is hawked from Court to Court in search of the highest bidder? The Emperor has offered the Tyrol, the King of Spain has sent a special envoy, the Queen Mother of France would have me married to a lad no more than half my age, the Queen of England would rather I remained a widow for ever. Yet none of them suppose me dishonoured by such huckstering. May a Queen never follow where her heart leads? Must she obey the hoary counsel of her statesmen and marry from expediency, whether their choice be idiot or dotard? "

They stared at her in astonishment. Bred, like their mistress, at the Court of France, they knew that royal marriages were arranged with the precision of a game of chess. They too had seen the heartbroken young Lady Elizabeth of France set out on her dreadful journey to the frontier as the bride of the frigidly pious widower, Philip of Spain. Though she was the daughter of one of the mightiest Kings in Christendom, yet she had no more control over her destiny than if she had been the daughter of a slave.

"Yes, I too was thinking of my cousin, Elizabeth," said the Queen. "I do not believe she slept for a single hour of the night before she said farewell to us at Poitiers. She, who was to be the bride of his Most Catholic Majesty, clung to me in terror and begged me to save her from her fate. I could do nothing," she said, suddenly tragic. "What can any of us do if we are born to be bartered for a great alliance?"

"Madam, this is wild talk," said Mary Seton anxiously. "Are you unwell?"

Queen Mary laughed. "Dear, troubled Seton! Perhaps I have a touch of the sun that we see so seldom in Scotland. No, no, I spoke in jest. Perhaps I was also jesting when I said much else. But it is true that I have as yet no mind to marry again."

"Madam," said Mary Fleming impulsively, "I swear that while you remain unwedded I will be no man's bride."

"I swear it also," said Mary Livingstone.

"And I," said Mary Seton.

"And I," said Mary Beton, with a sigh.

Queen Mary stretched out her arms, as if to enfold them all in her embrace. "Dear loyal hearts," she said. "I will have no such sacrifice."

"But we have sworn it."

"We cannot go back on our word."

"How could we be happy while you were still sad?"

"But perhaps you will change your mind," said Mary Beton hopefully.

The Queen laughed. " Perhaps I shall," she said. " And now our little respite is over. I have not yet decided what jewels I shall wear for the Riding of Parliament. And alterations may be needed to my gown."

" Oh, Madam, it will be such joy to see you in bright colours again," said Mary Fleming. " Heaven be praised that you have decided to lay aside your mourning and ride in splendour from Holyrood——"

" Have you a fancy for crimson, Madam? Worn with cloth of silver——" urged Mary Livingstone.

" We shall sparkle like the stars round the Queen of the night——" cried Mary Fleming.

" Nay, her Grace must shine like the sun in splendour. Madam, pray choose cloth of gold——"

The hubbub of high excited voices was like the twittering of sparrows in the eaves. Laughing, the Queen put her hands over her ears. " Children, children, your clamour will deafen me. Yet you are both right, Flem and Livvie. I will wear crimson velvet and cloth of gold, with my ruby cross and chain, my great collar of pearls and——"

" Oh, Madam, Madam, it will be like the fair days gone by——"

" Hush, then, for we are near the gates of the Palace," Queen Mary warned them, a finger to her lips. " Do not let us compel Master Knox to complain again of the levity of the Queen and her ladies. Already I have listened to enough scoldings to last for the rest of my life."

Obediently they caught her mood, pacing gravely after her, heads held high, towards the guards on duty at the entrance to the Palace, the little dog trotting meekly at the Queen's high heels. Halberds clashed on the stone flags as the guards presented arms, and the Queen inclined her head in response. But she also paused to speak to the tall men-at-arms. For she had inherited her father's love of simplicity as well as splendour, her grandfather's royal knack of knowing a surprising number of those who served her by sight.

" I have not seen you here before. What is your name? "

The big man with the lean dark face flushed with pleasure. " Angus MacDowl, your Grace. I am but new come to Edinburgh."

" Where is your home? "

" By Inverness, your Grace."

" Alas, you are far from it." The Queen turned to his companion. " And you, are you also from the north? "

The squat, sturdy fellow whose mop of fair hair was shaggy as an ill-thatched barn, shook his head glumly. " I am frae the Border country, your Grace."

" Who is your lord? "

" The Earl of Bothwell, Madam. I served in his troop as Sheriff of Lothian, and since his exile I have waited on his return."

Queen Mary smiled at the ugly, obstinate face. " May I too find such loyalty," she said. Then, with a little sigh, she passed on. As the descendant of a line of Kings whose people had adored them for their forthright ways, such contacts came more naturally to her than the formalities of France, where the common folk scarcely presumed to breathe the same air as those who ruled them. Things were different in Scotland. For the Scottish Court was in the very midst of the people of Edinburgh. Housewives marked the Queen's comings and goings with inquisitive, eager pride as they gossiped at their stairheads, speculated on the business of those who visited her. Her splendour was their splendour; her justice, dignity, prestige, even her happiness their intimate concern. Because she was so near to them she was dear indeed. The knowledge of it reached her as surely as the blessed warmth of the sun.

But the Scottish people's very identification with the personal conduct of their Queen gave the plain speaking of such men as John Knox additional power. The house of Stewart had been not only loved and obeyed in Scotland by the common people but supported by all the authority of the old faith. Against such a combination, the efforts of the most arrogant nobles to defy, even to drag down the Crown, had usually failed.

It was Mary's misfortune that things were different now. Since the Reformation the Scottish ministers of religion were inevitably at odds with a ruler who adhered to the old faith. So the balance of power wavered, with the Queen on one side, the Kirk on the other, and the people, gentle and simple, turning some this way and some that. As a young Queen, inexperienced and unmarried, she faced a nightmare task. Mary knew that well. She had returned to Scotland after careful instruction, bound by treaty and affection to France, sufficiently obedient to her alien education even to change the spelling of her family name. But no Stewart had ever been patient in bondage. Those who had schooled her for her part were now all dead, save only the Queen Mother, Catherine de Medici, whom she cordially detested, and the Cardinal of Lorraine, who had somewhat damaged her reverence for him by presuming to make arrangements for her second marriage without her knowledge or consent. She was now ready to seek advice elsewhere, perhaps even to free herself from the need to seek advice at all.

But John Knox, who had already published his *Blast of the Trumpet against the Monstrous Regiment of Women*, saw it very differently. " Such stinking pride of women as was seen at that Parliament was never before observed in Scotland," he declared in the pulpit of St. Giles at the first opportunity. And for good measure he took the chance of speaking against the Earl of Moray, whose earldom, as he truly observed, needed confirming. It was a remark which Moray was not inclined to forgive. The great building was crowded to its doors, for the opportunity of hearing a preacher of such pyrotechnic eloquence as John Knox was never neglected. Lords and their ladies, prosperous citizens and their wives had settled themselves on the stools their servants had borne to the Church, and the common people were packed as close as kindling, their faces a pale blur among the shadows as the preacher, beginning on a low and earnest note, mounted gradually to his peroration, was leaning forward with his arms rising and falling, his eyes blazing in the yellowish pallor of his face, no longer sour as a moulting eagle but superb in his eloquence as the same bird about to swoop upon his appalled congregation.

" And now, my lords," he cried in the harsh, oddly compelling voice which struck at his hearers as if a gnarled forefinger had touched each one in the solar plexus, " to put an end to all I hear of the Queen's marriage. Dukes, brethren to Emperors and Kings, strive all for the best game. But this, my lords, will I say—note the day and bear witness—that whensoever the nobility of Scotland consents that an infidel —and all Papists are infidels—shall be head to your Sovereign, ye bring God's vengeance upon the country, a plague upon yourselves, and perchance ye shall do small comfort to your Sovereign."

As the strident voice ceased, the hollow silence was broken only by the hiss of indrawn breath. Even Knox had never before spoken so explicitly, nor with such evident intention of claiming the Kirk's right to coerce the Queen.

Mary had a full report of the sermon before the shocked and startled congregation had sat down to their Sunday dinners, and its effect on her was all that the most avid of trouble-makers could wish. Even the Earl of Moray, waiting on his sister in her small withdrawing-room at Holyroodhouse, was surprised by the violence of her indignation.

" It is intolerable that one of my subjects should presume to speak so. I will endure it no longer," said Mary furiously.

" Master Knox has indeed exceeded his duty," Moray agreed sententiously. " And many of his own folk have been offended in consequence."

" Offended ? I am outraged," Mary retorted. " Proceedings shall be taken against him for high treason. I will have him hanged."

" It is scarcely treason, Madam, I fear," said Moray warningly. For he had the habit of judging any problem according to its probable effect on his own affairs, and the fall of John Knox might endanger the new religion. If it did, he himself might have to surrender his share of the confiscated Church lands. " Knox spoke boldly, but with the greatest solicitude for his sovereign lady."

" He shall answer for his boldness," Mary said, twisting the lace kerchief between her fingers with the vehement gesture of one wringing out clothes. " I have borne all and more than any sovereign may. Summon him, brother, to appear before me to give an account of his conduct forthwith."

" It shall be done, Madam," said the Earl of Moray, not ill-pleased with his errand.

But John Knox received his summons with composure. Several of his supporters escorted him down the Canongate to the Palace, but only the quiet and gentle minister, Erskine of Dun, was allowed to enter the Queen's presence with him. Mary was seated under her canopy of state, with Moray by her side, and her ladies, as usual on such occasions, had withdrawn to the far end of the chamber. She greeted him without preamble, anger exaggerating the trilled French r's till her soft voice was blurred with them, the jewels on her fingers flashing as she clasped and unclasped her hands on her black velvet gown.

" Master Knox," she said, " I have been patient with you too long. I have endured your rigorous manner of speaking, both against myself and my uncles. I have sought your favour by all possible means. I have offered you presence and audience whenever it pleased you to admonish me, yet I cannot get quit of you. It is too much. I vow to God I shall be revenged."

Erskine of Dun turned his troubled face to his companion, murmuring a plea for moderation. But John Knox was not to be restrained. He smoothed his beard with complacent fingers and nodded, as if at the petulance of a child.

" True it is, Madam, that your Grace and I have been at diverse controversies. And yet I never observed your Grace to be offended with me. Outside the pulpit, Madam, I think few have occasion for offence. But there, Madam——" Knox raised a hand in a patriarchal gesture, his voice dropping an octave towards the organ notes with which he entranced his congregations, " I am not master of myself. I must obey Him who commands me to speak plain and flatter no flesh upon the face of the earth."

Mary made a little movement as if to shrug away the enchantment with which he sought to eclipse her keen wits, and her curt question brought the preacher back from the cloudy kingdom of rhetoric to the matter now in hand.

" But what have you to do with my marriage? "

John Knox avoided the direct issue. " God has not sent me, Madam," he rumbled, " to wait upon the Courts of Princesses, nor upon the chambers of ladies, but to preach the evangel to such as please to hear it. It has two parts; repentance and faith. In preaching repentance it is necessary to tell all people of their faults. But since your nobility is for the most part too affectionate to do this, I have no choice but to speak as I have done."

Mary surveyed him with distaste. " And still I ask what you have to do with my marriage? And what are you within this commonwealth? "

" I am a subject born within the same, Madam," Knox retorted with unusual precision. " And though I be neither earl, lord nor baron, yet has God made me—however abject in your eyes—a profitable member whose duty it is no less to forewarn you of such things as may hurt, if I foresee them, than any lesser citizen. Both my vocation and my conscience demand plainness of me, and therefore, Madam, to yourself I will repeat what I have but now said in the pulpit . . ."

But Mary could endure no more. She was aware that she could do nothing against such a man. She had spoken gently, regally, calmly and violently, and all her words had rebounded like the gaudy balls she had tossed against a stone wall as a child. She felt helpless with fury, dismayed by the violence of her longing to take a horsewhip to such an obstinately defiant heretic. She bit her lip, drew a long shaken breath and burst into a passion of weeping.

Moray made an imperious gesture of dismissal. But John Knox ignored it. Thrusting his hands into his sleeves, he folded his lips and remained. At the far end of the chamber the Queen's ladies rose in consternation, whispering together, uncertain what to do. Then Erskine of Dun stepped forward, his kindly face creased with distress, and knelt by the Queen's side.

" Madam, I beg you to take comfort. My friend Knox may have an over-forceful manner of speech. Yet I promise he has your welfare as closely at heart as any of your subjects. My sweet lady, calm yourself, I beg you . . ."

But Mary could not check the sobs which shook her. " Will you not believe," implored John Erskine, " that all your subjects, of the old faith or the new, unite in reverence for their sovereign lady? Nor is there a Prince in Europe who would not be honoured to have you as his bride. Be not troubled by plain speaking, Madam, which is offered awkwardly, it may be, yet for——"

The Queen reached for a handkerchief and dabbed at her eyes. Uncertainly she smiled at the minister whose loving duty was so evidently sincere. But at that moment John Knox intervened, and his harsh voice set her shivering, like a thoroughbred gouged by the spur.

" Madam," Knox declared, " in God's presence I speak. I never delighted in the weeping of any of God's creatures. Much less can I rejoice in your Majesty's weeping. But since I have offered you no occasion to be offended, but have spoken the truth as my vocation craves, I dare not hurt my conscience or betray my commonwealth by my silence——"

Mary's sobs shook her, she could scarcely speak, but through the tumult one word came clearly. " Go . . ." she cried aloud. " Go . . . I will hear no more."

Honestly bewildered, John Knox looked about him. But

he saw only hostile faces. Moray glared, Erskine shook his head at him, the little group of the Queen's ladies faced him with clenched fists and angry eyes. He sighed, opened his mouth as if to speak again, then realised the impossibility of making himself heard against the Queen's tempestuous weeping. With the air of a man most outrageously misjudged, he gathered his gown about him and strode out of the presence chamber.

The ante-room was crowded, not only with those whose duty it was to wait on the Queen at that hour, but by every member of her household who had been able to devise an errand which would bring him there. He opened the door upon a perspective of astounded faces and arrested movement suggestive of a masque during which the performers, at the advent of a magician, had been turned to stone.

The Lord Chamberlain with his staff of office, the Earl of Morton with his hat-brim pulled low over his eyes; lords of the old faith such as Seton and Athol, or of the new, like Argyll and Kirkcaldy of Grange, stood stricken, and as Knox approached, ostentatiously turned away. On a window-seat, a dark-haired singer's fingers hesitated over the strings of the lute he cradled on his lifted knee, then hastily he began to strum again as Knox turned his way, ducking his head till his face was hidden by his velvet bonnet's bobbing plume. Round a table piled high with bright silks a group of ladies sat with needles poised and round eyes fixed on him. Suddenly, out of sheer nervousness, one of them giggled, and Knox whirled on her and her appalled companions like an accusing conscience.

" Oh, fair ladies," he rasped, his thin smile ranging from their jewelled, close-fitting hoods, and high, jewelled collars to their richly brocaded farthingales and the medley of vivid silks in their uncertain hands, " how pleasant were this life of yours if it should ever abide, and we might pass to heaven with all this gay gear."

With bitten lips and streaming eyes they watched his long forefinger rove round their shaken circle, every now and then jabbing with special vehemence towards a splendid gown or helplessly convulsed face. " But fie on that knave Death," cried Knox, " that will come whether we will or not; for when he has laid on his arrest, the foul worms will be busy with this flesh, be it never so fair and so tender, and the silly soul, I fear, shall be so feeble that it can neither carry with it gold, garnishing nor precious stones! "

They cowered beneath his sarcasm. But the contrapuntal effect of formidably wagging beard and yet more formidably wagging finger was too much for one of the Queen's French attendants who spoke no language but her own. Her laughter escaped at last from her control, though she still gasped and hiccuped with anxiety to check herself, while the others, catching the infection of hysteria, compelled Master Knox to complete his indictment unheard. For a moment he stared down at the helpless company with the frenzied irritation of a man thrashed by nettles. Neither imprisonment, starvation, nor the back-breaking ordeal of long months chained to his oar in the galleys, had been able to quench his zeal. But ridicule, for the moment, defeated it. He shook his fists at the circle of laughing faces, turned on his heel and swept away.

As the hubbub of speculation, laughter and indignation at last diminished, Lord John of Coldingham, most evidently in a towering rage, stormed in.

" What is this I hear? " he shouted at the Lord Chamberlain, now confronting him in a dither of uncertainty.

" My lord, the Queen has just given audience to Master Knox. I do not know if she will receive you——"

" But I know very well that she will," retorted Lord John furiously. " I have but now had the news of the fellow's impudence. Let me pass——"

He hurled himself at the heavy door, wrenched it open without waiting for the services of the grooms of the chamber who leapt forward, slamming it behind him before those outside could catch more than a glimpse of the wan smile and outstretched arms with which the Queen greeted her favourite brother. But some of these who had contrived to thrust themselves nearest to the door fancied they saw the Earl of Moray scowl. And to all those in the ante-chamber Lord John's words carried clearly.

" I am as fervent for the new faith as any man, but if these knaves do not keep their tongues off the Queen's Majesty I will have them run through in their very pulpits."

And Lethington, returning from his embassy shortly afterwards, was nearly as angry as Lord John had been. For Master Knox could scarcely have chosen a more awkward moment to make public the names of those with whom he had been in negotiation. Apart from less personal considerations, the Archduke Charles had been one of Queen Elizabeth's suitors and Catherine de Medici would rather see her daughter-in-law in her grave than imperilling the balance of power in Europe by a marriage with Spain.

But Lethington, at his first audience with Queen Mary, had no intention of dealing with the main purpose of his journey. He preferred, instead, to please her with lesser matters.

" Welcome, my lord of Lethington," she said warmly, as he knelt to kiss her hand. " What—word have you from France? "

" Madam, I bring you the greetings of my lord the King, of his young kinsfolk, of the Queen Mother——"

Mary sighed.

" But also something that I believe will gladden your heart still more. This portrait——"

Alert at once, Mary clapped her hands. " The little portrait of my mother that I asked you to obtain? You have it indeed? "

" I have it here," said Lethington, drawing a small parcel from an inner pocket, and undoing the chamois leather which protected the miniature of Mary of Lorraine. " I knew it would be the first thing your Grace desired to see. It is a fair likeness, I believe——"

She almost snatched it from him, kissed it, then held it at arm's length.

"A fair likeness indeed," Mary cried. "So I have seen her look—ah, heaven, how many times? My lord of Lethington, from my heart I thank you——"

Lethington smiled. "My greatest pleasure is to serve your Grace," he murmured. "I also brought some few fancies, since I thought it might amuse you to know how fashion fared in France."

"Then have them brought in forthwith," cried Mary, eagerly. "And bid my ladies join us. They too, will rejoice."

Soon the floor was covered with bolts of red velvet and white satin, cloth of gold figured with blue, cloth of silver, and dove-grey satin. Mary Beton paraded about in a coat of green silk, Mary Fleming in another of white velvet, while Mary Livingstone draped herself in scarlet, and the Queen laughed as Mary Seton snatched her mistress's little dog off the strewn brocades.

"My lord, you too have a fondness for small creatures. Tell me, how did your monkey fare while you were gone?"

"Alas, Madam," said Lethington, with a little grimace which made him for an instant surprisingly like his pet, "my people had too little understanding of its nature. It died within a week of my departure."

"But why, my lord," said Mary in distress, "did you not entrust the little beast to me? I would have cared for it."

"Madam, I thank you," Lethington said. "But I could scarcely think of burdening you further. You have many graver matters on your mind."

"Yes," she said softly. Stillness came down on her like a veil as she spoke, and the excited chatter rose about them like a wall of sound. As he leant confidentially over her they might almost have been alone.

"I brought little out of England, Madam, to compare with what I obtained in France. Her Majesty could not be persuaded to commit herself as regards the succession, and I was scarcely able to credit the proposal she made for your Grace's marriage."

"Indeed?" Mary tossed her head. "I do not care to hear it. What of the other matter on which I have twice written to the English Queen's Majesty? It is not our pleasure that the Queen of England should retain one of our subjects in captivity. Has the Earl of Bothwell been given permission to depart forth of England?"

Lethington stroked his chin. "Madam, I pray you to believe that the interests of Scottish justice are always very near my heart. But with more urgent matters of personal concern to your Grace in hand I did not venture to press the cause of a man who has scarcely endeared himself in the past to the Queen of England."

"And yet, my lord of Lethington," said Mary gravely, "may that not be the better reason for offering him a chance to serve the Queen of Scots?"

CHAPTER FIVE

SHARP, resinous and sweet, the scent of sealing-wax hung on the damp air as the Earl of Bothwell folded the sheet of parchment, addressed it in his fine, flowing hand, and turned it over to apply a daub of wax before the sand with which he had briefly sifted it was dry. He had arrived in Paris in November, 1563, and it was now February, 1565. He was shabby, cold, and savagely disillusioned as he blew on his numb fingers and reached for his quill, to write yet another begging letter, wry-faced at such an ignoble necessity.

Imprisonment and exile had embittered him. He had never expected the Queen to permit his enemies to keep him so long out of Scotland. He was too casual to be covetous, but it was exasperating to realise that he was one of the few Scottish noblemen pledged to the new religion who had not been enriched with the temporalities of the old. On the contrary, it now seemed as if he had lost even the possessions he had inherited. The command of the Liddesdale stronghold of Hermitage, his headquarters as Lieutenant of the Border, had been given to one of the Elliots, and such news as he had received indicated that even his family estates had been annexed by those in favour at Court. Worse, he had lost his best friend in Scotland with Lord John of Coldingham's sudden death on the journey through the Highlands which he had been making with the Earl of Moray, nominally to assist his half-brother in his administration of justice. But from Janet's distraught account, it sounded as if someone who had wanted him out of the way had used poison to dispose of him. Bothwell had raged helplessly, discounting much of Janet's description of the Queen's distress, her kindness to herself and the baby, and her wish that he should be called Francis, after her own dead husband. And then, Janet said, the Queen had wept, declaring that all those she loved were taken from her. Those without that distinction, thought James Hepburn sourly, might rot where they lay.

Nevertheless, he waited hopefully on the Cardinal of Lorraine from time to time. The two men respected each other in spite of their religious differences, and Bothwell's loyal service to Mary of Lorraine had not been forgotten by her kinsfolk in France. But the letter which the Queen had promised to write to the French King requesting that the command of his royal bodyguard of Scottish Archers, which was in her gift, should be given to her trusty servant, the Earl of Bothwell, had not yet produced any result. This was a pity, for the appointment would at least enable him to pay his servants, so that it would not be so easy for ill-disposed persons to bribe them to murder him. The attempt had come to nothing, but it had, paradoxically, cheered him considerably. Men did not try to dispose of an enemy who was no longer dangerous. But he would have liked to find better quarters than the rat-ridden rooms in an unsavoury neighbourhood which were all he could afford without additional funds. He received a small loan and the Cardinal's assurances of goodwill. But the months dragged leadenly.

Scots passing through Paris on business of one sort or another brought him news of Scotland that made him rage against Moray's arrogance, Lethington's machinations, and the indifference of the Queen. He petitioned everyone even remotely likely to have influence to use it for his return. Instinct warned him that dramatic events were imminent, and to have no part in them, imprisoned as inexorably by poverty in his Paris garret as he had ever been imprisoned in the Castle of Edinburgh, would be more than he could bear.

It was during an audience with the Cardinal that he learned of Queen Elizabeth's outrageous proposal that the Queen of Scots should marry her own dubious admirer, Lord Robert Dudley. But to Bothwell's surprise the Cardinal of Lorraine was even angrier at the reports that Mary had countered the insulting suggestion by summoning the Earl of Lennox back to Scotland. Bothwell looked blank as the Cardinal groaned aloud, his clear mind already divining her purpose. The Countess of Lennox was the daughter of Margaret Tudor and her son's claim to the English throne second only to the Scottish Queen's own. Furthermore, young Lord Darnley, tall, athletic and extremely handsome, was only a few months younger than his cousin Mary. But the Cardinal, who had seen something of the pretty, spoilt boy when he visited Paris to bring his parents' condolences for poor young Francis's death, beat the table before him with his clenched fists.

" That popinjay! " he exploded. " He will ruin all. She must not marry him."

In Scotland, though the burning question was still that of the Queen's marriage, there had also been some alarm for her health, and yet another sensation about the preaching of Master Knox, who had gone from one excess to another, and eventually been taken to task by Lethington for actually calling the Queen " a slave of Satan " from the pulpit. The Earl of Lennox's return had been well received, except by a few people who had good reason to regret it. The Duke of Chatelherault, head of the rival house of Hamilton, had left Court rather than meet him, and only the assurances Lennox brought that his Countess, a Douglas by birth, renounced all claim to the earldom of Angus, placated the Earl of Morton, head of the Douglas family, who had been comfortably drawing its revenues while the child who bore the title was his ward. It was thought that Moray, on the other hand, actually favoured the Dudley marriage, which struck less sharply at his own greatness. But he was careful not to let this appear to the Earl of Lennox.

At Candlemas, 1565, Bothwell was at last made Captain of the Scottish Guard in Paris, at the Queen of Scots's request. The appointment gave him great pleasure. He took it, typically, as a sign that his affairs were mending. He also found the Cardinal willing to arrange a period of leave for him, in order to obtain a first-hand report of affairs in Scotland. So Bothwell returned to his dismal quarters in such an exuberant state of mind that his bewildered page, staggering under a cheerful buffet, thought his master must be drunk.

" Our fortunes have turned, my friend, at last," said Bothwell. " Send Dandie Pringle out to buy us wine, meat and firewood. And start packing."

" Packing, my lord? Whither are we bound? "

" For Scotland," roared the Earl of Bothwell.

His instinct for crisis had been sound, though the farce of Mary's proposed marriage with Lord Robert Dudley, now Earl of Leicester, had not yet been played to a standstill. Moray and Lethington had actually met Bedford and Randolph at Berwick to discuss the marriage treaty, and Randolph was still urging Dudley's preposterous cause. Incautiously, he pursued the Queen to St. Andrews, where, in the snug little house in South Street, he found her quite determined to discuss no affairs of state.

" Master Randolph, if you join us you must be merry,"
she declared. " I shall not permit you to interrupt our pastimes
with your grave and great matters."

Randolph sighed. " I humbly pray your Grace that you
will inform me when I may do my Queen's business," he said
stiffly.

Mary hummed a few bars of the latest dance tune from
France, sketched a step or two with Mary Livingstone and
spoke over her shoulder. " I pray you, sir, if you be weary
here, return to Edinburgh and keep your gravity until the
Queen come thither. I assure you, you shall not get her here.
I know not myself where she can be. You see——" she
pirouetted, her empty hands spread wide, " here is no cloth
of estate. Why should you seek a Queen in this merchant's
house in South Street?"

" I was given to understand your Grace would be found
there," said Randolph, smiling reluctantly at Mary Beton,
who was shaking her fist at his long face.

" You shall share our dinner, and see whether we do not
cook better than all those that crowd our kitchens at the
Court," Mary promised. " You shall sit next to my dear Beton,
who thinks the world of you."

Meanwhile Lennox, alarmed by the persistence of those
urging Dudley's suit, had summoned his son in haste. But he
could not tell when he would arrive. For young Lord Darnley
was an English subject, and his mother was still resident in
England. If Darnley left for Scotland without the English
Queen's permission it might be disastrous for her. The
Queen of Scots merely laughed when Lennox spoke of such
difficulties. " If my cousin is the man I think him, he will
find a way." But she let Lethington proceed with the negotiations for the marriage with Robert Dudley, which might still
prove a useful red herring.

She was in a strange, restless mood that spring. It puzzled
the persistent Randolph. But her Highland subjects would
have called her " fey." She seemed to have been transported

into a state of mind far beyond the cares and complexities of daily life, an unreal, dangerous condition from which the victim is apt to be roused only by the impact of disaster. The little house in South Street was full of her friends, and her singers, led by the lean and swarthy Piedmontese, David Rizzio, seemed never silent. Randolph's head ached from the strumming, fiddling, laughing and dancing, and the dourer citizens were scandalised by the blaze of light, the babel of sound borne down South Street on the snell wind. He was able to secure only one serious discussion with the Queen as she rested by the fire, while her ladies cleared the supper so that the evening's music could begin.

Incautiously, Mary let the astute ambassador persuade her to talk of France, and of her French kinsfolk's desire that she should make another French marriage. "Not to marry, as you know, cannot be for me," Mary said. "To defer marriage long would be unwise. How privy to my mind your mistress hath been——" She looked quickly at the English ambassador's blank, attentive face—"you know. How willing I am to follow her advice I have shown many times, and yet——" She made a little gesture of impatience, "I can find in her no resolution. My meaning unto her is plain, and so shall my dealings be."

"Would it not be better, Madam," Randolph said, careful to avoid any direct mention of the English succession, "to let your desire come by time, than to force it by importunity?"

But the recognition of her claim to the English succession was not one Mary was prepared to defer. She flared up at once.

"When have you heard me speak of these matters before?"

"Not of yourself, Madam," said Randolph patiently. "But your ministers bear always your mind in their words."

"I gave them charge," said Mary quickly, "to consider what was fittest for me . . ."

She was flushed now, so that Randolph, who was not

disposed, either by nature or profession, to praise any woman unreservedly, surveyed her with admiration. ". . . I believe they will advise me for the best. But if your mistress will guide me I will leave their advices and follow hers alone. This is no sudden impulse," she began. Then, biting her lip, she rose as if to avoid the risk of indiscretion.

"I beg your Grace," said Randolph, rising with her, "not to cut off your talk here. Your speech has been so wise, well-framed and comfortable——"

But she had already regretted her departure from her former elusiveness. "I am a fool," she said suddenly, "thus long to talk with you. You are too subtle for me . . ." Her voice broke and she turned away.

"I protest upon my honesty," stammered Randolph, "that my purpose was but to nourish a better understanding——"

But he had lost her confidence. Her brown eyes, so strangely flecked, it seemed, with sunshine, even on a lightless winter's day, were glancing hither and thither in search of distraction. "At Edinburgh we may perhaps commune further . . ." she promised, with one of her gossamer gestures of dismissal.

There Randolph was obliged to leave it. He went from South Street to the Priory and conferred with Moray, whom he found as anxious for his sister to marry Robert Dudley as Morton himself could be. For Lennox had further alienated him by bringing jewels and presents for the Queen, her four Maries, Lethington and Athol, but had been tactless enough to bring nothing for him. Afterwards Randolph rode in haste to Berwick, for a secret report had reached him that a nobleman of the greatest importance was riding north through England, and with all his heart he hoped it might be Robert Dudley.

But at the same time Mary, who also had her sources of information, left St. Andrews, escorted by her personal attendants, to journey further through her frigid, echoing land. Frost had gripped the countryside so that earth, air and water seemed congealed. The very sea was frilled with ice, the ground rang beneath the horses' hooves, and the breath of the Queen and her small cavalcade hung on the piercing air like phantoms, between the distant mountains, sullen as pewter beneath the snow-line, and a nearer sea of lead.

It was mid-February when she reached Wemyss Castle, brooding on the cliff-top from which it guarded the coast of Fife, confronted by the misty outline of Edinburgh, on the far side of the Forth, a city crouching like a hoary lion on its rock. And Master Randolph, who had hurried to Berwick in the confident expectation of being the first from Scotland to meet Robert Dudley, now created Earl of Leicester, when he came to press his suit in person, was dismayed to find the lounging lad Darnley being entertained by the Governor of Berwick, after a headlong ride during which, he grumbled, he had outdistanced all his followers and foundered his only riding horse. But Randolph was first a diplomat and only long afterwards a partisan. Some change of heart must have occurred in Queen Elizabeth for the boy to be there at all. He bowed before it.

" I would be honoured, my lord, if you would consider completing your journey on the beast which has borne me hither."

" I take that very kindly, Mr. Ambassador," said Darnley cheerfully. He was a toppling tall, over-confident boy, brought up to be well aware of his good looks, and inordinately pleased with his accomplishments. His beardless face, taut now with hard riding in the cold air, was charming when he smiled. And he smiled often, provided that things were going well. Those meeting him for the first time were not in a position to know how sullen his face became when they went otherwise. For the present he was in exuberantly high spirits, eating enormously and swallowing great draughts of wine as he described his last interview with Queen Elizabeth.

" Heaven knows what moved her Majesty of England," Darnley said, between mouthfuls, glancing so pointedly towards the haunch of venison on the side table that the attendants hurried to replenish his trencher. " One day she swore roundly that she would see me damned before she gave permission for me to visit my father in Scotland. But the next she snapped her fingers in my face and told me to be gone."

The Earl of Bedford, recently appointed Marshal of Berwick, surveyed his guest in perplexed disapproval, and speculated on the extent of his habitual indiscretion. If it was his habit to babble so, without regard to the company he kept, Queen Elizabeth might well have concluded that he would do his own cause in Scotland as much harm as she could wish.

" It came about when I was in attendance on her Majesty and obliged to pace behind her while she took the air on the terrace of her Palace at Greenwich." Darnley giggled, choked, and filled his mouth again. " You should have seen me, my friends, mincing and ogling with the best while she lifted her skirts to give us all a chance to admire her well-turned ankles. Lord, what a woman! "

" But you were about to tell us of your journey, my lord," said Randolph hastily.

Darnley shook his knife at him. " You shall not spoil my tale! All shall be told in its place. Next I had to escort the Queen's Majesty to her apartments, aye, and help her choose the gown she would presently wear to receive the Spanish ambassador. Believe me or not, she refused the service of her ladies and had my lord of Leicester loosen her from the one she wore to give the morning's audience." He grinned at the memory. " Only the blessed saints can know how she contrived to constrict herself within such a farthingale! My lords, her stays were of supple steel——"

The Earl of Bedford jerked his thumb over his shoulder, and the servants scattered. But Randolph, sitting opposite Darnley, fancied he could still hear them sniggering behind the screens. He drummed on the table-top with impatient fingers and wondered what further revelations were to follow.

But the lack of enthusiasm in his audience seemed at last to have made some slight impression on the young man's self-esteem. He left his account of Queen Elizabeth's under-wear incomplete and launched loudly on an account of his own escape.

" All was prepared. I had warned my mother to order my people to have my horse saddled and my gear bestowed. Within an hour I was on the road for the north——"

" Unaccompanied, my lord? " murmured Randolph. It might be in the best tradition of chivalric romance, but he could scarcely credit the folly of a prospective consort of the Scottish Queen who arrived in Scotland without either attend-ants or gifts. Lethington, for instance, would not lose the opportunity of quoting his favourite tag about the folly of those who sought to lure hawks empty-handed.

Darnley leant back, replete at last, and smiled com-placently. " I am not such a fool as that, Master Randolph. I have not come as a beggar. My fellows are somewhere behind me on the road with all my gear."

" And what will you do now, my lord? " inquired Randolph.

" Why, ride on to Edinburgh," said Darnley carelessly.

" If it would be of service to your lordship," said Randolph, " I will gladly bear you company. I have some knowledge of the Scottish people, having resided among them."

" As you wish," said Darnley, yawning hugely. It was evident that he considered himself fully capable of dealing with the situation, and had no mind to be patronised by Court officials, whether Scots or English. " I shall go to Holyroodhouse."

" The Queen is still, I believe, in Fife," said Randolph.

" Then I shall follow her thither," said young Darnley gaily. " But it would please me well enough to see something of Edinburgh, of which my mother has told me much."

" Pah, a poor small place by comparison with London," said the Earl of Bedford, who had seen more than enough service in the north, and blamed its climate for the rheumatism which, in such winters as the present, seemed to set every old wound aching.

But Darnley humoured him with his enchanting grin. " And yet, my lord, it may be that one sees a city somewhat differently from the steps of a throne."

Bedford laughed. " I admire your confidence, but I do not envy you. I had rather test my fate astride the wildest stallion foaled than set my foot on the steps that lead to the throne of Scotland."

Darnley sniggered. He had drunk freely, and the wine was beginning to take its effect. Still boastful, but muzzy-headed now, he pushed back his stool and stood swaying. " Ah," he mumbled, shaking an admonitory finger at the hazily-seen figure of his host, " in this case it is no stallion I must mount, else I might also have doubts of the enterprise. But when it comes to a pretty mare, I fancy I am as fair a horseman as any . . ." He yawned, belched, and closed his eyes. " As you shall dis-dishcover in due course. But firssht . . . ai . . . I must sleep . . ."

The Earl of Bedford stepped forward, nodding to Randolph who gripped the boy's other arm. Together they marched young Darnley, now babbling loudly of his amorous adventures, off to bed. He set out for Edinburgh on the following morning, with Randolph by his side, and a straggle of disgruntled followers with their pack-beasts strung out along the iron-rutted track behind them, their voices sounding querulous on the frosty air.

Darnley was well received at Holyroodhouse. Lord Robert, the secular incumbent of the Abbey, and another of King James's bastards, was too comatose and comfortable to attempt to rival his half-brother of Moray in his ambitious schemes. His father had made him Commendator of Holyrood, and the temporalities which went with his sinecure offered him a very pretty living. He therefore saw no reason to endure the discomforts and anxieties incident on a quest for greater things.

But he entertained his young kinsman lavishly, for he enjoyed the pleasures of hospitality.

Randolph was relieved to find Darnley on his best behaviour. The few words of advice he himself had offered had been so casually received that he did not repeat them. But Lady Lennox had evidently coached her son well in the part he was to play, and his lapse on arrival at Berwick was not repeated. On the contrary, his charming smile and pretty manners were much in evidence as he towered above his fellow guests.

As far as the watchful English ambassador could tell, most of the nobility were prepared to consider him as an acceptable suitor for their Queen. Even such extreme Protestants as Argyll and Glencairn admitted that he offered less danger to the new religion than a foreign prince, though nominally at least, he was, of course, a Papist. But, since both he and his father were willing to attend the preaching, even Knox considered that there might be hope for them yet.

On the other hand, as Randolph reported to Cecil, the Hamiltons, headed by the Duke of Chatelherault, could see nothing good in him, and the Earl of Morton, head of Darnley's Douglas kinsfolk, greeted him warily. Many thoughtful citizens, delighted by his splendid youth, yet shook their heads and wondered whether his character promised sufficient stability for the help and succour of their young Queen.

It was decided that Darnley should not wait till the Queen returned to Holyroodhouse, but seek an audience with her at once in the Castle of Wemyss. A snowstorm was pending as he was rowed across the Forth, irritably conscious that he was not looking his best, numbed and shivering, with a streaming nose and a premonitory pricking at the back of his throat. For even Darnley's immense conceit was disturbed by the ignobility of catching an inopportune and unbecoming cold from the rigours of that northern winter he had reckoned to take in his stride.

But once in shelter he was so eager for the encounter with the cousin who could make a King of him that he forgot everything else. Impatiently he swore at the fumbling servants who helped him to change his sodden clothes for the splendid outfit of white and gold in which he would presently appear before the Queen's Majesty.

His cousin Mary was impatiently awaiting him. As she watched the boat slowly approach her anxiety had been almost more than she could bear. Her passionate hope that he would prove worthy, her sick fear that he would not, alternated like the double beat of her heart. All that day it had been impossible to please her. Thrice she had sent for her musicians, only to declare their harmony no better than a jangle and dismiss them. She had begun a new piece of embroidery, pricked her finger till the blood came, and pushed the frame aside, to pace about the presence chamber like a disconsolate spirit. On one side, the narrow windows looked out on the central courtyard, their small lozenges of heavily leaded glass sombre against the drifting snow. On the other the perspective of sea, land and sky had all day long been merged in a vast uncertainty.

" Oh, Seton, you do not think it is an omen? " the Queen whispered.

" Nay, Madam," said Mary Seton firmly, " it is but a hard winter, at which we should rejoice, since it gives the promise of a fair summer to follow, which mild green winters do not."

Queen Mary laughed. " Whatever should I do, Seton, without you and your good sense? "

" That, Madam, I hope you need never discover," said Mary Seton gravely.

" Dear Seton . . ." Queen Mary murmured with absent-minded affection. But she was too restless to be still, and presently she wandered from her well-warmed chamber across the passage to the smaller room in which a muffled figure was painfully writing with fingers almost as purple with cold as the broken seal of the letter from France to which he was composing a reply.

" Why, David, you will catch your death in this unfired

chamber," said Mary in dismay. " Leave your scribing till we have gone to dine, and you may have the other. There at least you will be warm."

Rizzio swung round and rose. Outwardly subservient, an odd expression smouldered in his dark eyes for a second before his hastily lowered lids concealed it. He had received much indulgence during recent years, both as a singer in Chapel and hall, and as a discreet and useful secretary, able to take over the Queen's personal correspondence in the absence of Lethington. So the hint that he would not be expected to dine with the Queen's royal guest on his arrival stung him sharply. But he hid his resentment, well aware that any such display would serve him ill.

" I thank your Grace," he said meekly. " I have all but done."

" Then leave the rest," said Mary imperiously, " and bring your lute to the fireside. Let us try the part-song once more, and see if we can please you this time. Come." She held out her hand in one of the casual gestures of kindness so typical of all her gracious family, exclaiming as she touched his fingers, " Why, you are half frozen, like the poor bird I picked up in the snow. Take this stool near the fire and warm your hands while we set out the music."

David Rizzio huddled himself as he had been bidden on the stool to one side of the chimney breast. But the grimace which creased his thin face was only partly due to the agony of returning circulation. He had seen the emaciated starling which the Queen herself had borne indoors to be revived in this very chamber, and was aware that the giggles of the ladies as they hunted their scores from among their brightly coloured personal belongings indicated the aptitude of the comparison. Grizzled, beaky and cadaverous, in his rusty black, he was not unlike the wretched starling, who had also been privileged, for a time, to occupy a place by the Queen's fireside. But when the starling had recovered sufficiently to gobble the crumbs put down for it and make blundering flights about the room, dropping unpleasant little messes everywhere, it had been exiled to the kitchen quarters where, Rizzio privately suspected, some scullion had unceremoniously wrung its neck. No, he did not care for the comparison.

" We are ready now, David," Mary cried.

" Here is your lute," said Mary Seton.

" Give us the note."

" Sing your part softly, David, or we shall stray from ours."

Rizzio stretched his cramped fingers till the joints cracked, then swept them across the lute in a sure, strong gesture. No longer a cringing, aggressive nonentity, he was another creature when he played or sang, aware of genius and delighting in it. On Parnassus he was King and the Queen a mere commoner. He believed that Mary, herself a musician, knew that her kindness, at such times, was no more than the homage rightfully due to him.

Uncertainly at first, the voices gathered strength, blended and soared. Soft and low, the Queen's voice wove a pattern of sound with the Italian's baritone, so that they were like the trunk and tendrils of a climbing rose which threw out leaves of song sustained by Mary Fleming and Mary Seton, to burst at last into flower with the lovely soprano of Mary Livingstone.

The young man in the doorway, whose whim it had been to appear unheralded, stood listening. It was not difficult to seem entranced as the singers, anxious to maintain a harmony which was not yet familiar, glanced only from Rizzio to their scores, frowning with charming concentration, unaware of being observed.

Rizzio saw him first, his voice failing on an indrawn breath so suddenly that the others stared, then turned, leaping startled to their feet in a confusion of little cries. Only the Queen sat motionless, still as a fawn in a thicket as the hunters crash by, her eyes widening as she stared at the glorious figure of the tall boy who seemed all white and gold, from his shining hair to the gilded rosettes on his white shoes. As her ladies fell back with deep curtseys, the cousins faced each other across the whole length of the chamber. Outside, the gale seemed to have fallen, within, the fire to have ceased its snap and crackle as Mary stared at him, incredulous with joy. She had set more store than she had dared admit on the chance to show the Queen of England what she thought of her outrageous proposal, and at the same time strengthen her own claim to the English throne. But now she scarcely dared believe in the beauty of the young man she meant to marry.

It was not their first meeting. But during the month of complete seclusion which had followed her French husband's death, she had been in no state to take note of the pretty boy of fifteen who bore his mother's condolences to the crape-shrouded Court of St. Germain. Now, at nineteen, full-grown and beautifully intent as a grave young angel, his early promise seemed most gloriously fulfilled. The bright, inquisitive faces of her ladies, the Italian's shrewdly sceptical stare, faded into nothingness. Mary held out her hand in a regal gesture.

" You are most welcome, Cousin. . . ."

PART TWO

February, 1565—February, 1567

" Avand Darnley! "
Motto of Henry Stewart, Lord Darnley

CHAPTER SIX

THE Lady of Morham, a village a few miles from Edinburgh, looked severely down at the young man who lounged, long fingers clasped about his ankles, among the rushes at her feet. It was easy to tell that they were mother and son. Both had the same strong bone structure, the same proud carriage of the head. The same laughter creases fanned out from the corners of their bold dark eyes. But the hair which was visible under the crisply goffered linen edging the close French hood was dark, scarcely threaded with grey, while the crisp crop that curled however close he cut it, was dark red. The former Countess of Bothwell leant forward to grip a fistful, then gave it a tweak which made her victim shout.

"There are times, James, when I think you must have taken leave of your wits."

James Hepburn screwed his head round to grin at her affectionately.

"Why, Mother, I had thought you would be pleased to see your prodigal son."

"Tuts!" said the Lady of Morham. "I am. But not such a fool as to let you know it unasked."

"Why not?" Bothwell looked injured.

"It would but encourage you in your folly. Since Moray means to be the death of you yet, what possessed you ever to leave the Court of France?"

"Perhaps to boast of my new commission. I am Captain of the Scottish Archers of the French King's bodyguard."

"Is such an honour likely to overwhelm the Lord Admiral of Scotland?"

"Then perhaps to discover in the interest of a certain eminent party how his kinswoman is faring."

"I should have thought," said his mother tartly, "that the Cardinal of Lorraine might have found a messenger less likely to pay for such a discovery with his life."

"It may be that I offered," said James Hepburn, "for reasons of my own. To see you, Madam, for instance."

She smiled at him wryly, as if life had made her as wary of those she loved as of more obvious enemies. And the twisted grin with which he answered her made them yet more evidently akin. They understood each other too well to attempt the expression of devotion which both found difficult.

"Be that as it may," said the Lady of Morham, "I am persuaded that no good will come of it. Your enemies' tongues have been busy."

"They are seldom at rest."

"But this time you have your own to thank for it," said his mother severely. "You have been talking too much to your visitors in Paris."

"Who says so?"

"Reports of your indiscretion have not only reached Cecil of England, but Moray and Lethington at home."

James Hepburn rubbed his nose ruefully. "It is true that I may have spoken what was in my heart. I did receive less than justice at the hands of those in authority."

"They claim that you now deserve none."

"Who says so?"

"Your cousin, Alexander."

"He at least is a true man. I will ride over to Riccarton——"

"You will do no such thing," said his mother quickly. "A fine time, James, to go cantering about the countryside in search of your relations. I have already summoned Alexander to Morham. Promise me that you will remain within doors till he comes?"

"I will remain," Bothwell said reluctantly. "Though I am persuaded that Alexander will have little news of importance."

But his cousin's account of the latest charges against him made his mother's anxiety seem reasonable enough. Sir Alexander Hepburn, Laird of Riccarton, was not an alarmist. But he shook his head like a great bear when James announced his intention of brazening it out. If he persisted in thrusting his head into the trap prepared for him, opined Sir Alexander, James had every chance of finding himself without it.

" I had thought," said James hopefully, " of presenting myself at Holyrood to report my appointment as Captain of the Scottish Archers and thank the Queen's Grace for her good offices with the French King's Majesty."

" Man, you must be demented," rumbled the Laird of Riccarton. " Have you no idea of what you are supposed to have been saying? "

" None. Except that it no doubt bears little likeness to what I said."

" Did you swear to be the death of both Moray and Lethington once you were back in Scotland? "

Bothwell, who had been pacing impatiently to and fro, swung slowly round to face Sir Alexander, shamefaced as a lad caught robbing an orchard.

" I may have said something of the sort," he admitted reluctantly. " I am very sure that Scotland will not hold the three of us."

" But what a time to say so," Sir Alexander grumbled. " Yet that is the least of it. What frenzy made you speak against the Queen? "

" Who says I did? "

" Not only your guests, but Dandie Pringle, formerly in your service."

" Surely they will not take the word of a lout dismissed for theft? "

" Mebbe not. But there are enough without him. Did you or did you not," boomed Sir Alexander, " say that both the Queen of Scots and Queen Elizabeth rolled together would scarcely make one honest woman? "

Bothwell grinned. "It was but a figure of speech. Yet right dishonourably indeed have I been treated by both."

"Pringle further maintains that you called our Queen the Cardinal's whore."

"That I did not!" said Bothwell violently.

"Yet Pringle swears it."

"He would swear snow to be scarlet and blood as white as snow if he were paid enough."

"But where has he got such a tale?"

Bothwell looked blank. But presently an idea struck him. He glanced sidelong at his mother, then said uncertainly: "My father had a tale about Cardinal Beton and Queen Marie of Lorraine. I may even have repeated it because another Queen had angered me. What other accusations have been made against me?"

"Sorcery, black arts, sodomy . . ." said Sir Alexander.

"I will ram such lies down any man's throat with my dagger," said Bothwell furiously. "May I not study the properties of metals, the humours of the flesh and the secrets of earth, air and water, as laid down by the learned men of Paris, without being charged with black arts? And as for the rest——" He laughed harshly. "Do they suppose there are no pretty maidens in Paris?"

"We did not think his accusations were true, James," said his mother, soothingly. "But we wished you to know to what lengths those who have the Queen's confidence will go to damage your reputation."

"Surely the Queen's Grace would not listen to such scurrilities?"

"She has authorised Moray to proceed against you on the old charge," said Sir Alexander gloomily. "His summons will be proclaimed by the heralds outside this very door before the week is out."

"He knows, then, that I have returned?" said Bothwell quickly.

Sir Alexander shook his head. "The summons is also

to be read at Crichton, Hailes, Haddington, Duns, Lauder, Selkirk, Hawick, Hermitage and Jedburgh."

" My lord of Moray certainly leaves nothing to chance," said Bothwell dryly. " He has a mind to stop every earth from which the fox may bolt. What think you, Alexander? Shall I answer his challenge? "

Sir Alexander pondered.

" Truth should have nothing to fear," Bothwell maintained.

" I doubt," said Sir Alexander, " that my lord of Moray will rely less on truth than the testimony of a thousand pikes."

" Nevertheless, let us surprise him. Answer the challenge, Alexander. Give surety on my behalf."

" The Justice Clerk is asking two hundred pounds."

" It shall be found. I have a mind to challenge those men who are so glib against me in my absence. I might appeal to the Queen."

"And what would come of that after Moray has had the pleasure of repeating your—figure of speech? " said the Lady of Morham dryly. " Besides, she thinks of nothing nowadays but the beauty of my lord of Darnley and the wisdom of David Rizzio. There is to be such dancing, mumming and feasting as has not been seen in Scotland this fifty years. And Darnley is the sun, moon and stars of her sky."

" There is talk in Paris," Bothwell admitted, " that the Queen's Grace has been bewitched."

" Bewitched or not, it is common talk that there are to be many marriages at Court before the summer is out. The wedding of Mistress Livingstone with the Englishman, Sempill, is to set the fashion. The Queen herself has promised each of her ladies a splendid bridal. Some say she has even promised to be of their party."

Wryly, Bothwell considered the situation. He knew enough of women to be sure it would be useless to ask the Queen to decide between a slandered exile and her powerful brother at a time when Moray's complaisance was essential to her personal

plans. " It might be better to wait on events at Hermitage. I
can be sure of the Borderers," he said.

" Moray has given the custody of Hermitage to Robert
Elliot of Redheuch," said Sir Alexander gloomily.

Bothwell grinned. " I shall soon have him out by the ears."

In Edinburgh young Lord Darnley was the centre of
interest. The Earl of Moray took him to hear Knox preach,
in the hope of placating the people whom the Queen already
considered his subjects. Mary herself was not yet prepared to
go to such lengths. But she did what she could towards understanding the viewpoint of her Protestant subjects by seeking
a staunch Protestant to act as her personal adviser.

She had first asked John Knox to accept the office of unofficial confessor. But he refused the honour as brusquely
as if she had offered him a rose which hid a serpent. Her
next choice was a layman and a diplomat. James Melville—
he had not yet received his knighthood—was startled by the
suggestion. But he did not undiplomatically refuse. " Yet
surely," he suggested, " such a commission would be more
fittingly carried out by my lord of Moray or Mr. Secretary
Lethington? "

Mary smiled. " Master Melville, I would take criticism
more happily from a man who has nothing either to gain or
lose."

" I fear, Madam," said James Melville unhappily, " that
it will cost me your favour."

" Alas, Master Melville, have you such a poor opinion
of my constancy and discretion? " said Mary earnestly.
" Tell me if there is anything you would have altered and you
will see how meekly I accept correction. I know I have already
made mistakes for lack of admonition. Courtiers most commonly flatter princes. But you will speak truly, I believe." She
paused. " At this very moment there is something in your
mind. I am convinced of it."

" It may be but a small matter," said Melville uncomfortably. " Nevertheless——"

" Nevertheless," she mocked him gaily, " I cannot amend it till I know what it is."

" There is some feeling among the nobility," Melville admitted reluctantly, " against the foreigner, David Rizzio."

Mary's dark eyes widened in astonishment. " If you had said Lord Darnley, I would have been more dismayed," she admitted. " But what can they have against poor David, save perhaps that Lord Darnley has become his friend ? "

" It is said that you yourself show him too much honour, Madam, now that Lord Darnley's favour has puffed him up, seeking his advice on other matters besides music, wherein you would be more ably advised by my lord of Moray or by Secretary Lethington."

He had made her angry, just as he had expected. Her quick flush contradicted her determined smile as she answered him. " My lord of Lethington would have me married to that upstart Leicester. To speak truly I would rather die, unless it would ensure the English succession. Yet I will bear your counsel in mind and show all the discretion in the world towards David. And—I thank you, Master Melville," she added, belatedly. James Melville kissed her extended hand and accepted his dismissal with alacrity. For it was evident to him that though the Queen had been able to force herself to accept his advice, she was most unlikely to take it, and he wished fervently that he had not offered it at all.

He admitted as much to his brothers, Robert and Andrew, when they next met, as was their habit when in Edinburgh, at his lodging in the Canongate after Sunday sermon. The Melvilles were members of an ancient and illustrious family in Fife, friends and contemporaries of the Earl of Moray. For such men life had not been easy during recent years. The tradition of their house demanded loyalty to the throne, friendship with France and mistrust of England.

But now, not only for the Melville brothers, but for thousands of honest gentlemen like them, tradition had been thrown into confusion. Since the Reformation those of the new faith in England must be considered their friends, and those in France who still adhered to the old religion their enemies. Even their family record of unswerving loyalty to the house of Stewart was no longer a sure guide, since the slip of a girl who was now their Queen had acquired both her education and her faith in France.

Many honest men in Scotland had welcomed the country's liberation from the spiritual hierarchy which, professing poverty, yet owned more than half Scotland's wealth, who undertook the spiritual guidance of the people, yet kept them in deliberate ignorance, who had lived sumptuously while grass grew between the paving stones of their derelict Churches and the rain fell on their very altars. But the Melvilles were perplexed, at a time when individual freedom of conscience was undreamt of on either side, by the contradictions involved in obeying a Popish Queen while working for the eradication of Popery among her subjects. Most of the great nobles had stood either to gain or lose by the change of creed. But the middle classes on whose support the Scottish Kings had been able to count for centuries had not been involved in the scramble for Kirk lands. For them the issue was between conscience and loyalty, a cruelly difficult choice. The clergy, whether of the old faith or the new, were in a worse state still. Monks and nuns, bereft of their cloisters, had been declared free to earn their living as they might. But for the ministers of the new religion no equivalent of cloistered security had been proposed. They were expected to preach to the people without, as often as not, knowing where to find the price of their next meal. John Knox bitterly complained of the Reformation settlement, which had given two-thirds of the immense wealth of the old Kirk to the devil, as personified by the nobles who annexed it, and shared the remaining third between God and the devil, by halving it between the new Kirk and the Crown. It was with the bitterness, often, of near-starvation that the ministers saw the revenues of rich Abbeys annexed by Court officials like Morton or Moray, or bestowed on secularised priests such as George Buchanan, the Queen's Latin tutor, who might be one of the greatest classical scholars in Europe, but was without interest in charitable works.

Consequently, the Crown was in a fair way to lose not only the support of the Kirk but that of the common people who looked to it for guidance. And since the support of the great nobles was uncertain at the best of times, such losses must tend to leave the Crown, at a time of supreme crisis, most dangerously alone. Knowing something of this, loyal and troubled men like the Melvilles could only grope their way among the contradictions of their position as best they might.

Sir Robert, eldest of the three brothers, shook his head as James Melville concluded his report of the Queen's commission. " I have half a mind to go back to Murdochcairnie and rear my family in peace. I see nothing but trouble ahead of us——"

" The Queen, poor lass, needs warmhearted folk about her," Sir Andrew said. " If only to show her that she need not expect kindness only from Papists. Master John Knox's conviction is like a burning brand. It lightens the darkness when he holds it high. But it cannot but injure the poor Queen when he seeks to cram it down her throat."

" She has a smile to turn any man's head," groaned James. " I thought I was sufficiently armoured against guile but I was limp in her hands as a sun-warmed candle."

" And yet I cannot see," said Sir Robert judicially, " that much harm can come of honestly offered counsel, brother."

" Nor much good either," said James Melville.

" As to that," said Sir Andrew, " time will show. I am glad you accepted her request for counsel. It would be a poor thing if we were to withdraw from the service of the house of Stewart when the Queen's Grace herself has need of all her good friends."

" So has her brother of Moray," worried James.

" Yet if difference comes between them I would serve the Queen," said Sir Andrew.

" And I," said Sir Robert, less positively.

But James Melville shook his head. " It is to be hoped no such difference arises," he said. " For it will not be easy to keep the Queen from folly. She is as sweet as a rosebud, yet a man might bleed to death, I believe, on the shrewd thorns that surround her. She is set on marriage with my lord Darnley, as all the world can see. But she would still throw him over, I believe, if Queen Elizabeth would promise to name her next in succession. Her desire for the Crown of England is beyond all reason. Why will not that of Scotland suffice? "

" Did Lethington bring any promise back from Queen Elizabeth? " asked Sir Andrew.

" No," said James Melville. " What is more, I came forth from England, and not long since, entirely certain that she will never agree. If there is one superstition from which the Queen of England cannot free herself, it is that of the ill-fortune of naming her successor. I have heard her declare that she would as soon have her own winding sheet hung up before her, as let her choice be known."

" I thought her a brave woman," said Sir Andrew. " Does she so fear assassination? "

" Can you doubt it? " said James Melville. " She must know that once she names a Papist as her successor, she puts herself at the mercy of any Catholic subject whose disordered mind expects remission of a few centuries in Purgatory for bringing about her death."

" A woman who sits alone upon a throne may be an inspiration to honest men. But she is a temptation to all others," said Sir Robert. " I shall be thankful when her Grace is safely married, be her choice what she will."

" Yet I could wish her fancy had lit on a better man," grumbled Sir Andrew.

" Young Lord Darnley has won golden opinions from

even those who dislike his Popery," objected his brother
James. " Morton and Glencairn have now waited on him at
Holyroodhouse. And Moray likes him well enough."

But here he was mistaken. Moray had no longer any
liking for young Lord Darnley. He had been willing to accept
him as long as he seemed merely a decorative cipher, a pretty
boy who would keep the Queen amused with his versifying and
lute-playing, dance like one of the princes from an old romance,
and companion her at the hunting and hawking for which
his enthusiasm matched hers. During his first weeks in Scotland Darnley had seemed happy to drift on the surface of a
golden dream, taking up so much of the Queen's attention
that the reins of government were left in Moray's willing hands.
And then, unexpectedly, at a hint of less welcome character-
istics, Moray was at once on his guard.

Darnley had been dining with a party of the more irrespons-
ible young noblemen, as the guest of Lord Robert, Commendator of Holyrood, in his quarters at the Palace. Afterwards they amused themselves by inspecting their host's
treasures, for Lord Robert was as greedy as a jackdaw. He
collected oddments of altar plate, jewelled Toledo blades,
obscenely carved wooden figures or strings of ivory and jet
in much the same way as a jackdaw accumulates bright
objects, for which it can have no possible use, among the
sticks and straws of its untidy nest. Young Darnley, who had
drunk enough to be careless, led his host by the arm towards a
map of Scotland.

" Show me the lands of my lord of Moray," he demanded
loudly. Someone grinned. Another winked. Apparently the
young man who seemed so harmless was not quite such a fool
as he looked.

Lord Robert yawned. He had had enough of his guests,
and wanted to be left in peace to sleep off the effects of the
rich meal he had given them.

" Lands? " he said vaguely. " What lands? "

" What property does my lord of Moray own in Scotland? "

demanded Darnley, with the persistence of the semi-intoxicated.

Lord Robert lurched a little as he leant towards the map, and began to prod it with a pudgy forefinger, squinting with the effort to focus his eyes. " Here, in Fife . . . and here . . . and here. And of course, as Earl of Moray he holds all the lands to the north. Here and here. And he has also acquired lands . . . here . . ." He almost overbalanced with the effort. Darnley casually righted him, then frowned, shaking his head.

" It is too much," he said thoughtfully. " Far too much . . ."

" Aye, indeed," said Lord Robert, now bumbling uncertainly towards the high-backed chair in which he was accustomed to settle himself for his afternoon nap. " Far too much. But you know my fair brother. Or, if you do not, you had better learn. What was the motto you showed me on that ring of yours? "

Darnley looked surprised. " *Avand Darnley*," he quoted with some pride.

Lord Robert reached the chair and lowered himself into it with exaggerated caution. His head fell forward on his chest, his lids drooped. It was difficult to open them again. But he shook a wavering finger at his guest before sleep overwhelmed him.

" ' *Avand Darnley*.' " he echoed. " But besher be careful . . . how you set about it." He belched, sagged further down against the crimson velvet cushion and began to snore.

Darnley laughed. The old sot would have forgotten all about it when he woke. Unfortunately for him, he was mistaken. Lord Robert not only remembered Darnley's i n—discretion, but took pains to annoy his brother with it. And the Earl of Moray was so infuriated to find that the young fool he had supposed so suitable, so happy to divert the Queen's attention, had already cast an envious eye on his personal property, that he swung from calculated approval towards equally calculated hostility. But this did not at once appear.

For Mary and Darnley, the horizon seemed still unclouded. She was glad to be leaving Edinburgh, with its Council Meetings, disapproving ministers and inquisitive crowds, for Stirling. For there, safe in the Castle above the plain across which the silver Forth meandered, they would no longer be haunted by the grim scimitar of Master Knox's down-turned mouth. There they would be free to dance and sing, and David would lead both the chanting in Chapel and the part-songs round the fire. They would ride far into the mountains, loud with swollen streams which tumbled like skeins of floss silk, fed by the melting snows. They would canter across the meadows, hawk on wrist. And in the evenings they would dance to the sweet wild music of the fiddles and the twanging of lutes, the latest and most daring of dances from the Court of France. They would sup by candlelight, listening to David's glorious voice as he sang of love while his listeners sighed, smiling at each other. They would hold hands among the shadows that came and went around the high-piled log fire.

All such things wove themselves into a pattern of delight in Mary's mind, vivid as the tapestry on her embroidery frame, as she rode at the head of her holiday-making cavalcade. She was thankful that the rigours and sorrows of Lent were over, blessed at last by the rejoicing of Easter, with the great festivals of the summer ahead, and Henry riding with his arm about David's shoulders, as if they had been friends for years, not newly met a month ago. Surely, she let herself think, as the fresh air and the keen wind and the pale, tentative sunlight began to exhilarate her as they always did, surely this was love? The mere thought of Henry's lazy smile, his splendid vigour, his superb grace and strength in the dance, made her breath catch in her throat. When he stooped over her, brushing her cheek with his lips in the movement of the latest frolic from Paris that made the sour-faces purse their mouths as if they had swallowed vinegar, she felt dizzy with desire for him, almost ready to faint. When they paced up the hall together, with the fiddlers' bows moving so fast that they made a pale blur in the shadows, and the two lines of dancers clapped a furious rhythm that was like the racing of her heart. . . . Surely what she felt then, that melting, aching, burning tumult within her . . . was love?

And yet . . .

She frowned as she thought of Lethington riding once more to the Court of the Queen of England. If Elizabeth would name her as next in succession, could even the price of consenting to the absurd marriage the Queen of England had suggested be too high? For of course, consent was one thing and ratification another, as those who kept demanding that she should ratify the Treaty of Edinburgh had already found.

But of course Queen Elizabeth would never agree. James Melville, who was an honest man, had been quite sure of that. Lethington had her instructions to ask first whether Elizabeth would name her successor if Mary would consider marriage with the Earl of Leicester. And then, when she had said it was out of the question, he was to make it clear that the Leicester marriage was out of the question too.

As the outline of Stirling Castle on its crag floated out of the mists like the prow of an enchanted galleon, Mary laughed aloud, switching her horse so sharply that it sprang forward, setting the whole cavalcade streaming across the countryside in a chaos of flying plumes and billowing cloaks and spraying divots, Darnley's melodious view-halloo bringing the men on duty to the battlements, ready to swing the guns out against their unknown enemies.

But their holiday at Stirling did not turn out as she had pictured it at all. The dancing and the singing and the feasting were shadowed by Darnley's sudden and disconcerting moodiness. He complained of his lodgings, his attendants, and his entertainment. He picked a quarrel with the Earl of Moray, who objected to the fully choral services in the Queen's private Chapel, so beautifully led by Rizzio. And Rizzio himself, encouraged by Darnley's support, strutted about as if he too were a prince of the blood, interrupting the Queen in the very presence of her nobles, as if he had been asked for his opinion, till their muttered comments were audible above the fiddling. The Earl of Moray finally presented himself before his sister in a rage, brusquely demanding a private interview, with a meaning glance round the pleasant room in which Rizzio was playing a duet with Darnley on the virginals, while the Queen's ladies amused themselves with a new kitten. Disturbed by his rudeness, she retired with him to her small cabinet.

" I ask your leave to withdraw from Stirling," said Moray, without explanation. " I must proceed with matters more urgent for the welfare of this realm than these gay revels."

The happiness drained from Mary's face, and some of the wild rose colour went with it. She would not find it easy to oppose her formidable brother, but if this were an indication of his disapproval of the marriage to which he had at first agreed, she would not hesitate. Not even Moray should come between her and what she had now convinced herself to be her heart's desire. But she would not be the one to start the quarrel.

" Why, brother, has anything displeased you ? "

Moray glowered at her. " I cannot find it in my conscience to ignore the superstitions and idolatries practised by your servants and their associates——" He spat out the word as a deliberate insult—" in your Chapel Royal. With your permission, therefore, I will return to Edinburgh to prepare for the trial of the felon Bothwell."

Since Mary had given her consent to the original summons against Bothwell she could scarcely forbid Moray to convene his trial now, however much she might suspect that his purpose was to dispose of Bothwell as summarily as he had attempted to dispose of the eldest remaining son of the unfortunate Earl of Huntly.

" Provided that you proceed according to the law which governs such assemblies, I can have nothing to say against it."

" I shall conduct myself, Madam, as circumstances may

make expedient," said the Earl of Moray insufferably. " And since the matter is urgent I will now take my leave."

Mary turned back to her chosen companions with a sigh at the shadow which her brother's hostility had cast over their pleasant interlude, to find David Rizzio seated alone before the virginals, picking out a sad little melody with one finger. He rose and came to her at once, anxiety widening his dark eyes.

" My lord Darnley asked me to make his excuses. He has been feeling unwell, it seems, for some little time. I have advised him to return to his chamber."

" Oh David, yes. That was well done. I have noticed his indisposition. He has not been at all like himself," Mary agreed, glad of the excuse for Darnley's sullen behaviour. " Did he turn worse during my absence? "

" He is now in a sorry case, Madam," said Rizzio. " He said his head ached as if struck by the clapper of a passing-bell."

" Send at once for my physician from Edinburgh, David. He will advise us. You do not think——" her voice sank to a whisper, " that he can have caught the plague? "

Agitatedly Rizzio crossed himself. " May our Blessed Lady forbid such a terrible visitation, Madam. I will send for the physician."

" At once, David. Do not delay."

" I will not, Madam."

" Already," said Mary, terror-struck, " it may be too late."

When the venerable physician, huddled upon a rawboned nag whose movements rattled the remaining teeth in his head, reached Stirling next day he was hurried without rest or refreshment to where Darnley lay in his darkened chamber. As he afterwards emerged the Queen almost ran to him, with hands outstretched and eyes imploring.

" Ah, Monsieur, tell me the truth. Is it the plague? "

The old physician, who had known the Queen all her life, gave a sudden cackle of laughter. " No, Madam. It is the measles," he said.

CHAPTER SEVEN

RUMOURS scrawled uncertainties across the Scottish sky like jags of summer lightning as the year progressed. Lethington, received in audience at Greenwich, in vain wove his habitual cobweb of subtleties to enmesh a declaration of her purpose from Queen Elizabeth. At last he was driven to ask a plain question. Would his mistress be recognised as the heiress to the English throne if she were disposed to please the Queen of England in the matter of her marriage?

" I must first be assured, my lord of Lethington," said Elizabeth tartly, " that the Queen of Scots is still free to marry."

Such a retort startled even Lethington out of his elegant composure. " Madam, I do assure you—I have no reason to think—dare I suggest that your Grace has been misinformed? "

" Do you take me for a simpleton? " snapped the Queen of England. " Randolph would not presume to blunder on a matter of such moment. Return to your mistress and advise her to see that her ambassadors are better informed on the matters they are sent to discuss. My time is more precious than my jewels, my lord."

Lethington did not suffer himself fooled gladly. He returned, fuming, to Scotland, determined to discover the truth regarding the secret marriage, witnessed only by the Queen's ladies and David Rizzio, of which Queen Elizabeth's ambassador seemed to have been better informed than the envoy of the Queen of Scots. But when he reproached his Queen for laying him open to a scolding from Queen Elizabeth, she only laughed and blushed and murmured that at the time of his departure she had not known her own mind. Indeed, she was still undecided now. Lethington, bowing stiffly, took his leave unconvinced. It was an affront which he was not prepared to forgive. And Moray had not, it seemed, returned to Stirling.

At Hermitage, from which he had soon ejected Robert Elliot, Bothwell was still laughing at the news of Darnley's measles when his personal servant, Gabriel Sempill, came hammering on the postern door, incoherent with panic as he tumbled off his sweating horse.

" My lord——" he stammered—" take me to my lord——"

" Well? " Bothwell, alert as a man in constant danger had long since learned to be, swung round from the supper table, reaching for his sword.

" The Earl of Moray is upon us with a great host . . ."

As a Scottish Borderer, Bothwell was more inclined to put his trust in the familiar hills from which he could assess the strength of his enemies than in a fortress within which he might well be trapped with insufficient provisions. But since Moray's muster had not, in fact, left Edinburgh, he returned to Hermitage next morning in a temper which was not improved by discovering one of his servants rifling his clothes chest. Exasperated already, Bothwell now took the man by the throat. " So that is where my new shirts are disappearing. I will have you flogged for this."

" Have mercy on me, my lord," gasped his victim. " And I will tell you something of more value than all the shirts you possess."

Bothwell relaxed the pressure on the unfortunate man's windpipe. " Speak on."

" My lord, it was in Paris. Money was given us to bring about your death by poison or the sword."

" I thought as much," said Bothwell grimly.

" My lord, we could not do it."

" Evidently not. Was the price too stingy? "

" No price would have served, my lord."

Bothwell grinned. " I wonder? " The man's eyes rolled in his head as his master's grip tightened on his throat. " But who was to reward you? "

" It was—my lord of Lethington," his victim gurgled.
" Or so I was told."

" Bah! That fox," said Bothwell in disgust. " I am obliged
to you for the warning. But pilfer from me no more. There
may be no such tale to tell next time." His parting kick sent
the fellow half-way down the spiral stair which opened on
the small central courtyard. As he picked himself up and
bundled across it towards the comparative safety of the
kitchen quarters, his master's laughter pursued him like an
echo. It was not easy to intimidate the Earl of Bothwell.

But Moray's muster was no matter of moonshine. He and
his brother-in-law, the Earl of Argyll, did not intend to leave
legislation unaided by force. Moray knew that Argyll, as the
Lord Justice of Scotland, might be relied on to conduct the
inquiry as stringently as he could wish. But if Bothwell did not
come alone his supporters might seek to influence the course of
justice. So when the Marchmont Herald summoned the assize,
six thousand pikemen under Moray's orders moved in to occupy
the Tolbooth, within and without, where the longstanding
trial for treason was at last to be held. But the expense of this
manœuvre, to his great annoyance, was unjustified.

The accused did not appear. In his place rose Sir Alexander Hepburn, to repudiate the charge on his cousin's behalf
and explain his absence.

" It is due to no uncertainty as to the justice of his cause,"
said Sir Alexander, looking pointedly at the military array
about him, " but rather to the certainty of the purpose in the
heart of his most potent enemy, the Earl of Moray."

Asked for further information as to his cousin's whereabouts, he stolidly observed that it was not his concern. But
when it was suggested that Bothwell had returned to France,
the Laird of Riccarton did not trouble to deny it.

Rising in fury, Moray demanded that Bothwell, defaulting
by his absence, should be outlawed. Argyll would have been
glad to oblige him, but the matter was unexpectedly taken
out of his hands. The Queen had heard of Moray's attempt

to force the cause against Bothwell by the illegal show of force. And such force might on another occasion be turned against his Queen as now against a man whose faults had only been those of over-zeal.

She sent therefore a peremptory message to the Lord Justice commanding him to dissolve the Court. Bothwell's surety was forfeit, but he should not be outlawed unheard. The snub infuriated Moray, though the Queen's popularity was too great for him yet to risk defiance. But he fancied that he could rely on Darnley to damage the royal cause sufficiently. He himself need only bide his time.

For things were coming to a head now. The wildfire blaze of rumour had been followed by the premonitory rumble of forthcoming events. In mid-May the Queen publicly announced her intention of marrying her cousin, Henry, Lord Darnley, her father's sister's son by the Earl of Lennox.

Lethington, still smarting from Queen Elizabeth's whiplash comments, found the official announcement of the Scottish Queen's prospective marriage a further exasperation in view of the rumoured secret alliance of which she had not troubled to inform him, and of which he still had no definite confirmation.

But he would have guessed it, Lethington told himself, had he been in Scotland. Half an hour in the presence of Lord Darnley would have indicated his changed status. For Darnley was not being careful any more. During Lethington's absence he had changed almost out of recognition. The formerly charming, diffident, and romantic suitor was now an irritable and demandingly spoilt lout. He was, admittedly, scarcely more than convalescent from his childish complaint, but it tried Lethington's suave patience almost to breaking-point to see him lolling in the great chamber at Stirling which the Queen had fitted up as a music room, the centre of the solicitous attention of the Queen and her ladies, content only when everything but his amusement was set aside, sipping possets and scribbling verses which the sycophantic Rizzio set to music and the Queen's Grace praised as if they were the work of genius.

In the Council Chamber, to which Lethington presently returned, doubts were already being freely expressed. The lords had, as they now thought, been persuaded to give too indulgent a consent to a marriage which should have been more cautiously debated.

"He—he is a blustering young coxcomb!" blustered the Duke of Chatelherault. "He has vowed to crack my pate once he is well enough. That, my lords, is an unseemly threat."

Smiles were checked, sympathetic heads shaken.

"He threatened to draw his dagger on me when I ventured to contradict him on a point of law," rumbled the Earl of Argyll. "On me, mark you, the Lord Justice of Scotland."

"He is pampering that Italian singing fellow as if he were a prince of the blood royal."

Lethington's lips tightened as he listened to them. But he kept his resentment to himself, as was his habit. He, too, had reason to complain of the behaviour of David Rizzio. As Secretary of State, Lethington had taken considerable trouble to ingratiate himself with the Queen, and he believed himself to have succeeded. She had been delighted with his gifts, amused by his fantastic pets, and appreciative of the attentions of a courtier who, like Master James Melville and the disgraced Earl of Bothwell, knew France almost as well as herself.

All was changed now. Until his latest journey to England, Lethington had been accustomed to deal with the Queen's French correspondence, on personal as well as diplomatic topics, and had expected to resume such duties on his return. It appeared, however, that in his absence David Rizzio had taken on the task, and the Queen blandly announced herself well pleased with the new arrangement.

"Do not let it irk you, my lord," whispered Mary Fleming, as Lethington paused in the lobby outside the royal apartments at the sound of her following feet. " It is but her kindness of heart. The little fellow was so glad to be of service in your absence that she will not have him thrust aside now."

" Am I then so deprived of natural feelings, that such treatment is likely to irk me less ? "

" Oh, *no*, my lord," murmured Mary Fleming.

" You would not say so ? " He touched her cheek with a lean, cold finger tip.

" Indeed I would not."

" Then her Grace's opinion matters less."

He took a step forward, catching her by the arm. But Mary Fleming twisted away with a little giggle of delight. " Oh no, my lord——"

" Do I displease you ? " Like all men who pride themselves on their remoteness, Lethington was quick to resent any suggestion that his discriminating advances might be spurned.

" On, *no*," Mary Fleming protested vehemently. " It is—it is only——"

" What then ? "

" It is—you will say I am foolish——"

" I think it unlikely. But I cannot tell while you clap your hands over your mouth. Come—try my understanding——"

" It is only that we, all four of us who are her Grace's maids of honour, have taken an oath that we will accept no man's attentions till her Grace herself is wed."

Lethington did not mock. Instead he nodded gravely, recognising the chance to exchange surmise for certainty. " I must respect such an oath. But surely the time for it is past. Her Grace is wedded already."

Mary Fleming gasped. Her eyes grew round. She bit her lip. " How—how did you know that, my lord ? "

" That does not matter," Lethington said, with an airy gesture. " Only that it is true."

" Yes," Mary Fleming said softly. " It is true. But we thought it a secret so well kept that none knew but ourselves."

Lethington laughed briefly at the innocent delusion.

" You—are not angered, my lord? " asked Mary Fleming anxiously.

Slowly Lethington brought his attention back from the spider's web of diplomatic complications which this admission implied. As he looked down at her, unseeingly at first, his expression softened. In the ash of his intellectual indifference a spark of emotional warmth, still unexpectedly smouldering, brightened to a small glow. " On the contrary. I must rejoice," he said.

But others were displeased. Moray was not idle. He lost no opportunity of inflaming all the nobles who were so pledged to the new religion that they could be relied on to oppose the Queen's marriage with a Papist after its disastrous effects had been sufficiently indicated. He also did what he could to inspire Master Knox to preach against it, though with less success than he had confidently hoped. For since his own recent remarriage, John Knox had for the time being mellowed most disappointingly in regard to the Queen's personal conduct. And Mary herself made matters more difficult by unexpectedly announcing that she would gladly make any concessions towards freedom of conscience which she could.

" Will you then consent to put down the Popish religion? " Moray demanded at the beginning of June, on the eve of the Queen's return to Edinburgh, during the first private interview he had had with his sister since his departure from Stirling two months ago.

But Mary neatly parried this shrewd thrust. " That is not in my power," she said. " It must be left to Parliament. As for myself, I am not persuaded towards any religion save that in which I have been brought up."

" Will you hear conference and disputation? "

" Yes," Mary said. She smiled at his astonishment. " I will hear public preaching too, provided it is offered by someone who is pleasing to me. I will not be harangued by my enemies."

" Who will you hear, then? " Moray demanded disagreeably.

Mary pondered. " I will gladly hear Master Erskine, who
did all he might to moderate Master Knox's severity when they
came to Holyroodhouse. He is a mild man of true honesty and
goodness."

" I will see what can be arranged," Moray mumbled,
and took his leave. He did not believe in Mary's sweet reason-
ableness. But he was sufficiently disturbed by it. If she were
able to convince those pledged to the new religion that she
was not unfriendly towards it, disaster might well overtake his
own plans yet.

Mary too was disconcerted as she returned to the lighthearted company with whom she could not share her
anxieties. She had agreed to the secret marriage in a high
mood of over-confidence and romantic excitement, expecting
to have no difficulty in winning the enthusiasm of her subjects
for their sovereign's choice. Any opposition, from whatever
quarter, must be overcome by force. The marriage vow was
irrevocable. So the sooner the public ceremony could be
performed the better, for she was increasingly aware of the
strain of a relationship at once legitimate and clandestine. If
knowledge of her secret marriage became general, the splendid
ceremony which her regality demanded must degenerate into
a farce. So she must still not only guard every look, word and
gesture except in the privacy of her private apartments, but
try to ensure that Darnley did so too. At first it had seemed a
romantic confederacy after her own heart, but as the very
difficulties of their relationship heightened her desire, it became
a frustrating conflagration of emotions which drove her towards
the limits of self-control.

For the forces of opposition were mustering. The Earl of
Argyll, it seemed, had not forgotten that Darnley had threatened him with his dagger. For he had summoned a great
convention of Protestant nobles to meet at Edinburgh in the
third week of June.

" Better you should do it than I, who am so close kin to the Queen that it would not be seemly," Moray had maintained smugly.

It was Rizzio who pointed out that the Queen and her Court should not remain at Holyrood, awaiting, as it appeared, the decisions of subjects of whose deliberations she could scarcely approve. Mary agreed. She would spend a few days with the Earl of Athol, who, as Darnley's kinsman, would not be expected to attend the conference in Edinburgh. So they set off, a small party escorted by only a few men-at-arms, to be Athol's guests at Dunkeld. Darnley rode with the Queen, blustering resentfully against the insolence of subjects whose assemblies could drive the Queen from her very capital.

" It will be a very different story when I am King of Scots," he boasted.

" It is to be hoped so. We have waited long enough," grumbled the Earl of Lennox, who rode on the other side of the Queen.

" We shall soon set things to rights now, my lord," promised David Rizzio, who had pushed his nag forward to hear what was going on. Lennox looked at him in distaste, his nose twitching like that of a nervous hare. Was he, the Lord President of the Council and father of the prospective King of Scots, to be reassured by a landless foreigner? But the Queen smiled at the little man with the swarthy, mobile face which could change on the instant from impish mirth to gargoyle-like misery. " Well spoken, Davie," she cried gaily. " Let us be thankful we have escaped from cities and council chambers on this golden day."

David Rizzio caught her mood as he hirpled along, clumsy as a meal-sack on his awkward pony. But the grotesque figure he made ceased to matter as he began to sing one of the part-songs in which the Queen and her young companions joined. For it was midsummer, with the countryside at its most glorious, and they were leaving controversy behind them for a few days of sheer delight. Since Athol was of her own faith, the Queen did not consider that the secret of her marriage need be kept from him, and the thought of a truce to dissimulation, a honeymoon in fact though not in name, intoxicated her. As she rode through the glens singing, Darnley held her hand.

But their pleasure was abruptly dashed on the morning after their arrival. A second party of horsemen, headed by Lethington and the English ambassador, appeared at the Castle gates. Randolph was the bearer of letters from Queen Elizabeth, it seemed, not only for the Queen of Scots, but for Lennox and Darnley besides.

"I will not see the fellow," Darnley said rudely. "We are to go hunting. Let him bide our convenience."

Without looking at him, their host turned to the Queen.

Mary had been trained for royalty. She sighed, but did not hesitate. "We shall have more heart for our sport, I believe, if we have first sent Master Randolph about his business."

Lennox hastened to agree. But Darnley sulked, slapping his leg with his riding whip, and would not meet the Queen's eyes.

"I shall be glad if you will summon the lord of Lethington and Master Randolph forthwith, my lord of Athol," Mary said. "Ill news is like a persistent creditor, best disposed of without delay."

Lennox, his nervously bulging eyes making him more like a hare than ever, stood beside her chair, but Darnley lounged insolently on a window-seat, as Lethington and Randolph knelt to greet the Queen. Mary received them coolly. She could very well guess the nature of their business, and found it more difficult to forgive Lethington for dancing attendance now on one Queen, now on the other, than Randolph for the espionage of which she had no doubt. Had not Mary Beton confessed, with tears, that though he protested his devotion at all times, he was most generous with his gifts when her mistress's plans were of the greatest interest?

"Madam," said Randolph, "I have here a letter from the Queen my mistress. Is it your pleasure that the lord of Lethington should read it to your Grace?"

"I thank you, Master Randolph, but I had rather you would briefly state your commission," said Mary.

Randolph glanced sidelong at Lennox and Darnley. "Madam, my commission is contained in the letter. Should your Grace be disposed to accede to the request of the Queen my mistress, I have no more to say."

Mary smiled remotely. "If the request be what I suppose, Master Randolph, the choice lies rather with those concerned than with me."

"Her Majesty of England," said Randolph, "is most gravely displeased."

"And yet it may be," said Mary sweetly, "that she has changed her mind by now. I have sent her other letters, this time by a most trusty ambassador——" Her glance flickered towards Lethington. "And therefore I can give you no other answer at this time."

Randolph bowed as deeply as if this reply had been all he could have hoped rather than just what he had feared. "Then will your Grace permit me to deliver the commands of the Queen my mistress to these noblemen?"

"I will," said Mary graciously.

The English ambassador seemed to grow in stature as he turned from the Queen of Scots to the defaulting subjects of the Queen of England. His voice took on a new edge, his pale eyes a marble glare. The transformation made Lethington smile thinly, but Mary's hands were cold as she twisted them in her lap.

"My lords," said Randolph, "I am commanded by her Majesty Queen Elizabeth to instruct you to return immediately to England. I have here her summons, my lord of Lennox, and yours, my lord Darnley. I must warn you," he added, in almost sepulchral tones, "that you will fail to obey her at your utmost peril."

The small sound of the breaking seal made Mary start as if
someone had cracked a whip. Lennox sighed, shaking his head
as if in sorrow for so much misunderstanding. But Darnley's
mouth fell slightly open as he read, and he swung first towards
Mary, then back to Randolph, his face patchily coloured like
a schoolboy in fear of a whipping.

"Why, Master Randolph," he said at last, "this is very
sad and distressing. What would you do in my case?"

Randolph's lip curled. "I am here only to discover what
your lordship's intentions are."

"I have no mind to return," said Darnley truculently.

"Shall I convey that as your lordship's answer?"

But Darnley's defiance was ephemeral as a soap-bubble.
"No," he said hastily. "You shall first give me time to think."

"It would seem to me," said Randolph, "that your
lordship's mind is already made up."

"That—that may be so," said Darnley. "And you need
not think to wait long for my answer. But you shall not have it
now," he added, as the thought of Queen Elizabeth's royal rage
disconcerted him again. He folded his arms across his chest
as if their pressure comforted him, and struck an attitude, one
foot on a stool, his head thrown nobly back. But the panic in
his eyes betrayed him. Randolph's expression was sleekly
satisfied. Like a well-fed fox he surveyed the little group from
which Lethington had pointedly dissociated himself. He had
shaken them badly, and he knew it.

"If your Grace will summon me at your convenience," he
murmured, "I will wait upon you to convey your answer to
the Queen, my mistress. Meanwhile, I will seek your Grace's
permission to return—to Edinburgh."

He gave the little pause its full significance. It was as well
to make it clear that her enemies would find him within call.
He bowed low to the Queen, more casually to Lennox, and
bestowed a jerk of the head on Darnley. Then, elaborately
backing and bowing, he withdrew from the royal presence.
As his three victims turned in wordless consternation to each

other, Lethington, after hesitating for an instant, unobtrusively followed him.

Tears stood in Mary's eyes. She had hoped so much, in spite of all past experience, that her recent letters would have produced a very different answer from Queen Elizabeth. Lennox surveyed her distractedly, his nose twitching. Darnley was the first to recover. After all, as prospective King of Scots, he could scarcely submit to be scolded by the servant of the Queen of England. He managed to laugh, even to swagger a little.

" Dry your eyes, Madam, the danger is not so great as it appears. Since we cannot retreat, we must needs go forward."

" We must go forward indeed," Mary said urgently. " Once we are married before the world, there will be nothing the Queen of England can do against you."

" Then let us hasten, Madam," Darnley said, stamping his foot. " Once Moray works his will on his convention of heretics we may never come into our own."

" I will make all the haste I may," Mary assured him. " But the wedding of the King and Queen of Scots must be as splendid as any in Christendom."

" What shall hinder it from being so ? "

Mary flushed hotly. " The lack of money," she said unwillingly.

" Money ? " Darnley's tone was contemptuous. " But you are the Queen. You can obtain it where you please."

It was an odd speech from a man already dependent on his wife's bounty. He and his father had brought little out of England, and spent it so lavishly that Darnley had recently been obliged to offer jewels in payment of a gambling debt. But the thought that the Queen should be short of money shocked him, for he had reckoned on future abundance. " Surely you have only to demand it from Parliament ? "

Mary shook her head. " It is a bad moment to make such a demand," she said uncomfortably. She did not admit that she had already sought to avoid making it by asking a number of Edinburgh merchants for a loan to defray her wedding expenses. Their elaborate excuses and pained refusal had given her the first inkling of the unpopularity of the marriage with which she had hoped to delight all Scotland. For what Darnley's arrogance and tactlessness had left undone, Moray was doing all he could to accomplish. A few days after the scene at Dunkeld his project for kidnapping both Darnley and the Queen as they returned from a visit to Callander, and conveying them to his mother's castle of Lochleven, was all but successful. The incident, taken in conjunction with a number of hostile demonstrations against her marriage, left the Queen in no doubt as to her brother's open enmity should she persist in her purpose.

As time went on, the nightmare sensation of creeping treachery, no longer held at bay by the loyalty of those most dear to her, but a contagion infecting even her next of kin, darkened her spirit. She sat silent, impervious to her ladies' bright chatter, even to the inspiration of David's glorious voice. The cold, mysterious melancholy which she had inherited from her tragic father crept over her like the blight on a rose. She had never been really robust. All her life she had been subject to fainting fits, to a pain in her side that dragged like the contracting scar of an inner wound. In times of crisis, she had always been able to summon the necessary strength. But afterwards she would pay the price of exhaustion in bottomless despair. She was in such a mood when the English Ambassador sought audience again.

" Let me send him away, sweet Madam. I will tell him you are indisposed," said Mary Seton.

But Mary shook her head wearily. " I will see him. If I can convince him of my constancy of purpose he may persuade the Queen of England to let me wed in peace."

Randolph entered the privy chamber as trippingly as if he brought proposals of enchanting novelty. The Queen of Scots, his manner indicated, could by no means fail to be overjoyed.

But presently they were going once more over the same well-trodden ground. His mistress was urgent in her desire for the return of her misguided subjects. If the Queen of Scots would despatch them there need in future be nothing but kindness between the sister Queens.

" To send them home I may not," said Mary. " Is there no other way? "

" That way would be the best," Randolph said. " But the wise men about you might accept somewhat else to stay the present evil, and the rest be gotten in time." He paused, tilted his head a little on one side, like a predatory blackbird, and surveyed her as if in thought. " What if your Majesty would alter your religion? " he suggested at last.

As Mary's temper rose, her despairing melancholy yielded like the mud flats of the Solway to the racing return of its tide. She was not yet a religious woman. The familiar practices of her faith were as much a habit as her royalty. But she was a Stewart. Generations of Kings linked her with the great Bruce. His spirit and hers rose up in wrath at such presumption. She turned on Randolph like a young lioness.

" What would that do? "

Randolph smirked. " Peradventure," he murmured, " it might move her Majesty to allow the sooner of your marriage."

" What? Shall I make merchandise of my religion? It cannot be," she told him roundly. Randolph sighed and took his leave.

Her ladies, urgently summoned, found the Queen's face flushed as if she had a fever, her pupils so dilated that her eyes seemed black. But she brushed their solicitude aside with as peremptory a gesture as her tremendous ancestor himself might have made.

" Let me be, Seton. I ail nothing. Call David. Bring us pens, ink and parchment——"

Rizzio arrived breathless.

" Sweet Madam, what is your will? "

" Sit there, David, at the table. Date the paper this

sixteenth of July, in the year of Our Lord fifteen hundred and sixty-five. Write a separate letter to each of the Reformed lords, assuring them that I have no thought to disturb the religion I found established on my return from France, but as I have always kept good faith with them, so I now expect them to keep faith with me. They are to convene at Edinburgh, this time at my command, with their servants and vassals in warlike array, bringing fifteen days' provisions with them to assist me in preserving the peace of this realm, which is now threatened by seditious and evil-disposed persons."

" Madam, I will," said David eagerly. His dark eyes shone and his ugly face was puckered with delight as he pictured the royal triumph which such heroic measures must surely bring about.

" Wait," said Mary slowly. " There is another matter . . ."

Rizzio, his arms full of parchments, paused obediently.

But Mary sat very still, no longer aware of those about her as she pictured the impudent grin of the ugly, harsh-voiced young man who had climbed down the Castle Rock of Edinburgh in utter darkness and offered her his most humble duty in the tone of a man who could not flatter and was too arrogant to lie.

" Write also to my lord of Bothwell," she said quietly. " Convey to him the assurance of my pardon and command his immediate return."

CHAPTER EIGHT

RIZZIO bowed himself alertly from the Queen's presence and set off in search of trusty messengers for the letters she had signed. As he went, he snapped the fingers of his right hand, cramped with so much quill-driving, and hummed a melody he had recently composed. Not a man in Scotland, he reflected complacently, now knew as much of the Queen's purpose as he. Not even my lord Darnley, so soon to be her consort in face of all the world.

But it would be a great weight off his mind to have the official marriage safely accomplished. Every day it was becoming more difficult to check the Queen's natural desire to see her husband held in as much honour as herself, and still more difficult, perhaps, to keep Lord Darnley from demanding such consideration as of right, rather than at the Queen's good pleasure. It would not be much longer now, Rizzio told himself, as he shook a handbell to bring a page running as he himself had once run at his betters' command. He laid the letters out before him on the bare table which, with a couple of stools and a clutter of sheets of music, a broken lute and a cloak flung down across a bench, was the sole furnishing of his unimpressive room. No arras masked the bare walls, no painted ceiling hid the rafters. That, too, must be set to rights, he told himself as he waited, impatiently now, for an answer to his summons. Such a chamber might be well enough for a varlet, but it was scarcely the sort of place in which her Grace's most confidential secretary could receive important envoys from other rulers, even from the Holy See. But what had come to the children of the household? Irritably, he rang the bell again.

This time someone could be heard approaching at a shuffling

walk, and a redheaded boy of perhaps thirteen, wearing the
red and yellow of the royal livery and staunching on his
sleeve a flow of blood from his nose, put his head unwillingly
round the door and scowled at him. There had been a scuffle
below stairs at the sound of the bell which the wee jumpit-up
strumming fellow liked to shake instead of clapping his hands
like his betters and the lad who got the worst of it had been
obliged to answer the summons. Sullen and resentful, he
received Rizzio's rebuke in silence. It was unwise to show too
much insolence to someone known to be in high favour with
the Queen.

As Rizzio raised a hand to cuff him the boy took a step
backwards, throwing up his arm in a habitual gesture of
defence. "But no then, I will not hurt you," Rizzio said.
" If you will listen, yes ? "

Warily, the boy nodded.

" Go down to the great hall," Rizzio commanded, " and
search for some who serve these lords." He ticked the names
off on the outspread fingers of his right hand. " So. Can you
remember ? "

" Aye."

" Then send such servants to me at once. And return
again. I have other names to give."

Rizzio put the letter to Bothwell carefully aside. Its
delivery would require thought. Who had answered for
Bothwell at the recent assize ? Drumming his fingers on the
table-top, Rizzio tried to recall the unfamiliar name of the
man who had stolidly defended his kinsman against Moray's
fury. At last, as the distribution of the Queen's letters was
completed, he remembered. Catching the disgruntled page
before he could make his escape, Rizzio swung him, yelping,
towards the table again.

" Another time, you shall remain in attendance till leave is
given to go."

Rubbing his scarlet ear, the boy muttered threats which
Rizzio diplomatically ignored. " Go now and find Sir Alex-

ander Hepburn. You shall request him to come here to
Holyroodhouse forthwith. It is a matter of urgency regarding
which I am commanded by the Queen's Grace."

" Sir Alexander Hepburn? Where does he bide? "

But Rizzio dismissed such a question with a wave of his
hand. "How shall I know? Ask the Master of the Household. If he is not in Edinburgh then take a horse and ride till
you find him. But hasten. Am I to wait your convenience
while you finish picking your nose? "

As the boy shambled off, Rizzio turned to greet Darnley,
who had lounged along the lobby and now stood in the doorway, his smile vague, his elegant doublet, short cloak and
blue trunk hose slashed with silver looking as if they had
recently been slept in. His hat was on the back of his head,
and he did not trouble to raise his hand to hide a prodigious
yawn.

" Ah, there you are, Davie. Have you set those verses I
left with you to music yet? "

Rizzio sighed. It troubled him to realise how often young
Lord Darnley was to be seen, if not actually drunk, at least
obviously having already drunk so much as to have been
obliged to sleep it off before presenting himself at the Queen's
dinner table. But let censoriousness be left to heretics. The
young man whom her Grace had chosen was of the true faith,
though perhaps not yet as diligent in his observance as might
have been hoped. But he was young, and her Grace's darling,
and much might also be forgiven him for his graciousness
towards an exile like himself. Rizzio tried not to sag as Darnley
brought a hand down on his shoulder with the force of one
felling an ox, " Well, Davie? "

" The verses are ready for you, my lord. Would it please
you to try them to the music before you go to dine? "

Darnley belched expressively. " It would not please me,
Davie. I shall have enough ado to hold my wind as it is
without venturing on such an extravagance." He swayed
slightly, so that Rizzio wilted under his weight.

" Then it might please your lordship to walk for a while out of doors to cool your head? "

But Darnley lifted his arm from the little Italian's shoulder, gave him a playful buffet which sent him staggering across the room, and flung himself down on a stool, his arms spread wide across the table-top among the scattered parchments, his cheek pressed against the cool surface of the wood.

" You are a good friend, Davie. The only—hic—friend I have. Bring a pitcher of water and sluice it over my head . . ."

Somehow Rizzio contrived to sober him, to smooth and straighten his clothes, to pummel the fair hair dry with a towel and comb it so that it shone like floss silk. Darnley set off for the Queen's apartments at last, his flat plumed cap gallantly askew, his short blue cloak with its silver cords swaying slowly in time with his stately stride. In the doorway he paused to turn his head and wink.

" Smile, man. I swear I shall do you credit."

But David Rizzio, left alone to clear up the mess of strewn papers, spilt ink, dripping water and sodden cloths, shook his head and sighed. He scarcely knew, at times, whether to light a score of candles to the Queen of Heaven for having sent such a splendid young man to captivate the Queen's Grace, or to bombard all the saints with anxious entreaties in case her choice should prove to have been mistaken.

But as the date for the wedding approached, Darnley steadied himself for the ordeal. When Randolph presented Queen Elizabeth's request that the Queen of Scots would refrain from taking up arms against her best subjects, as she described Moray and his party, Darnley, lounging near, laughed aloud and shook a finger in the English ambassador's face. Randolph drew himself up, rigid with offended dignity.

" My lord, I have not yet had your answer," he said stiffly, " in regard to the matter of your return to England, which the Queen my mistress commands."

" I find myself very well where I am, Master Randolph, and to return I intend not," said Darnley negligently. " What is more," he added, encouraged by the indulgent smile which Mary could not check, " the Queen of Scots and I have so strong a party in England that Queen Elizabeth has more cause to go in fear of us than we of her. Aye, Master Randolph," he declared, drawing himself to his full height, " I take more note of the Papists in England than of all the Protestants in Scotland can do."

Randolph turned his back on him. Bowing low, he spoke only to the Queen. " Madam, it seems that since you are of this mind, there is no more that I may profitably say."

" Master Randolph," said Mary coldly, " I fear that that is so."

Before the English ambassador was out of hearing, Darnley's wild laughter scandalised everybody but the Queen. For she was exultant, too, now that the wedding day was so near. The approval of the King and Queen-Mother of France had arrived that day, and the banns of marriage were at that very hour being solemnly cried, by the minister of the Kirk in the Canongate, at the request of the Justice-Clerk.

" Between Henry, Duke of Albany and Earl of Ross on the one part, and Marie, by the grace of God, Queen of Scots, Sovereign of this realm, on the other part," the stately phrases ran.

It was not till the following day that the dispensation from the Pope for the marriage of the Queen of Scots to her cousin Lord Darnley was brought to Edinburgh by the Bishop of Dunblane, and the Queen's presumption in having the banns cried without it was afterwards remembered. That evening Darnley took supper with his bride. Anticipation tingled in the air, bright as hoar frost, as the small company afterwards listened to Rizzio's love-ballads or danced to the music of the fiddlers he had trained to play for the new French dances. As it grew late Darnley drew the Queen imperiously from the dance floor into an embrasure. He had been drinking less than usual, but he was more exhilarated than she had ever seen him.

"How much longer must we wait, sweetheart?" he demanded. His arm was round her as they stood together looking out, through the lozenges of thick, greenish glass, at the outlines of the moon-washed Canongate, wavering as if seen through water.

"It will not be long now, my dearest," Mary said softly. Sometimes his urgency excited her own desire, and sometimes, as now, it made her oddly aware of his unguided youth.

"In a week's time I shall be King of Scots." His voice was loudly defiant.

"You will be my beloved consort," Mary said.

"I shall be King," Darnley repeated.

"What is the difference?" she asked tenderly.

"All the difference in the world," Darnley retorted. "Am I to trail after you like one of the disgusting lapdogs who enjoy your favour? Surely the Crown Matrimonial can be as easily conferred as the Dukedom of Albany and the Earldom of Ross?"

Mary caught her breath as if a death-chilled finger had been drawn down her spine. For a second she seemed to stare at the future, the solid ground yawning like a living thing to show her the precipice prepared for her unwary feet. For the instant of illumination she could neither hear nor speak. Then, from an inconceivably alienating distance she was aware of Darnley's peevishly reiterated complaint. But it seemed half a lifetime before the incoherent sounds of aggressive indignation began to reassemble into words, to form questions, to demand a reply.

". . . standing there like a marble statue," Darnley was saying. "Am I never to be answered?"

Mary forced her stiff lips to smile. "Yes, indeed."

He stopped to stare at her. Her face did indeed seem like marble in the pallor of the moonlight, marble just touched by the golden glow of candles as she turned towards him.

" You have not been listening," he accused her indignantly. Then, as she shook her head in helpless silence, he began to say it all over again.

She knew then that she had been consciously trying not to hear him, because, with every petulant word, he was breaking the glorious image she had made of him as ruthlessly as any heretic who took a hammer to destroy the smiling serenity of an alien saint. If she did not listen, if she could shut her mind to the stupid folly of his destructive talk, the shrine of her devotion to him might yet escape.

". . . that is all I ask. Since I am already Duke of Albany, Earl of Ross . . . the Crown Matrimonial will enable me to rule by your side . . ."

" I beg you . . ." Mary whispered, " only to be patient. This must take time . . ."

He was at once as delighted by the hint of surrender as a little boy by the promise of a sweetmeat. He did not at once realise that she had promised nothing. Within her the training of a lifetime, the reiterated precepts of the great Cardinal of Lorraine, still strove against the clamour of her senses. Even her woman's instinct was itself in conflict. For the second time she was to take a consort whose infirmity or youth made him seem less a husband and protector to be revered than a child to be cherished or indulged.

" Then you will do it? You will bestow on me the Crown Matrimonial? " he persisted.

Tormented by indecision, she swung towards him again. Those dancing saw only the charming posture of two lovers, the Queen's black velvet and white veil yielding a little towards the towering splendour of blue and gold brocade, Darnley's fair head inclined as if to catch her faintest whisper. The music of the violins soared, underlaid by the whisper of taffeta, the tapping of high heels. Here and there an eyebrow was raised, a nod answered a smile, while seasoned dowagers, heads on one side like attentive terriers, sighed gustily as they watched the couple in the embrasure.

" Ah, what sweethearts they are . . ."

But Darnley, his smile as beautiful as that of a young warrior angel, was murmuring: " I shall hold you to that promise, Madam, when the time comes."

" I promised nothing," Mary whispered, but so softly that she spoke more to her own conscience than to the jubilant young man who now caught her about the waist and whirled her into the surge of dancers which parted to receive them and closed behind them again. The tide of enchantment, which had ebbed so far, rose over her head again as she yielded to the compulsion of his arms.

" *Avand* Darnley! " he shouted as they went. And the indulgent laughter of the company who had seen nothing but the sweet solicitude of lovers, answered him with the mindless fidelity of an echo.

The date of the marriage ceremony had been fixed for Sunday, 29th July. It was not till after sunset on Saturday night that Mary signed the warrant which commanded the Lord Lyon King of Arms to proclaim Henry, Duke of Albany and Earl of Ross, as King of Scots, on the Queen's personal authority and by reason of the marriage to be solemnized between them next day. The royal title, so conferred, was only a courtesy, unlike the Crown Matrimonial, which must be set on his head in the presence and with the consent of the Three Estates of Parliament, entitling him to a sovereign's authority, wealth and privilege. But since, from that time forward, the Queen wished him to receive the royal title, all documents must bear both their names.

Master James Melville shook his head unhappily as he stood at the stairhead outside his lodging and listened to the proclamation, duly made with trumpet call and beaten drum at the Market Cross and the gates of Holyroodhouse, as the stillness of dusk was pricked with the first lights. " I had hoped," he said to his brother Andrew, who now stepped out to join him, " that her Grace might have abstained from this.

I warned her, as she made me swear to do, that it would be to her dire loss."

" You have more knowledge of the mind of those against her than I," said Sir Andrew. " Though I can well imagine that it will enrage my lord of Moray."

" It will also give him the cause for rebellion that he lacked," said Master Melville with a troubled face. " Nor will the Queen of England be disposed to see him fail. The country seems like to be reft asunder. The supporters of her Grace are already assembling. But several have left her for my lord of Moray. And more intend to go."

" I am for her Grace," said Sir Andrew gravely. " And Robert likewise." He looked uneasily at his brother. " You will not let your friendship for Moray divide you from the Queen? "

" I will remain in my lodging to-morrow and bar the door, and send out word that I am sick," said James Melville. " For truly I am in such perplexity that I know not where to turn. All is changed from the days in which a man's course lay straight before him, with his worship pledged to God and his service to his sovereign. Now he is pulled first one way and then that. Between his loyalty and his conscience, a man can make no move without being in some sort a traitor."

" You trouble yourself too much with subtleties," Sir Andrew said. " As I see this matter, it is for the Queen's Grace to choose whether she will put her trust in the old usage or the new as regards the worship of God. It is for me to choose likewise. What if she chooses one way and I another? She is still my sovereign lady. I shall be at the Palace to-morrow."

" And I shall bide where I am," said his brother.

The marriage ceremony was to take place at six o'clock in the morning, as much to prevent the attraction of probably hostile crowds by the Popish ceremonies in the Chapel Royal as to free the rest of the day for rejoicing. It was only half-past five, and something of the innocence of dawn still lingered

when the Queen, wearing the familiar black and white of
her royal mourning, but with her richest jewels, was led by the
Earl of Lennox on the one hand and the Earl of Athol on the
other, to the Chapel Royal, followed by a hubbub of excited
ladies in their newest gowns. All the nobility of Scotland who
could stomach the old religion were already assembled, and as
the bride entered, the congregation rose, the sponsors went to
bring her bridegroom, and the ceremony began.

When it was over, Darnley did what he could to placate
the Protestant section of those he now considered his subjects,
by rising to lead them out of the Chapel before the Nuptial
Mass. He had been pale with anxiety as the marriage service
began. Now, as might have been expected, he was jubilant.
There was much loud laughter as his party waited for the traditional disposal of the mourning robes the Queen must wear as
a royal widow until she actually became once more a wife.

Unexpectedly shaken between laughter and tears, she submitted, after the pretty protests which were as traditional as
the pins by which her black robes had been secured, while
her husband drew out the first pin. Next, her ladies, joining
hands as if to protect their mistress, let first one and then
another of the impatient courtiers take his turn, till the black
velvet fell about her feet and she was revealed in a shimmer of
gold brocade. At last, with hand-clappings and shrill, delighted
cries, they swooped upon her like a cloud of brilliant flowers
as they hung a necklace of great rubies about her neck,
others like drops of blood in her small ears, and exclaimed at
the beauty of the three new rings which had been added to
those with which her fingers blazed.

In the background, forgotten by them all, David Rizzio
clasped triumphant hands. " *Te Deum laudamus!* It is done
and no man can undo it! " he cried aloud. But his voice
went unheard. For as soon as the Queen's transformation
was completed the procession which was to escort bride and
bridegroom to the great hall for dinner was quickly formed,
and Rizzio, his work done, was content for once to remain in the

background, suddenly weary as the weight of responsibility he had carried ever since the secret marriage slipped from his shoulders. It had not been his first attempt at high diplomacy, but there had been times when he had trembled to think of his fate had his plans gone astray. But now, seated uncomplainingly at one of the lower tables, watching the Earls of Athol and Morton carve for the Queen, and the Earl of Crawford offer her wine from a golden goblet on bended knee, Rizzio smiled loftily round his humbler neighbours. Soon, soon he would reap a golden reward for his faithful service. His place would not be among those base fellows. At the high table he would rub shoulders with the greatest in the land.

And Darnley—how difficult it was to remember that he was now the King—his friend Darnley was being served by the Earls of Eglinton and Cassilis. Even Glencairn, that fervent supporter of the new religion, was now creaking to his knees, holding the goblet ready. Rizzio smiled as he remembered the day when he had soused Darnley's fair head and towelled it dry in order that his friend might be fit to present himself before the Queen at dinner. It was Darnley himself who had called Rizzio friend, the only friend he had. Well, that was no longer true. Kings had more friends than they could count. But Rizzio was sure that the new King of Scots would remember his services in time of trouble. It might mean a knighthood. The little foreigner drew himself up. Perhaps even more. Men had been given earldoms for less. . . .

Those taking part in the festivities had now begun to notice that others were missing. The names of the absentees were whispered from group to group with shrugs and head-shakings. Most conspicuous of all, undoubtedly, was the absence of the Queen's half-brother. But next to Moray, the English ambassador's vacant place was most marked. That of the Duke of Chatelherault might be due to indisposition. And Lethington's attention was given so much to Mary Fleming that he might indeed be indifferent to the diligence with which Rizzio was now performing for the Queen a score of confidential services which would once have come from him.

At noon, the Queen commanded the Lord Lyon King of Arms to proclaim her husband's new title as King of Scots, once more, in the presence of all the nobility assembled at the banquet. Soon the splendid phrases rolled like thunder over the heads of the company.

". . . Henry, the most high and mighty Lord Darnley, Duke of Albany, Earl of Ross, husband of the Queen, our most sovereign lady, by the grace of God, King of Scots."

" God save his Grace! "

In the emptiness which engulfed his words, the homage of the Earl of Lennox echoed like one lone pebble thrown down a well.

Hurriedly, the Queen gave the signal for the royal largesse to be scattered by the heralds to the oddly silent crowds outside the Palace. Dancing followed, with masques and pageantry which should have delighted everyone with sound and splendour. As evening approached, the tension mounted indeed. But the sultry quality of apprehension was more noticeable than either triumph or joy.

In every interval between dances those nearest the long windows of the Palace were aware of the crowds gathering outside it. At first it was possible to suppose that the people of Edinburgh were assembling to offer appropriate congratulations to their Queen on the occasion of her marriage. Had they not assembled in just such a way at her homecoming from France four years ago? Her ladies made little jokes and pantomimes of covering their ears as they remembered the loyal sawing of fiddles and wailing of bagpipes.

" Let us hope that the enthusiasm of the citizens will to-night be somewhat more restrained," said Mary Fleming, flickering her dark eyelashes up at Maitland of Lethington, " for truly, my lord, none of us slept a wink all night long when her Grace first returned."

But Lethington's answering smile was absent-minded.

He had heard enough of the noise made by crowds in various moods, both in Scotland and elsewhere, to be reasonably sure that any demonstration was unlikely to be enthusiastic. It was more of Moray's work, no doubt, though he guessed the ministers had also had a hand in it. For the sounds outside suggested that the proclamation of Darnley's regal title had incensed the common people of Edinburgh as much as it had alienated the nobility. Had he been consulted, reflected Lethington sourly, he would have known better than to permit such incredible folly. But since her Grace had not thought fit to ask his advice, she must take the consequences of doing without it. He smiled grimly and quoted a Latin tag, to the mystification of Mary Fleming.

" *Quem deus vult perdere, prius dementat.*"

Mary Fleming giggled nervously. " What does that mean, my lord ? "

" When the gods plan a mortal's destruction, they first deprive her of her wits."

" *Her . . . ?* " whispered Mary Fleming, round-eyed.

" A somewhat free translation," said Lethington negligently. " Ah, here come the fiddlers again. Mistress Fleming, let us dance."

At the other end of the ballroom, Sir Andrew Melville turned to look out of the window beside which he stood at the bobbing tide of pale faces swirling outside the forecourt. Mouths opened and shut. Clenched fists were shaken as the intermittent clamour rose and fell between peaks of indignation that rose like the wave-crests of an angry sea. As far as he could tell the crowd was not out of control. But their hostility saddened him. What a pity for the Queen to win so much affection by sheer hard-working charm, only to risk losing all and more to gratify the ambition of a young man he personally considered unfit to hold her stirrup, let alone share her throne. It was the waste that angered him as he turned away, the stupid, needless waste of so much goodwill. Uncertain what to do for the best, he went in search of the Queen.

But to his amazement Mary seemed utterly unaware of anything wrong. Surrounded by a laughing, chattering crowd of young noblemen, she was holding out her hands to Darnley, as he boisterously sought to reach her, protesting that he could not get anywhere near his own wife. As Sir Andrew watched her, he remembered the nonsensical rumour that the Queen had been bewitched. For her cheeks were flushed, her eyes brilliant, and her movements like those of a woman walking through a dream. He stood on the edge of the group about her for some time. But he could not catch her eye.

Then the dancers paused to rest, the fiddlers laid down their bows to gulp down the wine they were offered, and the snarling roar from outside the Palace rose high above the laughing chatter within it. This time the hostility of the cries against her " Popish marriage " was beyond all doubt. Could the people have overwhelmed the guards and got into the forecourt itself, Sir Andrew wondered, turning back to the window. Shrieks wild as seagulls' cries rose at him, and David Rizzio, white-faced, rushed at the weary musicians, gesticulating frantically. " But play, then," he screamed against the threatening noise. " Are we to wait all night for the dance while you sit there idle ? "

Sir Andrew glanced quickly at the Queen. But Darnley had reached her side at last. He was whispering something to which she listened enraptured. As far as he could make out, she had still heard nothing. But it was evident that nearly everyone else had.

" Play louder ! But louder still, I tell you ! " Rizzio urged the musicians.

" Bring more wine," Darnley shouted to the frightened servants.

" It would be as well to double the guards, I believe," Lennox said uneasily.

" I will see it is done," Athol agreed.

" Will they break into the Palace, think you ? " Lennox

asked. His narrow face, with its hare's teeth, was taut with
anxiety.

"No. They will do no more than bawl themselves hoarse.
It will not take long," said Glencairn.

But he was mistaken. The hubbub outside the Palace
went on all night. Nobody knew at what point the Queen
became aware of it, but in the morning she sent for the Provost
and took him to task. She also promised that if her people
would allow her the same freedom of conscience as they asked
for themselves, she would undertake to defend their liberties
as jealously as her own. With this they seemed satisfied.
But the problem of Moray and his threatened rebellion
remained, and the crestfallen return of Sir Alexander Hepburn
suggested that Queen Elizabeth and her representatives were
not indifferent to its success.

Mary received the Laird of Riccarton pleasantly. "You
have wasted no time. Is my lord of Bothwell with you?"

Sir Alexander looked down at the bonnet he was twisting
between his hands. "Madam, he is not," he admitted unwillingly.

"But I—I had counted on him," said Mary in dismay.

"Madam, the fault was mine. I thought to make greater
speed by passing through England," Sir Alexander admitted.
"But at Berwick your letter was taken from me by my lord of
Bedford, and though I protested it was your Grace's commission, I was bundled empty-handed whence I came."

The Queen stamped an imperious foot. "How dared
he meddle with my messenger in time of peace?" she cried
indignantly.

"The Earl of Bothwell's loyalty is too well-known for those
who serve the Queen of England to welcome his return,"
said Sir Alexander proudly. "Indeed, I regret the letter's
loss the more because I fear they will do all they may to
prevent him from reaching Scotland, now that they know
your Grace's command."

"You must go to France by sea. He will indeed come,

will he not, once he receives my summons?" Mary's voice was anxious. As always, opposition had hardened her purpose. She had recalled Bothwell only because she was recruiting all those likely to oppose her brother Moray. But Bedford's intervention had now persuaded her that his return was essential to her campaign's success.

"Yes, Madam," said Sir Alexander proudly, "he will come."

CHAPTER NINE

SHE would have to fight Moray before the summer was done. So much was now obvious. His recent actions had made it clear that he meant to force civil war on Scotland. Equally obvious was Mary's need of a leader whose sheer ability would compel on her supporters the unity they lacked. Her Councils were clamorous with dictatorial, conflicting voices, and bedevilled by the sardonic figure of Maitland of Lethington, not yet openly against her, but no longer to be counted on with confidence. The Queen, his expression seemed to indicate, would presently discover the consequences of preferring such an upstart as David Rizzio before so infinitely more experienced a secretary, as himself.

Darnley, as she was almost maternally aware, as maternally reluctant to admit, showed no aptitude for leadership. He was but young, she told herself, younger than she had ever imagined. He would learn in time. Meanwhile, were his beauty and his passion not enough, or almost enough, for her? (He had only been teasing, of course, when he begged for a respite from her ardour.) But he must not be inflicted with the thankless business of composing the quarrels of older men. The Duke of Chatelherault had promised Moray that the Hamiltons would join him, less on account of their dislike of a

Popish marriage than because of his resentment at its probable effect on his chance of the succession. More genuinely
religious objections had brought into Moray's camp such
extremists for the new faith as Argyll, Rothes and Glencairn.
And hostility to the house of Lennox was enough to add the
contingents of Maxwell and Boyd.

Against them, Mary did not yet know on whom she could
count. Athol, Seton and Erskine would join her as habitual
allies of the house of Lennox. But that was not enough. She
must use her happiness, her royalty and her youth to bring in
many others. She kept Rizzio hard at work, writing to every
nobleman whose attitude was still unsure.

" Has Sir Alexander set out for France with my lord of
Bothwell's pardon, David? " she asked uneasily, while she
waited for their replies.

" Madam, I myself saw him go."

" Write also to the Captain of Dunbar commanding the
immediate release of George Gordon. Promise him the restoration of his honours and earldom if he acquits himself well
against my brother of Moray."

Rizzio chuckled. " He will need no such inducement,
Madam. Everyone knows that it was Moray, not your Grace,
who sought the ruin of his house."

" That is why I wish him to know that it is not Moray who
now plans to right that wrong," Mary said. " Is there anyone
else, Davie, that my brother has despitefully treated? "

" There must be many, Madam. But they will need no
summons."

During August both sides reckoned their resources and
felt for their opponents' weak spots. On the 19th, Darnley
hoped to reassure those who considered him a Papist by
attending sermon in St. Giles, where a special throne was put
up for his convenience. But John Knox had been informed
that Darnley had recently tossed the newest metrical version
of the Psalms, as used by the Reformed Kirk, into the fire, and
was not therefore sufficiently convinced of his conversion

to receive him with the deference Darnley expected. On the contrary, he launched into such a diatribe against the government of boys and women, and the punishment meted out to Ahab and his posterity for failing to control the harlot Jezebel that Darnley would have won more genuine sympathy if he had ordered the reformer's arrest then and there. But when Knox was summoned before the Council, and forbidden by Lethington to preach again in Edinburgh while the King and Queen were in the city, Knox boldly defied him.

"My lord, I will preach or abstain as the Kirk commands me," he declared.

Before she left Edinburgh, Mary summoned Randolph and warned him that if he abused his position as ambassador by entering into negotiations with her rebels, she would have no alternative but to confine him to his lodging and surround it with a guard. And from Stirling, where on the 28th of August, she went to inspect her troops, she sent Queen Elizabeth a letter which, she hoped, made her mastery of the situation quite clear. It had been the result of careful thought, but she wrote it rapidly, with her own hand, a little smile curling the corners of her mouth now and again.

"Madam my good Sister,

Having had news from the King my brother-in-law, I despatch this gentleman of mine expressly to make report to him of the state of my affairs in this country, and would not do this without sending you a line to recommend myself to your good graces, and to pray you to let him be expedited, that his letters may not be old. And because I have no leisure, being on the march with the King my husband against our rebels, I cannot write you a longer letter than to pray God to give you, Madam my good Sister, health, and a very long and happy life.

From Stirling, this 28th of August.

Your very affectionate good sister and cousin and faithful friend,

Marie R."

There was mischief in the final twirl of the triumphant R, and her eyes were shining with amusement as she handed the sheet to Rizzio.

" There, David. I believe that should make all clear. Read it and afterwards be sure that it is sent."

" I will, Madam," said Rizzio happily.

From Stirling, Mary rode westward with her supporters, but the rebels eluded her and her uncertain army was baffled, first by a thunderstorm and afterwards by the flooded rivers which obstructed their path. Meanwhile, Moray took advantage of the absence of the royal forces and rashly attempted the capture of Edinburgh, only to be driven out by the threat of the Castle guns. He retreated first to Lanark and then to Dumfries, while Mary rode at the head of her forces to receive the surrender of Argyll's fortress of Castle Campbell and recruit support in Fife. When she returned to Edinburgh, it was in triumph, to proclaim in her own and her husband's name her determination to maintain liberty of conscience and security of property for all her subjects and plan a further campaign against the rebels in the autumn.

Darnley, quite uninterested in the technicalities of government, was glad of their return to Holyroodhouse, where the gilt-inlaid breastplate and morion he had ordered to be made to his measure by the best armourer in the city should now be waiting for him to try. He hurried, therefore, to his own apartments, bawling for his servants, too impatient to encase himself in his warlike splendour to remember that Mary had asked him to help her with a number of urgent problems.

Mary sighed and turned to Rizzio. " There is the question of the subsidy despatched by His Holiness, on which I sent James Melville to interview the Duke of Northumberland.

I understand Master Melville is here with his report. I will receive it in the small supper-room, since it would be better heard in private. Bring him to me there."

The small supper-room, as it was called, was particularly well adapted for confidential discussions, since it lay at the end of the range of royal apartments, only to be approached through the Queen's bedchamber, out of which it opened, or by a private stair, concealed behind the hangings, which led from her bedchamber to Darnley's on the floor below, and continued downwards to offer a means of leaving the Palace by the corridor connecting their apartments with the Chapel Royal. Here Rizzio brought in James Melville, who looked both downcast and ill at ease.

" Well, Master Melville, did you contrive to persuade the Duke of Northumberland to part with the eight thousand crowns from His Holiness ? "

" Madam, I did not," said James Melville, " to my great vexation. I fear the Duke of Northumberland is no true friend to your Grace," he added somewhat smugly, " though of the same persuasion."

" That must be some slight satisfaction to you, Master Melville, since you are not," said Mary dryly.

James Melville looked down his nose. " Be that as it may, Madam, I did my utmost to persuade the Duke to recognise your right to the gold. But he maintained that, since by ancient usage he was entitled to the contents of all ships wrecked within his bounds, the gold, which he admitted he had seized, was consequently his."

" I shall complain to Rome. See to it, David," Mary protested.

" I have done my utmost, Madam," James Melville said, in a tone which suggested he considered it unlikely that Rizzio could do more.

" I am sure of that, Master Melville. But something else, I think, is troubling you. Will you not tell me, speaking with the freedom I invited, what it is ? "

"Madam," James Melville blurted out, "I entreat your permission to leave your service."

Mary looked stricken. "Surely you would not take service with my brother against me?"

"No, Madam. But this is a time full of suspicion, and I feel unable to carry out my duties towards you as I would wish."

"But, Master Melville, you must have some better reason to seek to desert my service."

"I believe, Madam, I could serve you better abroad."

"I am afraid," said Mary in a troubled voice, "that you no longer use such freedom of speech with me as I had hoped you always would."

"It may be, Madam, that my opinions would be unpleasant to you."

Mary smiled. "My dear Master Melville, that would be no novelty. Have you a sharper tongue than Master Knox?"

"Heaven forbid, Madam."

"I knew you would say that. I know also that you have a liking for the Earl of Moray," said Mary earnestly. "But not so much as to approve of his action in taking up arms against me."

Uncertainly, James Melville shook his head.

"Your enemies, I know," said Mary impulsively, "do their best to give a bad character of you to the King. But I hope you will give no more credit to those who speak evil against me, sir, than I give to those who seek to discredit you. Wait on the King with the same wise counsel that you have offered me. He is—but young, and much in need of wisdom. As I know I am also."

"I am so beset," said James Melville wretchedly, "I know not which way to turn."

"Turn back, Master Melville, to your former place," Mary begged, with a tentative, imploring little gesture which he found hard to disregard. "Have a care of David also," she added in a lower voice. " I know he is hated by those who think they have suffered some loss of position because of him. It is not so."

" I am glad to hear it, Madam."

Mary held out her hand. " I promise that all you will tell me or the King we will take in good part, as spoken by a good and faithful servant. Will you remember that? "

James Melville almost groaned aloud.

" You will remember? " she repeated softly.

" Heaven help me, yes," James Melville said.

Mary laughed. It was a sweet, soft laugh of relief rather than triumph. She held our her hand, and he knelt to kiss it.

" Master Melville," she said gaily, " I believe you take me for a very sorceress. And yet I am but a poor Queen in need of all her friends."

To this, James Melville, bowing himself through the doorway, thought it best not to reply. But as he left the Queen's presence he almost collided with a newcomer in the doorway, at the sight of whom Mary clapped her hands like a delighted child.

" My lord of Bothwell! Now all our warfare shall go merrily forward."

" I trust it may, Madam," said Bothwell, with his wry grin.

He was leaner than she remembered him. Harder, too, with bitter lines on the face which had been merely weather-beaten a few years ago. He was shabby, not with the darned thrift of a man who accepts such necessity as a commonplace, but with the defiance of one who prefers a rent to a patch and wears his old clothes with the contempt that his poverty deserves.

So much she noticed before Darnley came clattering up the stairs, superb in his gilded armour, foolishly disconcerted to find that the Queen, whose immediate admiration he required, was not alone.

Mary spoke quickly. "Dear heart, you seem the very god of war! And here is the Earl of Bothwell, new returned from France."

Darnley frowned as Mary turned to Bothwell.

"You are most welcome, my lord," she said graciously. "For things have reached a pretty pass. My brother of Moray has taken the field against me."

Bothwell nodded. "Madam, could you have looked for him to do otherwise? For years he has had an understanding with the Queen of England."

"Yet I had hoped——" Mary said, "to have been able to avoid bloodshed between Scots."

"Have no fear," Darnley said loudly. "At the first sight of our conquering host his rabble will turn tail and run. Is that not so, my lord of Bothwell?"

"Without doubt, my lord the King," said Bothwell cheerfully.

"Madam," broke in Rizzio, from the doorway, "may I suggest that we have yet much to arrange in regard to the campaign before us? Who would your Grace be pleased to put in charge of the baggage? Is each contingent to be separately provisioned? With what funds are those in the royal company to be paid?"

Mary sighed. "You are right, David. There is much to be seen to. My love, shall we now choose our commanders?"

But Darnley had lost interest. With a wave of the hand he dismissed such a necessity. "Have we not chosen? My father, as President of the Council, must lead the van, and my lord of Morton, as Chancellor, the advance guard. I shall command the centre and defend my sweet lady. But first I will tell the armourer who awaits my verdict where the cuirass irks me. It must be altered."

He went into the bedchamber, parted the hangings which hid the private staircase, and went whistling down it to his apartments below.

Mary turned towards the Earl of Bothwell, relieved

to find his expression abstracted and grave. He showed no
resentment at Darnley's choice of leaders. As usual, he was
more concerned with winning the campaign than the choice
of those to lead it.

" I trust, my lord, that your journey was uneventful? "
Mary said. " When my first summons fell into English hands
I feared they would afterwards be on the watch for you."

" They were, Madam. I came by way of the Netherlands,
where I obtained as good a store of arms and explosives as they
would spare for what I could pay. It is a sorry collection, no
more than a dozen nags could bear. But it is already at your
command in the forecourt below. I have also the promise of
two thousand men who wait upon your orders in France, and
I would gladly raise the Borders if I may have leave to ride
thither."

" All you can bring will be most welcome," Mary said.
" We are not too badly placed, for Moray has been driven
out of Edinburgh, and has betaken himself to Dumfries. My
main force lies at Stirling, though two thousand men are
with my lord of Lennox in the west."

" I will raise as many from the Border."

" Take note, David," said Mary formally, " that my lord
of Bothwell is to be confirmed anew in his offices as Lieutenant of the Border and Lord Admiral of Scotland."

" I will, Madam."

Rizzio's quill squeaked busily, and Bothwell bowed. So
byegones were to be byegones? Well, as far as he was concerned
such belated justice suited him well enough.

" Have I then your Grace's permission to return to
Hermitage? " With the chance of settling scores with Moray
dependent on rousing his fellow Borderers, Bothwell had no
wish for delay. " I have thrown Robert Elliot out once, but it
may be I shall now have it to do again." He grinned, in
anticipation.

Mary laughed. There spoke a man of action after her own
heart. " Then set about it forthwith, my lord," she said.

Almost before she finished speaking he had bowed and gone, leaving her exhilarated by the brief contact with such vitality. But the contagion of warlike preparations made it harder to return to the tedium of administrative business. Impatiently she pushed the piled documents away.

"The King and I will attend to these later," she said. "Run down now, David, and ask him to send the armourer to me when he has done. I, too, must consider what I shall need for our autumn campaign."

"What, Madam, will you lead your troops in person?" faltered Rizzio.

"Why not?" she said gaily. "Have I not done so before? If the King means to wear armour, so shall I."

She swept out of the little supper-room and through the bedchamber beyond almost as vehemently as Bothwell had done, clapping her hands for attention as she entered her presence chamber.

"*Mes enfants*," she declared excitedly, "we are about to chastise the rebels and put them finally to flight. Prepare yourselves for battle!"

She paused, her face gravely mocking for an instant, then convulsed with laughter at their candid dismay. "What, have you no heart for the rigours of another campaign? I shall have my lord the King's armourer make me a light breastplate to wear under my riding-dress, and a casque which will fit snug under my velvet riding-hat with the cock's plumes——"

"Sweet Madam," wailed Mary Fleming, "I beg you not to venture. You will ride to your death!"

"The King," said Mary proudly, "will be riding by my side. Will he allow any harm to come to me? And I shall carry a pair of pistols at my saddle-bow."

"Oh, Madam . . ." Their indrawn breath was like the silvery shudder of aspen leaves.

"Now as to my costume. It shall be of scarlet velvet, since that is the aptest of all colours for war, and richly embroidered with gold lace to match my lord the King's gilded armour——"

" Oh, Madam, why will you not leave such rigours to the men who are our rightful defenders ? " wailed Mary Beton.

" I look for none of you to share them——" said the Queen proudly.

" Yet I will share them, whether you will or no," protested Mary Seton.

But no voice echoed hers. Shrinking a little, shivering as a sudden scurry of rain lashed the panes, they looked at each other in horrified inquiry, their protests shrill as the twittering of small birds threatened by a cat.

" Oh, Madam . . . surely it is no season for such a venture . . ."

" We were soaked to the skin when we rode from Stirling . . ."

" Will you not stay snug at Holyroodhouse and let their lordships fight for us all . . . ? "

" I shall fare forth. But you may stay as snug as you please," said the Queen indifferently.

Mary Fleming sighed with relief. She did not think that Lethington would ride with the royal forces. He was no longer even nominally Secretary of State. Her Grace had recently bestowed the office on Sir James Balfour, a nimble-witted lawyer whose ambition, his enemies whispered, was matched only by the unscrupulous means he was prepared to use to achieve it. It was also said that his present protestations of zeal for the old faith, when it could be of service, effectively hid his cynical indifference to the things that all faith stood for, whether old or new.

But the new arrangement suited Mary Fleming well, since it left Lethington free to pursue her, and his ardour was now such that she did not mean to resist him much longer. Mary Beton, troubled by Randolph's fall from favour, said no more. She did not know whether she would see much of him even if she remained at Holyroodhouse, for it was rumoured that the Queen was about to expel him from her Court. And now, after those first shamefaced moments, they all turned to planning and measuring and wrangling about the Queen's riding-dress of scarlet and gold.

But the pretty preoccupation over her personal equipment did not prevent Mary from worrying about the campaign before her. She was determined now to refuse all compromise. Had her brother and his allies not boasted of their intention to kill her husband? How could there be any peace of mind for her while they remained in Scotland? Here she was supported by both Huntly and Bothwell, who presently returned to Court, their preparations completed. With loathing of Moray and loyalty to the Crown as common ground, the two young men, in other ways so different, now struck up a friendship which delighted the Queen. She reinstated George Gordon in his disgraced father's earldom, and added him, with Bothwell, to her Council.

" As my Lieutenant of the Border I shall put my lord of Bothwell in command when we march against the rebels at Dumfries," she told Darnley, as they conferred in his privy chamber over the final arrangements for the coming campaign, a large map spread out on the table between them. But Darnley protested angrily.

" Bothwell? Why should he command? His business is with the Border, and our army is mustering at Biggar, in the west. It is my father, your Lieutenant in the west, who should lead it. Is he not President of the Council? "

Mary frowned in perplexity. " But your father is fully occupied elsewhere. Bothwell and his Borderers are already at my disposal. It will be a week before your father can join us at Biggar."

" Nevertheless, he shall not be passed over," said Darnley obstinately.

" But, my dear love," Mary implored, " if you would but look at the map before us——"

" If you would but confine your attention to tasks fit for

ladies and leave warlike decisions to the men whose business they are, we should fare better," retorted Darnley pettishly. " It is my father's right to command in the west, and our forces are mustered at Biggar——"

" Our enemies are at Dumfries."

" That is of no consequence."

" Your father must journey from the borders of Argyll. Bothwell and his Borderers are already within a short march of Dumfries," said Mary, less patiently.

Darnley stamped first one foot and then the other till his spurs rang. " My father stands close to the throne of Scotland. Bothwell is but a moss trooper that you have hauled out of his native bogs because he has a way with the Border barbarians! I tell you, if he leads I shall stay at home. You can ride without me, scarlet velvet, gold braid and all."

Mary bit her lip. It was their first real quarrel, and she knew enough of Lennox's dilatory disposition to be sure that her choice of a faster moving leader was the right one. But she guessed that Darnley would carry out his threat, and the consequences of such a public disagreement might well be graver than those of a week's delay.

" It shall be as you wish, my dearest," she said.

Darnley's sullen petulance vanished like ice at midsummer. He swung round and caught her in his arms. " There's my Mary. We will summon my father to lead us all to victory."

So Mary and Darnley rode in state from Edinburgh, and spent, as she had predicted, a week at Biggar waiting for the chosen commander's arrival. Huntly shook his head at the news of Lennox's preferment, but Bothwell greeted it with his usual enigmatic grin, and his raised eyebrows might have indicated either scepticism or indifference.

Lennox came at last, complaining and flustered in his haste, and the army moved off just before it became evident that the delay had given the rebels the time they needed to withdraw from Dumfries and take refuge in Carlisle.

" I am not sorry that they got away," Mary assured

Darnley, eager to minimise his humiliation. " I have little stomach for shedding Scottish blood. Their exile shall suffice."

He accepted her generous gesture with an ill grace. " I have had enough of such tedious warfare," he declared. Then he threw his expensive armour into a corner and went hawking again. Mary was left alone to attend Council meetings and deal with an accumulation of State affairs. Too proud to complain, she could not hide her anxiety from Rizzio.

" When both our names are needed, and the King's Grace has been detained elsewhere, I am at my wit's end to know what is to be done. Deeds, charters, letters, they are piled like snowdrifts on my table. I may not sign alone, since they are made out in both our names, yet if I leave them everything will presently be in confusion."

" Madam," said Rizzio, " if I were to take a sample of the King's signature, and have a cunning workman prepare a stamp in wood or metal—after the fashion of a seal, cut in reverse, you could then soak it on a pad of ink——"

" And press it on the parchment beside mine! Well thought on, Davie. See that it is done! My lord the King may have his pleasure and yet his business shall be done besides. He is but young, David. Remember that," she added with sudden urgency. Her voice had the vehemence of one seeking not only to reassure others, but herself.

" I will remember," Rizzio promised gently.

" There is so much to do, now our enemies have been driven from the country, that my head swims," said Mary. For a moment she covered her face with her hands, leaning forward across the parchment-strewn table. Rizzio was alarmed.

" Madam, are you unwell ? "

" No . . . it is nothing." She often felt sick and dizzy nowadays. Her ladies smiled and nodded to each other, thinking she did not notice. It might well be as they supposed. An heir for Scotland . . . it would be one of her many duties done.

" At least Queen Elizabeth has disowned the rebels who thought to enjoy her favour, after their defeat," she said, with one of her swift changes of mood. " Master Melville has been pleading with me for their pardon, and hinting that if I would not, it might be the worse for me."

" He has spoken to me also," said Rizzio cheerfully. " In the same threatening vein. But I despised his fears. Thus I answered him." He snapped his fingers briskly. " What need I fear from banished traitors while I am under the protection of the Queen's Grace? "

" Why, nothing, David. No man dare touch my trusted servant," said Mary warmly. " Oh, David, my arm aches with writing. Let us leave our labours. It wants but a little to supper time. Afterwards let us occupy ourselves with singing and dancing in the old way."

" With all my heart, Madam," said Rizzio. " If the King has returned shall I tell him what merriment is planned? "

" Yes, Davie, do. It would complete my pleasure to have him by my side."

Darnley was back, in high good humour again. He sat by the Queen's side under the royal canopy at the centre of the high table, and her recent comrades in arms, Huntly and Bothwell, one to her right and the other to his left, shared the jokes which sent roars of appreciative laughter echoing round the hall. Here and there were less cordial, more secret faces. The Earl of Morton, whose loyalty was no longer above suspicion, brooded in silence, and Lord Ruthven, whose saturnine face made Mary shiver for no reason she could name, sat glumly near him. But Mary was determined to enjoy herself, and refused to notice their alien mood. After the boards had been cleared, Darnley led her out to dance before all the rest, and her face, upturned to his, as they met and parted in the elaborate movements of the pavan, was dazed with happiness.

When they paused to rest she found herself near the lounging figure of Bothwell, unpartnered for the moment.

He looked, she fancied, both lonely and sad, and out of her bright mirage she sought instinctively to comfort him.

"Why, my lord, you shall not stand there solitary. I will put all to rights. They call me the busiest matchmaker at Court. And so I am. Oh yes, I have plans for you."

"Indeed, Madam?" said Bothwell sombrely. "May I ask what they are?"

"I have not yet given the matter sufficient thought," Mary said gaily. "But only this very instant it came to me that the loyal service shown by the houses of Bothwell and Huntly might well be secured by closer bonds than friendship. Huntly's sister has lately come to Court. Have you taken note of the Lady Jean, my lord?"

Bothwell looked blank. "No, Madam."

"Then do so. She is both good and beautiful, I believe."

"Madam, in this, as in all else, I am your Grace's obedient servant," said the Earl of Bothwell tonelessly.

CHAPTER TEN

DARNLEY rolled vague eyes at the Earl of Morton, who was slyly refilling his beaker, though he had already drunk enough wine to loosen his tongue and disturb his feather-duster wits. Lolling on a high-backed chair at the head of Morton's well-covered supper table at Douglas House, he continued to recite his grievances in the loud, toneless voice of the partially drunk.

". . . and what is the use of it? I am King but in name. It has not profited me by a single bawbee. When I ask for the funds which should be at a King's disposal, what comes of it? I am told that my lords of the Treasury cannot spare it. The soldiers must be paid, the royal castles repaired, artillery renewed at my lord Bothwell's whim, workmen set to work on newer fortifications . . ."

"Aye, it is a sore thing to see so great a lady so ill advised," agreed Morton. His little pigs' eyes swivelled towards Maitland of Lethington, silent and watchful at the far end of the board as his industrious machinations approached their culmination.

Times had changed since he and the Queen had laughed together over the antics of his monkey and she had clapped her hands with delight at the pretty things he had brought home from France. Ever since her preference for David Rizzio had capped his humiliation at being sent to discuss the Leicester marriage with Elizabeth when Mary was already secretly married to Darnley, Lethington had been working for the little Italian's destruction, but so subtly that his purpose had been unperceived by those he had used to achieve it. Rizzio himself did not wonder why Lethington had told him that the Earl of Morton was unfit for the office of Chancellor, and the country would fare better if he asked the Queen for the office himself. Nor did Morton suspect Lethington's purpose in warning him subsequently that Rizzio intended to be Chancellor in his stead. Least of all did Darnley guess why Lethington hinted that it was Rizzio's influence with the Queen that kept him penniless. Now, in answer to Morton's questioning glance, Lethington gave an almost imperceptible nod.

"I fear, my lord the King, you have been cherishing a black-advised viper in your bosom," Morton said sententiously.

Darnley gaped. "Eh?"

Only by warning Morton that Rizzio had been advising the Queen against Douglas interests had Lethington persuaded the Chancellor to speak so clearly. It was not the sort of risk he often cared to take, especially since the long-legged lout he had been flattering all the evening was such a bairnly creature that he might well blurt out all he had heard to the Queen at their next quarrel. Unless, of course, they could entangle him so fast that he must hold his tongue for his own safety. Had it been possible, Morton would have preferred to act without him, and Moray, with the other exiled lords, was still doubtful about the value of Darnley's co-operation. But Lethington had pointed out that only those on the spot could accurately assess the situation. If they found they needed Darnley, Moray must take their word for the necessity.

" Surely, my lord the King," rumbled the Earl of Morton, " your generosity has not blinded you? Can you not see that you have but the one man to thank for all the differences between you and the Queen's Grace? The man with whom she shuts herself away from even her most devoted ladies, hour after hour. On affairs of state, says he. Aye, mebbe. Ihmhm! "

" You mean—David? " said Darnley in amazement.

" Who else? Give the matter a wee bit thought," Morton mumbled.

Darnley swung one long leg over the arm of his chair and lay back to consider such an astounding possibility. His arms lay limp, one on his knee and the other across the table. His mouth sagged open and his eyeballs rolled in his head as he tried to focus his befuddled brains. At first he had been kind to the little Piedmontese secretary in the casual way he would have been kind to a dog that fawned on him. But he had also found David Rizzio's enthusiastic support for his courtship of the Queen most useful. Rizzio had set his verses to music, thumbed out new variations of the mediocre tunes he had himself composed. He had never supposed the ugly little fellow's interest in him to be other than genuine, for his own vanity had made it impossible to think of such an ill-favoured varlet as a rival.

" It—it is not possible," he stammered.

Morton's movement to refill Darnley's beaker was checked by Lethington's slight but definite shake of the head. To fuddle the young fool further would be dangerous. " Who was it persuaded the Queen's Grace to pardon Chatelherault and

bring the Hamiltons back to Court in all their arrogance? ”
Morton asked.

“ You—you think it was David’s doing? ” maundered
Darnley.

“ Who else has the Queen’s confidence nowadays? ”

Darnley swung his leg down and sat square to the table,
bringing his clenched fists down on the board with such force
that the pewter plates leapt from it. “ It may be so, indeed.
It was David who had the pretty idea of counterfeiting my
signature, so that I might take less part in the ordering of
affairs. I tell you, she has been false to her own proclamation.
I have received neither the revenues nor the rights of the
Crown Matrimonial——”

“ And who, think ye, advised her to withhold them? ”
inquired the Earl of Morton.

“ Saints in heaven, but it is too much,” shouted Darnley.
“ I will spit the little toad with my dagger. I will nail his ears
to the door of the Queen’s chamber. I——”

“ Gently now, my lord, gently,” rumbled Morton, somewhat alarmed. “ This is not a matter for you to adventure
alone.”

“ Huh,” said Darnley. Then a smile in which stupidity
and cunning were outrageously blended lightened the drunken
blankness of his flushed face. “ You will help me? What
have you in mind, my lords? ”

“ A bond,” said Lethington, speaking for the first time,
“ between true friends who will promise to rid you of your
enemy, and afterwards to obtain for you all the privileges of
the Crown Matrimonial.”

“ Now that,” said Darnley, “ is a rare and splendid thought.
Would you both swear to it? ”

“ Aye,” said the Earl of Morton. “ But only so long as
you swear also that you speak of our purpose to no man, no,
not even to the Queen’s Grace——”

“ I will be silent.”

“ Do you swear it? ”

" I swear it. When shall we set to work? "

Lethington moved unobtrusively from his place at the far end of the board to take a stool opposite the Earl of Morton.

" As soon as may be," he promised. " But there is one small matter which must be set against all the benefits we promise you, my lord."

" Eh? " Darnley's expression was vacant again. It was doubtful if his pale, blurred eyes saw Lethington as he checked his irritation sufficiently to speak slowly and clearly, shaping each word as if he were addressing one either deaf or demented.

" In exchange for our loyal co-operation in securing the Crown Matrimonial and all the privileges and benefits so far withheld, we ask you to receive again at Court the lords who have been banished for their opposition to the Queen's un-reasoning tyranny——"

Darnley frowned. " I thought," he said bemusedly, " they were banished because of their opposition to me? "

" So you were led to suppose, my lord," said Morton blandly. " But it is not so. They are your most loyal and loving subjects, and ask only the opportunity of proving it."

" Oh," said Darnley vaguely. " Well, in that case, I will think on it."

" I am sure," said Lethington, with the concentration of a hypnotist impressing his will on an uncertain subject, " that your lordship is well aware that one warning word to the Queen would mar all? "

Darnley nodded.

" Nor must any word of it reach David Rizzio," Lethington went on, with sufficient intensity to drive his meaning into any but the most fuddled brain. " If it does, all hope of the Crown Matrimonial is quite gone."

" No word must reach David Rizzio," Darnley repeated parrot-wise. " Or all hope of Crown Matrimonial quite gone."

" You must make him believe," Lethington droned, " that he is still as much in your lordship's favour as ever."

"Aye, as much in favour as ever." Darnley's head had begun to nod on his shoulders.

Lethington thrust his lean, hawklike face close to Darnley. "You must take pains to play with him, sing with him, and consult him as closely as ever you did, my lord. If you do not, all will be lost."

"All . . . will . . . be . . . lost," droned Darnley between slack lips. His head lolled forward, jerked up again, then fell sideways as he slumped back in his chair. His breath snored through his nose. Beyond recall now, he slept.

"You plied the wine too freely," said Lethington in exasperation. "Now the work will all be to do again."

"Then it shall be done again," said Morton doggedly. "With the young fool so short of money that he cannot pay his gaming debts, it will be easy to persuade him here to dine."

"If he should babble of our purpose to the Queen——"

"Not he," said Morton judicially. "He is as like to seek a harlot's bed as the Queen's, from all I hear. By to-morrow he will remember nothing."

"I am not so sure," said Lethington.

As if in confirmation of his words, Darnley's eyelids flickered, and his slack lips curled in a sly grin as he contrived to raise himself enough to confront his confederates with an admonishing finger.

"Mark me, my lords, not a word—mussht—mussht be spoken of this. Shilence is golden—as the Crown—Matri-tri-trinomial," he concluded owlishly, and sagged once more into stentorian sleep.

His hearers turned to each other. "One thought at least seems to have found lodging in that bat-hung belfry of his," said Lethington. "Shall we leave him where he is or carry him to bed?"

Morton measured the slack limbs of the unconscious young man with a judicial eye. "Let him be. Are we to break our backs for any young sot who thinks himself fit to wear the

Crown Matrimonial? Come away to the fire now, while I tell ye the story I heard of the fisher-lassie and the minister . . ."

In due course Darnley woke, stiff and wretched, to be given a beaker of the claret Morton had mulled over the scandalous stories at which Lethington wearily smiled. Then he was huddled into his cloak by his servants, who had been dozing in the hall below.

" Ye'll find him," Morton murmured confidentially to Darnley's valet, " a wee bit wandering. But pay no heed, pay no heed."

" Never fear, my lord," the man said. " We ken him fine."

But there was something now that his most trusted servants did not know, something that Darnley had grabbed as eagerly as a child which hides its coveted treasure from the world. His obsession with his own importance made it easy for him to believe that men such as Lethington and Morton might really be willing to run the risks they contemplated for the pleasure of making him the ruler of Scotland. And, conversely, he regarded the Queen's reluctance to accord him that position as an injury so monstrous that she deserved all she was likely to get.

Darnley was not a virile lover. Soon after their marriage he had begun to find Mary's ardour wearisome. For he was only able to enjoy sexual intercourse if he stimulated his senses with a frequent change of partner, so that the tenderness of a mature relationship was unknown to him, and he was quite without pity for the sick squeamishness which now afflicted the eager young woman who had been so anxious to believe herself in love. Her pregnancy had been definitely established by December, but Darnley was not inclined to set aside any of his amusements for her consolation. His secret understanding with Morton and Lethington had made him more arrogant than ever. But his impatience still goaded him to pester the Queen on the subject of the Crown Matrimonial at every opportunity.

" I cannot understand," he complained, stalking about the bedchamber in which the Queen was resting after a wretched night, " why you will not perform what you promised, by proclamation, as long ago as our wedding day."

Mary looked at him out of the depths of her sick misery. An incipient migraine made his face visible in wavering bands of light and shade. If she remained quiet, she might have a chance of throwing off the attack. But if she were compelled to argue, she would presently be overwhelmed with the familiar, blinding pain from which, for the next forty-eight hours, there would be no relief.

" I have told you many times," she said faintly, " that the Crown Matrimonial and the income which goes with it must await the consent of Parliament. Since the autumn campaign, we are at the end of our resources. So much was bestowed on my brother of Moray——"

" Then why not take it back now we have beaten him ? "

" His lands may only be taken when Parliament declares them forfeit, with those of his confederates. Will you not try to understand ? "

As she closed her eyes against the thudding pain, Darnley stood looking down at her, a spiteful leer marring his handsome but already bloated face. His memory of the evening at Morton's lodging was somewhat blurred, but he retained the impression that he had been assured that if the Queen would not bestow the Crown Matrimonial on him, others would. As to her explanation that there was no money for him to have, he simply did not believe it.

" All that you do against me is done by ill advice," he blurted out.

Mary lifted her heavy lids. " What advice? " she asked in surprise.

" No matter," said Darnley hastily. " Where is David? "

" What need have you of him? " said Mary uneasily.

" I would have his opinion of my new verses. He sets them to music more sweetly than any man."

" You will find him in the little . . . supper-room," said Mary, clenching her teeth against the assault of pain. " Send . . . Mary Seton to me first . . ."

" I will, Madam," said Darnley, and forgot the request before he reached the door.

That Christmas, Darnley delighted Rizzio with his new attentiveness to the rites of the old faith. Since his failure to impress the ministers of the new religion by a few yawning appearances at their sermons, he had determined to avenge their indifference by returning to the old. He attended Midnight Mass in the Chapel Royal, returned for Matins in the small hours, and later for High Mass. The Queen, he fancied, showed less diligence than usual. It was pleasant to be able to look down on her from the eminence of his ostentatious piety, exasperating that she should receive his scoldings with a smile, as she busied herself with the preparations for the marriage alliance between the families which were proving themselves her staunchest supporters. Though it seemed unlikely to be the love-match she had hoped for, its advantages were obvious to everyone, except perhaps, to the bride.

Lady Jean Gordon had no wish for a brilliantly diplomatic marriage which would unite the greatest title in the north with the greatest champion of the Crown on the Border. Pale, mulish, and marble-cold, she listened to her brother's enthusiastic approval of the Queen's proposal as if another woman were concerned. She might bow her head to the Queen's command, but her determination to marry Alexander Ogilvie of Boyne remained unshaken, even after the unfortunate man took the opportunity offered by her unwilling betrothal to try and make Mary Beton forget the flatteries of the now disgraced Randolph.

Bothwell himself treated the marriage arranged for him with detachment. Such contracts were fairly common among members of the Scottish nobility, after the fashion which had always been followed in France. He appreciated the advantages of a closer alliance with the family of his good friend, but he did not expect to make much from Lady Jean's dowry, since most of it would be needed to redeem from his creditors the Castle of Crichton which was to be his marriage gift to his bride.

The Queen sent for him while the marriage contract was being drawn up. Candlemas was coming, and Lady Jean was one of those whom Mary's example had persuaded to return to the old faith. She smiled, therefore, on Bothwell as he knelt to greet her, in anticipation of a similar triumph.

" My lord of Bothwell, it will give me much pleasure to attend your wedding."

" Madam, such an honour must give even greater pleasure to us," said Bothwell. But his eyes were watchful and his lips twitched slightly, for he fancied he knew what was coming next. In this he was not mistaken. But Mary did not proceed at once to essentials. " I am hoping," she said, " to offer your bride her wedding gown. I have bespoken twelve yards of cloth of silver for it, and six yards of white taffeta with which to line her sleeves and train. She looks her best in white. I myself have not yet decided whether to wear white or crimson. It may be that the crimson would be more seemly. I shall be after all but one of the matrons in attendance . . ."

Bothwell had no definite opinions on women's dress. He only knew that the Queen was talking fast because she was nervous, and waited for her to come to the heart of the matter.

" Since Lady Jean is a Catholic once more, it would be most suitable for the ceremony to take place in the Chapel Royal. I believe I can arrange a Nuptial Mass."

Bothwell's chin jerked up. His face was grave, his eyes amused, at the confirmation of his premonition.

" To that, Madam, I regret I cannot agree."

" And yet, my lord," said Mary quickly, " you said that you were in all respects my most obedient servant."

" My life may be in your keeping, Madam," said Bothwell almost roughly, " but my conscience is not."

Mary sat silent. It was a new idea to her that those whom

her Church taught her to call heretics might consider themselves also bound to put the claims of conscience before all others. In some odd way, she found it reassuring. She had already received sufficient proof of Bothwell's loyalty. To discover that he would actually oppose her because of his religious principles made that loyalty seem a more precious thing.

" Then where would you wish the ceremony to be? " she said at last.

" I will have the banns cried at the Kirk of the Canongate," Bothwell said. " As those of your Grace were. But the marriage must be performed there also by the hand of the minister."

" Then I will receive the wedding guests at Holyroodhouse afterwards," Mary said, giving way with a good grace which hid her disappointment. " We will have rare junketings— our last before Lent. There will be a banquet for you and your lady, my lord of Bothwell. Bid whom you please. We will have the jousting and warlike games which you like, besides the dancing and mummery that I know you do not care for over much."

Bothwell grinned up at her in silence.

" I will confer knighthood on the five esquires who excel most, in honour of the occasion," said Mary, happy as she always was, when planning merrymaking.

" You do me too much honour, Madam," Bothwell said.

" You have done me more service than circumstances permitted me to reward," said Mary. Then she broke off, abruptly, biting her lip. Without disloyalty to her husband she could not explain how Lennox had been given supreme command of the recent campaign.

There were other comings and goings, that February, at Holyroodhouse. The French ambassador brought the Order of St. Michael, with which to invest Darnley, on the 10th, as a friendly gesture from the boy-King of France and the Queen-Mother. He had travelled through England, calling at the Court of Queen Elizabeth, where both the Queen and the Huguenot ambassador to her Court had urged him to persuade Mary to pardon Moray and the other leaders of the rebellion.

But his advice, on the contrary, was to do nothing of the sort. This, he assured her, was also the opinion of such experienced diplomats as her uncle, the Cardinal of Lorraine. So Mary, always readier to pardon than condemn, reluctantly agreed to proceed with the forfeiture of the estates of Moray and his friends when Parliament met at the end of the first week in March.

The presence of the distinguished French guests gave David Rizzio further opportunities of displaying himself as the Queen's most confidential adviser. And Darnley, with the cunning which offset his decorative stupidity, encouraged him to strut about the presence chamber in satin and velvet, loudly instructing the servants, and making the most of his intimacy with the King. Some of the Frenchmen were amused, others disturbed by the display, for the mounting hostility of the Scottish lords was obvious. Before they left, a member of the ambassador's suite took the little man aside to murmur a few words of advice.

" In your place, my friend, I would have a care. I have seen some ugly looks come your way lately."

David snapped his fingers jauntily. " That for those ugly looks, *mon vieux*. I have no fear."

" You count on the Queen's protection? Yet she is but a frail woman——"

David looked over his shoulder, then went on in a lower tone. " For the Queen's protection I am grateful, yes. But that is not all. The astrologer Damiot once said to me: ' Beware of the Bastard.' I am a good Catholic——" he crossed himself hastily, " but I respect such hints. Ah, yes. I will take very good care, believe me, that Moray never sets foot in Scotland again."

" In your place I would beware more of the Scots who hate you than of any astrologer's warning against bastards," said the Frenchman dryly.

Rizzio spread his hands wide and shrugged his indifference. " These Scots will boast. They rarely perform their brags."

" May you be right."

" Fear not. In such matters I am always right," said David gaily. " But now I must return to the Queen. We have vexatious news of the English ambassador."

But to Mary the news was welcome. At least she could now dismiss the man she had mistrusted for so long, now that evidence had reached her that, in spite of her warnings, Randolph had supplied Moray with an English subsidy of three thousand crowns. After the rebellion failed, the confidential agent who had acted as go-between offered the Queen this information in exchange for his own pardon. When Randolph denied it, she confronted him with the man he had employed, ordered him to proceed, under guard, to the frontier, and forbade him to return.

" Do you not think, Madam," suggested Rizzio, as the disconcerted Randolph withdrew, " that we would now do well to send a letter of explanation to Queen Elizabeth by the hand of Sir Robert Melville? It would show her you will not tolerate such abuse of an ambassador's privilege."

Mary agreed, thankful only to have got rid of Elizabeth's most dangerous agent in Scotland. But David's influence had been so evident that he acquired, at the same time, another, and most vindictive enemy.

Darnley's comings and goings were now quite incalculable. The Queen scarcely dared ask where he was, or, on his return, where he had been. Bothwell and Huntly, who had never been closely associated with him, had their military duties, and took little interest in the complexities of Court intrigues. Besides, they had much to do before Bothwell's wedding day if the jousting and knightly exercises were to be ordered as the Queen desired.

And so, under cover of such preoccupations, Darnley came and went. At Morton's residence, he was presented to the other conspirators, several of whom were his kinsmen, for James

Douglas, Earl of Morton and George Douglas, known as the Bastard of Angus, were related to his mother, Lady Lennox, and the emaciated Lord Ruthven, who had been mortally ill for months, was the husband of Lady Janet Douglas. Often present at Douglas House were Sir John Bellenden, the Justice-Clerk, Ker of Faudonside, and inevitably, Lethington. At a distance waited the exiles, Moray, Rothes, Glencairn, and a number of lesser men, all impatiently on the watch at Newcastle for the signal to return.

Darnley was carefully informed of the arrangements for which his help was required. But he was not present when the probable consequences were discussed. It was thought better to leave him unaware of them. The Queen was five months pregnant, and any acts of violence carried out in her presence might well endanger her life and that of her child. If not . . . there were even darker possibilities . . .

Bothwell's wedding was almost as splendid an affair as the Queen had hoped. The company attended the ceremony in the Kirk of the Canongate and went on to the banquet at Holyroodhouse. There the masques, mummings and dances, the feasting, jousting and athletic games went on for five days. Bothwell looked less exuberant, it was thought, than might have been hoped, but as things turned out, his air of constraint was not surprising. For Lady Jean, in the cloth of silver gown which had been the Queen's gift, moved through the brilliant ballroom like an icicle which no sun could thaw. Bothwell did not appear to try, and even Huntly was disconcerted. He had taken it for granted that his sister, when commanded to devote herself to the Earl of Bothwell, would obey him. But her cold, resentful eyes sought only Alexander Ogilvie.

The honeymoon was brief, for Bothwell had his duties at Court in connection with the Riding of Parliament on the 6th of March. Leaving his bride at Crichton Castle, to reorganise the mansion which was now her personal property, he returned to Edinburgh by way of Morham, in order to see his mother.

She regarded him quizzically as he crossed the parlour to her high-backed chair, still in its winter place by the hearth, put a hand lightly on each shoulder and stooped to kiss her cheek.

" Well, James, you have scarcely the air of a bridegroom, for all the fine fuss they made of your wedding. Is the girl pleased with Crichton? "

" She is having the plenishing haled hither and thither, complaining of this and demanding that. I scarcely know how to content her," said Bothwell.

" And she, does she content you? "

Bothwell laughed grimly.

" Her face is as blank as a duck's egg, and she has worn black for Alexander Ogilvie ever since she folded her wedding gown away in lavender and turned the key of the chest for fear one of her maids should presume to peep at it."

This time he really had startled her. The fine dark brows arched almost up to the goffered frill of her French hood. " Black! In the first month of her married life! I cannot credit it! "

James Hepburn paced to the far end of the room, head down and thumbs hooked in his broad leather belt. " It is true."

" But, man alive, how did you ever come to marry such a woman? "

" It was the Queen's wish, her brother's pleasure, and my consenting folly," said James with the bewilderment of a successful man confronted by his first failure. " I never thought her reluctance more than a maiden's whimsy. The match is a good one, Huntly my sure friend, and the alliance gives our houses the greatest strength in Scotland. I believed she would soon respond. I am not inexperienced——"

" Let us deal with your present troubles," said his mother dryly. " She has repulsed you? "

" She shot the bolt of our bedchamber against me on our wedding night. I had the choice of rousing the household with the noise I made breaking it down, or going elsewhere."

" Which did you do ? "

" I—went elsewhere," James Hepburn said blandly.

" She will come to her duty," said his mother.

He shook his head. " I care not greatly now whether she does or not."

His mother nodded. Her own experience of married life had been too bitter for her to attempt to give either the advice or sympathy which she herself would have found useless. They talked, instead, of other things for a while.

" Are the King and Queen yet returned from Seton ? "

" They return to-day, I believe," said James, " for the Riding of Parliament which also brings me back to Holyrood. I have now my part to play in the procession," he added, with an unexpectedly youthful air of gratification.

His mother smiled at the scapegrace son whose faults everyone knew, while his gifts had been so long wasted. " And so you should. Who are to bear the Honours of Scotland ? "

" Huntly will ride before her with the Crown, Crawford with the Sword——"

" And you with the Sceptre ? "

" Yes."

" You will acquit yourself right bravely," she said.

The pride and joy in her voice touched him sharply. He had not known, till then, how much she had hoped and feared for him during the heartbroken years. Nor had he realised what pleasure his new position of trust would bring her. When at last he took his leave some of the cynicism with which the inauspicious beginning of his married life had seared his face afresh had gone. He was, after all, unused to domestic comforts. For him, as for any soldier and adventurer, the world lay wide. He jingled peacefully back to Edinburgh to set his men to work furbishing his gear for the traditional splendours of the opening of Parliament.

On the following morning the Queen rode out of the fore-court of Holyroodhouse, a superb figure in crimson and gold

on a great white charger, led by two gentlemen-in-waiting
in the royal livery of scarlet and yellow. Her sovereign's
canopy was held over her by four others, all bareheaded.
Before her clattered a great company of horsemen in the royal
livery, their breastplates and steel morions glinting in the pale
spring sunshine, the Provost and Bailies of Edinburgh, in their
scarlet robes, the dignitaries of the Reformed Kirk in black
gown and white bands, and representatives of every loyal and
noble house in Scotland on magnificent horses. The vivid
colours of their silks and velvets, the white spray of plumes,
blended into a rainbow ribbon which wound up the Royal
Mile as the great officers of State emerged from the forecourt. First Huntly, in crimson and gold, rode out on a bay
horse, with the Crown, on its purple velvet cushion, resting
on the front of his saddle. Bothwell followed, in blue and
silver, on a black, cherishing the Sceptre; then Crawford
in wine-dark velvet on a grey horse, bearing the Sword of
State.

And then, at last, came the Queen, riding quietly out of the
forecourt and into the Canongate where the citizens had hung
their gayest carpets from their stairheads and crowded every
vantage-point to see her go by.

Very straight she sat on her high saddle, turning from side
to side with gracious little gestures of head or hand, and the
smiles which transfigured the pale oval of her face like the
sunshine about her, conveying warmth as well as light. As
she entered the Canongate the roar of delight made her
horse dance apprehensively and the hands of her attendants
tightened on the leading reins as she moved forward between
two almost visible walls of sound. Though the crowd's
friendliness was evident, the first impact of its enthusiasm made
her gasp.

" God bless her bonny face . . ."
" The Queen . . . God save her . . ."
" The Rose of Scotland . . ."
" The Rose frae the highest bough . . ."

" God bless her . . ."

" Heaven save her Grace . . ."

Bowing and smiling, lifting her jewel-sewn glove in response, no one would have guessed at the furious scene Darnley had just made, refusing either to take part in the ceremony or submit to her authority while she presented him to her Parliament, as she must, before asking that Parliament to grant him the funds he required. As the procession was assembling in the forecourt, Darnley's hysterical voice had been heard by all those in the presence chamber, demanding to be allowed to act as the Sovereign of Scotland and open Parliament himself. She argued, implored, commanded, but at last she could only turn and leave him, hoping vainly that he would follow her, so that they might ride together as arranged. But instead Darnley shouted for his attendants. Let horses be saddled. He would go hawking at Leith.

Outside the Tolbooth, the gorgeous procession had swung round to line the street, so that those bearing the Honours might escort the Queen into Parliament Hall. There, that day, the business before the Three Estates would be brief and formal, in preparation for the session proper, which would begin on Monday. From her throne, the Queen, robed and crowned, first heard the names of the new spiritual and temporal Lords of Parliament recited. The First Estate was represented by four ministers of the new faith and three of the old, and among the temporal lords of the Second were the Earls of Lennox, Athol, Morton, Huntly and Bothwell. Then the summonses for Moray and his associates to defend themselves against the accusation of treason on the following Monday were formally proclaimed.

Afterwards Mary returned to Holyroodhouse, intending to spend the next few days as quietly as possible, for the quarrel with Darnley had shaken her severely. It was the most recent of a series of degrading scenes, in which Darnley, oftener drunk than sober, had taunted or tormented her, either by railing against her religious toleration, her choice of advisers, and her inability to supply him with money, or clamouring for the royal authority which every exhibition made him more evidently unfit to bear.

That Saturday evening she felt too weary to face the publicity of her usual evening meal. Instead, she ordered her supper to be served without ceremony in the small room off her bedchamber. In attendance were only her half-brother and sister, Lord Robert and the Countess of Argyll; Lord Keith and her French physician. David Rizzio had come to carve, her equerry, Arthur Erskine, was cupbearer, and one or two servants stood in the background. It was, as Mary had wished, a quiet, informal occasion. As David carved, one of the servants, napkin on arm, bore to the Queen the meat which, though it was Lent, had been prescribed in her special circumstances. They were speaking French, sipping their wine, companionable in the soft radiance of candlelight, when at a sudden clash of steel below their voices ceased. Hasty feet could be heard stumbling up the private stair to the bed-chamber behind them, though when only Darnley burst through the hangings they felt surprise rather than fear, and the Queen received him as graciously as if there had never been trouble between them. " My lord, have you supped? "

" Aye, and I had thought you would have finished also by this time," Darnley mumbled vaguely. He kissed the Queen and came to sit beside her while she called one of the servants to bring wine. But he was evidently restless. Even while she was speaking, he kept turning his head on his shoulder towards the hangings which hid the doorway through which he had come.

Standing by the sideboard, David laid his carver down. His glance followed Darnley's, as the hangings parted again to show the emaciated figure of Ruthven, his face ghastly beneath his morion, his limbs borne down by the weight of full armour, his lips writhing back from his teeth in a grimace of pain.

At the sight of that awful figure, some of Rizzio's jaunty confidence forsook him. But it was not until he caught sight of George Douglas, nicknamed the Bastard of Angus, that he began to scream.

CHAPTER ELEVEN

SOMEONE clapped a hand roughly over his mouth, stifling the outcry to a gurgle, as the Queen rose. Pale as an altar candle, she challenged Ruthven proudly.

" My lord, I had thought to visit you in your chamber, having heard of your sore illness. But now you enter our presence in your armour. What does it mean? "

Ruthven reeled forward, to sag on to a stool as if he could no longer stand. " I have indeed been ill, yet I am well enough to come here for your good."

" And what good can you do me? " Her voice was curt now.

" There is no harm intended to your Grace," Ruthven muttered, " nor—nor to anyone else but that poltroon David——"

" Why, what has he done? " she demanded sharply.

" Ask your husband, Madam."

Mary swung round on Darnley. " What is the meaning of this, my lord? "

Darnley's sullen face was livid as his glance flickered from his confederates to his wife. He muttered: " I know nothing of the matter . . ."

Ruthven's cackle of laughter, hollow as a raven's caw, fretted Mary's nerves beyond bearing. " Leave our presence, my lord," she cried.

Slowly Ruthven shook his head. The gesture was eerie as if made by a corpse.

" Seize him," Mary commanded.

But as Lord Keith and Arthur Erskine advanced, Ruthven staggered to his feet, gasping with the effort of jerking his rapier from its sheath. Sweat furrowed his ghastly face as he croaked: " Lay no hands on me! "

While they circled warily round his swaying figure, the hangings parted again. Mary's eyes widened as the little room filled with armed men. But still she faced them.

" What is this? Do you seek my life? "

Her clear voice dominated the agitated conference of her attendants, the chime of steel, the shuffle of feet, the low-voiced commands of someone who did not yet appear.

" No, Madam," grated Ruthven. " But we will have that villain Davie."

As he lunged unsteadily at the now frantic Rizzio, the Queen herself caught his wrist.

" If my secretary has been guilty of any offence, my lord," she declared, " I promise to bring him before the Lords of Parliament, and have him dealt with according to the usual forms of justice."

But Ruthven, with a sudden access of strength, wrenched his sword-arm free, and lurched towards Rizzio, who, cornered in the window embrasure, had drawn a foolish, elegant little dagger, though he was shaking too convulsively to use it. " Madam," he groaned between colourless lips, " I am a dead man."

Mary turned to him with a smile of desperate courage. " The King will never permit you to be killed in my presence. I am sure of it——"

The assassins were closing in upon them, and Ruthven had lost patience. He jerked his head angrily at the irresolute Darnley. " Sir," he grated, " take the Queen to you."

As he spoke, a splintering crash of timber rose from the hall below, where the main body, organised by Morton to take possession of the Palace, had overwhelmed the guards.

" A Douglas! . . . A Douglas! . . . A Douglas! . . ."

The voices grew louder, were backed by the clash of swords,

as Huntly and Bothwell, at the head of the great staircase, defied four score of Morton's yelling followers in a desperate battle for the royal apartments. But both knew it could not last long.

"Back to my quarters," Bothwell shouted, as his expert eye reckoned the suicidal odds. Murder, not robbery, was evidently the purpose of those against them. With their shoulders against the heavy door they barred it against the invaders. "It will hold them but for a moment," Bothwell panted. "Quick, out by the window. We'll raise the city for her Grace——"

"A Douglas! . . . A Douglas! . . ." yelled Morton's men as they beat the door down.

In the little supper-room the arrival of reinforcements had so encouraged the attackers that even the presence of the Queen could no longer restrain them, and as his enemies closed in, Rizzio's nerve finally broke. He ran to the Queen, and fell on his knees, his despairing convulsions shaking her from head to foot as he clung to her gown.

"Madam, Madam, save my life, for God's dear sake!"

"You shall all die for this!" she defied them.

"A Douglas! . . . A Douglas! . . ." The shouts were louder now as the doors of the presence chamber burst open with a crash, above which the Queen could hear the shrieks of her terrified ladies while her attendants struggled helplessly in the grip of men who threatened to run them through if they interfered.

"He shall have justice. I will see to it," Mary cried.

"Justice . . . justice . . ." babbled Rizzio.

But Ruthven took Mary roughly by the shoulders and forced her into Darnley's arms, as George Douglas, the Bastard of Angus, reached over her shoulder and stabbed Rizzio in the neck. The blood sprayed both Douglas and the Queen as Darnley, scarcely knowing what he was doing, dragged her aside and pushed her back into her chair.

"Madam . . . blessed Saints . . . Mary, Mother of God . . . save me . . . save me . . ."

The blades rose and fell. The piercing clamour wavered. Ker of Faudonside pressed a cocked pistol against the Queen's side.

" Fire, then," she whispered, " if you have no thought for the royal child I bear."

As Darnley struck the pistol hastily aside, the table went over with a prodigious crash. Lady Argyll snatched the candle-stick as it slid, and holding it high against the ultimate horror of darkness. Antony Standen, the Queen's page, thrust away a rapier with which another fanatic was menacing his mistress, while the conspirators dragged the still shrieking Rizzio out of the supper-room, and through the Queen's bedchamber to the presence chamber, where the Douglas men from the main staircase fell on him like wolves.

" Ah, poor David," cried Mary, " my good and faithful servant. May God have mercy on your soul."

But George Douglas was now forcing his way back through the crowd. With a sly grin he snatched Darnley's dagger from his belt. When accounts came to be made up Darnley must not be able to say that he had no part in the business. He shouldered his way back to the presence chamber.

" This is the blow of the King," he yelled. Then he thrust the dagger into Rizzio's body and left it quivering there.

" Our work is not yet done," gasped Ruthven. He plunged through the dreadful chaos of the supper-room, in one corner of which Darnley still pinioned the Queen, close to the over-turned table, while broken glass crackled under foot and wine and blood mingled in half-seen horror as Lady Argyll still cherished the wavering light of the remaining candle.

" Leave them there together," Ruthven commanded, with an unsteady gesture towards the King and Queen. " Get the servants out and turn the key on them." He staggered across the wildly disordered bedchamber which Morton's men had begun to loot, hauling down the rich hangings, snatching up everything that had the glint of jewels. But Ruthven, looking so ghastly that they fled in horror, drove

them before him with the flat of his sword. At the head of the
staircase he met Morton and Lindsay.

"Is Bothwell dead?" Lindsay roared.

"Where is Huntly?" shouted Morton.

"My lord," confessed a breathless man-at-arms, "we
broke down the door of Bothwell's chamber. But——"

"But what, idiot?" growled Morton.

"They have both escaped us, sir. The window shutter
stands wide."

"You wretched bunglers! This will mar all," groaned
Ruthven. "Those two we should have silenced above all
others."

"They can do nothing," said Lindsay contemptuously.
"We have the Queen."

"Aye," said Ruthven. "We have the Queen. Let us
make sure she does not also escape us. That fool, her
husband . . ."

They surged back towards the supper-room. Darnley
had released the Queen, who had sagged back in her chair
in utter exhaustion. Tears streamed silently down her face,
and she scarcely moved as the bolt shot back. But her eyes
opened as an agitated equerry tiptoed towards her.

"David?" she said faintly.

"Madam," said the man soberly, "David is dead."

"Oh, Madam, it is true," cried Mary Seton, who had
rushed in after him. "How have you fared, sweet
Madam——"

But the Queen scarcely heard the frantic inquiry. At that
moment she realised just how sorely Darnley had betrayed
her, and turned on him in fury.

"Ah, traitor and son of a traitor, is this your thanks for all
I sought to offer? What offence have I given you, that you
should do such a shameful thing?"

"I——" Darnley began wretchedly, "I sought only
to——"

He broke off, for Ruthven had come in, looking almost

at the point of death, as he flung himself down in a chair. The hollow eye-sockets from which he glared at Darnley and the Queen seemed full of blood.

"Bring me a drink," he croaked. "I am sore felled by my sickness."

"Help me from hence," the Queen whispered to Mary Seton. "I can endure no more."

Lady Argyll came hastily to take the Queen's other arm. "Let us pass, my lords," she said imperiously. "This may be the end of her Grace in her condition."

But still they would not leave her in peace. Darnley trailed after her into her ravaged bedchamber, and while her distressed ladies did what they could to restore order, his querulous voice railed on as he sought to justify what he had done. Too weary to protest, she could only endure. ". . . and since that fellow David came in credit with your Majesty, you neither regarded me, entertained me, nor trusted me after your former fashion. Every day you were wont to come to my chamber before dinner, and pass the time with me. This long while you have not done so . . ."

Mary lifted her head. Could he have already forgotten the language in which he had told her, before all his drunken companions, that she was unwanted? Sick at heart, she let him drone on.

". . . and when I came to your Majesty's chamber, you bore me little company, except David were the third person. And after supper your Majesty used to sit up at cards with David till one or two after midnight . . ."

Poor David, she thought wretchedly. Was even the kindness with which he had tried to devise little entertainments to take her attention off the lateness of her husband's return to be held up against him? At last the injustice of his reproaches stung her into speech.

"It is not a gentlewoman's duty to come to her husband's chamber," she retorted, "but rather that of the husband to come to his wife."

Arms folded, feet astride, Darnley leered down at her, his grin both lascivious and inane. " Changed days then, Madam! Changed days," he taunted. " In the beginning you were ready enough to seek my chamber. You were warm and loving enough, until you had gotten what you wanted. Then I became of no more account than the stud dog——"

Fire blazed from the ashes of her weariness. " Enough. I will hear no more. For this night's work I will live as your wife no longer, that I swear."

She broke off, startled by an unearthly cackle from the shadows. Propping himself on his sword, Lord Ruthven advanced with shaking forefinger and dreadful smile to give her a lecture on her duty.

It was too much. Mary rose, shaking with anger. " My lord," she said, " I know well whom I should thank for so much misery. May God, who beholds us from the high heavens, avenge my wrongs and move that which shall be born of me to root out you and your treacherous posterity."

Ruthven recoiled from the impact of her rage. She saw the whites of his eyes roll like those of a terror-stricken horse. Ruthven knew himself for a dying man, but Mary had uttered at a venture the only threat that could still touch him. Her words had the ring of truth. In the silence that followed, their echoes seemed to roll down the years towards the day, a quarter of a century later, when her son was to see them so strangely fulfilled. Then the spell broke. Outside the Palace, torches were bobbing and the hubbub of voices broke against the windows like the spray from an angry sea.

" Who's below? " shouted Ruthven.

" The Provost of Edinburgh," a gruff, troubled voice shouted back. " What's amiss in the Palace? "

" Nothing, friend," Ruthven assured the eerie figure of light and shadow outlined by the glare of pine-knot torches. About him were grouped his fellow citizens, their apprentices and labourers, craftsmen and lads, armed with pikes, axes, swords or pitchforks, some in their steel caps, others in their blue bonnets, a shambling, uncertain, loyal and bewildered multitude which had mustered in response to the alarm Huntly and Bothwell had raised.

"Where is the Queen?" shouted the Provost. Behind him a score of voices took up the cry in a long, wavering roar. Torches flared as pitchforks were shaken and the roar mounted to a scream. Mary heard them from her chair and rose with a cry of hope. But Ruthven, moving with uncanny speed for so sick a man, caught her arm in an ice-cold grip.

"By heaven, Madam, if you seek their aid, you shall end as David did." He jerked his head towards Darnley. "Speak to them. Tell them all is well."

Darnley flung the casement wide. "All is well, good people," he cried, his voice wavering on the verge of hysteria. "The Queen and I . . . are . . . are merry."

"Let her Grace speak for herself," the Provost demanded. But the words stung Darnley's pride.

"Provost, am I not the King? I command you, on your allegiance, to order your company to their homes."

The roar of defiance wavered uncertainly. Then Ruthven spoke, his voice strident against a background of protests and catcalls. The Queen caught only a few words here and there, of quarrels among her French servants, of justice meted out to Rizzio, who had intrigued to bring back Popery to Scotland. Popery . . . the hated word doused their ardour, as he had known it would. The defiance diminished, died at last mutteringly into silence. As the shadowy figures, dark against their flaring torches, turned away, Mary bowed her head and wept. When at last her ladies were permitted to take her away to bed, she was too weary to sleep and unable to endure the thought of darkness. Candles burned beside her and Mary Seton held her hands all night long.

But though she had not slept, the returning daylight

brought fresh courage with it. On that strange Sunday morning her one thought was of escape. Her ladies, coming and going on their domestic errands, under the suspicious stare of the guards placed by Morton outside her bedchamber, contrived to receive a message from Bothwell, Huntly, Athol and a dozen others who planned either to attempt a rescue or to meet the Queen once she was free.

But sufficient forces to overwhelm those now in control of Holyroodhouse could not, she knew, be raised on the instant, and with such fanatics as Ruthven in charge any attempt at rescue might mean the death of his prisoner. Escape was little easier, for the guards let no one either enter or leave the Palace unchallenged. It seemed clear to Mary that she must contrive to seduce one of her captors to her assistance. And, sorely as the idea revolted her, it was also evident that she would have most chance with her already uneasy husband. She sent a friendly message, though it sickened her, inviting him to her chamber.

But Darnley had much to do that Sunday morning. As agreed beforehand, he now proclaimed, in his own name and on his personal authority, that the convention of the Three Estates of Parliament was dissolved. All members must leave Edinburgh within three hours, under pain of loss of life, lands and goods, except such as the King, by his special command, caused to remain. Bewildered and uncertain, the delegates obeyed.

Next, he duly welcomed with his personal pardon Moray and the other rebel lords from Newcastle, who now presented themselves at the gates of Holyroodhouse and demanded audience with the King. So far Darnley had enjoyed his tasks. They were in keeping with the sole authority which he had been promised. But Moray's curt greeting was almost an insult, and he was smiling to himself as he mounted the great staircase which led to his sister's apartment. Mary, who had been pacing about her bedchamber in desperate anxiety, turned as the door opened, hands clasped, suddenly still.

Moray faced her calmly. He was sure that she knew nothing of his part in the Rizzio affair. And the rebellion for which he had been exiled was, after all, a mere nothing by comparison with the murder in which her husband was now safely involved.

"Ah, Madam," he said unctuously, "it grieves me to the heart to see you in this state." Raising a hand to his eyes, he appeared to brush away a tear. His concern seemed real enough for Mary, forgetting all their disagreements, to run to him with outstretched, imploring hands.

"Oh, my brother," she cried despairingly, "had you been here, you never would have allowed me to be so treated."

"Never," said Moray, patting her awkwardly as he glanced round to be sure that nobody was present to contradict him. "Never! Tch, tch, what a dreadful thing. Had you but thought to recall me——"

"It was by no will of mine," said Mary, "that your exile was so prolonged. But for the displeasure of others——"

"I know that well." He sighed. "Had my advice been taken——"

"Brother, all that is past," said Mary quickly. "It is now a question of regaining the liberty and position these men and my deluded husband have taken from me."

Moray pondered. "Aye . . ."

"You, with your influence, will see to that, I know."

Mournfully, he shook his head. "I would do all in my power to see this wrong righted," he assured her. "But I am utterly without authority nowadays. What else can you expect? I am but a returning prodigal——"

"Yet you will try?"

"I will, Madam, I will indeed."

She saw no reason to doubt him. But because she also believed that he was without power to help her, she prepared to do what she could to help herself. Which was fortunate, for Moray went straight from his sister's room to confer with Rizzio's murderers. Darnley, who had served his turn, was now contemptuously excluded from their debate, to wander about his own quarters, angry and frightened by the turn things had taken. For there was no more talk of the Crown Matrimonial now. He had heard that some of his former associates were in favour of keeping the Queen in close confinement. Others even advocated her death. In either case the dreadful question haunted him: would his own life be safe? Once the Queen, his wife, were dead, what were his own chances of long remaining alive? That evening, when the confederates set off to sup elsewhere, he remembered his wife's summons. It was not easy to obey, for the Queen's apartments were formidably guarded. But reconciliation seemed to be his only chance.

Outside the Queen's bedchamber door the guards looked at each other uncertainly. They had no orders to refuse admittance to the King, and Darnley had just enough sense left to take their obedience for granted. But, once inside, his knees sagged beneath him till he had safely shot the bolt.

Mary was sitting by the fire in the dusk. Two or three of her ladies curtseyed to the King and withdrew. Then Darnley, in a state of penitence stimulated by terror, threw himself on his knees at her feet.

" Oh, Madam, most humbly I implore your forgiveness. I—I know not what to say——"

" What is done, is done," she told him sadly. " David is dead. But he would not have me withhold my forgiveness."

Fumbling for her hand, Darnley covered it with kisses.

" What is to be done now? " she asked presently.

" Madam, I fear greatly that your life is in danger," he babbled.

" That does not surprise me," she said calmly. " But if I am in danger, so are you——"

" We must needs save each other then," bleated Darnley.

She gave him a small, cold smile. " Such a thought comes somewhat late. But better, perhaps, than not at all. What do you know of their purpose? "

" Your own death is at debate," said Darnley. " They proposed besides the death of David, to hang Sir James Balfour at your chamber door——"

" I wonder why? " she said in astonishment. " He is nothing to me. Go on."

" Bothwell, Huntly and Livingstone were to be beheaded. Certain of your ladies were to be drowned——"

" Who made these plans? " she asked. " Besides Ruthven and Lindsay, whom I saw——"

" Morton was in it, with Lethington, from the first——"

" Lethington? " her fine eyebrows rose. Then she nodded. " I should have guessed."

" The bond was signed also by those exiled at Newcastle—"

" By my brother of Moray? I cannot believe it."

" Him above all," said Darnley viciously. " And what is more, I heard him but an hour since, listening to those who argued for your death. You must escape, Madam, from their hands forthwith——"

" And you must certainly come with me," Mary said with an unexpected, almost mischievous smile. " For they will never forgive you now that you have betrayed them. You are doomed, as surely as poor Davie."

Darnley stared up at her, his eyes widening as the terror of his position was borne in upon him. He who had resented his dependence on his wife now depended on her more than ever. Wildly he looked round.

But she laughed for the first time since the night's terror, as the prospect of adventure revived her like a draught of wine. " Do not be afraid," she said. " We have friends outside Edinburgh. I will send word to my lord of Bothwell. He is nearer than Huntly, who will have gone to the north. I shall tell him to meet us on the road to Dunbar."

" To-night? " Darnley faltered.

She pondered. " No. We shall need more time. Erskine and another shall have horses ready by the churchyard to-morrow night at moonrise if you will persuade those who were formerly your confederates——" Darnley winced at the whiplash edge of her voice, " to withdraw the guards and confide me to your safe keeping. Let it be known that I have been so prostrated by recent events that I can scarcely raise my head."

" And if they will not heed me? "

" They must heed you," Mary said, gripping his hands as if to infuse him with her own courage. " Do you understand? Your life as well as mine will be the price of failure."

As he went, Darnley promised to do what he could. But she doubted very much if the rebels would ever trust him. On the Monday morning she summoned Lethington, who was debonair as ever as he kissed her hand, his graceful talk drifting as lightly over the recent tragedy as thistledown over a shambles. Like Moray, he professed the deepest concern for her predicament. Unlike Moray, he felt sure he could help.

" If your Grace would condescend to receive all the lords concerned in audience——"

" Not Ruthven," Mary said, shuddering. " I will not endure his presence. No, not if my life hung on it."

" Saving then my lord of Ruthven," said Lethington smoothly. " I will arrange for them to present themselves for an audience at which they will receive your Grace's pardon and promise to let byegones bide. Afterwards you will be in a position to ask that the keys of your Palace shall be restored to your servants and the care of your chamber to your own officials——"

" Only thus," said Mary earnestly, " shall I be able to obtain a night's rest. My lord of Lethington, I have not slept since I saw David fall——"

" Madam, I understand. You are at the end of your resources——"

" My lord, as heaven is above me, that is true. I can scarcely hold up my head . . ."

" I will arrange the audience forthwith," said Lethington.

All except Ruthven were ultimately satisfied. The Queen expressed her willingness to give them the assurance of her pardon forthwith, reminding herself as she did so that she spoke under duress, so that no promise she made was binding. If they freed her now, she went on boldly—and her doctor would assure them that this was a matter of urgency, both for her health and the safety of her child—she would proceed, God willing, to the Tolbooth and there make an act of remission to them all for crimes committed. Then she faltered, put a hand to her head and turned tremulously to her husband, imploring him to help her from the presence chamber, to summon her ladies, to send for the midwife. . . .

It seemed impossible that any woman in her condition, exhausted as she was by two nights without sleep, could think of escaping them, even if Darnley did not, for his own sake, keep her safe. So, after some hesitation, they agreed to surrender the keys, and all left Holyrood to sup with the Earl of Morton at Douglas House. Mary and Darnley retired early, knowing that they might still be watched. But at midnight they were roused by Bastian, the valet whom her personal maid, Margaret, was soon to marry, to creep down the private stair by which the murderers had reached the supper-room, out of the Palace by the entrance to the Chapel Royal, and so to the churchyard where Sir William Standen, Master of the Horse, waited with the Queen's equerry, Arthur Erskine, and three extra horses, one of which bore a pillion seat for the Queen and another for her maidservant.

The men were tense and silent in the darkness, and even the chime of a bridle made Darnley gasp with fear, though Mary was almost gay as she gripped Erskine's belt. Under her breath she was humming a French air. But Darnley grew more uneasy every minute. For he had now had time to consider what would happen to him, if his former confederates discovered his escape. He looked often over his shoulder as they left Edinburgh, urging the others to make haste.

" We are making all the speed we dare, my lord," said

Sir William, " in view of her Grace's condition. There is little fear of pursuit now."

Still Darnley was not satisfied. Again and again he swung round in the saddle to listen. In the utter silence of the night the whoop of an owl from a distant wood made the hair on the back of his neck prickle. At the sudden bellow of a cow by the wayside Mary laughed. But Darnley swore aloud.

" We are nearly at Seton," she murmured.

" I hear horsemen behind us," Darnley cried hysterically.

" Surely not, my lord," said Erskine.

" I heard them. Listen. There they are again."

He was not mistaken. Now the others could hear them too. Horsemen were on the track behind, coming nearer, coming fast. Darnley lost his head completely.

" Faster, faster," he screamed. " By God's blood, they will murder us both ! "

" My lord, I dare go no faster," protested Arthur Erskine. " It would endanger the life of her Grace and the child." Darnley raised his whip to flog Erskine's horse. But the equerry struck his arm aside.

" What matter ? " Darnley cried wildly. " If this child dies we can get another."

" My lord," said Mary, " I beg you to ride on and leave us, if you are afraid."

" By heaven, I will," said Darnley, driven beyond shame. As he thrust his spurs at his horse's flanks, the startled beast plunged forward at a gallop. Soon the sound of his headlong progress died away.

" Madam," said Sir William Standen quietly, " there are indeed horsemen behind us. What would you wish me to do ? "

" Turn to face them," Mary cried. " And draw your swords."

They waited on the roadside, the sword-blades gleaming coldly as the moon slid from behind a cloud. But at the sight of the valiant little party the oncoming horses checked. Their riders peered ahead, dark, anonymous shapes seen against the moon.

" Where is the Queen's Grace? " their leader demanded.

He was no more than a bulk of shadow, but that harsh voice was unforgettable.

" My lord of Bothwell! "

It was not a question but a cry of joy.

CHAPTER TWELVE

BOTHWELL swung himself from his horse and disappeared into the shadows. Then his face swam up again, wavering, like the moon's reflection in ruffled water, before her over-strained eyes.

" Your Grace is well? "

" Better than I have been this long while, my lord! "

His answering chuckle, with its suggestion of a fighting man's comradeship, pleased her.

" I brought a horse from Seton for your Grace," he said, " knowing that you prefer to handle the reins yourself."

She flushed at his recognition of her small vanity. " You did not doubt our coming? "

" Why should I, Madam? " She saw his teeth gleam as he smiled, felt his hands on her waist. Then his great strength sustained her for an instant as he swung her down. For an instant, but no more. As a soldier in charge of an anxious operation, he was concerned only with her safety; and the nearest refuge was the royal castle of Dunbar. As the other horse was led forward he lifted her to the side-saddle with the same swift efficiency, expertly examining all straps and buckles as she picked up the reins.

" The stirrup is as your Grace would wish it? "

" It is." Her voice was impersonal as his.

"We have yet many miles to ride," he warned her, glancing over his shoulder at the sound of approaching horses. "Here are Lord Seton's men."

Darnley was with them. Even in the dim light, she recognised her husband, towering between the lords of Fleming and Livingstone, his loud voice mocking his former panic now that he was safe among friends.

"Heaven be praised, Madam," said Lord Seton, "that you are free. His Grace made all haste to reassure us."

"Indeed?" said Mary. She sat in the midst of her rescuers, less aware now of comradeship than of remembered treachery. For the first time since they had set out from Holyroodhouse, she shivered.

"Madam," Bothwell urged her, "we had best proceed. By now your departure will have been discovered."

"Let us proceed, then, by all means," said Darnley, with a nervous, whinnying laugh. But Bothwell turned his back on him, awaiting the Queen's answer.

"I am ready, my lord," she said.

They rode all through the night, to reach Dunbar before daybreak. But Bothwell's stentorian roar sent men of the garrison scuttling for the great gates.

"There is little here of comfort for your Grace," he said, as she took the arm he offered to escort her into the desolate hall, disused since the last change of officers. Ashes lay white on the hearth, the merciless chill of the salt-soaked walls of red sandstone was like a tangible weight, and their breath hung in clouds about them on the cold air.

But Mary laughed. "Have I not always wished to share the rigours of campaigning? Let them bring wood to kindle a blaze that will bake the chill out of these walls. There must be eggs, also, hereabouts, for I heard the cocks crowing as we waited before the gates. I myself will cook them."

The tired men's spirits rose with hers. Soldiers hurried in with kindling and logs. Cloaks were tossed down as the first crackle on the hearth grew into a roar. And the Queen

herself laid the eggs snugly in the embers, watching over them
while she ordered the others to their tasks.

"Pile on wood, my lord of Bothwell. Draw forward the
lesser table, my lords of Seton and Fleming. Let us eat as near
the fire as we may. Have you bread there, my lord of Livingstone? If we lack trenchers, then cut a slice for each of us. My
lord of Bothwell, can we make shift to mull some wine?"

Bothwell nodded. "I have here a vessel that will serve.
Yet we have but one beaker——"

Mary laughed, shielding her hot face with her hand as she
prodded the eggs out of the embers. "Then it shall be a
loving-cup, and we shall drink to the restoration of our kingdom."

"That, Madam, is no longer in doubt," Lord Seton
said.

"Do not be too sure of that," said Darnley disagreeably,
as he lounged towards the fire. He was tired of being in the
background, yet reluctant to perform any of the menial duties
allocated to the others. Still obsessed with the dignity appropriate to the Crown Matrimonial, he was too stupid to realise
that his own greed and folly had diminished his chances of
wearing it still further.

"Our enemies have a great force at their disposal, and
their plans are deeply laid."

"You know something of them, no doubt, my lord?"
Bothwell asked. It was more a question than a taunt, but
Darnley snatched, scowling, at his dagger, so that Seton took
him hastily by the arm and steered him towards the table at
which the Queen was now seated, tossing her egg from hand to
hand to cool it, one cheek smudged with ash, and strands of
bright hair astray.

When the meal was over they hoped that she would rest.
But she shook her head. "I must write so many letters—and
in my own hand now," she added, her face sad as she remembered David. "Otherwise my kinsfolk in France may hear
worse tidings than the truth."

"While you write, Madam," said Bothwell reassuringly, "we will set about collecting a sufficient force to escort you back to Edinburgh in triumph."

She smiled uncertainly, blinking now to keep back weary tears. "Will that take long, my lords?"

As a compass needle swings towards the north, each head now turned to Bothwell, who accepted the implied leadership as a matter of course. Darkly he brooded, drumming a brisk rhythm on the table-top with his lean, fine finger tips. "Give me a week, your Grace," he said presently, "and we shall be ready to re-take the city, if need be, by force of arms."

He was, characteristically, better than his word. Within three days he had mustered three thousand Border pikemen, and when Huntly arrived with his contingent their camp fires were hazing the country for miles about Dunbar. News of the Queen's escape and martial prospects spread rapidly, still further shaking the confidence of the rebels already disconcerted by Darnley's defection. Soon the more prudent were seeking to make terms, and, to Darnley's incredulous consternation, Mary seemed willing to accept them. Though he did all he could to dissuade her, she received the humble submission of the Earls of Glencairn and Rothes in the great hall at Dunbar. She herself was not vindictive, and as Bothwell had observed, the break-up of the rebel organisation was a hopeful sign.

"Once the first rats scurry down the ropes, Madam, the ship's not long for the sea."

As news reached the capital that the Queen, escorted by the Earls of Bothwell and Huntly, was returning at the head of a formidable fighting force, those most deeply concerned in the recent plot thought it prudent to leave the city in order to avoid being either lynched by the people or captured by the Queen's men.

Even Lethington, whose part in the conspiracy had been so devious that it might have gone unrecorded had it not been for Darnley's defection, thought it best to retire to Dunkeld; and Knox, who had been even more outspoken than usual in praise of the killing of " that poltroon and vile knave, Davie," went off on a preaching mission to Galloway. Morton, Ruthven, George Douglas, Lindsay and Ker of Faudonside set off for Moray's former quarters at Newcastle. But before leaving, Morton wrote to the Queen. He protested his utter innocence and deep regret for the recent disaster, provided her with a list of those involved, and explained that he himself had only been associated with their conferences through the threats and insistence of her husband, and his father, the Earl of Lennox. Mary read the letter in silence, but Darnley flew into an almost hysterical fit of rage and terror after glancing at the first few words.

" It is a most wicked and monstrous lie! "

" Is it? I wonder? "

" That fellow Morton is the vilest of all traitors, saving only the Bastard of Moray——"

" My lord, you are speaking of my brother," Mary said coldly.

Darnley's jaw went slack as he stared. " But—b-b-but you do not mean to pardon those malignant devils who slaughtered poor David at your very feet? How can you forgive——"

" I find it harder to forgive the man who came to me with a Judas kiss," said Mary, as her temper rose. " Who held me helpless while the work was done, and then ran hot-foot to inform against those for whom he had betrayed both his wife and his trusting friend? "

He cringed, as her scorn lashed him, then returned to the attack. " If you pardon these felons you will not only endanger your life and mine, but that of the child who must soon be born. And I——"

" I had rather entrust my life to men of whom I can be sure, whether for good or ill," she said, " than to those capable neither of love nor hate. To you, as my husband, I am com-manded by Holy Church to show my wifely duty. But to your father I owe nothing. He shall not enter my presence again."

"Madam," said Darnley in dismay, "I cannot believe that you will be so harsh."

"My lord, my mind is made up. There is no more to say."

He followed her about all day, nevertheless, like a great whipped hound, railing against his former associates at every opportunity, declaiming his own innocence, and protesting against her injustice to his father. But by the following morning he had forgotten it all, and as their newly constituted army set off for Edinburgh in the strengthening sunshine of the third week in March, he was preening himself once more. To the amused disgust of Bothwell and Huntly, he behaved as gloriously as if the muster had been all his doing.

They rested at Haddington over Sunday, the 17th of March, 1567. There Mary held her first Court since Rizzio's assassination and announced the necessary changes in her Council. Huntly became Lord Chancellor instead of Morton, and Sir James Balfour, the suavely unscrupulous lawyer whom the confederates had unfortunately failed to hang at the Queen's chamber door, was given a congenial position in the justiciary under Argyll. Lethington was merely deprived of the revenues of the Abbey of Haddington, which were restored to Bothwell, less as a favour than as a tardy act of justice. Bothwell was also confirmed in his appointment as the Queen's Lieutenant, formally restored to the hereditary office of Lord Admiral, and, as a tribute to his recent services, made Captain of Dunbar.

So much was pleasantly achieved. But the arrival of James Melville, upon confidential business, was another matter. His friendship with Moray was too well known for his errand to be in doubt, and the earnestness with which he seemed to be reassuring the Queen caused those who were watching their conference from the far end of the great hall some anxiety. Huntly turned to Bothwell in dismay.

"Can you credit it? I believe she will yield. He is undoubtedly demanding forgiveness for that schemer, Moray."

"Aye, very likely," said Bothwell, stroking his chin.

"Heavens above, James, do not stand there grinning. Already Moray has done his best to ruin us both."

"And no doubt he will again, George," Bothwell agreed. But at the sight of his companion's consternation, he began to shake with perverse, exasperating laughter.

"I can see no cause for mirth," raged Huntly.

"Come, George," Bothwell murmured, "surely you must laugh at that righteous hypocrite's monstrous impudence? I swear Moray has now convinced even himself that he had neither art nor part in the regrettable affair——"

"I believe he devised it from the start."

Bothwell nodded. "No doubt," he said dryly. "But control yourself, man, for her Grace is beckoning us, and I doubt we shall care but little for what we are to hear."

Mary watched them stride together up the hall with some little apprehension. But, though she dismissed Melville, she did not attempt to appease the two grave-faced young men.

"My lords," she said, "I have listened to Master Melville with care. It seems that my lord of Moray has entirely severed relations with his former associates——"

"Madam," burst out the Earl of Huntly, "surely your Grace does not believe such a tale?"

"Why not? He admits his former friendships, but says he has been shocked beyond belief by their murderous act. Those are his own words, my lords. Why should he lie?"

"Madam, because falsehood is his nature," Huntly said.

Mary sighed. "Do you not recognise the possibility of penitence, my lord?"

Huntly ran his fingers through his thick fair hair. "How shall we tell, Madam, the difference between penitence and expediency? Do not both present the same smooth face?"

Mary made a little gesture of entreaty. "My lords, he is

my brother," she said. "Shall I not give him the benefit of such a doubt?"

"Madam," said Huntly wretchedly, "your will must be our law."

Mary turned to Bothwell. "And you, my lord, are you in accord with my lord of Huntly in this?"

"No, Madam," said Bothwell, with his wry grin. "But I shall do what I may to endure what you have willed."

She looked at him sharply, checking an imperious retort. "Then let us talk instead of our entry into Edinburgh."

The Queen's return was as splendid as she could have hoped. Bothwell led the Border contingent of pikemen; seven earls in their finest silks and velvets rode about her; and behind her came the lesser lords with their followers, dressed also in their best. At Musselburgh the Archbishop of St. Andrews with his Hamilton kinsfolk joined them, and all the streets of Edinburgh were narrowed by shouting crowds.

But Mary refused to return at once to Holyroodhouse. Tragedy lay so dark about her Palace that the idea was unendurable. Lord Home offered her the use of that house in the High Street which had once belonged to the Bishop of Dunkeld, and Bothwell himself attended to the mounting of guns for its defence. Even so, she found its security inadequate. She was still suffering from shock, unable to sleep without appalling nightmares or to check her dread of any unexplained sound. When Huntly suggested to the Council that, in the circumstances, a move to the greater safety of the Castle might be expedient, she did not for once protest that she was not afraid.

Darnley was thankful for their change of residence. The Queen had caused a proclamation to be made at the Market Cross forbidding anyone, under penalty of treason, to say that the King had had either art or part in the murder of David Rizzio. But his guilt was too well known for the diplomatic fiction to have any effect. He moved in a sort of vacuum, disowned both by the loyal nobles and his former friends.

Mary tried sincerely, as she prepared for her confinement, to be friendly with the father of her prospective child. But she had learnt one lesson. She permitted him no further share in public affairs.

He sat by her side, however, when the Earl of Moray, at the end of a month's probation, was received in audience in the hall of Edinburgh Castle on the 21st of April, and did his utmost to maintain his usual air of haughty indifference.

Moray looked well, in spite of his complaints of dire poverty, and looked round his sister's improvised Court with a complacent smile.

" Well, Madam, I am glad to see you delivered from the wickedness of my former friends. But you have a poor, peaked look. We must take better care of you. Are you eating enough ? "

" I think so, brother."

" How do you sleep ? "

" Indifferently."

" Ihmhm. I thought as much." He nodded, looking scornfully round the assembled lords. " Frightened out of your wits, no doubt. Aye, that'll be the way of it. But we'll fettle all that."

In spite of herself, she smiled. His masterful air reminded her of the old days in France, when her indulgent elder brother came to visit her after illness had doomed her to dreary days in a shadowed room. His intercession had often gained her permission to walk with him in the gardens or listen to the fiddlers who played for the more fortunate to dance in the great hall of the Palace of St. Germain.

And so Moray established himself at the Castle. At first he was careful to seek no part in the government as he edged his way back into favour. The administration was now in the hands of Bothwell and Huntly, the most effective members of the Council. They were working to stabilise the country's disturbed economy, sponsoring a Currency Act to check imports of counterfeit coin, new Game Laws to prevent the

unauthorised slaughter of deer, or the exploitation of Scottish
lochs by alien fishermen. Bothwell, as Lord Admiral, also set
about checking piracy, and advocated local Courts of Justice,
to be held wherever the Queen made a progress about her
kingdom.

But Huntly was physically incapable of being civil to the
now complacent Moray, and Bothwell did not see why he
should try. So neither was anxious to remain at close quarters
with him in the Castle. Besides, both were married men,
and Huntly at least was anxious to see as much of his wife as
his duties permitted, while Bothwell's uncompromising lady,
though still wearing mourning for her lost Ogilvie, was now
willing to take up residence at Haddington, having reorganised
Crichton Castle, it seemed, to the last tenterhook and bunch
of lavender. On arrival at her new home, she had appeared
favourably impressed, but her righteous indignation was soon
roused by the discovery that during her preoccupation with
her own house-proud affairs, Bothwell had found more lighthearted occupation. Bessie Crawford was only a little sewing-
maid, but it took Bothwell's gift of yet another estate, with
castle and lands in life-rent, to appease his lady's wrath against
a husband who went elsewhere for the diversion she was
unwilling to provide. But Bothwell had now too much on his
hands to fret over the failure of a relationship from which he
had never expected much personal satisfaction. And his
apartments in Holyroodhouse offered an alternative to the
cold comfort of Haddington.

For the Queen, awaiting her ordeal in the Castle, the days
dragged as they had never done before. Withdrawn from
the outside world, the significance of the routine of government, the intrigues of friends and enemies, even her husband's
blatant infidelities and excesses, dwindled as her personal crisis
approached, to the mimic rivalries of puppets on a distant
stage.

She spent many hours making and copying out her Will,
a task she found oddly comforting. She had always loved

giving presents, and she was happy as she pored over the inventories of her jewellery, dresses and furnishings, smiling at the thought of the pleasure of those surprised by her carefully chosen gifts.

Her husband first. . . . She sighed. He should have the more because their marriage had fallen so far short of her first childish hopes. She listed rings, chains, seals, brooches, in particular the great diamond ring he had put on her finger on their wedding day. Her French relations must also be splendidly remembered, and some of her most valuable possessions go to the Crown of Scotland for her child. Something for her brother of Moray. . . . Surely Bothwell had been mistaken when he said bluntly that Moray would choose the day of her accouchement to bring his friends back to Scotland? But if he asked her to make an Act of Grace and recall them as a thank-offering for her deliverance, that might be different. Pretty Flem was crying her eyes out for her beloved Lethington, and she herself might well need his quick wits to help persuade the Queen of England to acknowledge her child's rights.

Bothwell . . . Huntly . . . the other members of her Council . . . she returned to the inventories. Bothwell's masterly management of the recent crisis had put her greatly in his debt. She selected for him a fine diamond, table-cut, and mounted on black enamel, adding the jewelled figure of a mermaid that he had once admired when she wore it at a ball. It was a pretty thing in diamonds, complete with diamond mirror and ruby comb. Belatedly she remembered Lady Jean, and chose her a tiara of rubies, pearls and garnets with bracelets to match.

The list went on and on. Nobody must be forgotten. So many people had been kind. Her Maries must each have something special, of course. As she listed all the jewels she had loved to wear, the terrifying events of the last few weeks jangled more faintly in her memory. That dreadful Ruthven. . . . But he was dead, they said, in England. She crossed herself. God rest his misguided soul.

Her quill scratched busily. Her attendants, her servants, all must be remembered. How fortunate it was that she had enough pretty things to give even the shyest page and newest laundry-maid a memorial of their royal mistress. As she grew tired her attention began to wander a little, so that she had to go back and scratch out occasional mistakes.

The Queen of England was being very civil. Had she really got the smallpox? What would happen if she died? Robert Melville reported from the English Court that many said she could not live. Was it unchristian to dream at such a time of becoming the Queen of both countries as well as the mother of a fair son? It would be pleasant to be the greatest ruler in Christendom, greater than her mother-in-law of France had ever been. James Melville, she knew, was determined to be the first to convey to Queen Elizabeth the news of her child's birth. He was the most ambitious of the three Melville brothers, though Robert, she thought, was the most diplomatic. And yet, it was the unassuming Andrew she liked best.

Her wrist ached, and her head swam, as red-hot arrows of pain stabbed through the leaden bulk of her unwieldy body till she caught her breath. Sudden fear set her heart-beats scurrying.

" Seton," she called, in a high, strained voice, " Oh, Seton, come quickly . . ."

But it was another two days and nights before the Prince of Scotland gave his first querulous cry. His mother lay speechless, unaware of the thunder of the Castle guns overhead, or the gratified buzz from the ante-room in which the officers of state had waited throughout the difficult birth. But by the afternoon she had recovered sufficiently to face her first traditional duty, that of presenting her child for his father's acknowledgement.

Darnley shambled sheepishly into the small, many-angled room, his blond head rising high above the flurry of apprehensive ladies who whispered that the Queen must be spared all possible strain. She lay, frail as a foam-bell, on her violet velvet pillows, a small reddish object asleep in the crook of her arm, watching his approach with dark-ringed eyes. As he stooped awkwardly over the gorgeous bed, she spoke, in a small resolute thread of a voice.

"My lord, God has given you and me a son, begotten of none but you."

Then, with a little, proprietary movement, she turned the shawl back from the crumpled face, her voice gathering strength as she went on. "I protest to God, and as I shall answer to him at the great day of judgment, that this is your son and no other man's. Let all here, both ladies and others, bear witness that I fear he is so much your son that it may be the worse for him hereafter."

Awkwardly, Darnley stooped and kissed the minute face, and at once the tiny mouth opened on a high, thin cry. "Sweet Madam," he said sulkily, "is this your promise to forgive and forget all?"

"I have forgiven all," said Mary. "But I can never forget." Her arm tightened round the child by her side. Her voice was suddenly strong. "What if Faudonside's pistol had shot? What would have become of him and me both?"

"Madam," said Darnley, "these things are past."

Wearily, Mary turned her head against her violet velvet pillow. She could endure no more. Slowly her eyelids closed. "Then let them go . . ."

Darnley made no protest when a rush of ladies, headed by Mary Seton, urged him from the room. In the ante-room grave-faced noblemen and their ladies, ministers of the new faith, ambassadors from France and England, were all jostling for an opportunity to convey their congratulations to the Queen. But Darnley plunged boorishly past them without acknowledging their greetings and went in search of lighter-hearted associates.

Bothwell was in Liddesdale, riding home after an irritating day of conference with the English wardens, when he saw the northern sky redden with the last links of the chain of bonfires that had snatched the news from the Castle rock and sent it flaring from end to end of Scotland. So the Queen's child was born at last. He cocked his bonnet more gaily as he wished the poor bairn joy of its heritage, be it lass or lad. Then he put the matter out of his mind as he jogged on towards Hermitage.

Some days afterwards he returned to Edinburgh to offer his congratulations and take command of the Prince's body-guard, which would in due course escort the heir to the throne of Scotland, his wet nurse and all the rest of his household, to Stirling Castle, second stronghold in the kingdom and tradi-tional nursery of the reigning monarch's eldest son.

As Lord Admiral, it was also Bothwell's duty to escort the Queen on her first convalescent journey by ship across the Forth to confer with her son's hereditary guardian, the Earl of Mar, at Alloa. While they were Mar's guests he first heard of the Queen's decision to admit Lethington once more into her presence, and liked it even less than Huntly had liked the return of Moray. For if Lethington persuaded his former associate to back his demand for the return of Haddington, Lady Jean would be seriously displeased. He should not have it, Bothwell determined. When the Queen decided to remain with the Prince at Stirling he returned to Holyroodhouse, in a very bad temper, to deal with army accounts which had been accumulating since the spring campaign.

The Queen had not been in residence at Holyroodhouse since Rizzio's murder, and those who remained there avoided the supper-room and the bedchamber adjoining, for rumour already said that Rizzio's ghost wandered there, wringing translucent hands and wailing for revenge. Bothwell, who was not superstitious, ignored such tales. But he did not deride them, since he had taken to working in the little supper-room for the sake of quiet.

His possessions were strewn about it as usual. An old doublet was tossed down on a bench beside a coil of tarred rope sent for his inspection by a shipwright of Leith, an empty powder-horn and a torn glove lay beside it, and one of the Queen's little dogs, which had attached itself to him on his return, had dragged his cloak on to the floor and muddled it into a softer resting-place than the bare boards.

When Huntly arrived, obviously disgruntled and anxious that Bothwell should share his grievance, he showed no signs of setting his papers aside.

" How you can work so calmly, James," Huntly grumbled, " I do not know. I tell you, Moray means to ruin us both."

" Eh, what's that? " Bothwell paused half-way up a long column of figures. " Moray? No doubt of it. And Lethington besides. He picked a quarrel with me at Alloa. He means to have Haddington back. I care not for all her Grace's efforts to make us friends again. What use is such wheedling of men that fate makes enemies? Yet it angers me more to find that the fellow who provided mouldy fodder for her Grace's horses at Dunbar in March has made a profit on the reckoning as well as on the stuff my men had to feed to the pigs."

" Fodder! " exclaimed Huntly. " Of what account is petty pilfering at a time like this? "

" You speak as a rich landowner, George. Her Grace is a poor one."

" Then I will return when you have retrieved her Grace's fortunes," said Huntly, swinging impatiently towards the door.

Bothwell continued to count on his fingers. It was dusk now outside, for already, in mid-September, the nights were lengthening. Soon he could scarcely see the crabbed script before him. He sat back and bawled for the French page, whom nobody called Hubert, because he came from France.

" Paris! "

The lad came running. His master's temper had been uncertain of recent weeks.

" Bring candles."

" At once, my lord."

As the door opened again, Bothwell could hear the distant

scrape of fiddles and hands clapping to mark the rhythm of a dance. Had her Grace already arrived? It was as well that she had refused to occupy her former apartments, or he would have been bustling with the rest of them, ever since yesterday's news of her sudden decision to visit Edinburgh. The gay sounds beckoned him. But he had work to do. Jerking his quill towards a space between the shoals of papers, he began to count on his fingers once more.

CHAPTER THIRTEEN

"I LOOKED for her Grace's arrival before now," Mary Seton murmured an hour later, under cover of the hubbub of conversation in the crowded presence chamber, to Mary Livingstone, who, with her husband, was also in attendance at Holyroodhouse that evening. " I wish I had been permitted to accompany her from Stirling instead of going ahead with the rest to see that the new royal apartments were in order. It is to be hoped that there has been no further unhappiness between her and the King."

" Why should you suppose it? " said Mary Livingstone airily. " They were well enough agreed when I saw them last. You take their squabbles too sorely. Such trifles, believe me, dear Seton, are of no account between married folk."

" I trust you may be right," fretted Mary Seton. " Or that her Grace had not forced herself to come to Edinburgh again. I am persuaded that their lordships of the Exchequer will not deny her the sum she asks for the Prince's christening."

" I think she does well to make sure," Mary Livingstone said. " Twelve thousand pounds is a great sum, and it is already mid-September."

But Mary Seton was no longer listening. From the great staircase echoed the thud of grounded pikes, the chime of spurs, the sharp rattle of commands from the captain of the guard.

" At last! Here comes the Queen's Grace! "

Her words brought the drowsy company to their feet. In a flutter of little movements many hands adjusted ruffs, pushed strands of hair under jewelled nets, grasped skirts in readiness to sweep a curtsey or snatched bonnets off to make a bow. As the double doors were flung back by two grooms of the presence chamber, the Queen passed between them, with the Earl of Bothwell by her side.

She received their greetings with her usual grace, laughing a little at the flurry they made of taking her riding-cloak and gloves, accepting the chair by the fire, the cushions for her back, the little stool for her feet. But her eyes were blank, her movements almost those of an automaton.

" Why, Madam, how cold your hands are," worried Mary Seton, enclosing them between her own. " And how pale you look! I cannot imagine how we did not hear your Grace arrive. How came I to miss the sounds from the court-yard? Who dismissed your attendants? "

" I did," said Bothwell. " Calm yourself, Mistress Seton. Her Grace has not been neglected."

" I am glad to know it, my lord," said Mary Seton. But all her mind was on the Queen. " Madam, you are shivering. And your hands lie leaden in mine. Such an hour to make the journey from Stirling! I wonder the King permitted it."

" It was his wish," the Queen said, just above a whisper. " He rode with me to Edinburgh."

They were all alert now, heads turning, lips curling at the news.

" But Madam, where is he now? " cried Mary Seton.

" He—he found he had other business which—he had overlooked and must deal with—at once," the Queen said slowly. But the flush which spread across her face belied the careful words.

" Tch, tch," said Mary Seton. Behind the Queen's back she shook her head at Mary Livingstone. It was just as she had feared. There had been trouble again. The King had turned his horse, as like as not, on the outskirts of Edinburgh and ridden back to Stirling, or to his father's mansion outside Glasgow.

" But still . . . we should have heard . . ." Mary Seton was too deeply devoted to the Queen to be unaware when something was being hidden from her, something that intuition could guess but not define.

" I came in by the private entrance with the King," said Mary wearily.

" But the guards——"

" It was their duty to recognise, not to raise the alarm," the Queen pointed out. " No more questioning, Seton, I beg. For I am tired to death."

" Your posset, Madam," said Mary Livingstone, nudging Mary Seton with a headshake which indicated that she would do well to leave her mistress in peace. There were times when Seton took too much upon herself. Such a commotion because her Grace's return had taken her faithful watchdog unawares. " It was most fortunate that my lord of Bothwell was at hand——"

" Most fortunate," the Queen agreed.

" I thank your Grace," Bothwell said, dryly.

But she did not turn to him, as in the ordinary way she would have done, with her quick, warm smile. " Let us speak no more of the manner of my arrival," she commanded abruptly. " Who shall make music for us? " It was a question she had so often asked when she was weary or disturbed, always confident of the answer, when Rizzio was at hand. But now the very thought of music recalled the six months' old tragedy so sharply that she rose, her hands extended as if to thrust memory from her, her voice breaking on an upward note. " No, no, no. No music to-night. Escort me to my chamber——"

Her urgency threw them all into confusion. Pages,

hurriedly roused from the shadowy corners in which they had been dozing, grabbed their ponderously branching candlesticks, gouts of grease beading their gay livery as they took their places with the ladies in attendance on the Queen.

Left behind with the other lords, Bothwell bowed formally as the procession moved off. His face was enigmatic as he turned to watch the game of chess in which his brother-in-law was being beaten by the Earl of Argyll. Huntly's mind, it seemed, was not on the game, for he glanced up at Bothwell as he waited for his opponent to make his next deliberate move.

" Well, James, still brooding on the sins of that fodder merchant of Dunbar? "

Bothwell stared. His preoccupation with the figures for the spring campaign now seemed as remote as last year's snows. " What fodder merchant? " he asked vaguely.

Huntly surveyed him in astonishment. " Have you been drinking, man? The fellow's punishment was all you cared about an hour since."

But Bothwell was in no mood for teasing now. Without another word, he swung on his heel, swept up sword and bonnet from the chest on which he had laid them, and wrenched the double doors apart before those in attendance could step forward.

" Now what," said Huntly in an injured tone, " did I say to make him take his leave in such discourteous haste? "

Argyll shrugged. " What is strange in the discourtesy of my lord of Bothwell? The man is as wild as a whaup from his own hills. Your move."

Frowning, Huntly tried to bring his attention back to the game.

" Strange," he thought aloud, as he moved a bishop, " that the King was not with her Grace . . ."

" Check," said Argyll.

" What could have made him leave her . . . ? " Huntly moved his Queen up to protect the threatened King, his attention less on the board before him than on the drama it mimicked, so that he did not see the lesser Queen's danger until it was too late.

" Tch, tch. Checkmate," said Argyll, sweeping his opponent's Queen from the board. " Had you been more attentive, I should not have given you such a beating." As he snapped his fingers, his page came yawning forward to pack the pieces away. " We shall no doubt hear what her Grace has in mind in the morning. Moray and Lethington will be here, too, before we have broken our fast."

" I do not doubt it," said Huntly gloomily.

Argyll surveyed him ironically. " Do not forget, my lord, that we are all sworn to be good friends together now, with byegones forgotten, at the express command of the Queen's Grace."

Huntly nodded. " Yet, as they say, one swallow does not make a summer. Neither does one fair promise make a friend. I bid you good night, my lord."

The Earl of Argyll chuckled dryly as Huntly left the royal apartments in as evident ill-humour as Bothwell had done. These hot-tempered fools, for all their romantic attachment to the Crown, when a pretty woman wore it, had not the sense to safeguard their own interests. He himself had taken care to obtain the useful office of Justice-General in the recent reconciliation, with men of understanding under him. Queens had come, and Queens would no doubt go, sooner perhaps than later, but justice must still be done in Scotland, though the skies fell, he reminded himself, as he too prepared to withdraw to his lodging.

Next morning, as Argyll had predicted, Moray and Lethington waited on the Queen, though they were obliged to leave without seeing her. She had not recovered from a wretchedly sleepless night.

" Her Grace's health will no doubt improve," Moray said disagreeably, " when she learns that the subsidy has been agreed at the twelve thousand pounds she sought."

With little cries of delight the ladies-in-waiting hastened

back to the Queen's darkened bedchamber. Surely twelve thousand pounds would provide all her Grace could wish? Their excitement roused her, as they had hoped, to laugh at their rapaciousness. But she herself listened to their joyous outcry as if to the clamour of sparrows under the eaves. Not even dear Seton must know the reason why her husband had refused to remain at Holyroodhouse. Uneasily, she sought to obliterate it from her own memory.

" Twelve thousand pounds, Madam! It will obtain all the splendour in Scotland! "

" It will purchase the fairest stuff in France, Madam, for your new gowns . . ."

" The lords in attendance will have the new suits we planned for them. How were they to be? " cried Mary Fleming.

" I have forgotten," she said remotely.

" Why, Madam," said Mary Beton, " I remember very well. My lord of Moray's was to be of green, my lord of Argyll's red, and my lord of Bothwell's blue, all at your Grace's personal charge. These colours will become them excellently, I believe——"

The Queen put her hand to her head. " I have graver matters on my mind," she said. " We will leave lesser decisions till later."

" There is also," said Mary Seton, " the question of the Bishop of Mondivi, whom His Holiness has appointed as nuncio at the Court of Holyroodhouse. My brother asked me to press your Grace to grant him at least an interview."

" No! " said the Queen. " I will not do it, Seton."

" My lord of Athol is most earnest that you will receive him, Madam," Mary Seton persisted. " In so doing you would best serve the true faith. His Holiness maintains that the Protestant cause is ready to decline if you will show a proper zeal for the cause every Catholic ruler must have at heart."

Mary shivered slightly. " I will hear no more of it, Seton."

" But, Madam, why? "

" Because—because I will have no more bloodshed between Christians," said Mary vehemently. " Have I not seen France torn apart——"

" But for the faith, Madam, is it not our duty to endure all things—? "

" I do not believe that the cause of true religion is so served," said the Queen. " Do not stare at me as if I had taken leave of my wits, Flem and Seton. I am Queen of Scots. It may be that half my people are heretics. But I am still their Queen. I tell you I will not see in Scotland the butchery I was compelled to witness at Amboise and Orléans. While I am Queen, there shall be no more such bonfires in Scotland."

" It is said that the Bishop is likely to complain to His Holiness if you refuse to receive him," murmured Mary Fleming.

" I have refused," said Mary indignantly, " to endanger his life."

" He is prepared to take the risk."

" And I am not."

" It is said," persisted Mary Seton unhappily, " that your toleration of heretics is the first cause of the King's anger, Madam."

" We will not talk of the King, Seton," said the Queen more sharply than her ladies had heard her speak before. " On such questions I am answerable only to my conscience. It is time for me to rise and prepare to attend the Council. Do not mention this again."

" As you wish, Madam," said Seton sadly. She had not brought up the question of the Papal nuncio merely to oblige her brother and Athol, but because, as almost everyone except the Queen seemed to realise, Darnley had turned back to the old faith, both complaining of the Queen's lukewarmness in her religion and protesting his own ardour. Already her good friends were wondering what use might be made of his change of heart by those who led the Counter-Reformation.

" If your Grace would but consider giving some proof of your own zeal for the true religion . . ." Seton ventured.

" The true religion, to my mind, has no need for such proofs as the axe and the stake can provide," the Queen said coldly. " I will wear my black velvet for the Council Meeting, Flem, and my rubies with it, lest I should lack colour. You shall attend me——"

" Most gladly, Madam," said Mary Fleming, mischievously amused by poor Seton's disgrace. But it was not in the Queen's nature to be angry for long with those who loved her. She paused beside her disconsolate lady on her way to the Council Chamber, while Mary Fleming importantly scolded one page for his awkwardness with her Grace's work-basket and another for dropping her embroidery frame. Smiling, the Queen kissed Mary Seton's tear-stained cheek.

" Do not distress yourself too much, dear Seton," she said softly. " You are my most loving friend, and the best dresser of hair in Scotland. Shall I complain because you have not the makings of a diplomat? "

The members of the Council rose at her entrance, and the Queen graciously acknowledged their salutation as she passed before them to the raised dais.

" Proceed, my lords," she commanded, after the usual formalities. It was not her habit to intervene much in debate, but rather to occupy herself with whatever embroidery she had on hand while her ministers argued, occasionally pausing, needle poised, to follow a speaker's argument with a frown of concentration or an approving smile. But unobtrusively, she noticed everything. This morning, for instance, she was aware of the whispered conference between Moray and Argyll which her arrival had interrupted; the uneasy glances which passed between the Earl of Athol and the Bishop of Ross; the stolid cheerfulness of Adam Bothwell and Alexander Gordon, Protestant Bishops of Orkney and Galloway; Huntly's troubled face and Lethington's thin smile as he waited for her to be amused by the sight of the little dog whose narrow muzzle and twitching nostrils projected delicately from the puckered wristband of his full sleeve.

But she carefully averted her eyes from James Hepburn, Earl of Bothwell. And it was not till the Council began to debate the royal progress to the Scottish Border which she and Darnley were expected to make at the end of the first week in October, and the assize she had undertaken to hold at Jedburgh for the sentencing of various offenders, that Bothwell himself took any part in the discussion.

Then, as his colleagues turned towards him for news of the preparations he had made for the Queen's reception, he rose, leafing through the papers in his hand, his harsh voice indicating only preoccupation with his duties as Lieutenant of the Border.

" There are a number of offenders against the royal authority whom I shall summon to answer for their conduct before the Queen's Grace," he said. " I have their names here—if I can find them——" He frowned down at the papers he held. " Ah, yes. In Liddesdale the most culpable are the Lairds of Mangerton and Whithaugh, Jock Elliot of the Park, and sundry lesser folk whose names and offences I have set down. It is my purpose to send my people such summonses forthwith, so that they may present the culprits betimes to the Queen's Grace after I have been privileged to escort her to Jedburgh."

Heads nodded, hands were held out to take the papers that Bothwell now passed to the Earl of Moray, who perused them warily, then left his place to bear them to the Queen, whose needle, arrested by the first word Bothwell had spoken, was now plunging in and out among the crimson petals of a silken rose.

" Madam, as you have heard," said Moray pompously, " it is the purpose of my lord of Bothwell to summon the offenders listed here to present themselves before you at Jedburgh next month. Is it your pleasure that he should do so? "

The Queen inclined her head towards him, then spoke at some length in a rapid undertone. Moray bowed and stepped down from the dais, pausing to return the papers to Bothwell as he passed.

"It is the pleasure of the Queen's Grace that you should proceed in person against the offenders whose names appear hereon," he said blandly. "Otherwise, she does not consider it certain that they would acknowledge the royal authority. It is therefore her command that you should proceed to Liddesdale forthwith, and retain them in custody at Hermitage until the time of the assize. Touching your escort, her Grace thanks you, but will relieve you of that duty so that you may fulfil another of greater urgency. . . ."

Even Bothwell's iron control scarcely concealed the fact that the Queen's dismissal stung him as sharply as if she had struck him across the face. Incredulity, incomprehension, finally wrath, seared his stare like jags of lightning. He had not looked to be so treated by her Grace. She had been thankful enough for his presence the evening before, when her sudden cry of pain had brought him crashing down the private stair from the supper-room. Darnley had forced her back against the wall of his bedchamber and was twisting the arm she had flung up to shield her face with the vicious zest of a cruel child. It had been pleasant to take the great, gangling fellow by surprise, without word spoken, toppling him backwards like a swaying poplar, to struggle helplessly against the wrestler's grip and the knee hard in the small of his back. When he caught the Queen's eye he could have sworn she, too, was struggling against laughter. What could her coldness mean now?

He had drawn no weapon against the King. He doubted whether Darnley had even recognised him in the gathering darkness. Once released, he had slammed out, sobbing wild threats against his wife rather than her defender. They had heard him shout for his horse in the forecourt, the tumult of hoof-beats on the cobbles, dying away. Afterwards, the Queen had recoiled from the private stair and its dreadful memories. So he had attended her by the main entrance. What else could he have done?

"It is understood," Moray concluded, "that the King will ride with her Grace to Jedburgh, and members of her Council escort both, my lord of Bothwell."

Bothwell's eyes were now as blank as the Queen's. "As her Grace pleases," he said tonelessly. "But since I am to carry out these arrests in person, I humbly ask that she will now hold me excused to do so."

Huntly followed his brother-in-law's disdainful departure with troubled eyes. What had gotten into James lately? And how had he now come to displease the Queen?

"Let us turn," said Moray, as the ushers swung the doors shut behind the Lieutenant of the Border, "to the amount of the levies to be made on each of the Three Estates to provide for the christening of the Prince . . ."

Mary could not at first believe that Darnley would carry his grudge so far as to absent himself from the royal progress to the Border. She wrote to him, formally and informally, she sent Athol, his kinsman, to plead with him, she waited at Holyroodhouse in increasing anxiety, throughout the first week of October. Surely, even at the last moment, he would join her? But when the 7th of October did not bring him, she could wait no longer if she were to open the proceedings at Jedburgh on the 9th.

As the great cavalcade, splendid in silks and velvets, mounted on their tittuping, restive horses, paced up the High Street and down the West Bow, the thunder of hoof-beats on the cobbles brought workers from their benches and housewives from their hearths to wave and cry a blessing. It was a clear, frost-crisp morning, with the leaves drifting, golden and scarlet, from the wayside trees, to echo the scarlet and yellow of the royal livery. In different circumstances Mary would have delighted in the ride to Melrose, where they were to break their journey that night.

But for once she scarcely noticed her surroundings. The

old pain that anxiety always increased dragged at her side. Her heart lay heavy as a stone within her, while her thoughts swirled hither and thither, wildly as birds distraught by an oncoming storm. She turned from the distress one man had caused her, to remember that she had driven the other away. For instinct had warned her that only at the cost of her peace of mind would she ever admit Bothwell to her presence again.

At Melrose, Sir Alexander Hepburn, Laird of Riccarton, sought urgent audience with the Queen before she had even dismounted from her horse. As he looked up at her, his craggy, troubled face reminded her unexpectedly of his kinsman, and she was suddenly cold with fear.

" Madam," said Sir Alexander, " I bring sore news of my cousin of Bothwell. It seems that he was grievously wounded by the outlaw, Jock Elliot of the Park, as he resisted arrest. It is not thought that he can live."

CHAPTER FOURTEEN

THE Hermitage Water fretted its way between bracken and boulders under a frosty arch of cloudless sky. To the man who lay between worlds, the vociferous medley of small churning sounds seemed only just short of speech. Drained of blood and fevered with the pain of roughly tended wounds, James Hepburn lay inert on the bed to which they had borne him from the sheep-cropped turf of Kershope Haugh on which he had fallen, after the headlong chase down Liddel Water had ended in the catastrophic encounter with Jock of the Park. For Jock's feigned surrender and his captor's unexpected stumble had given the outlaw a chance to make a savage, unexpected attack which had been all but fatal.

There had been trouble, meanwhile, at Hermitage. The Armstrongs, imprisoned there, pending armed escort to

Jedburgh, had taken advantage of Bothwell's absence to overwhelm the guards and seize the Castle. When the party returned, with their leader unconscious on a sledge, they were glad to accept the compromise suggested by the relatively peaceable Robert Elliot, laird of nearby Shaws, and offer the Armstrongs safe conduct as far as Whithaugh and Mangerton, on condition that they left the Castle forthwith. Since the Armstrongs had already devoured the Castle's stocks of meal and meat down to the last bannock and salted carcase, they graciously accepted the offer, and rode home scathless, inordinately amused by the trouble Bothwell's servants were taking over a man as good as dead.

But they had underrated their enemy's tenacity. Reports of his death spread up and down the country. But he had no intention of dying as he lay and listened to the murmur of the Hermitage Water from the bedchamber in which the shutters had been flung wide by his command.

If he could only hear what they were saying . . . Bothwell fretted. Why could he not raise himself and confront them . . . all those people who stood and muttered to each other about his bed? Was he in chains? His horror of imprisonment caught him by the throat, and his distraught croak brought his page running.

" Give me . . . a drink . . ."

" It is here, my lord." Anxiously French Paris held a beaker of water to his master's lips. Bothwell gulped it greedily, then grimaced as its tastelessness angered him. " God's . . . blood, boy, bring . . . me . . . wine."

" My lord, the physician has forbidden it."

" Do . . . as . . . I bid you . . ." Bothwell whispered, his lips drawn back from his teeth in a grimace of pain so ferocious that Paris fairly ran from the room. But when he came back his master's mind was wandering again, and he turned his head away.

" They are . . . talking of me, yonder. What are they saying, boy? "

" Who, my lord ? "

" All those folk behind you . . ."

Nervously, Paris jumped round. " My lord, there is no man here save myself."

" Have . . . you gone . . . deaf? "

" I hear nothing, my lord, save the dirl of the Hermitage Water."

" More . . . fool . . . you! They are conspiring . . . against the Queen's Grace. The King is in it . . . and the men of Rome . . . they do not know I am . . . listening to their debate. Keep quiet, boy——"

" My lord, I have not stirred," faltered Paris, his eyes rolling till the whites showed like those of a frightened horse.

" If . . . I could but . . . hear . . ." sighed Bothwell. His lean face puckered. Two tears of weakness poised for an instant on the edge of his sunken eye-sockets, then wandered down the deep furrows that ran towards the angle of his jaw.

" Against the Queen's Grace . . ." A rigor shook him into silence, and his teeth dirled on the edge of the beaker of wine that his terrified page held once more to his lips. Then sweat broke out on his forehead and he lay quiet for the first time since they had borne him back to Hermitage. The heavy lids fell over the wild eyes, flickered once or twice, and were still, his shallow breathing barely lifting the blanket they had thrown over him.

In the Court of Justice at Jedburgh the first day of the assize was nearly at an end. The Queen had attended to all the preliminary business brought to her, fixing the prices of bread, ale, stabling and meals for retainers after consultation with her advisers. Now the local offenders were coming up for trial. There were not as many of those as had been expected, for the most interesting criminals had been able to turn Bothwell's misfortune to good account, and the lesser folk presented for the Queen's judgment seemed a pitiful collection of unkempt, hungry-eyed creatures who stole, she fancied, out of desperation rather than villainy. When Moray recommended their execution, she forbade it, and he had perforce to submit to her Grace's preference for a fine.

" With imprisonment, naturally," he added, " till they produce the money."

Mary forced herself to listen carefully to the charge brought against each of the defiant, villainous-looking Borderers who were hustled in and out of the dock. Only by keeping her mind on the numbers of sheep stolen, steadings fired, enemies wounded in murderous assaults, could she obtain any respite from the despairing conviction that if Bothwell died, she must share responsibility with the man who had struck him down.

" May it please your Grace, we here present for judgment one Walter Elliot, on a charge of theft . . ."

Against her will she could see Bothwell's irreverent grin more clearly than the scowl of the sullen fellow before her. She clenched her fists, compelling herself to listen to the sing-song voice of the clerk as he recited the tale of Wattie Elliot's misdoings.

" May it please your Grace to pass judgment accordingly ? "

" Fine him as before," she said. What was James Hepburn to her ? Nothing. But she did not wish him to die.

" May it please your Grace . . ."

The proceedings dragged on. Mary began to stifle weary yawns behind her clasped hands, as she rested her elbows on the table before her and cupped her chin on her fists. None of the minor offenders had received the death sentence which all had phlegmatically expected. Had they caught Jock of the Park, she thought fiercely, it would have been very different. She would show no mercy to a murderer, whoever his victim might be. But Sir Alexander had regretfully informed her that Jock had got clean away after doing his best to kill in cold blood the man to whom he had already surrendered. Treachery made her angry, and some half-starved fellow's petty pilfering did not.

Her thoughts wandered again. How many of the members

of her Council shared her anxiety for Bothwell? Very few, she guessed. It would suit those who liked to play a double game to know that the man who had remained untempted by all offers of English gold was safely out of the way. What more could it mean to her, Mary wondered, as she sat, still as a statue of justice, beneath the canopy of state which she herself had embroidered with its cryptic motto. " *In my End is my Beginning*," high above the whisper and stir of the Court.

" May it please your Grace . . ."

At the end of the day's proceedings she rose, graciously acknowledged the salutation of the assembly, and laid her fingertips on the rich stuff of Moray's sleeve as he crooked his arm to escort her from the chamber. Afterwards, when she was back in the pleasant little house, standing in a well-tended garden, which had been rented for her accommodation during the assize, she invited the lords of her Council and some of those from the neighbourhood to attend her in the withdrawing-room on the first floor which overlooked a glowing, autumnal orchard. Sipping her wine, she fondled the ears of the little dog which had made the journey on Maitland of Lethington's saddle bow, and asked what news had come from Stirling.

" His Highness the Prince is well," said Lethington smoothly. " My lord of Mar is confident that your Grace need have no anxiety."

" No despatch has yet come from the King? "

" None, Madam."

She sighed. " And—what is the news from Hermitage? " She forced herself to ask it, her whole body rigid as she waited to hear that Bothwell was dead.

" No change is reported in the condition of my lord of Bothwell," said Lethington flatly.

So the days slowly passed, till she left the Court-room for the last time. Her head was aching with the strain of long hours in such an atmosphere, and she leant heavily on Moray's supporting arm as the pain dragged at her side. For once she lacked the spirit to make the usual inquiries. She only knew, lying back in her chair to receive the comforting solicitude of the ladies who eddied about her, that she had done all she could. She had administered the Queen's justice and maintained the Queen's peace on the Borders. Now she could rest. She would see no one this evening. Her ladies should say she was not fit to receive the lords as usual. Thankfully she reflected that she could count on the Maries to send everyone else away.

Mary Seton was dismissing them now. The Queen smiled as she listened to dear Seton's gentle inflexibility. " My lords, her Grace is weary with the day's proceedings. She can receive no one, my lord of Lethington. My lord of Huntly, I fear your questions must wait. Her Grace is not fit to sign any documents to-night. Sir Alexander, I beg you will not trouble her Grace with ill news from Hermitage——"

" But the news is good," said the laird of Riccarton indignantly. " I have ridden these twenty-five miles to inform her Grace——"

" You shall inform her in the morning," said Mary Seton, pausing uncertainly as she heard her name called. " Yes, Madam ? "

" Send Sir Alexander to me," said the Queen imperiously.

He looked askance at the ladies he had interrupted in their small tasks. With smelling-salts, aromatic herbs, and fragrant lotions in their hands they reluctantly drew back from their mistress, who sat, pale as parchment, in her high-backed chair.

" Well, Sir Alexander ? " Her voice was toneless.

" Madam, for all but a week my cousin of Bothwell lay like one dead, so that we despaired of him," said Sir Alexander tersely. " But yesterday he seemed somewhat to mend. And this morning he wakened with the will to eat and the strength to mock our long faces——"

The Queen laughed. " So he would. We—we have been much distressed for our trusty servant, Sir Alexander."

" Madam, your solicitude does him great honour," said the laird of Riccarton. " I will see he has word of it."

" We have lacked his shrewd counsel on matters concerning the Border this last week," the Queen said slowly. " And there are many things since this assize which will presently require his attention. Sir Alexander——" she frowned, hesitated, suddenly reached a decision. "—if my lord of Bothwell is fit to receive us, it would please me well to ride with the lords of my Council to Hermitage and thank him for his devotion to his duty."

It was an impulsive plan, but neither out of character nor alien to her family's record. By just such spontaneously gracious acts her ancestors had won the love of the Scottish people they ruled. And Sir Alexander recognised the tradition with delight.

" I know nothing, Madam," he said heartily, " more likely to complete his recovery."

" Then," said Mary, faltering a little now that the decision was taken and its implications began to present themselves, " I—I will think on it and consult the lords of my Council. I would be glad to inform my lord of Bothwell of what has passed at Jedburgh in his absence. Yet—is it an arduous journey to Liddesdale ? "

" At this time of year, Madam, it is the sweetest in the world. I myself will guide you, since I know the way well."

She smiled. " Thank you, Sir Alexander. It will be pleasant to spend a day in the open air again, after so many within doors."

The news of the Queen's project did not cause much surprise. The assize had been sufficiently tedious for her desire to exercise to be easily understood. Huntly, in particular, welcomed the chance to see his brother-in-law, while Moray and Lethington were too newly back in favour to venture opposition to her small fantasy. Her ladies were glad of a change from the days which had hung heavy in Jedburgh, though they raised their plucked eyebrows at the thought of riding to Hermitage and back in a single day. For her Grace had already made it clear that the visit must be both formal and brief, since she did not wish to tax the resources of the sick man's household by seeking accommodation for the royal party overnight.

" We shall rise at first light," she said gaily. " Sir Alexander warns us that the going will be rough. We are to reach Hermitage an hour before noon and start back an hour after it." She broke off to shake a finger at Mary Fleming. " No use to sigh, Flem. It is our only hope of returning to Jedburgh before darkness comes down."

" That, Madam, I can well believe . . ."

" Think how much pleasanter it will be to canter over the moors than stifle in a Court of Justice! "

" Yes, indeed, Madam. But even pleasanter, do you not think, to lie late abed after such a weary week? "

" No, Flem. I long to be out of doors," said the Queen, throwing her arms wide. " I must get the stench of that Court-house out of my nose."

Early as it was when they started next morning, half the population of the little town, it seemed, had paused on their way to work to gape at the splendid cavalcade now mustered outside the Queen's lodging. Her Grace, pale after a week indoors, laughed with delight when her palfrey, fresh and skittish in the bright, cold air, bucked under her. Her riding-dress was of dark green serge, frogged and stitched with gold, under a warm black cloak with a gold buckle, and she wore a high-crowned black riding-hat with a rolled brim and bobbing green plume. The hands which so masterfully restrained her plunging palfrey were gloved in black velvet, stitched with gold thread and sewn with pearls, and the lace at her neck and wrists was as white as the foam that already flecked her eager beast's arched neck.

Moray and Huntly were to ride on either side of her. But Lethington held back his big bay horse till Mary Fleming appeared.

" Oh, my lord, I am glad indeed to see you," she said. " For I am but an indifferent horsewoman, and her Grace is in one of her wildest moods. If she sets too fast a pace I do not know how I shall hold this foolish beast of mine."

" Never fear, I shall be at your side," said Lethington gallantly.

As Sir Alexander had promised, it was a glorious ride. Once clear of the town, they went by Bedrule and Bonchester, pausing to water the horses at the well midway up the farther slope, then followed a green ribbon of sheep-cropped turf round the contours of the hills that guarded the approaches of Liddesdale, past Earlside, Stobs Castle and Priesthaugh Burn. They were on the high moors now, with Cauldcleuch sombre on their right and a vivid perspective of hills surging to the Border line. As they drew rein at the highest point of their journey, before beginning the descent to Braidley, Mary caught her breath. In the distance, the silver sword of the Solway Firth thrust deep into the wine-dark land. Beyond again, veiled in mist, lay England.

She sat her palfrey a little apart from the others, comparing the Scottish hills, in the gold and bronze of the autumnal bracken, the crimson and purple of faded heather, glorious as her own royal robes, with the dream-pale contours of that England over which, in the most secret, scarcely conscious recesses of her farthest ambition, she sometimes let herself fancy that she already reigned.

" How much farther is it, Sir Alexander ? "

" Not far now," Sir Alexander said. " We need no longer hasten if your Grace is weary. Once past Braidley, we are all but there."

" Have no fear for me," she said dreamily. " I am never weary on horseback. I wish . . . we might ride on for ever . . ."

Her voice was suddenly forlorn, for the hours of pleasant exercise had been sheer joy. Too soon now, she must be a Queen again, walking the knife-edge between rival factions, dreading yet another scene with her unpredictable husband, as much as the terrible loneliness. All her life she had turned towards those who loved and understood her as instinctively as a sunflower turns to the sun. When she was loved her response was the very heart-beat of joy. But when love was withdrawn from her she no longer cared to live. She had inherited both the nobility and the gaiety of her race. But over her, paradoxically, lay also the dark wing of despair, despair which had brought both her father and great-grandfather to the circumstances of their death.

"There lies Hermitage, Madam," said Sir Alexander, pointing.

She turned to look along his arm. Far below them, the Hermitage Water looped through a smudge of alder and birch between the golden hills, and beside it the Castle stood on a green bluff within its girdling moat.

"That little box?" she cried, deceived by the dwarfing solitude.

Sir Alexander chuckled. "It will seem larger when we stand beside it, Madam," he said.

Their arrival did not take the Hermitage household by surprise, for Sir Alexander had sent a man ahead on a fast horse to warn them. But the news had caused consternation to Bothwell's second-in-command, who, as a Sinclair cousin of his mother's family, did not wish his kinsman to be disgraced, yet was at his wits' end to know how adequate hospitality could be contrived in a fortress which was, at the best of times, equipped only for garrison duty. The Lady Jean did not care to come there, though on this occasion she could scarcely be blamed for absence, since Bothwell had so flatly refused to have her sent for. And the recent depredations of the Armstrongs had left scarcely a bone or a bannock in the place. But Bothwell, when consulted, had been unconcerned.

"Calm yourself, lad," he said in a hoarse whisper. "Why . . . should I feed . . . the curs that . . . fawn on . . . her Grace?"

"For the credit of our house, at least."

" Ach, roast a sheep and beg a sack of meal from Shaws for bannocks."

" I will. And I'll send Paris to redd up your chamber."

" Do not dare," groaned Bothwell. " His clatter makes my . . . head . . . ache . . ."

He drifted off again into the uneasy sleep from which the problems of hospitality had roused him, and his young kinsman, clashing frantically down the stone spiral which opened into the small central courtyard, realised that he must complete the arrangements for the Queen's reception alone. Bawling for the men who had gathered outside the Castle to stare stupidly up at the hills between which the royal cavalcade would presently appear, he sent them scurrying to slaughter a sheep, kindle the fire on the kitchen hearth and bespeak meal and wine from their neighbours of Shaws.

When the royal cavalcade arrived at last he was sweating with anxiety as he pulled off his bonnet and dropped on one knee before the Queen. He was not surprised at the contempt with which Moray and Lethington surveyed his preparations. But the frank delight with which the Queen greeted the good smell of roasting meat made it of no consequence. " I am famished," she said as she dismounted, looking up at the windowless, sheer cliff of the fortress which seemed to survey her from its arrow-slits as if out of narrowed, hostile eyes. " How —how fares my lord of Bothwell ? "

" He is better than he was, Madam. Would your Grace be pleased to see him ? "

" Yes," she said.

" You will eat first, Madam ? "

She said, simply, " It would be better, perhaps. I am forgetful when I am hungry, and I must entrust him with as much business as he has the strength to bear."

The meal was served in the hall above the kitchen, on bare boards hastily laid across trestles round which benches and stools had been collected from all corners of the Castle to seat the illustrious company. They were glad of the peat fire which

had been blown to a glow on the hearth, for the stone walls
seemed to hold the chill of centuries. Some of the ladies
whispered and grimaced at the plain fare, but the Queen
ate her meat and bannocks with appetite.

"You may convey our appreciation to the cook," she
told young Sinclair, wiping her lips daintily on her lace-edged
handkerchief because no one had thought to command a
page to wait on her with a basin of scented water and a towel
over his arm.

"Madam," said young Sinclair, flushing furiously, "I will
cherish your praise all my life. This is the first time I have
attempted to roast a sheep whole with Border pikes for a spit."

"Do not let your wife know it, or she will never employ
another cook," laughed the Queen. Then, under cover of the
general amusement, she looked round the board to attract
the attention of the members of her Council.

"My lords," she said, "Sir Alexander has warned me that
we must not delay long before starting homewards if we are
to reach Jedburgh by dusk." She turned to young Sinclair.
"Will you now guide us to my lord of Bothwell's chamber?"

"At once, Madam. It is above this one. Shall I lead the
way? The stairs are not well lighted."

In silence she inclined her head, and in silence the lords
of the Council followed her, the chime of their spurs rising
towards her in the confined space like a fantasy rung by
unearthly bells.

The windows of the chief bedchamber were larger than
those in the room below. As she paused in the doorway she
saw that Bothwell's bed had been drawn across the window.
The towering white clouds now massing outside it were the
only things that moved, for he himself lay so still that she
thought him dead. At the sound of her indrawn breath young
Sinclair turned reassuringly.

"He is asleep, Madam. He was asking for you but now.
Will it please your Grace to enter?"

Mary forced herself to cross the room, her eyes fixed on the man she would scarcely have recognised. His skin was drawn taut across the bones of his skull, his eye-sockets were pools of darkness on which his closed lids seemed to float, and clumsy bandages were wound turban-like about the wound which had only just missed an eye. One hand, also swathed with bandages, lay across his chest, the other arm was flung wide in a gesture of exasperated weakness that stabbed her with compunction. Then Bothwell's lips parted in a ghostly grin. Under the shadows he had been watching her.

" My lord," she said, aware of the shuffle of boots, the heavy breathing of full-fed men behind her, as if they belonged to another order of creation from the emaciated figure on the bed, " we—we are sorely grieved that you should have been brought to such extremity in our service."

" Madam," the hoarse voice whispered, " it is not so easy to kill James Hepburn——"

" Let us not talk of killing," she said quickly, thankful that he seemed to bear no grudge for the dismissal which had so nearly been the death of him. " We have come, my lords and I, to thank you for your devotion and urge you to return to Court as soon as your health permits."

" Madam, you may be sure of that," he said. " Yet . . ." he paused for breath, then went on more strongly, " I trust I need . . . not delay so long before doing you . . . some service. It was but my left hand which was stricken . . . Already I can handle a quill. Not yet, perhaps, a sword . . ."

" I am well pleased to hear it." She was still formal, well aware of the silent company at her back. " Particulars of the justice done at Jedburgh shall be brought to you for further action." She was talking fast, conscious of a contradictory tumult of emotion, glad of the impersonality of such grave words as law and justice. " I shall empower you to hold a Court to confirm what I have decreed, here at Hermitage, since you are not fit to go elsewhere. Have you a likely clerk in your service? You will need assistance yet awhile."

" My kinsman, George Sinclair, might serve."

"He has already done us good service in the kitchen."
She smiled at her small joke. "He shall have our royal
authority, to do all you may require. My lords—" she turned
regally to her silent Councillors, "can you call to mind
anything else we have to say to my lord of Bothwell?"

They shook their heads. Their faces, except Huntly's,
were indifferent, but in her odd state of heightened sensibility
she fancied that their expressionless eyes could see through her
armouring regality to the bewildering pain with which she
heard herself say that they must now take their leave.

Moray agreed at once. "It is a sorry country in which to
be benighted." He stepped forward, crooking an arm for her
to lay her fingertips upon it while he conducted her formally
to the head of the stair. As they went down, Huntly paused
for a few words with his brother-in-law, while Maitland of
Lethington, standing aside by the doorway, looked thoughtfully from Bothwell to the Queen, his slim fingers twisting the
sparse sandy beard that just covered his long chin.

During their stay at Hermitage the weather had changed
so completely that it scarcely seemed the same landscape,
unreal now in the gathering rain as the deathlike outlines of
Bothwell's bandaged head which her imagination printed on
land and sky. Her attention was so little on the track that she
let her palfrey flounder into the mire near Braidley, and she had
lost a spur when they were with difficulty extricated by Sir
Alexander. Thereafter he took the precaution of riding by her
side, while Moray and Huntly followed.

"Sir Alexander, is it possible that he should recover?" she
asked forlornly.

"Alas, Madam, who can tell?" Sir Alexander answered.
"But he himself said it was not easy to kill a Hepburn. If
your Grace is not too weary, we should ride faster now. From
the look of the sky I fear we shall have a storm before dark."

She did not greatly care. For the violence with which the
wind and rain presently beat about them matched the desolation that threatened to overwhelm her soul. Where now was

the bright promise of her marriage with Henry? Were not her dearest brother, Lord John, and her devoted secretary, David Rizzio, both gone? Was it not by her command that Bothwell had received the wounds from which he too might die? It seemed her fate to bring disaster on all those she loved. Without realising how instinctively she had included Bothwell in that company she saw the days of her life closing in upon her as relentlessly as the wind-whipped rain-squalls which walked across the hills like the grey ghosts of forgotten giants.

Huddled in their cloaks, the royal party made their way homewards as best they could, their horses plunging wretchedly through the churned mud of the narrow tracks along which Sir Alexander, now in the lead again, guided them. By the time they reached Jedburgh all were shivering, and Mary's head felt red-hot. The pain in her side was so bad that she could scarcely stand once she had been helped from her horse. Vaguely she was aware of being carried up to bed. And after that nothing had any more stability than the card houses she sometimes amused herself by building for others to blow down.

At first the pain in her side died to a dull ache. But afterwards it became so bad that she cried out. Fever blurred the outlines of day and night. The musicians played no more in the evenings, and they spread straw on the cobbles to muffle the sounds of passers-by. She vomited again and again till she was so weak that she could scarcely lift her head. As her physician tried first one remedy and then another, Mary Seton scarcely left her. It was better that others should not hear her Grace grieving less often for her sins than because she had sent the Earl of Bothwell to his death.

But the Queen had some lucid intervals. In one of these she saw her brother Moray tiptoeing about the bedchamber and collecting her jewels as confidently as if she were already dead. Her unexpected protest scarcely disconcerted him. He was quick to assure her smugly that it was his duty to make sure they did not fall into unworthy hands in any emergency.

Darnley came once, and looked at her discontentedly. They had haled him away from his hawking because she was thought to be in extremity. But she did not die, and he left next morning. She cried a little because he had stared at her with such distaste that she knew she must be looking hideous. And then sickness overwhelmed her again, and she vomited dark clots of blood which frightened her. Her legs and arms grew cold, and she could neither hear nor see those about her. Anxiously she asked that both those of the old faith and the new should pray for her. Then she made her confession and received the last rites of her Church. But her physician bandaged her limbs tightly, blistered her, and refused to believe in the appearance of death.

Mary felt as if she were being slowly dragged from the dark depths of a bottomless well. Very far away, someone was talking indignantly to her physician.

" If her Grace has been poisoned, sir, by all that is holy, I can make a good guess at the name of the man who did it. And, by God's wrath——"

" She has not been poisoned, my lord," said the physician hastily.

" Then what ails her ? "

" As a layman, my lord, it is not to be expected that you should understand these mysteries——"

" Bah ! " The sharp sound cracked like a whip. " I do not believe, sir, that you understand them either."

The faintest suggestion of laughter invaded the darkness about her like a shooting star. Incredulously, she struggled against the mortal lassitude that weighted her lids like lead. As if she were experiencing a dream in reverse, she fought to open her eyes. Someone was standing by her bedside, someone, surely, by whose bedside she herself had recently stood. Summoning all her strength, she felt the leaden lids roll back at last as she looked bemusedly into the angry eyes of the Earl of Bothwell.

CHAPTER FIFTEEN

" SO . . . you did not . . . die." Her tongue seemed so
much too big for her parched mouth that it was a
ponderous task to shape each word. And afterwards the sweat
of sheer exhaustion drenched her whole body as she wondered
whether he, like Darnley, would turn from her in distaste for
what she had become.

James Hepburn straightened himself and grinned. Thumbs
thrust through his belt and feet astride, he turned his shoulder
on the affronted physician, now gobbling like a turkey cock
because his authority had been flouted. And his triumphant
vitality glowed like sunshine.

" No, Madam. I lived. And so will you."

" Shall I, my lord? "

It was less a question than an entreaty. If she must live,
what assurance could he offer that life would be worth living?
It would be so easy to die, to surrender to the dark tide which
was tugging her away. To live would be much harder. She
could not do it alone.

Almost as if he had guessed her thought, Bothwell held out
his hand for her inspection. It was still bandaged, and, looking
up, she saw that his head was, too. " If I can cheat death so
nearly, Madam, so can you."

She smiled faintly, for his arrogance was as heartening as
aqua vitae. Her pulses began to throb against the physician's
bonds. " It may be . . ." she began.

Her fingers were no longer ready to loosen their precarious
hold on the life she still pictured as a despairing struggle against
a dark, engulfing flood. Nor was she merely holding the
unresponsive branch of the tree that had stooped over the

water in her feverish dreams. She was sustained by the cool, hard strength of a man's hand.

" It may be . . . that we can . . ."

Bothwell knelt awkwardly beside the bed. Though the Queen now seemed asleep, he did not wish to unclasp her feverish fingers. But his own injured leg had begun to throb beyond endurance. He had been borne to Jedburgh in a horse litter, breathing wrath and destruction against the Queen's murderers, to attend the emergency Council meeting at which preparations for a regency were to be discussed. Now, as he felt her slowly relax into peace, his face hardened into a determination as austere as his own hills. There should be no regency for Moray to annex with all the rest.

" My lord, I must ask you to go," insisted the physician at his elbow.

" Very well, my friend," Bothwell agreed. " But you must help me up. This business has left me as stiff as an old tree."

" Tch, tch," The physician hauled, panting, on Bothwell's uninjured arm, as Paris ran from the doorway to grasp his master round the waist. " You have been in as parlous a state as her Grace. Why are you now out of your bed ? "

Bothwell grinned. " Because I have work to do which it would be folly to leave to others." With a wink which made the physician raise his tufted eyebrows, he turned to limp out, his arm across the shoulders of his page.

The emergency Council meeting was held on 25th October, and Moray's attempt to discuss the measures which would be necessary in the event of the Queen's death provoked such caustic comments from both Bothwell and Huntly that he was forced to abandon it. And by the end of the month it was evident that they would not be required. Once the crisis of her illness had been overcome, the Queen's recovery was rapid. As soon as the physician allowed her to sit up for an hour or two Mary summoned her musicians, ate with good appetite and discussed with her ladies the material she would need for new dresses. She dictated the appropriate order to the Treasurer in Edinburgh on her second day out of bed.

"Command him to send, at the sight of this writing, twenty ells of red silk, with twenty ells of white plaiding——"

"I pray you, Madam, give me time," cried Mary Fleming. "I have not yet reached the end of the second line——"

Impatiently the Queen waited, her forefinger tapping on the little table which held her workbox. "Are you ready now?"

"Yes, Madam."

"Also four ells of black taffety, three of fine black velvet, four of small Lyons canvas, six ounces of black silk——"

"Six ounces of black silk," murmured Mary Fleming, scribbling frantically.

"Two ells of black buckram, six ounces of black stitching silk. Is there aught else we shall need, Seton?"

"We shall need black thread, Madam."

"And a pound of black thread. He is on no account to fail in this. Tell him to keep this writing as his warrant."

"It is done, Madam." Mary Fleming rubbed her aching wrist, then brought letter and quill so that the Queen might add the bold, candid signature which, in its fire and haste, was so like that of her grandfather, the fourth James, greatest and most unfortunate of all the Stewart Kings.

"Now! How are they to be made?" the Queen demanded, knuckling the wax on the folded parchment with her personal seal. "Hasten out to find a trusty messenger, dear Flem. I am somewhat thinner since my illness, so I shall be able to wear the new stomacher very well. The red silk will make a gallant show, and the black velvet for the farthingale save it from seeming gaudy. I most earnestly hope the Treasurer will not delay, or we shall never get the fitting done before we start on our progress through the Border."

"Are you fully persuaded, Madam," worried Mary Seton, "that you feel well enough to ride about the country before returning to Edinburgh? Would it not be wiser to postpone the progress until Spring? It is already November."

But the Queen shook her head till her long ruby and pearl ear-rings swung. "No, Seton, it must not be put off for one day. After so much talk of my death the sooner I am seen alive the better."

"Yes, indeed. But . . ." said Mary Seton doubtfully.

"And what is more, I shall enjoy it. I have come to love the Border country," said the Queen.

"I marvel, Madam, that you can ever bear to see it again," shuddered Mary Fleming.

"The world looks very wonderful, Flem," the Queen said gravely, "when seen through the eyes of Lazarus."

"But you will at least wait until the physician considers you fit to make such a journey," begged Mary Seton.

The Queen laughed. "It is he who recommends it. He is all for the healthful air and exercise of riding about the Border hills."

"I trust my lord of Bothwell is sufficiently recovered to go with you?" Mary Seton persisted. "I would not count on the wild men of the Marches without him to keep them in order."

"No more would I," said the Queen gaily. "Have no fear, Seton, as Lieutenant of the Border and Sheriff of Lothian, my lord of Bothwell must ride ever at my right hand."

"That will not please my lord of Moray," said Mary Fleming mischievously.

"Nor my lord of Lethington," Mary Seton retorted.

"My lord of Lethington," said Mary Fleming indignantly, "seeks but the opportunity of serving the Queen's Grace, however he may be maligned."

"Dear Flem!" said the Queen indulgently. "And now shall we settle what I am to take? Several sumpter beasts will be needed, for I must wear a different dress every day, and it is my lord of Bothwell's purpose to show me as much of the Border countryside as time permits."

"Will the King join us, Madam?" Mary Fleming wondered.

Stillness came down on the Queen like frost. But at last she said: " I have written to beg him to come. But as yet I have had no answer."

Her ladies-in-waiting exchanged significant glances. They had their own ideas regarding Darnley's silence. Ought they to warn the Queen that persistent rumour declared him to be in most diligent communication with the extremists of their faith ? But they said nothing, fearing to spoil her pleasure in the progress about the Borders on which her heart seemed set.

And yet they remained uneasy. They knew that Darnley was with his father at the Lennox mansion near Glasgow, and, as Catholics, they had heard that both he and his father were now showing a devotion to their religious duties which exceeded that of the Queen. But they were not aware of the increasing intimacy between Darnley and Sir James Balfour, whose religion varied with the expediencies of the moment, and who was unlikely to have forgotten the Protestant conspirators' plans to hang him after they had disposed of Rizzio.

Mary, too, had been vexed by Darnley's recent threats to leave the country, but she had not taken him seriously when he boasted of his assignation to meet King Philip of Spain, when his most Catholic Majesty visited the Netherlands to discuss with his terrible governor, the Duke of Alba, the latest Counter-Reformation measures against his Protestant rebels. Darnley, on the other hand, was taking himself very seriously indeed, in view of recent hints that Pope Pius might look kindly on his claim to the Crown Matrimonial of Scotland if he could bring his intransigent wife to a better understanding of her duties to her Church.

He did not, therefore, wish to accompany the Queen on the triumphal progress about the Borders which would so undesirably stress her reliance on heretics. He wrote at last to say so, with disagreeable emphasis on the levity of her behaviour.

The letter followed Mary to Kelso, where she was to spend the night of 9th November, in a merchant's house which had once been the hospice of the ruined Abbey which Henry VIII's rough wooing had so grievously despoiled. Moray, accompanied by Lethington, brought it to her in person, and watched with interest as she shrank from it as if it had been a snake.

At last, with obvious reluctance, she put out her hand. But she did not break the seal at once. Instead, she turned it this way and that, as if seeking to guess the contents from the direction: " To the Queen's Majesty," in Darnley's flamboyant scrawl. If he had refused to join her, his absence must indicate that he cared little where she went. If he had accepted, would she be able to bear it? The seal crackled as she unfolded the single sheet. Then his angry words seemed to leap at her, words so vindictive that their assault was as bewildering as that of a swarm of wasps.

She crushed the letter between her hands and threw it into the heart of the fire. The flames licked it to ash in an instant. It was gone. But the pain remained. She was shaking from head to foot now, and the tears she could not check ran between her fingers as she pressed her palms against her eyes. Darnley hated her. So much was evident. But as his wife she was bound to him for the rest of her life. For the rest of a life that might last fifty years.

" I cannot bear it! I had rather kill myself! "

She did not realise that she had spoken aloud till Moray's shocked voice answered her: " Why Madam, do not talk of such extremities. Let us journey pleasantly together and leave our troubles behind. Afterwards we must see what can be done."

She let her hands fall into her lap. " There is nothing . . ."

" Do not be too sure of that," said Lethington pleasantly. He was delighted that Darnley should have written in such an alienating strain. Had he accepted his wife's invitation it might not have been possible to avoid the reconciliation which the Queen would no doubt consider her duty. But now the young fool might well, if fortune served, have thrown all chance of that away.

Mary was still staring into the flames which had consumed Darnley's letter but failed to lay its ghost. It fluttered there as a mere blackened wisp, seared with occasional livid strokes, in the midst of the burning logs. When she spoke at last, it was without turning her head or raising her voice.

" I pray you, my lords, to leave us."

Mary Fleming came to kneel beside her mistress, but Mary Seton, uncertain for once, hung back. Taking the Queen's hand in hers, Flem laid it against her cheek.

" Sweet Madam," she said softly, " I beg you not to grieve. What's done cannot be mended. What's to come, may be."

" Dear Flem," said the Queen tonelessly. " Would that I could believe you."

" Why, then Madam, will you not try? You know that we all love you. We break our hearts at the sight of your grief. While we are young, life must hold better things——"

" No, Flem. I am bound until I die to a man who has come to hate me. How can you ask me to be gay when I look ahead? "

" Oh, my sweet mistress," Mary Fleming cried, " are we not bidden to take no thought for the morrow? Surely then it is a sin to look so far down the years? Is it not our duty to enjoy the pleasures of each day rather than to seek to bear the burdens of the next ? "

For the first time the Queen smiled, though less because of what Flem had said, than because her joy in being loved was in some subtle way contagious. " I had not thought to hear you in the pulpit, Flem," she said.

" I would mount the gibbet, sweet Madam, if it would lighten your heart," said Mary Fleming. " I pray you, then, consider my little sermon and ride out with us to-morrow as we planned. Let us be like the school-children and leave our sorrows behind with our books . . ."

" I will try——"

" There speaks my sovereign lady. Now, which of your new dresses will it please you to wear first? How fortunate it is that the mild weather still holds. But now that the days are darker, you must shine before the people like the sun in splendour. Will you wear your riding habit of black and gold or the other in crimson, with the white Highland mantle and the red hat with the red and yellow feathers? "

" I believe I will wear the black——"

" Yet the crimson is the richer——"

" That is true . . ."

Mary Fleming felt the cloud lighten a little, as the Queen's innocent pleasure in elegance broke through the cloud of her despair.

" If I am to wear the crimson, word must be sent to the stables to see that my palfrey's trappings are changed accordingly. But we must also take the purple velvet trappings for great occasions."

As she reached out for the little silver handbell to summon a page, Mary Fleming relaxed. Once her Grace began to talk of clothes, she knew that the battle had been won.

Next morning Bothwell ousted the servant whose business it was to help the Queen into the saddle, taking her crimson-shod foot on his own hand. At his grunt of pain she looked down in compunction.

" My lord, I had quite forgot your injury."

" So had I," said Bothwell ruefully. " It is no matter. Is the stirrup to your liking? We have some distance to ride."

" I am ready to ride to the world's end," she assured him.

He turned from her abruptly, shouting for his own horse. When it was brought, she was surprised to find it little bigger than her own palfrey, and he answered her glance of inquiry as they moved off down the street.

" We use such beasts in Liddesdale," he explained, " because they fare better among the mosses than such great chargers as the one Moray rides to-day. Where it would sink like a stone mine would leap like a stag."

She nodded. "That I can understand. But tell me, my lord, can you arrange for us to ride to the very Border line? I have a fancy to look across it into my cousin's kingdom, which may yet be mine."

Bothwell grinned understandingly. "Why not?" he said. "I will speak to the Deputy-Governor of Berwick and invite him to meet us at the Bound Road."

The progress followed its appointed course. The Queen spent two nights as the guest of Lord Home, Warden of the East Marches, at Home Castle, stopped for the next night at Cowdenknows, then rode on by Langton to Wedderburn. As she rested there that evening Bothwell came to tell her that all arrangements had been made for her to ride to the Bound Road the following morning. Delighted, the Queen commanded her ladies to prepare her most striking habit of royal purple and gold, with as many jewels as they could contrive to hang about her, with purple trappings for her white palfrey. The distinguished company summoned to escort her included Moray, Lethington, Huntly, Bothwell and Lord Home, with that industrious diplomat, James Melville, to meet the English contingent, headed by Sir John Forster, Deputy Governor of Berwick, on the Border line.

All the Queen's melancholy had disappeared as she sat among her ladies and gentlemen, sparkling with mischievous delight at an encounter which would almost certainly infuriate the Queen of England. In the distance, veiled by the autumn mist from the sea, lay the English hills among which her grandfather had died on Flodden Field. Between them rose the menacing fortifications of Berwick. Had that town changed hands for the last time, she wondered, while she watched the puffballs of white smoke leap from the walls as the artillery fired the royal salute which Sir John had ordered in compliment to the Scottish Queen. Or might it one day be part of her dominions yet again?

It was an elegant, international occasion. But Sir John Forster's quarrelsome stallion resented the close presence of so many strangers. As the governor, cap in hand, was talking to the Queen, it reared up with an angry squeal, striking out so suddenly that one hoof grazed the Queen's leg before its rider could regain control. In the subsequent confusion, horses whirled and men shouted, hands closing on sword-hilts as Sir John flung himself in consternation from the saddle and rushed to the Queen's side. Scots and English glared at each other and the Queen gasped, white with pain. But her clear voice controlled the situation.

"Do not disturb yourself, Sir John. It was an accident by which no harm has been done."

"Madam," stammered Sir John Forster, "I would have died rather than injure you."

"I know it well," said the Queen. "I beg you will give the matter no further thought. We thank you heartily for your honourable reception. But since we have still some distance to go we must now take our leave."

"We had hoped," said Sir John uneasily, "that you would have remained longer."

"I wish it had been possible," said Mary graciously. "Pray commend me to the Queen of England, my good sister, if you care to inform her Majesty of how we have presumed on her friendship. My people will give you largesse for the gunners. Farewell, Sir John . . ."

"It was a shrewd blow, Madam," said Bothwell, looking at her with new respect as they trotted out of earshot of the English contingent.

She flushed at his evident admiration. "Indeed, I thought it had broken my leg."

"Yet you did not flinch."

"I should hope not, my lord," she rebuked him gaily.

"But you cannot ride as far as Coldingham to-night."

"As to that, we shall see."

But she grew stiffer as the bruise came out, and by the

end of the day she was thankful to break the journey again at Home Castle. Next day she was able to continue the return journey. The progress was over, and the weather was breaking. In other circumstances she would have been quite content, for Craigmillar Castle, near Edinburgh, was one of her favourite residences in Scotland. But now she was sad.

"Alas, my lord of Bothwell," she said, turning her head on her shoulder for a last glimpse of the veiled Border hills, "how soon all pleasant things end."

"Your Grace looks the better for the journey," Bothwell said.

"And so do you, my lord. We were a pair of sorry folk a month since."

"Madam, we were indeed."

"It was a strange business," she said thoughtfully.

He nodded without speaking.

Could it have been by mere chance, she wondered, as they rode on in silence, that first one and then the other had stood at the very gates of death? His arrogance had often angered her, but it was with the same arrogance that he had persuaded her to live. Did he also feel that, whether he wished it or not, for the rest of their lives they could never be quite indifferent? "When we are old," she said at last, only half laughing, "perhaps it will mean something that our deaths so nearly came on the same day."

"Do not talk of growing old," he said abruptly. "I do not care to think of it."

"For you or for me?"

"For either."

"I wonder why?" She smiled up at him, demanding compliments as a child asks for sweetmeats. But he felt awkwardly at a loss. His tongue had none of the courtier's art. "For such speculation," he mumbled, "you should call on Lethington's quick wits."

"No," she said. "I have heard enough pretty speeches from those who do not mean them. I would sooner have the truth, for once, my lord of Bothwell."

"That I will always try to give you, Madam," he said sombrely, as Moray cantered up to join them.

At Craigmillar, on the day after her return, the Queen held a Court to receive the first of the foreign guests invited for the Prince's christening in less than a month's time. The Comte de Brienne had come to represent Charles IX of France as godfather of the heir of Scotland, and with his arrival the great day loomed suddenly near.

But Darnley's unexpected appearance at Craigmillar brought a reminder of another sort. He was in a vile temper, made no inquiries about his wife's health, and gloomed about the Castle, speaking to nobody, for days. But one morning, suddenly and without ceremony, he burst into the Queen's presence chamber, ignoring her assembled Council as he beat with clenched fists on the massive table-top.

"Are you aware, Madam, that the Queen of England proposes to offer me a deliberate insult?"

The Queen sighed. "Surely not, my lord?"

"She does, and I believe you know it," said Darnley offensively. "I am creditably informed that she is instructing her ambassador to deny me the royal title in the country whose Queen is my wife, at the christening ceremony of my own son."

"If this be true," said the Queen wretchedly, "I must protest——"

"*If* it be true!" railed Darnley. "*If* it be true, indeed. Madam, do you call me a liar?"

The insult drained all colour from her face. But her voice was steady. "My lord, to say it is possible for a man to be mistaken is scarcely to call him a liar."

"I am not mistaken. Ask any of your chosen company," cried Darnley, with a wild, disdainful gesture towards the men who had once been his friends. "But I tell you this.

If I am to be so treated by a servant of the Queen of England, I will not present myself to receive his insults. You may have as splendid a ceremony as you wish, Madam. But I shall not be there."

He turned, without word of farewell, and a hollow silence followed the explosive violence of the slammed door. Moray sighed gustily, Bothwell raised an eyebrow at Huntly, and Lethington surveyed the Queen sidelong as she cried in despair:

"Would God, my lords, I had died at Jedburgh!"

"Tch, tch," said Moray reprovingly. "Never say such a thing, Madam." He cleared his throat. "You will recall that I forecast no success from your marriage. Be that as it may, we must decide what now to do about it."

"Madam," said Lethington quietly, "we have discussed this matter much between ourselves of late, since the King's ingratitude to you for the honour done him has been so evident and continuing every day from evil to worse. And we have recently bound ourselves not to obey him in anything, but only your Grace. What is more, we are ready to seek means now to make divorcement between your Grace and the King."

She looked at him wearily. The rules of her Church laid down that no marriage, once entered into, might be broken. But she knew that this, of all its rules, was the one most often evaded. It was so easy to discover belated grounds of impediment; affinity or kinship which had been overlooked. Until recently, she would not have considered such a possibility. But now—she had been so battered by Darnley's violence, chilled by his neglect, and revolted by his debauchery that she was ready to seek any means of escape. But what effect would a divorce have on her son's position?

"It could only be entertained," she said uncertainly, "if such a divorce were lawful and did not prejudice my son's right to succession, whether here or to the throne of England. Otherwise, I assure you, my lords, that I would rather endure all torments and abide whatever perils my marriage may bring."

"Surely, Madam," said Bothwell, in the harsh impatient

voice which offered the short shrift of the battlefield to the
circumlocutions of the Council chamber, " a divorce would
prove no barrier to the Prince's succession? My own case was
somewhat the same. My parents were divorced, yet I
inherited."

She looked at him in silence, startled by the comparison.
It was Moray who answered, softly and thoughtfully, as he
looked from the Queen to her impetuous subject.

" Why yes, indeed, my lord of Bothwell, that is very true,"
he said. " And much comfort may be taken from it."

In the silence that followed the shape of things to come
seemed almost visibly to stir and move.

CHAPTER SIXTEEN

MORAY'S narrowed eyes glanced from the Queen to
Bothwell, then flickered sharply back to Maitland of
Lethington as his own name was spoken.

" Though my lord of Moray, here present, is little less
scrupulous for a Protestant than your Grace is for a Papist,
I am assured he will look through his fingers at such doings
and say nothing . . ."

" Eh, what's this? " Moray demanded.

" I meant that neither her Grace's religious scruples nor
yours need hinder such a divorce as we have been discussing,"
said Lethington in his high, ironic voice.

" Quite so," said Moray, huffily uncertain, as usual,
whether Lethington, in his waspish way, were making fun
of him.

" I would sooner let the matter rest," said the Queen
wearily, " than that you should do anything to lay any spot
on my honour or conscience. You may seek to do me service and
yet act to my hurt and displeasure."

" Madam," said Lethington, " let us guide this matter
for you among us. I can promise your Grace that nothing
but good will come of it and all be approved by Parliament.
We will bind ourselves to obey you in all things where your
commands shall happen to conflict with those given by the
King."

She put her hand to her head in a distraught little gesture.
" There let the matter rest, then," she said. " I can listen to
no more at present."

Lethington bowed his obedience, well satisfied with the
Queen's reception of his proposal. And next day a bond was
drawn up by Sir James Balfour, who was once more dancing
attendance on the Queen and her Council. Thanks to his
diplomatic dexterity, he was now enjoying the confidence of
both parties and able to come and go between them while he
decided on which he should finally rely. Before reporting to
Darnley in Glasgow, therefore, he was interested to witness
the Councillors' signature to the document which seemed
superficially so respectable yet offered an implicit suggestion
of violence. Evidence of the Queen's confidential association
with such notorious heretics as Lethington, Argyll, Huntly and
Bothwell, must, he believed, discredit her in Rome. It might
even justify her inclusion in the tentative proposals for the
elimination of the refractory elements in Scotland recently
recommended to the Pope by the affronted Bishop of Mondivi,
who had been prevented from performing his duties as
Papal nuncio by the Queen's refusal to receive him.

At Craigmillar the Queen was engrossed in preparations
for the royal christening at Stirling, though the task of ordering
new and splendid outfits for all those concerned had lost some
of its usual delight. She could not forget that if Darnley carried
out his threat and refused to appear, his absence would constitute a public insult both to her and to the son he had already
acknowledged as his own.

Bothwell, meanwhile, was preparing to leave Craigmillar.
As her Lieutenant, he had plenty to do before the 17th of

December, and organisation was work he usually enjoyed. It struck him, as he took his leave, that she lacked something of the fire and spirit he had appreciated as they rode through the Border country. But it did not occur to him to suppose that her distress might have anything to do with him, even though, as he knelt to kiss her hand, it lay as inert on his hard, dry palm, as a small frozen bird.

"You must go so soon to Stirling, my lord?"

"I have much to arrange for the christening, Madam."

"You will not forget to be fitted for your new suit among so many other concerns?"

He grinned at her. "Madam, I am, they say, a vain man. Has your Grace not observed it?"

She laughed. "I have. But I did not think you knew it."

"My good friends," said Bothwell dryly, "lose no chance of pointing out my faults." He shrugged. "My shoulders are broad enough to bear such burdens."

His voice was indifferent, his mind already busy with the problems awaiting him. She knew it, but because both his harshness and his strength were so astringently comforting she was reluctant to let him go.

"We have seen your lady wife less often at Court than formerly," she said. "Is she not well?"

"She is well enough, I believe, Madam. But since you were graciously pleased to restore my lands in Haddington she has been much occupied with the plenishing. She cannot rest till everything is to her mind."

"But she does not feel that you neglect her for your duties at Court?"

Bothwell shook his head. "No, Madam. I doubt if she marks it greatly whether I come or go."

The Queen raised her delicate eyebrows. "Indeed?"

He was aware that the news had pleased her. But the shadowed lids fell over her brown eyes as if she sought refuge from his blue glare.

" We will detain you no longer, my lord," she said hastily. " We shall not meet till the eve of the christening. I shall go to Holyroodhouse, then on to Stirling, to greet the Earl of Bedford when he arrives from England. I wish we had news of Savoy's ambassador. It will be a sore affront if Moretta does not arrive in time to represent his master. The Duke is one of the Prince's godparents."

" As to the ceremony, I know nothing," said Bothwell indifferently. The Queen's lips twitched. In spite of her distress it amused her to see a man with Bothwell's reputation for recklessness so nicely observant of the distinctions of the new faith.

But she herself had no intention of being slavishly subservient to the technicalities of the old as she sent for the Archbishop of St Andrews, head of the house of Hamilton in the absence of the Duke of Chatelherault, asking him to bring the Bishops of Dunkeld and Dunblane to go through the order of service with her. It was, of course, to be according to the Roman rite, but to the Archbishop's indignation the Queen refused either to allow the traditional ceremony of the spittle or to give her reasons for her decision till the affronted cleric had retired.

Afterwards she was more candid with Mary Fleming. " I'll have no pocky priest spitting in my child's mouth," she whispered, and Mary Fleming giggled with delight. For the Archbishop's indignation at the fee charged by the Milanese doctor who had treated him for the pox was better known at Court than his lordship supposed.

On the 7th of December she reluctantly declared her intention of leaving Craigmillar. She liked the place, both because of its high, open situation between the Pentland Hills and Duddingston Loch, and because French was to be heard as often as Scots in the street of the adjacent hamlet which had been nicknamed 'little France' on account of the number of her French craftsmen housed there. But she felt she must return to Holyroodhouse. However wrong things had gone between them, it was Darnley's birthday, and if he should wish to make amends, she must be at hand.

But he did not appear at sad Holyroodhouse, either on his own birthday or on hers, next day, and in spite of all her attendants could offer in the way of celebration, it was the unhappiest she had ever spent. Darnley was now twenty, and she was twenty-four. In twelve months' time she would have reached her full majority, and be free not only to initiate what legislation she wished but to revoke all legislation carried out by her ministers on her behalf during her minority. But the prospect brought no comfort.

She was lonelier now than she had ever been. Always before, there had been someone to whom she could turn. In France there had been her uncles, especially the Cardinal, who had never failed her when she needed advice and would not trouble poor Francis for it. And at first, when she came to Scotland, she had taken it for granted that she could trust the brother she had so gladly made Earl of Moray. She knew better now. There had been others who flattered her pleasantly; Maitland of Lethington, Master Melville, Sir James Balfour, George Buchanan, even Henry, her husband. They had all spoken her fair. But Darnley had wanted only to be King of Scots. Sir James Balfour was fickle as a weathercock in a gale. Those she most loved were dead. As she remembered her dearest brother, Lord John of Coldingham, and David Rizzio, who had been such a faithful servant, the full force of her inherited melancholy returned with its haunting refrain: must those she loved always die?

No, not all. She shied away from the thought as a horse shies at a half-seen figure in the dusk, then swung back to face it with the courage which was as much part of her inheritance as the extremes of gaiety and despair. He himself had said, it was not easy to kill James Hepburn. But what was James Hepburn to her? There was nobody to whom she could confide that secret, the knowledge of the smouldering fire which must destroy them both if ever it burst into flame.

No one must know. But sometimes, since she had lain ill at Jedburgh, she fancied that Mary Seton guessed.

On the 10th of December, she set out with all her Court for Stirling, where Bothwell waited on her to make his report in the great hall of the Castle after supper. She was tired, less on account of the journey, which, as usual, she had enjoyed, than because of the conflicting reports already brought to her by officials who seemed more anxious to discredit each other than to get the work done.

" My lord of Bothwell, can the preparations ever be made in time? "

" Why not, Madam? I have no doubt of it." His voice was almost amused, his assurance as welcome as the feeling of rock underfoot to a traveller sunk in a quicksand. Hope returned to her as he made his report, for all, it seemed, was now ready for the reception of the distinguished foreigners expected for the christening. A sufficient force had been assembled, Bothwell declared, to ensure the safety of the Queen and the Prince. The food and wine for the banquets were the concern of others, the masques to follow them would be devised by the Frenchman, Bastian, and the master gunner would see to the firework display with which the rejoicings were to conclude. It was to be of prodigious and expensive magnificence, Bothwell assured her. The honours at table were to be done by Huntly as carver, Moray as cupbearer, and himself as sewer or taster of the dishes set before her Grace.

She smiled at that. It seemed scarcely likely that any of her subjects would try to poison her. The office was a survival of more troubled times. " All seems most ably arranged, my lord, as ever, when you have the ordering of affairs."

" I thank your Grace," said Bothwell rather wearily. For it had been an exasperating, thankless business. He would rather have organised half a dozen campaigns for such men as his own Borderers, whom he could curse into efficiency, than have to pick his way, as delicately as a man dancing among eggs, between the prejudices of the Scottish nobles, though these were as nothing, he knew well, besides those of the arrogant foreigners who would presently appear.

" Is there something else, my lord ? "

Bothwell nodded. " I understand that both the French and English ambassadors have instructions to petition your Grace to pardon those lords still in exile for the murder of Seigneur Davie, of whom my lord of Morton is the chief."

Mary sighed. " I feared as much. We will consider it when we must, my lord. I will release you now, since you will wish to return home so that you may escort your good lady to Stirling for the ceremony itself."

" I thank you, Madam." His voice was toneless, and as he knelt to take his leave Mary fancied that the strong lines about his mouth had deepened. A scrap of gossip drifted through her mind. On what grounds, she wondered, had one of her ladies so confidently assured the other that Lady Jean and my lord of Bothwell were already estranged ?

The distinguished guests were all arriving now. James Melville, with a party of Lowland gentlemen, met the Earl of Bedford at the Border and escorted him first to his lodgings in the pleasant Edinburgh suburb of Kirk o' Field, then on to Stirling which the Earl entered, at the head of eighty English knights and gentlemen, on the 14th of December. The Queen held a Court to welcome him, receiving from his hands the superb silver font, valued at over a thousand pounds, which Queen Elizabeth had sent for her godson's baptism. The French King's representative, the Comte de Brienne, had already been in Scotland for some time, but it now seemed that M. du Croc, the kindly French ambassador, who had been working so earnestly for the reconciliation of Mary and Darnley, would have to act as proxy for the Duke of Savoy's ambassador, who had still not arrived. The Papal nuncio had further distracted the Queen by announcing that he would be delighted to attend, but in the circumstances she thought it better to advise him for his own safety to stay away. The decision would be entered against her at Rome, she knew, but the knowledge did not shake her. There would be quite enough difficulty over the service as it was.

For all the Scottish lords pledged to the new faith had declined to come further than the chapel doorway, and in spite of anything that M. du Croc could say, Darnley had categorically refused to appear at all unless he could be assured that the English ambassador would defy Queen Elizabeth and address him as King of Scots.

Since this was not to be expected, the procession set off without him, between the two ranks of nobles bearing tapers who lined the way from the Prince's bedchamber to the Chapel Royal. The Queen came first, walking with the French Ambassador, who carried the Prince, followed by the Earl of Athol bearing the christening taper, the Earl of Eglinton with the salt, Lord Sempill with the chrism, and the Countess of Argyll representing Queen Elizabeth. Through the Chapel doorway the Latin chanting of the choristers and the sharp subtlety of incense assaulted the waiting ranks of nonconforming noblemen outside.

The absence of Darnley, inevitably noticed by all, was publicly remarked upon by none. Mary knew he was actually in Stirling and had confidently expected that he would at least join them for supper, or perhaps for the revels which followed. But the splendid meal, the dancing and the masque, went by, and still he did not come.

Next day the company was entertained by a wild bull hunt in the great park, watched by the ladies from a safe distance. On Thursday a banquet was followed by the masque for which the Latin verses composed by the Queen's tutor, George Buchanan, were sung by a choir of maidens. Unfortunately Bastian's French contingent of satyrs got somewhat out of hand during these proceedings, wagging their fork-tailed rumps at the English guests in a way which inevitably recalled the old French gibe about the demoniac tails of the English soldiers at Crécy and Agincourt. Last of all came the fireworks, a splendid, spouting, sizzling waterfall of light and colour which delighted the guests assembled on the Castle battlements, their faces bleached by the glare, their eyes and mouths dark circles of astonishment, like caricatures scrawled by a child.

It was all over at last, the christening, the courtesies, the banquets, the dancing and the *feux de joie*. And then, just before her guests began to take their leave, the Queen brought herself to make the announcement for which everyone had been waiting. With the exception of the three men who had actually threatened her person, the lords exiled after the murder of Rizzio were now free to return to Scotland.

The news pleased many people, alarmed some, and threw Darnley, still skulking in his rooms, into an utter panic. Of all the lords involved in the conspiracy which he had belatedly betrayed, he dreaded the return of his Douglas kinsmen most. Others might forgive the double part he had played. The Douglases, led by Morton, never would. Once Morton was back in Scotland, Darnley babbled to anyone who would listen, his life hung on a fraying thread. If the Queen, who must know that, pardoned his Douglas kinsfolk, it could only mean that she had no further use for him. She had turned to the heretics for support and he must look elsewhere for safety. He dared remain in Stirling no longer. Any moment, he assured his incredulous servants, might be his last. Feverish and distraught, ready to draw his dagger at a mouse's scuffle or the creak of an ill-oiled shutter, he left Stirling on Christmas Eve, without saying farewell or giving any indication of his intentions, though Mary, well aware of his father's hostile influence, could guess where he had gone.

The Court spent Christmas quietly at Stirling, and Mary was glad of the respite from both national and international diplomacy. The Earl of Bedford had gone to spend a few days in Fife with Moray before starting south, Lethington was preoccupied with arrangements for his marriage to Mary Fleming which was to take place on Twelfth Night, Bothwell and Huntly had taken leave to escort their wives home from

Stirling, and she was free to spend more time than usual in the Prince's apartments.

But once Christmas itself was over, she was restless again, longing for the outdoor exercise which always did her more good than any medicine. When Lord Drummond spoke of the excellent hunting he could offer in Perthshire, she accepted his invitation with delight. Bothwell and Huntly returned on the day after Christmas to find the Queen ready to set out for Drummond Castle, excited by the prospect of good sport in the mist-hung glens, but also aware of the chime of memories that haunted them for her race.

" My grandfather often came to Castle Drummond," she told Bothwell as he rode beside her under the archway and down the cobbled slope from Stirling Castle. " You know the story of the three Drummond sisters who were poisoned? They all died. But it was Margaret King James loved."

" I had heard of it," Bothwell said. " King James was a poet, was he not? "

" No, that was the first James. And yet we are all poets, more or less."

He looked surprised. " Do you also write verses, Madam? "

She laughed. It was a relief to find a man who did not seek to flatter her. " Oh, yes. There are many things which will not permit themselves to be said otherwise."

He pondered. " That I can understand. But I have not the way of it myself."

Checking a smile, she said: " I had not thought it likely. But you can believe that any poet must be haunted by the old tale of the King who loved unwisely, and the lady who died for his love? "

" I believe you to be most truly stricken by their story, Madam," said Bothwell candidly. " But I have no patience with the caterwaulings of those who do not care a jot for those they sing of. Love should be fierce and strong——"

" And true? "

" And true, if truth exists in love."

" How can you doubt it? " she asked.

" I have had good reason to doubt, Madam."

" Yourself, or others? "

" Both, Madam, heaven help me," James Hepburn said gravely.

" But, my lord—" Mary began. Then at the sound of a galloping horse behind them, her palfrey threw up its head and pranced, as the Earl of Huntly drew rein beside them with a gay greeting. And when they sp   , again it was of lesser things.

But the story of James and Margaret haunted her as they arrived at Castle Drummond. Would the fourth James, her own legendary grandfather, have married a commoner if she had lived? And if they had been happy together, need he ever have died at Flodden? Perhaps it was here, in this very Castle, that the story of Scotland had turned towards the shadows. They called him, after the Bruce, the greatest King Scotland had ever known. Surely he would have been still greater with Margaret Drummond as his Queen?

All that evening such questions seemed to echo through the music of the fiddlers who sawed so diligently in the minstrels' gallery while their betters ate in the great hall. As Mary grew drowsy in the warmth of the logs piled on the hearth, she could fancy that two figures stood beyond the dancers, hand-in-hand in the window embrasure, as if they must presently step out into the night. And when, later, she stood herself by the window of her bedchamber, the heartbreaking memory of Margaret's words seemed to drift up to her from the courtyard below, as if her own sorrow had mysteriously attuned her heart to an earlier passion and despair.

" *God speed you, dearest Lord. And come again. For if you did not . . . I think that I should die . . .*"

The words rang in her ears as she fell asleep. She woke, as if returning from an infinite distance, to pale winter sunshine, the hubbub of hunt servants and the whimper of hounds in the courtyard below. As the cavalcade set forth the last wreaths of mist were shredding away from the surrounding peaks. Her host rode on one side of her, Bothwell on the other, and though her face seemed almost luminous in its exaltation, its joy was less that of an earthly woman than the moonshine people of the shee. And Mary Seton, fearing she knew not what, crossed herself as she watched.

"We shall have a good day, Madam," said Lord Drummond, glancing approvingly towards the sky. "It will be my privilege to escort your Grace . . ."

But in such a countryside, with hounds in full cry and riders going pell-mell after them, it was not easy for riders to maintain touch with each other. The Queen, that morning, wore a black and scarlet habit which made her easy to distinguish, as she flashed in and out of the trees. But having noted the fact, Lord Drummond was deceived by it. After his horse had come down and thrown him, he remounted and rode bemusedly after a distant flash of black and scarlet, without realising that the wife of one of the local lairds had happened to choose the same colours as the Queen.

So it came about that when the Queen's horse went lame, only Bothwell was with her. They had checked their horses after a long gallop, and were pacing side by side, talking as they often did, in French, when her palfrey faltered. Bothwell swung himself to the ground at her exclamation of concern, and ran his hand over the trembling beast's fetlock. After his inspection, he stood up, shaking his head.

"He can carry you no further to-day, Madam. I had best send back to Drummond for another beast."

"If you shout loudly enough, my lord," she said anxiously, "perhaps someone will hear you and come back to us. If I change horses we may yet overtake the hunt."

Bothwell nodded sympathetically. But it was evident that the hunt had already left them far behind. They were alone in an unknown glen, with the melting snow churned into mud by scores of passing hooves, and the heather dripping in the sunshine as it overhung a shallow cave among the rocks.

" I doubt it, Madam," he said.

" Then I must dismount," she said, with hasty compunction, " and give my poor beast a chance to rest while you seek help."

She held out her hands for him to lift her down. How light she was, Bothwell thought, and yet, as he set her on her feet, her face was only a little lower than his. With the reins of his own beast over his arm, his hands still on her waist, he looked at her gravely. Her chin was lifted, her eyes on the far distance.

" There is the huntsman's horn . . . they are not yet so very far . . . if you were to call . . ."

" Do you wish me to call, Madam? " said Bothwell softly.

Slowly, she turned to him, amazed. She seemed to see him for the first time, so that every line that seared his weathered face, every curve of the lips now touched with such unexpected urgency, were the landmarks of an undiscovered country, dangerous as the whirlpool-guarded legendary territory of the Land-under-Wave that the Gaelic singers also called the Land of Heart's Desire. A lifetime's training urged her to resist, to repel him, to seek refuge in her royal destiny. But against such a warning rose the fierce wild blood of her race, pounding its refusal to be for ever denied. The hunting-horn sounded again, faint and far now among the dripping glens.

" Do you wish me to call? " said Bothwell gravely. She was still free to go. But after that moment, she might never be free again.

" I . . . do not know . . ." she said, in a high, strange voice. She felt his arms go round her, his lips move across her face. Before her eyes closed, she was aware of his, very close, very blue, still mocking, as if he too were well aware of, yet defied their darkling destiny.

" My dearest heart," she heard him say harshly, " have you not always known? "

CHAPTER SEVENTEEN

THE flurries of snow against the leaded panes were soft as the touch of children's fingertips, less a sound than a blurring of the silence in the quiet room in which the Queen had asked to be left alone while she wrote Latin verses for Master George Buchanan. Since she always said that she could never concentrate with others present, her request now occasioned no surprise. Mary Seton, tiptoeing in from time to time to make sure that the fire had not gone out, saw that her mistress was indeed writing verses, and was glad of it. It would do her Grace good to forget the recent news from Glasgow of the King's grave illness. She only hoped that her Grace's own health would not suffer because she had so promptly sent her personal physician to attend him.

Mary was writing verses, indeed, but in French, and not for the eyes of Master George Buchanan. She had taken up her quill with the intention of completing the classical exercise he had set her, but found herself writing, without conscious anticipation, words whose importunity had taken her unaware, as if all the tumultuous emotions of recent weeks had focused themselves on the point of her quill, to stream out with an urgency she could not check and barely control. Between the desolate hushing of the snow, the companionable snap and crackle of the flames, flowed the tide of words, pulsing like arterial blood, importunate as the petition of a stricken soul.

> " *O Dieux, ayez de moi compassion,*
> *Et m'enseignez quelle preuve certain*
> *Je puis donner qui ne lui semble vain*
> *De mon amour et ferme affection* . . ."

Rasping against the rough surface of the paper, her quill

spattered gouts of ink across it every now and then as her impatience drove it. Because she was the Queen, because she was a married woman, by such means alone could she find, for a few moments, peace. For such a luxury was only permissible when, as now, she had an excuse for solitude, a fire into which she might throw the verses which even he must never read.

That day they had spent together in the Perthshire glen now seemed alternately as remote as Paradise and as close as her own heart. Since it had been unforgettable, why had he been so sure that afterwards she would wish to forget? Was he mocking her? Was he defending her or himself from the fierce pain of separation? Why did he think she would find such a price too high? And how could she convince him of the contrary? She was the Queen. She must do nothing which would provide her enemies with the chance for which they were waiting, nothing which would damage her son's right either to the Scottish or the English throne. She must maintain before the world the smooth and passionless composure that her position demanded.

But the strain would break her unless, every now and then, she could break down the barrier between her outward and her inmost self, cast aside subterfuge and dissimulation like irksome shoes, and move barefoot across the asphodel meadows like any landless maiden, whose head bore no heavier burden than a wreath of flowers. How gladly she would give up everything she most cherished, all she had ever possessed.

" *Entre ses mains, et en son plein pouvoir*
Je mets mon fils, mon honneur, et ma vie,
Mon pays, mes subjects, mon âme assujettie,
Est tout à lui . . ."

As the latch clicked she whisked the pages over, spreading her arm, in its wide velvet sleeve, across them. Chin cupped on hand, she began to scrawl on the back of the uppermost sheet.

" Madam, surely you have worked long enough for Master Buchanan⁇ " asked Mary Seton anxiously.

" How often must I tell you, Seton," said the Queen in sudden fury, " that I will not be interrupted? "

Her startled lady-in-waiting recoiled.

" I ask your Grace's pardon, but it is an hour since I came to see if you would not take supper. It is long after eight o'clock."

" I do not care if it is midnight. Do not come in again."

" As your Grace pleases."

Much disturbed, Mary Seton retired, and the Queen drew her verses from their concealment. How could he still be uncertain of her devotion?

> "*. . . vous doutez de ma ferme constance,*
> *O mon seul bien et mon seul espérance . . .*"

But she could not go on. Mary Seton's stricken face seemed to rise between her and the page. She had lately learned so much of the pain of loving that the knowledge of having sorely hurt her faithful Seton was sufficient to keep her from writing another word.

Tossing down her quill, she picked up the scrawled sheets and read the verses through. Only an echo of the peace that had come to her as she wrote now remained, and yet she was reluctant to put them in the fire. They had come nearer to the truth than anything she had so far written. She would like to be able to read them again. On an impulse, she tucked them within the tooled leather carrying-case of a book of devotions till she could find a safer hiding place, then seized the silver handbell and shook it till a breathless page came running.

" Send Mistress Seton to me," she commanded.

" At once, your Grace."

But when the boy was gone, she took her head in her hands, aware of the world from which she had briefly escaped as a sufferer from frostbite is aware of the agony of returning circulation in a numbed limb. How was her daily life to be endured? And what would she do if her unreasoning anger had driven gentle Seton from her?

But a flurry of running feet told her that she had not yet been abandoned. Mary Seton's arms were about her, her lips on her hair, her warm, loyal, unresentful affection sharpening her own self-reproach.

"My dear Seton, I do not know what came over me. Forgive me for my harsh words."

"Oh, dearest Madam, there is nothing to forgive. We all know your anxieties. Is it to be wondered at that you should sometimes speak sharply?"

Weeping, the Queen shook her head and clung to the kind hands that sought only to comfort her. "It is wicked to take advantage of your loving patience. If I drive you from me I shall be well served."

"Nothing you could ever say, Madam, would do that," said Mary Seton. "Dry your tears, put away these dull exercises, and let us plan what we shall wear for Flem's wedding on Twelfth Night."

"Oh, happy Flem!"

"What, Madam? To marry Lethington?"

"To love and be so beloved," said the Queen, her voice wild with despair.

Mary Seton nodded. She had long known that at the core of her Grace's distress was the ruin of her marriage. And yet, poor lady, how could she have saved it?"

"I am perplexed by the lack of news from Glasgow," said the Queen presently. "The physician must surely have arrived by now. Send off another messenger, Seton. Tell him to ride without delay and bring me word again."

"I will, Madam. But I believe that if there had been news of moment, he would have seen we had it."

The Queen sat through supper like someone in a dream who cannot bear the thought of waking. As she listened to Mary Fleming's delighted tale of her plans for a married life which would still permit her to wait upon her sweet mistress, the verses she had been obliged to leave unfinished still echoed in her mind.

" Is it not fortunate that my dearest William also seeks only to serve your Grace? "

" Fortunate indeed, dear Flem." (" *O mon seul bien et mon seul espérance* . . .") How the words chimed still. It was torment to have to let them die away. How soon could she plead another task set by Master Buchanan to ensure further solitude?

" What have we to do to-morrow? " she asked. But the chorus which answered her made it clear that there could be little respite for her classical studies.

Deprived of the pretext for solitude, the lack of it fretted her like thirst. For her need to protest her love had been redoubled by Bothwell's perplexing incredulity. Like the fourth King James, she was ruler of Scotland. Bothwell was her subject as Margaret Drummond had been his. To Mary herself, as to King James, the sort of casual relationship which would have excited gossip rather than censure seemed an unthinkable parody of heart's desire. Had Margaret believed that? Bothwell would not. Yet, surely, on that December morning at Castle Drummond, he had also known that for them both a single destiny had been written, as if to shine from century to century, among the stars? Why then had he afterwards retreated behind the mocking barrier she had come to dread?

Had he indeed ridden to Whittinghame, as he told her, to help settle the affairs of the recently returned exiles? Could he have gone to Haddington instead? Could she believe that his wife, the Lady Jean, was still as inconsolable for the loss of Ogilvie of Boyne as Mary Beton insisted? Wretchedly she twisted her hands together. What was to become of them? What could become of them all?

In Glasgow, Darnley was now convalescent, but still plastering himself with every nauseating concoction recommended to him, in a hysterical attempt to preserve his threatened beauty. Could such a misfortune as permanent

disfigurement be the punishment of his infidelity to Holy
Church? If there were any risk of that, he had best make what
amends he could. And Father Hay, the Jesuit, was most
definite that his first duty was to be reconciled with his wife,
while the best course of action against her heretical advisers
was considered. He must protest to the Queen his fervent
desire for reconciliation. If she responded, none would rejoice
more fervently than those of the true faith. If not . . . then
mercy might have to be eclipsed, for a time, by justice.

Justice. . . . The word had an enticing ring to the young
man who believed himself to have been so grievously wronged.
The last thing he wanted to see offered to the Queen and her
heretical advisers was mercy. But he wrote as he was told.
And behind him the shadowy purpose of which he was not yet
aware began to take shape.

For those who desired the elimination of the Protestant
leaders, even that of the Queen who had come to terms with
them, preferred not to risk Darnley's knowledge of their
purpose till the last moment. But if the Queen were to take
the lure, he alone could offer it. In the background Father
Edmund Hay continued to work on the still nervous convalescent, while Sir James Balfour acted as a go-between for
him and Count Moretta, ambassador of Savoy, who had
belatedly arrived in Scotland when the risk of having to act as a
co-godparent with the heretical Queen of England was long
past. And at a discreet distance, on the far side of the Channel,
the Bishop of Mondivi, whom the Queen had refused to
receive as nuncio, waited on events and prepared to report to
Rome. Meanwhile, Sir James Balfour also took over the prac-
tical details of the reconciliation intended to provide the
background of the cataclysm which would leave Darnley,
once more fervent for the old faith, sole ruler of Scotland.

The choice of the site was easy. Balfour's brother Robert
owned property in the suburb of Edinburgh known as Kirk
o' Field. The Old Provost's House might be less impressive
than some of the other buildings of the former Augustinian

foundation, but it was, from a conspiratorial angle, very convenient. Though small, as befitted the lodging of a celibate official, it communicated by a covered way with a hall once used by the canons as an assembly room, which could accommodate the entire Court. The basement kitchens below the dwelling-house were still in use, but the cellars below the hall had been given over to bats and spiders since the end of the convivial pre-Reformation days.

Once Balfour had prepared the Old Provost's House as the scene of the drama, the task of getting the Queen and her Councillors there at the appropriate moment must be given to Darnley, and his part explained to him. Inevitably, everything depended on the success of the preliminary reconciliation. But it must not be too genuine, for Sir James Balfour at least had not forgotten Darnley's weathercock betrayal of his confederates after the murder of Rizzio. Would the bribe of the forgiveness of the Church, the glittering prospect of sole and supreme power in Scotland, be enough to keep his tongue from wagging this time? Balfour could only hope so, as Darnley wrote imploring the Queen to come to Glasgow and receive his humble protestations of repentance. The letter, with which he had received some assistance, read as an artless plea for help, a confession of past offences calculated to touch Mary's heart, and an earnest petition for her company. It filled her, in the circumstances, with dismay.

The members of her Council, when consulted, unanimously advised her not to go to Glasgow. But she herself knew that she must go. She might put it off as long as possible, grasping at such excuses as the Lethington-Fleming wedding at Holyroodhouse, the forthcoming meeting of the Council, the important legislation awaiting her signature and the departure of the last of her foreign guests. But in the end she would go.

For a breach with Darnley might adversely affect the status of Darnley's son, especially in view of the delicate negotiations which Sir Robert Melville had been instructed to initiate with Queen Elizabeth about the English succession. But this was something with which, she instinctively felt, Bothwell would have little sympathy. She avoided him therefore, until he practically forced his demand for an audience upon her.

" Promise me," he said abruptly, " that you will not go to Glasgow."

But she backed away. " Do not touch me, James. I—I cannot think calmly while you are so near."

He tucked his thumbs into his belt in the favourite gesture which made him a high-shouldered image of brooding power. " So much, then, for those assurances of devotion. It was well I was not deceived."

" They were true. All that I said was true," she protested in distress. But his crooked grin still mocked her. " You expect me to believe you—now ? "

" Why not ? You cannot think I would wish to go to Glasgow ? Or to be civil to Lennox, whose face I would never willingly see again ? And Henry himself, sick, wretched——"

" You know what ailed him ? It was the pox," said Bothwell roughly.

" I know it. But he is my husband still. And I must safeguard the future of my son. It might mar all that Robert Melville is striving to win from the Queen of England to have a breach with his father now."

" You are a strange woman," James Hepburn said thoughtfully.

She drew herself up to her full height. " I am the Queen."

He dropped on one knee, his blue eyes teasing her. " And I your most humble servant."

She ran to him then, holding out her hands. " Do not mock me, James. I must go indeed. But I will return as soon as may be. I swear it. I shall seek to persuade him to return to Craigmillar. There he can be cleansed, and I shall not be too far from the Prince at Stirling. Will you ride with me to Glasgow ? It is your duty, as Sheriff of Lothian, to escort the Queen."

" Then the choice is yours, and you need not have asked me whether I would or not. But I must go to Liddesdale, once I have set you on your way. Trouble is brewing there again."

" Is it? " He saw fear leap into her eyes. " Oh, James, have a care. Let me have news of you."

" There will be no news," he said. He was teasing her again. So it was between them nowadays. Sparks flashed and thunder rolled, as if they approached each other only at their utmost peril, yet under a compulsion which drew them so strongly that they could not keep apart. They were developing a new skill in seeming coldly distant when they spoke in public, their faces always at odds with their words when none was near enough to catch them. " But I will send Paris to wait on you, so that he can bring your news to me."

" I will write," she promised eagerly.

He shook his head. " It is too dangerous. Tell Paris only if you fare well or ill. The spoken word is safer."

" But writing," she said, suddenly piteous, " will ease my heart the more."

He looked at her in silence, his face enigmatic as death, his blue eyes suddenly tortured, like those of a man surveying the love of heaven from the hateful depths of his own unbelieving hell.

" I will wait upon your Grace at your pleasure," he said abruptly. " May I now take my leave? "

She nodded, speechless because her heart so cried against his going. All the discipline of her royal lifetime, all her searing ambition for the third crown which she believed to be hers by right, were needed to keep her from throwing herself at his feet and begging him to take her to the ends of the earth. She had been Queen of France, she reminded herself desperately as he paced backwards from her presence, she was now Queen of Scots, she should long since have been Queen of England. Even now, if her usurping cousin would but name her as her heir, all might be well. And at the worst, her son must one

day reign in England. Elizabeth, they swore, could bear no
living child. But there must be no breach with Henry, her
husband, now, above all, while success yet hung in the balance
in the negotiations with England on which Robert Melville
toiled.

She relaxed as the door closed behind him. He had gone.
And she had endured his going without crying aloud for
mercy. When she went to Glasgow, James would at least
ride by her side. He could do no less.

But he would do no more. When the Queen left Edinburgh on a fine sharp morning at the beginning of the third
week of January, he did indeed ride on her right hand, with
his brother-in-law of Huntly on her left. But once he had seen
her safe to Lord Livingstone's mansion at Callander, and she
had passed out of his jurisdiction as Sheriff of Lothian, he
requested her permission to attend to his duties elsewhere.
Was it, perhaps, because to ride farther would have been more
than he could endure? She comforted herself by thinking so.

But after he and Huntly had turned back she rode among
the gentlemen sent by the Earl of Lennox to escort her in a
leaden silence, which Mary Seton noted with apprehension.
She knew the Queen too well to miss the difference between
the desperate gaiety of the first day's journey and the lifeless
endurance of the second. She could only hope that those now
escorting her Grace considered her gravity appropriate in a
wife about to visit a suffering husband.

When the Earl of Lennox sent his apologies by the Laird of
Luss, explaining that he dared not venture into her Grace's
presence for fear of her displeasure, she did not attempt to deny
it. She was gracious, from sheer habit, to those about her;
but anyone who knew her well could tell that her gestures
were almost automatic. For she dreaded the prospect of meeting Darnley more with every mile they rode. In the loneliness
which had followed Bothwell's departure she was glad to know
that his French page, Paris, was trotting far to the rear of the
cavalcade, hunched against the bitter wind. She had noted

his lugubrious face, with reddened nose and ears, before they set out, with a little lifting of the heart. At least she was not quite cut off from his master. Perhaps she might find a chance to scribble a greeting, though Bothwell had advised her against it.

Darnley was still in bed, and his chamber was darkened because of his disfigurement. A great fire was heaped on the hearth, and the airless room stank so that she felt quite faint. She could not at once make out where he sat, against his high-piled pillows. He wore a mask to hide his suppurating sores. But their stench was heavy on the air.

" Is that you, my Mary? " His high, peevish voice was even more disagreeable than she remembered it, she thought, as a wave of nausea almost overwhelmed her. " You have been long enough in coming," he added disagreeably.

" Nevertheless, I am here now," she said. Slowly she approached the bed, as though each step cost her a separate effort of will. " Has the physician done good service? They told me you were better——"

" I am so heartily glad to see you, dearest love, that I am like to die of joy," said Darnley with oddly unconvincing vehemence. She had the impression that he was watching her closely from behind his mask. " In spite of all your cruelty."

" Cruelty? " She was startled.

" Aye, the cruelty of a hard-hearted wife who will not accept offers of amendment. You are the cause of all my sickness——"

" Indeed, there at least, you lie! " she said.

" I have done amiss, I own," he admitted hurriedly, " but only for the lack of my wife's tenderness. Many others of your subjects have wronged you. But you have pardoned them."

" I have also pardoned you, many times. And always you have returned to the same fault——"

" I am but young," wailed Darnley. " Have you not said so yourself? May not a man of my age, for lack of counsel, fall twice or thrice, and at last be chastened by experience?

I ask only your pardon, and that we shall be at bed and board once more, as husband and wife——"

" That cannot be till you are well again," she said hastily.

" If I may not have your pardon, I shall never rise from this bed," cried Darnley wildly.

" You must calm yourself. We will speak of this here-after."

" You will stay with me? You will share my lodging? "

" Not till you have been cleansed. It would be folly."

" But afterwards? When I return to Edinburgh? You will share my lodging there? "

His insistence on the point surprised her. To humour him she did not refuse outright. " That we will decide when the time comes. I thought to have you borne to Craigmillar where the mediciner and I shall do our best to help you."

Darnley sighed. " I will do all you say if you will but remain near me. I cannot sleep. Will you sit up with me? "

" Not to-night. I have been travelling these two days and I am weary."

" Then to-morrow? "

" We will see when to-morrow comes."

She had arranged to lodge in the Archbishop's Palace, which was near enough for her to visit her husband daily, but avoided the necessity of accepting Lennox's hospitality. She was almost too tired to eat, that first evening, when she was at last established in the apartment prepared for her. But the food and the warmth and the uncontaminated atmosphere restored her enough to be able to take the opportunity of scribbling a few pages to Bothwell, under cover of making notes to remind her of things to be seen to next day.

" Dismiss the servants, dear Seton," she said. " And go to your own supper. I am so weary that I am wakeful. It will help me to make a memorial of what must be done to-morrow."

" I have no wish for supper, Madam."

" But I wish you to have it, Seton. Go now. I shall be more content, I promise, when you return."

But Seton lingered. " Shall I send some of the others to you, Madam? "

" I would rather be alone."

" At least the bell is by your hand. And the guards are in the ante-chamber."

The Queen smiled. " Dear Seton, I was never less afraid. Go now."

As the door reluctantly closed the burden of concealment slid from her like a rain-sodden cloak. She dipped her quill and began to write, without haste, but also without hesitation, smiling to herself as she felt estranging time and distance swallowed up by the compulsive imagination which brought her into the presence of her beloved. She left the letter un-headed. James would know why she took up the tale from the moment of their leave-taking the day before.

" Being departed from the place where I had left my heart," she wrote, " it may be easily judged what my counten-ance was, seeing that I was no more than a body without a heart. Until dinner-time I spoke to nobody, and none dared present themselves to me . . ."

She was writing faster now, as she told him of the day's events, the escort provided, the absence of Lennox, her encounter with Darnley, and his unexpected protestations. Her wrist began to ache, and revulsion took hold of her, making her shudder as she wrote.

" I am weary, and half asleep, and yet I cannot forbear scribbling, so long as there is any paper. Cursed be this pocky fellow that troubleth me this much, for I had a pleasanter matter to discourse with you but for him." She broke off to rub her wrist. Somehow she must make James believe that duty and not desire had taken her to Glasgow. " He is not much worse, but he is ill arrayed. I thought I should have been killed with his breath. It is worse than your uncle's, and yet I was set no nearer to him than in a chair by his bolster while he lay on the further side of the bed . . ."

It was tiresome to have to use odd sheets of differing shapes and sizes, but it was all she had. To ask for more would attract too much of Seton's loving attention to her purpose. If she wrote on the back of the memorial she had already jotted down, it would serve her need. And James would understand.

A sound outside the door made her hastily collect the various scraps of paper covered with her large, flowing script, and stuff them once more inside the carrying case of her book of devotions, which she could without comment bear about with her, till a chance came to finish the letter.

Meanwhile, its very presence was a sort of consolation, as she sat by Darnley's bedside next morning, shuddering away from his attempts to grasp and draw her close. Now and again, when she thought that he was sleeping, she drew out the closely scribbled pages and looked them through, unaware how instantly the change in her expression betrayed her to the man watching from behind the mask that turned his pustuled face into a pool of darkness as he snored ostentatiously on his rich pillows.

What he saw confirmed what Father Hay and James Balfour had told him. She was no longer faithful, no longer worthy to be his wife, still less to be Queen of Scots. It was he, Henry Stewart, who should rule Scotland. If all went as had been planned, he need waste no anger over the woman who had so cruelly despised him. He would soon be rid of her and all the rest besides. He need only persuade them, at the appropriate moment, into the chosen place at the Provost's lodging which was already being prepared for the reception of such heretics. But presently Darnley found that the effort of snoring made his throat ache. He closed his mouth and moved on his pillows, grinning to see how quickly she pushed the papers out of sight.

" Are you still there, my sweet wife? " He was pleased with himself for the conviction he contrived to put into his voice, and he did not miss the way she stiffened, as if to resist further entreaties.

" I am still here."

" Stay with me, then, to-night."

" Not to-night," she said, rising from the stool by his bed with such abruptness that it went spinning. " I will come back in the morning, I promise you. But I must return to my lodging for supper now."

The attendants in the far corners of the chamber sprang up, thankful for the chance of leaving it. Darnley smirked as he watched their haste to escort her from his presence. Fools! They thought him of no account, a mere stinking hulk that did not demand even the courtesy of a farewell.

That night Mary finished her letter. It was very long, and seemed longer because of the odd scraps of paper on which it had been scrawled. It was late, and her poor women would be weary. But she herself seemed to have passed beyond sleep into a state of burning wakefulness that ached behind her eyes. She was reluctant to put the letter away, as if even its ephemeral contact had power to evoke the comforting strength of his hand, the harsh vigour of his voice. Remembering his warning against the written word, she echoed it.

" Burn this letter, for it is too dangerous . . ."

If Paris was to take the bulky packet in the morning she must now thread it with the ribbon for the seal. But the slots would be hard to make in such odd scraps of paper.

" Excuse my evil writing, and read it over twice. Excuse also that I scribbled, for I had yesternight no paper and took the paper of a memorial. Pray remember your friend and write to her often . . ."

Her hand hovered over the last words, as she checked the impulse to add the signature that all the world knew. Slowly she folded the clumsy budget, then held it close, as if suddenly uncertain whether to send it after all. Now that the letter was written she was aware of such relief that its despatch seemed almost irrelevant. James had said the written word was too dangerous. He was probably right. At least it might be wiser to keep it for a while. If the rumours which had been reaching her from time to time, ever since the christening at Stirling, had any foundation, she was now in the midst of her enemies. Paris might be a trustworthy messenger, but he would be alone against many. And the road to the Border at mid-winter was a lonely one indeed.

Frowning thoughtfully, she rose from her place by the fire and crossed the chamber to the table by her bedside on which, with her rosary and books of devotion, was the little silver-gilt coffer with its crowned initial F's which Francis had given her when they were first married. It was a pretty thing, and stronger than it looked, with a lock which would defy most pilferers who did not know the trick of it. Taking the key from her reticule, she opened it. Within lay some of her small treasures; locks of hair belonging to her son; an amulet; a letter from her uncle, the Cardinal; the verses she had recently written.

She sighed, hesitated, and glanced towards the fire, then laid the bulky letter beside the verses. She closed the lid and turned the key forward and back, pushing it further for the second twist, according to the trick of it. As she let her hands fall to her sides, she shivered suddenly, so exhausted that the voice from the doorway scarcely startled her.

" Why Madam, have you taken cold? " cried Mary Seton.

" Cold, Seton? Why, no." Forcing her face into the unconvincing creases of a smile, she tried to make light of her fatigue. " As we used to say in France, someone must have walked across my grave."

CHAPTER EIGHTEEN

THE Douglases no longer considered themselves King's men. Much had happened since the first Sir James Douglas had landed with Robert the Bruce on the west coast of enemy-occupied Scotland, to begin his country's liberation in February, 1307. Seven years later he had shared the leader's triumph at Bannockburn. But things were very different in February, 1567. Neither King Robert nor Sir James had been well served by his descendants, for a sorry series of royal minorities had bedevilled the house of Stewart, and the Douglas men had come to consider themselves greater than the royal children they bullied and kidnapped as occasion served.

Their successes had been intermittent, for the boy Kings invariably rebelled in due course against their captors, sending the house of Douglas into eclipse for a generation. Their supreme gamble came after Flodden. For the fifth King James was only an infant when his father fell, and Douglases and Hamiltons faced each other, as it were, across his cradle, ready to fight to a standstill for the custody of the Crown. The Douglases won only a boomerang victory, for at seventeen King James escaped from his gaolers, and banished the house of Douglas from the country once more. When they seeped back during the reign of his daughter Mary, the consequences were what might have been expected.

It had been George Douglas who first stabbed Rizzio, but behind him loomed the significant figure of James Douglas, Earl of Morton, head of that turbulent house. Darnley's betrayal affected Douglas fortunes only briefly, but he had made them his mortal enemies for life.

Morton was back from exile, though not yet received at
Court, by the beginning of 1567, and Archibald Douglas, a
renegade priest of ill reputation, had taken refuge with his
brother William at Whittinghame before the Queen's pardon
had brought all but his most obviously treasonable kinsfolk
back to Scotland.

Yet Darnley now fancied himself too illustriously supported
to fear even the Douglas malice. His headlong imagination
had magnified the exhortations of a zealous Jesuit and the sly
hints of an unscrupulous lawyer into the firm support of all the
Catholic powers. Was he not, therefore, the chosen instrument
of the Counter-Reformation, about to achieve eternal merit by
eliminating the most notorious heretics in Scotland at a single
blow? Balfour, he knew, had almost completed his preparations,
and though the details had not yet been explained to him,
he saw no reason to doubt his confederate's efficiency. What
he did not realise was that Balfour was too agile a turncoat
to stake life and reputation on the lighting of a fuse and the
discretion of Henry Stewart.

If possible, Balfour would have managed without him, for
Darnley was a bad risk and he knew it. But in the circumstances the risk must be taken. Balfour decided to safeguard
himself, however, by hinting to the Earl of Moray, that in
certain circumstances, he, Balfour, might be in a position to
do great things for the cause of the new faith. Pressed to be
more precise, he declined, knowing that if their plans went
astray, he could boldly remind Moray of their conversation
and claim credit for their failure. And if all went well Moray
would not be in any position to prevent him from claiming
his reward from another quarter.

So Balfour felt, by the end of January, that he had done his
best to safeguard the situation. Darnley was duly conveyed
in a horse litter from Glasgow to the Old Provost's House in
Kirk o' Field, escorted by the Queen and a large party of
Scottish nobles, most carefully wrapped in furs against the
mid-winter weather.

The suburb of Kirk o' Field could be reached from Holyroodhouse, if necessary, without travelling through the city. It was therefore specially suitable for a patient convalescent from what had been politely called smallpox. The Old Provost's House, formerly occupied by the head of the community, stood at the south-west corner of the quadrangle, with gardens at the back, and when the Flodden Wall, built at the time of the country's greatest need, had cut across the monks' south garden, a postern door been made for their convenience. Beyond it, an alley meandered along the backs of the Canongate gardens towards Holyroodhouse. Beyond again was open country. From the house itself one door opened into the garden and another into the quadrangle.

The Old Provost's House was the typical lodging of a man in authority over an ecclesiastical community. The personal accommodation consisted only of two chambers, one above the other, linked by a turnpike stair, with a smaller, intermediate apartment which could be used as ante-room or garderobe according to the needs of the moment. For Darnley's reception it had been equipped with his commode, upholstered in velvet and overhung by a canopy in the royal colours. The upper chamber, used as a bedroom by the Duke of Bedford when he lodged there on his way to Stirling, already contained an imposing bed, with hangings of black velvet, fringed with gold and silver, from the royal establishment, and a smaller green and yellow bed had been placed in the room below for the Queen, so that she could humour her husband by sharing his lodging, though not his bed, till the cleansing requirements had been fulfilled. Below the Queen's room were kitchen, store rooms, and sleeping places for the servants. It was close quarters even for those actually attendant on Darnley, and the lords and ladies of the Court were not expected to find room there.

For their reception the assembly hall on the far side of the covered way had been fitted up with tapestries from Holyroodhouse, and a dais, throne and canopy of state provided for the

Queen. Here, after Darnley's arrival, came the officers of state, the members of the Council, the lords of Parliament, with their wives and attendants. Here too came the musicians to play for them as they danced, the minstrels to sing to them, the servants to set out such refreshments as had not been seen since the last of the Augustinians' good red wine was rolled out of the dark and echoing cellars below.

Those who came to congratulate the Queen on her husband's recovery were probably unaware that such cellars existed, still less that they were empty no longer. Nor could they know that Sir James Balfour had recently been purchasing large quantities of gunpowder. His comings and goings attracted no attention, for both the assembly room and the cellars below it could be entered, by those who had the keys, either from the living quarters by passing along the covered way, or by a separate outside door. The nearest dwelling, the New Provost's House, was also owned by Balfour's brother Robert. It stood on the west side of the quadrangle, with Hamilton House, in which the Archbishop of St. Andrews was at that time lodging, quite near, and Douglas House in Blackfriars Wynd, where some of Morton's kinsfolk were usually to be found, on the far side of the High Street, but also in the vicinity.

Holyroodhouse, on the other hand, was nearly a mile away, so that Darnley could, with some show of reason, urge the Queen to remain at Kirk o' Field these wintry nights, instead of riding home through sleet and darkness after the evening entertainments devised to cheer his convalescence. And Mary was ready to humour him just then in almost all things. For he was now well enough to plan fresh excursions, he had often spoken of going abroad, and nothing, as she well knew, would more immediately make Elizabeth break off the present negotiations for the Scottish succession than the news that Darnley was visiting Flanders to confer with her mortal enemy, that figurehead of the Counter-Reformation, his most Catholic Majesty of Spain.

Since Mary's visit to Glasgow, Darnley had seemed unexpectedly amenable, though he had been talking even more wildly than usual of crazy schemes for advancing the Faith by seizing Scarborough and annexing the Scilly Isles as bases for the Spanish invasion of England which he seemed to consider imminent. It might well be no more than talk, but she could not be certain, and her anxiety mounted as Robert Melville left for England. The least rumour, whether of Darnley's intrigues with her Spanish enemies, or estrangement from his wife, might give her incalculable cousin Elizabeth an excuse to refuse Melville a hearing. Whatever the duplicity might cost her, however cruelly her motives might be misunderstood, Mary knew that she must, somehow or other, keep her husband not only safe, but quiet.

And so Bothwell's return, unscathed, from Liddesdale, only intensified her anxiety. She dared not make a pretext to see him alone in order to explain the reason for her friendliness with Darnley, for Darnley, once so indifferent, now seemed unwilling to let her out of his sight. She could only endure Bothwell's raised eyebrows and speculative stare. Sometimes she was angry with one, sometimes with the other, so that she scarcely knew whether love or hatred shook her. She was thankful only that the letter she had spent so long scribbling lay still with the verses in the little coffer by her bedside. Perhaps the French were right. Men should not be too sure of women's love. And yet, she could not quite bring herself to tear up the pages she had so wildly scrawled.

Nor could she bring herself to share Darnley's bedchamber at Kirk o' Field. But for some reason she did not understand, he seemed satisfied by her presence in the room below. She slept there on the nights of Wednesday and Friday, so that she might be there on Saturday morning to assist in the elaborate preparations for the cleansing bath prescribed by the physicians, about which Darnley was so exasperatingly unenthusiastic. But later on Saturday she returned to Holyroodhouse, in spite of his violent protestations that she might at least remain with him, now that he had consented to be cleansed, and celebrate the new beginning of their married life with appropriate tokens of forgiveness.

Mary had no means of comparing these proposals with the games of tennis he had played with Rizzio within a few hours of his carefully planned murder. She only knew that the prospect of closer relations with her husband was one from which she recoiled with loathing, though she knew her consent could not much longer be deferred. At least, however, she could postpone it by pretending that she was needed at Holyroodhouse to complete the arrangements for Darnley's return, or to make sure that everything was ready for the carnival on Sunday, 9th February, 1567. As Darnley knew, she had promised to attend the marriage of her servant Bastian in the Chapel Royal on Sunday morning, with dinner to follow at noon and a masked ball at night.

Between these festivities she must also make time to attend the supper party to be given the same evening by the Bishop of Argyll in honour of Count Moretta, the ambassador from Savoy who was now about to take his leave. It was at least essential, Mary felt, that she should attend the supper party in order to soften her refusal to join the league of ultra-Catholic powers, sponsored by the Pope and led by Spain and Savoy, for the forcible suppression of heresy throughout Europe. For in spite of all the pressure Moretta had been able to bring, and all Darnley's enthusiasm for the benefits such an alliance would confer, Mary had held out against it. She had already seen too many atrocities perpetrated in the name of God to be willing to permit the use of the rack, the stake and the inquisition for the counter-reformation of Scotland.

A hint that more was on foot than met the eye was given by the Earl of Moray, who presented himself on Saturday morning, and asked, without preamble, for immediate leave of absence. Mary was acutely disappointed. She had hoped that her recent efforts at reconciliation had been so successful. What had gone wrong now?

" But to-morrow is to be a day of rejoicing," she protested.
" Will you not share it ? "

" My wife has yesterday been taken with her labour pains,"
said Moray sombrely. " I must beg leave to go to her."

Mary put a hand to her head. She seemed to remember
that the Countess of Moray's pains had come upon her on
another occasion when her brother had cause to anticipate
events in which he would prefer to have no share. What
reason could he have now? She looked at him anxiously.
But his face was blank.

" Count Moretta will be sorely disappointed if the supper
to which we have all been bidden should lack your presence."

" I fear my wife's condition is a matter of greater urgency."

" That I can scarcely deny," she agreed. She gave her
consent, since it did not seem humane to withhold it. In spite of
her protestations, she did not suppose that Count Moretta
would be greatly concerned by the absence of a man with
whom he had so little in common. She herself was looking
forward to the masque at Holyroodhouse much more than the
stately ambassadorial farewell.

Most of Sunday passed uneventfully. The distinguished
company who took supper with the ambassador included
the earls of Argyll, Huntly and Bothwell, all in the splendid
costumes they would afterwards wear at the masked ball.
But Mary was glad to leave soon after supper on the excuse of
visiting her husband at Kirk o' Field. The ambassador,
kneeling to kiss her hand, made no attempt to detain her, but
as he rose, his calculating glance roved round the group of
nobles preparing to escort her, with barely concealed dis-
satisfaction. For Lethington, as well as Moray, had absented
himself. Mary had agreed to this with an indulgent smile.
What else could be expected of dear Flem's newly wedded
husband?

The royal cavalcade clattered noisily into the quadrangle
at Kirk o' Field, dismounting in the smoky light of torches
blown aslant by the keen night air, and trooping into the long

hall where the musicians were tuning up and the servants
setting out wine and comfits. Darnley was in an uncertain
temper, unwilling to leave his small and stifling chamber
to endure the stares of the assembled Court. In spite of his
treatment his face was still heavily ulcerated and he had lost
a great deal of his fine, fair hair. He had been drinking, as
usual, more than he could carry with dignity, and the Queen
was glad to think that she would soon be due at the wedding
ball for which she had promised to return to Holyroodhouse.

But when she spoke of it to Darnley, his anger startled her.
She had been sitting beside his bed, while Bothwell and
Huntly, with a couple of others, amused themselves by throwing
dice on the far side of the room. Darnley's passionate protest
made them look up in surprise.

"Why, Madam, this is but a sorry carnival. I am to be
left here, unwanted as an old coat, while you disport yourself——"

"I would not go," she said, "if I had not promised my
good servants to join the rejoicing. For you it is different.
Bastian has done you no service, but he has served me loyally."

"So you seek to honour a servant at the expense of your
husband——"

"Henry, to-morrow we shall be together at Holyrood——"
she said in a low voice.

Seeing the plan on which so much depended thus unexpectedly threatened, Darnley lost his head and broke out
almost hysterically. "To-morrow, to-morrow, to-morrow!
What use is to-morrow to me if I am to be left alone to-night?"

She stared at him in amazement. Could his illness have
weakened his wits? He might do anything, she guessed, if he
were thwarted. No longer an invalid now, he might call for
his servants and make good his threat of leaving Scotland,
and at a time when she needed him, above all, by her side.
She bit her lip and pondered.

"Would it comfort you if I promised to come back after
the ball?"

She was not looking at him but beyond him as she spoke. She noticed Bothwell's hand, lifted to throw the dice, arrested in mid-air above the board, his knuckles suddenly white. Then Darnley's delight recalled her attention. He was laughing and clapping his hands.

" Why, yes! " he cried. " That will be different altogether! You will return? We can all be gay together, if but for an hour or two. Then I shall be content. I will see that food and wine are set out in the hall for those escorting you. All those at Court must be my guests. I will take no refusal from my lord of Moray——"

" He has gone into Fife."

He made a gesture of impatience. " Then Lethington."

" I have given him leave of absence also, being but newly wed."

" The rest, then, must suffice." He was quite sulky again, so that she was bewildered by such abrupt changes of mood. But at least he seemed somewhat pacified by the thought of her return. If she would promise——

Laughing, she took off one of her rings. " Here is my pledge," she said. " Hold out your finger. And now we must be going, if we are to take any part in Bastian's merrymaking. Have the horses been brought forth? "

" They have, Madam," Bothwell said.

After she had left the room Darnley flung himself back on the purple velvet pillows of the richer bed with which he had asked the Queen to replace the sombre black hangings set up for the Earl of Bedford. He folded his arms behind his head, interlacing the fingers, and smiled up at the firelit ceiling as he listened to the hubbub of departure. How long must he still wait for the fulfilment of his purpose? How long, O Lord, how long?

At Holyroodhouse the Queen's uneasiness was swallowed up by the joyous hubbub of the masked ball, in which the strangely garbed creatures of Bastian's lively fancy leaped and pranced among the magnificence of their illustrious guests.

For a time, at least, Mary forgot Darnley and his strange
behaviour. He would wait for her to return, she felt sure.
After that . . . she shuddered away from whatever necessity
the circumstances might demand. "*Carpe diem*," was not a
motto of which Master Buchanan would approve, but when
to-morrow loomed so uncertainly, was it not permissible to
take pleasure in to-day? She smiled as she saw Bothwell
approach her. He was going to ask her to dance. It was
strange that they had not yet danced together. She had not
supposed him, somehow, to be much of a dancing man. Nor
was it his purpose now. He was grave and he spoke in a low,
curt voice.

"Madam, may I ask you to give audience to the Captain
of your Guard? He has news of the greatest urgency."

Mary's eyes widened with amazement. "What can the
Captain have to say at this time of night? Who is on
duty?"

"John Stewart of Traquair."

"Do you know what he has to say?"

"I do, Madam."

"Is it of such urgency that it will not wait till morning?"

"It is, indeed."

She sighed. "Then I will come. Bring him to my small
cabinet at the far end of the corridor. Then remain with us."

"I had not thought to leave you, Madam," said Bothwell
grimly.

She was already waiting for them when he returned with
Traquair, a bluff, soldierly Borderer so troubled by his incredible news that he at first stood speechless, and Bothwell spoke
only briefly.

"Your Grace, do you recall the name of Alexander
Durham?"

"Very well," Mary answered without hesitation. It was
her pride to know the names of all who served her. "Do you
speak of the father or the son?"

"Master Durham, your agent for the collection of rents,

came to me, Madam," said Traquair unhappily, " on a matter connected with his son, who is in the service of the King."

" I know young Sandy well," the Queen declared.

" His father was in great distress," said Traquair, " because of a tale brought home by Sandy, who fled from Kirk o' Field yesterday pleading sickness, on account of which he refuses to return."

" If he is sick, he had best bide at home," said the Queen mildly. " I see no harm in that." She looked in surprise from Traquair's appalled face to Bothwell's mask of silence. " I fear you must be more plain with me, my lords."

" Master Durham reports," said Traquair hoarsely, " that his son returned in such terror that he could scarcely speak for trembling at what he had been told, in all secrecy, by the King, when he waited upon him at supper and others were elsewhere. It seems he was often so trusted with such confidences as the King would not share with the rest."

" The King thought much of Sandy's discretion," Mary agreed.

" On this occasion, Madam, it may well be that his lack of it has saved your life," Traquair blurted out. " For what he told his father, under an oath of secrecy which Master Durham most properly felt unable to keep, was that the King boasted the cellars beneath the assembly hall at Kirk o' Field to be stuffed with gunpowder, so that when he pleased to order it, all those present would be blown into the air. He had but to excuse himself on the pretext of retiring to the garderobe, with those in attendance on him, stopping long enough on his way to the postern to give word to one waiting to light the fuse. By the time the house rose from its foundations, they would be up and away on the horses awaiting them; one for Sandy, one for Taylor, and the third for himself."

Mary felt his words beat about her like hailstones on bare flesh. As if borne down by them, she bowed her head between her hands. " Sweet Mother of God," she murmured, " I cannot—I cannot believe it . . ."

But even as she spoke, she remembered. This would not be the first time that Darnley had made it obvious that he cared less for her than for the benefits she had failed to bestow. On the dreadful night of Rizzio's death he had introduced armed murderers into her private apartments, knowing— hoping, perhaps—that the shock might kill both her and the child she carried, and leave him sole ruler of Scotland. She could not pretend that there had ever been any affection between them since, though she had cherished him as her husband because it was her duty, and sought to live at peace with him because he was the father of her son.

". . . what did he seek to gain?" Her voice was no more than a whisper.

"We know nothing yet, Madam," said Traquair, "except that your Grace must not return to Kirk o' Field to-night."

"No . . ." she said. Her voice was desolate. Letting her hands fall limply to her lap she slowly raised her head, her eyes wide and staring, not at them, but at the gulf of terror so suddenly opened at her feet. Hatred she could understand: she knew jealousy for love's dark shadow. But treachery bore about it the stench of the pit, and she recoiled from it with loathing. It was some time before she realised that Traquair was speaking again in his deep, worried voice, of the pre- cautions which must be taken, the things he would do for her greater safety.

". . . and my lord of Bothwell has undertaken that if I will make myself responsible for safeguarding the Palace while your Grace retires, he will go forth with his servants and see that a sufficient search is made at Kirk o' Field."

The words jerked her back to consciousness of her immediate surroundings. She turned quickly to Bothwell. "My lord, I cannot send you into such danger——"

Bothwell grinned. "Danger is no new experience for a soldier, Madam. May I suggest that you release Traquair to take the precautions he has proposed forthwith?"

She nodded. "Go then."

Traquair bowed, then took his leave so promptly that his relief was evident. Left alone with the Queen, Bothwell smiled with unusual gentleness. Then he took her cold hands in his own, shaking them as if he were trying to wake a sleep-walker. Presently her staring eyes began to focus again. She blinked. With relief he saw that she was looking at him.

" Is . . . it possible, James ? "

" Most possible," he said, curt again. " As you must know. But we have as yet no other accusation than that of a distraught serving lad who has run home in panic. The first thing is to make sure of the truth. And then——"

He paused, frowning, waiting for her to make the comment he expected, knowing her well enough to be sure her courage would not fail to face up to the gravity of the situation.

" Surely, James, even if it be true, now that no harm has been done, we can keep all quiet ? The King is easily mis-led——"

He laughed harshly.

" I do not believe he would do such a thing if others had not inspired it."

" No doubt. But with these others we have still to reckon. While the King remains a free man your Grace's life must be continually in danger. If the case be proved, I ask permission to take him into custody forthwith."

She sat before him like a statue, her hands clasped now over her heart, her eyes resentful, as his words blighted all her hopes of coming to terms with Darnley for their future great-ness. The little room was so still that the whooping of the dancers, the scrape and sawing of the fiddles, even the words of a song, rose towards them like bubbles through the still waters of a rock-encircled pool. At last she said:

" Do then what is needful, James. But . . . have a care."

" And you, Madam ? " He brushed her concern for him aside like a drifting feather. " Will you return to the dance ? "

She shook her head. " I have not the heart. I had promised

to help put the bride to bed, but now I cannot face it. Send
for my women. Tell them to speak of a sudden indisposition
which will excuse me. Heaven knows it is true enough!"

"I will." Stepping into the corridor, Bothwell shouted
for his page, and when Paris came running he sent him for
Mary Seton, commanding him not to leave the royal ante-
chamber till he could bring the news that the Queen was
safely in bed in the chamber beyond. Then he went to his
own apartments and thriftily changed his clothes. He had
made light of the possibility to the Queen, but he fully expected
to be set upon at Kirk o' Field, and had no wish to see his best
doublet spoiled. When Paris came to report, he was ready,
with the disgruntled servants he had routed out of their beds,
to belt themselves with their weapons and accompany him
on a midnight search for they knew not what.

At the Palace gate he was challenged. As he gave his name
he nodded approval of Traquair's efficiency, and swore at
Dalgleish for holding the torch askew. The moon, a mere
sliver, had already set, and it was dark as death in the Canongate.

"Hold up your torch, man," he commanded, "or we
shall flounder into every midden between here and the
Netherbow."

The Netherbow port was closed, and they had some
work in waking its custodian, who grumbled at the lateness of the hour and was only to be silenced by a well-known
voice.

"Open to the lord Bothwell."

The porter shuffled hastily down his short flight of stairs
and flung the gates back. His lantern confirmed the identity
of the Sheriff of Lothian as they passed through.

Within the city all was murky. But the streets were not
silent. Dalgleish had now beaten out his torch, which had
burned to the butt, as their eyes became accustomed to the
darkness. Others were astir about Douglas House in Blackfriars Wynd. Steel chimed on steel as armed men mustered.

Bothwell's servants huddled into a doorway for what shelter they could get against the keen night wind, while their master went forward to confer with those who were abroad as late as himself. Among them they recognised the great bulk of Archibald Douglas, moving soft-footed, though in armour, as if for some burglarious enterprise, noted the weasel features of Sir James Balfour in unexpected conference with their master.

He kept them waiting long enough to be half frozen when he returned at last, and ordered them, to their supreme relief, to return to Holyroodhouse forthwith. They were too weary to care why. But as they saw his face for a moment in the brief light from the closing doorway of Douglas House, it was evident that he was laughing to himself, quite silently, but with such concentrated mirth that the tears ran down his face and his lips were drawn back from his white, even teeth in a very rigor of mirth. They made their way back as they had come, and he spoke no word except to give his name, as before, at the Netherbow and the Palace gate.

At Kirk o' Field, Darnley had grown weary of waiting for the Queen's return. He was first angry, then sorry for himself, as he thought of the gay doings at Holyroodhouse which had so enchanted his lighthearted lady that she had forgotten all about her promise to return to her sick husband. So much the worse for her, and for those who returned with her in the morning. He would drink, and forget her till then.

" Taylor! "

" My lord? "

" Bring me wine. And see it is well mulled. Rout Bonkil out of his bed in the kitchen."

When the wine came, he drank it and called for more to take the edge off his disappointment. Like a child in so many things, he had a childish dislike of waiting. His father, too, would already be at Linlithgow, all agog to hear how their project had sped. Well, he would have to wait for one more day. The Queen would not come to-night. Never mind . . .

all was prepared . . . he had only to say the word . . . only to light the tow . . .

He had no idea of how long he had slept when Taylor, anxiously shaking his shoulder, waked him. " Wh-wh-at is amiss? " he mumbled. " Has the Queen returned? " His head ached. In the eerie light of the taper Taylor had kindled the room seemed to be spinning first one way and then the other.

" My lord," said Taylor anxiously, " I smell burning. Something is afire below. Shall I go and——"

But one sniff had sobered Darnley more effectively than a dozen buckets of cold water. With a wild yell he leapt from his bed, death itself clutching his throat with the reek of the burning fuse. Waiting for neither slippers nor gown he raced for the chamber door, clad only in his nightshirt, whimpering with terror as he blundered down the narrow stairs.

" My lord . . ." gasped Taylor, " surely there is time enough? I see no flame. Wait for your gown and slippers." Grabbing Darnley's shoes and gown, he shuffled his feet into his own slippers, snatched up his belt and dagger, then, wondering if the King might be the worse of his exertion, he dragged a chair after him down the stairs and out of the still swinging door in pursuit of his apparently demented master.

He was vaguely aware that it was not dark after all in the garden. He could see Darnley's tall, white figure racing ahead, checked by the sight of men with torches, then turning too late, as the figures converged on him. He only cried out once, in a high voice breaking into despair.

" Have pity on me, kinsmen . . . for his sake . . . who had pity on . . . us . . . all." The words died away into a gurgle, the velvet gown was snatched from Taylor's hand, then something was crammed over his head and shoulders, pinioning his arms by his sides. Vainly, he fought against the stifling, suffocating darkness, but at last, he too lay still under the leafless apple trees.

Back at Holyroodhouse the dance was over, the bride and

bridegroom tucked up in bed, the revellers dispersed. As the servants extinguished the candles, ghostly trails of pungent smoke were scrawled across the encroaching darkness as flame after flame went out.

Then the silence of exhaustion descended on the Palace, on the city at its gates, weary after the Sabbath's austerities, as its rulers after their carnival. A sleet-laden wind strayed through the small hours, setting a shutter clacking, a door swinging, up and down the sleeping city whose stillness emphasised the solitude of those who lay wakeful; anxious mothers beside their children's bedsides, forsaken sweethearts in their cold beds, restless sufferers watching for the morning, here a lad with toothache, there an old man with an evil conscience. At Holyroodhouse the Queen, distraught by conflicting emotions, had fallen at last into a doze, when an abrupt and awful roar seemed to split the heavens asunder and rend the earth beneath. She woke in terror, unable to stir or speak till the slam of doors flung back, the hubbub of terrified comment, the thud of hurrying feet, reassured her with the knowledge that she was still in the visible world.

Then Mary Seton's arms were about her. " Oh, Madam, I thought it the end of all things——"

" At least—it is not that——" said the Queen. Then the knowledge of what it must be drenched her in sudden sweat. " But—the King——"

" The King, sweet Madam? "

" So it was true—they told me . . . that crack was meant for me——"

" Mother of God! " Mary Seton crossed herself. But the Queen caught her by the arm.

" Go at once, Seton, and discover if the Earl of Bothwell has returned——"

As Seton hastened from the room, she sat without breathing, it seemed, in the midst of the clamour of her frightened ladies; some of them on their knees, sobbing as they clutched their beads, others peering out of the windows into the darkness, gabbling like fowls after a clap of thunder. Then Mary Seton was back, stricken by the sight of her mistress's ashen terror, but misunderstanding its cause even while she gasped her reassurance.

" He must have returned long since, Madam. He is but this instant risen from his bed."

PART THREE

February, 1567—May, 1568

" In my End is my Beginning."
Motto of Mary, Queen of Scots

CHAPTER NINETEEN

SHE could not stop shivering, though they piled fresh logs on the fire and more covers on her bed. Traquair's warning now conjured up too vivid a picture of the chaos of dismembered bodies, bloody and blackened, to which she and the Protestant leaders of Scotland would have been reduced had they returned to Kirk o' Field. But almost more dreadful than the fate she had escaped was the thought that it could have been prepared for her, and the wild question that followed: had her husband indeed been instigator as well as victim?

Sick with horror, she waited for the return of Bothwell, who had once more left the Palace for Kirk o' Field, thankful only that Huntly and Traquair had remained at Holyrood-house to ensure her safety and that of her son. For in the hurried conference between the three men which had followed the explosion there had been talk of an armed rising, anxiety for the Castle's custody.

Hours passed without news. Mary Seton sat by the Queen's bedside, trying now and then to persuade her mistress to take a hot posset, or ordering the serving women to change the hot bricks at her feet. About them the other ladies huddled, whispering and crossing themselves as they reminded each other of the Queen's first stricken cry. If she had been the intended victim, must they too not have died?

In the ante-room, where the lords and gentlemen quartered in Holyroodhouse had gathered, the wildest speculations were circulating. More restrained than most, James and Andrew Melville wondered what effect this cataclysm would have on their brother Robert's mission to Queen Elizabeth, and whether it would bring the Earl of Moray back from Fife.

Silence fell as Bothwell strode in at last; dusty, haggard and unapproachable. In silence still they made way for him to convey to the Queen the news no one dared demand. For his face was blank as granite, and his long fingers on his sword.

Mary received him promptly, surrounded by her ladies, and indicating with a weary gesture that she was ready to hear the worst. It was Bothwell who hesitated, as if he wished to mask the horror of what might have been her fate. When he spoke at last, his voice was hoarse after hours of questioning clamorous townsfolk, and groping for bodies among mountains of rubble and dust.

" Madam," he said tonelessly, " it seems that some powder deposited in the King's lodgings has taken fire. It has blown up the house and killed his Majesty with those of his bed-chamber. Their bodies have been found some distance from the ruins, in an orchard under the town wall."

She stared at him, still wordless, scarcely listening as he told her of the removal of Darnley's body to the New Provost's house, where he had left it, watched over by a guard of honour till the Queen's wishes were known. But she was so evidently in no state to issue instructions that he did not mock her by demanding them.

" I will return later," he said, more to Mary Seton, now agitatedly waving him away, than to the Queen. " In order to learn what is in her Grace's mind."

But in the ante-room, he was surrounded by those who could now control their tongues no longer. James Melville spoke first.

" What can you tell us, my lord, of this dire occurrence? "

Bothwell surveyed him under his heavy brows, then shook his head in evident perplexity. " It is the strangest thing in the world," he admitted. " The King's house at Kirk o' Field has been burnt up. We found his body some distance from it, under a tree——"

" Dead? " asked Andrew Melville gruffly.

" Aye. But with no hurt nor mark on all his person."

" No mark? Yet blown up by the explosion that rocked us here? How can that be? "

But Bothwell was in no mood for speculation. He shouldered his way through the crowd and went in search of Huntly. With the Queen on the verge of collapse, there was much for them to do.

That morning the Council met at the Tolbooth. Argyll, as Lord Justice of Scotland, was President, assisted by Huntly as Lord Chancellor, Bothwell as Sheriff of Lothian, and Lethington, now once more acting as Secretary of State. Bothwell recommended that the Queen and the Prince should at once be moved to the greater safety of Edinburgh Castle, under an armed escort led by Huntly and himself, until they saw what repercussions were likely from the tragedy of Kirk o' Field. They would have noticed, he added dryly, that the Earl of Moray had not yet returned from St. Andrews.

But this time Moray had nothing as crude as an armed rising in mind, though he had his own reasons for keeping out of Edinburgh while others did his work. In his absence, Argyll set up a Court of Enquiry, with Murray of Tullibardine to represent Lennox interests, and Bothwell, as the Queen's Lieutenant and Sheriff of Lothian, to assist him. They took testimonies from all the neighbours at Kirk o' Field, and made arrangements to have Darnley's body borne in state to Holyroodhouse.

The following day a belated letter from the Archbishop of Glasgow, Scottish ambassador in Paris, arrived for the Queen, warning her most urgently that the Spanish ambassador there had reported some formidable enterprise to be in preparation against her. As Mary read it, shock and confusion of mind overwhelmed her like a breaking wave. For of what enterprise would the Spanish ambassador be likely to know save one undertaken by those of her own faith? Moretta had been in Edinburgh, and Savoy was the close ally of Spain. The thought was more than she could bear. She took refuge in her darkened mourning chamber, leaving her ministers to do what they could. Lethington, who knew her epistolary style better perhaps than any man in the kingdom, took charge of her correspondence once more. He wrote in her name to the King and the Queen Mother of France, to the anxious Archbishop of Glasgow, to the stricken Earl of Lennox. He also arranged for the publication of her offer of two thousand pounds' reward for information leading to the apprehension of those guilty of the King's murder.

So for a week, the situation smouldered, like the ruins of Kirk o' Field. Darnley's body was embalmed, and lay in state in the Chapel Royal, while the last offices were sung over it by the priests of the Roman Church. The Earl of Lennox, back in Glasgow, gave no sign of having received the Queen's letter, but Robert Melville, shocked by the news of the tragedy, turned back from his mission to England to ask for fresh instructions. The Queen remained in Edinburgh Castle, under the care of her physicians, who announced that, once the funeral was over, they believed the only hope of improvement in her Grace's health to be for her to find rest and quiet outside the city.

She received their recommendations with the same indifference that she showed towards all suggestions for her welfare. Still numb with shock, she was subject to fits of shivering, and unable either to sleep or to control her tears. Such a condition seemed only appropriate to most people, though it might appear excessive to those who knew how unsatisfactory her relations with her husband had recently been.

But the physicians' ultimatum delighted Mary Seton. She assured the Queen that her kinsfolk would be honoured to receive her at Seton, and to this she agreed, but indifferently, as if it mattered little where she went. The Prince was to return to Holyroodhouse now that no rebellion seemed likely, under the care of her most trusted lords, Huntly and Bothwell.

She was reluctant to send him back to Stirling yet, though she had herself been in the care of the same Earl of Mar as a child. For she remembered uneasily that Mar's Countess had been a Murray of Tullibardine, a family more devoted to Lennox interests than those of the Queen.

Soon after the Court had left Edinburgh the city was shaken by an explosion of another kind. Early risers on the morning after Darnley's funeral were stupefied to read a placard found nailed to the door of the Tolbooth, which announced in tall black capitals that, in response to the offer of reward, the anonymous accuser declared the murderers of the King to be the Earl of Bothwell, associated with Mr. James Balfour and two others, " the Queen assenting thereto."

The hubbub caused by the announcement brought the keeper of the Tolbooth out of doors to shoulder his way through the excited crowd. Tweaking the placard off its nail, he hastened with it to the Provost, who read it with goggling eyes, then hurried off to Holyroodhouse. A few minutes later Huntly wrenched open the door of the room in which his brother-in-law was working out the proportion of wages due to the members of the Prince's household now in his charge, and slapped the placard down before him.

" What devilry is this, James ? "

Bothwell nodded grimly as he read it. " This sort of thing is commoner in France," he said at last. " I have seen such placards many times in Paris."

" But—' the Queen assenting thereto——' "

" That, before heaven, she never did," Bothwell agreed. " Rather was it planned that she, and you, and I, and all in whom she trusted, should have died while the King lived, if I mistake not."

" Aye, but by whom ? "

Bothwell grinned wryly. " Your guess will serve as well as mine, George. One, at least, of those that planned it got what he deserved. The others have no doubt by now put many miles between them and the city of Edinburgh. I will not trouble the Queen with this." He took it between his fine, strong hands, then tore it decisively, across and across. " We shall hear no more of such mischief," he said with confidence.

Huntly looked doubtful. " May you be right," he said. " For I can see that much evil might be done by placards like this."

" Could anybody be found to believe them? " Bothwell asked contemptuously. " Hold fast, George. For the Queen needs all her good friends. Moray will not return to help her, you will see, and if you waver, others will follow you."

" I shall not waver," Huntly said. But under Bothwell's bold stare his own gaze faltered. For the friendship between them had suffered from the estrangement between Bothwell and his lady. And Bothwell's firm handling of the present situation seemed to suggest that he, at least, now believed himself to stand nearest to the Queen.

As the days passed the fog of suspicion which hung about the ruins of Kirk o' Field thickened till men peered fearfully at each other's faces, haunted by the possibility that when the murderer struck again they might not escape. Men such as James Balfour and Archibald Douglas had disappeared as if the ground had swallowed them. But the placards continued to appear. At first other names were mentioned, apparently at random. Only two remained constant; those of Bothwell and the Queen. And what was at first received with incredulity, began with constant reiteration, to have an increasing effect. What if it were true, men and women began to ask each other. For what is often repeated is ultimately believed.

On the 7th of March the Queen returned from Seton to give audience to the English ambassador in Edinburgh Castle and receive the condolences of Queen Elizabeth. But she was only dimly visible in the black-hung chamber, and spoke so little that the Englishman afterwards wondered whether he had really seen the Queen or whether one of her ladies had played her part because she was too ill to face him.

There was talk of a decline, even of " the falling sickness."
Two days later, Mary returned to Seton, distracted by Lennox's
insistent demands for a further inquiry, and by the vile accusations now being plastered all over Edinburgh, the knowledge of which could no longer be kept from her, since at any
moment she might be confronted by one on the door of her
own Palace.

She was thankful to get away from Edinburgh, where
silent crowds now gathered daily to stare speculatively up at
the windows of Holyroodhouse. Even Bothwell's nerves were
fraying: his friends heard him swear to wash his hands in his
anonymous enemy's blood. In the presence of the Queen,
however, he made light of a situation which would otherwise
have been intolerable, and she was thankful to know that the
Prince and the peace of the city were in his keeping.

For Moray, disregarding her distracted summons, had not
returned to Edinburgh. It suited his purpose very well that
his sister should now turn to Bothwell in the atrocious predicament they had been compelled to share. For it gave him just
the excuse he needed for assembling about him men such as
Morton, Lindsay, and, eventually, Lethington, once more
alienated from the Queen by her preference for Bothwell's
advice. To him also now came such Catholic Earls as Caith-
ness, shocked by suspicion of the Queen, and Athol, a kinsman
of Lennox. James Balfour came too, choosing this time to
remind him of their earlier conversation, and was made
welcome in his Councils.

By the middle of March Moray's plans were far enough
advanced for Lethington to inform Cecil triumphantly that
they were planning a marriage for the Queen which would
complete her breach with Rome which was already well
advanced, and presently involve her and the man bold enough
to marry her in one ruin. Even the alienation of the two
friends who might have stood together for the Queen against
them all seemed likely to be accomplished. For such a
marriage as they contemplated would not be possible without

the prior dissolution of Bothwell's own, and the affront to Huntly's sister must surely irk the Gordon pride.

The persistent series of placards was now beginning to have so serious an effect on public opinion that Bothwell went about the city with an armed escort. For Lennox had now begun boldly to call for the summary execution of all those who had ever been placarded in connection with the murder, apparently indifferent to the fact that such a demand must require the death of the Queen. In answer, Bothwell put the search for his anonymous enemy before all other business, and he was identified in consequence, before March was out, as James Murray of Purdovis, a Lennox man who had heard some of Bothwell's most unguarded remarks in Paris. But when the Council sent a strong force to arrest him, he had already left Edinburgh for an unknown address.

Bothwell went to convey the news to the Queen at Seton, where he found her, forlorn among her anxious ladies, her face leaden, her hands for once idle in her lap. She surveyed him bleakly, after the estranging events of the last six weeks, as if across the havoc of a searing fire which had blackened a fair woodland prospect with the breath of hell. Far away, he stood now, under the skeletal arms of once blossoming trees, surveying the charred ruin of a relationship once beckoning-sweet as a May morning.

He made no attempt to speak with her alone. But her gesture sent her ladies out of earshot, so that, though they might still be seen, they could speak, as Queen and minister of state, in confidence. Her mood had changed now, as anger at the wreckage of an intimacy which had brought her so much comfort took the place of grief.

" Have they found him, my lord, this contemptible fellow who has made so free with my name and yours ? "

" They have. It is to speak of that matter I am here," said Bothwell. " For what Murray of Purdovis has said against the Queen's Grace he should die."

She shook her head. " It is not necessary for me to silence

a man who accuses me falsely. Such an action would suggest that I feared him."

" The Queen's Grace may show mercy, since she is above the law. I demand a public trial by my peers," Bothwell retorted.

Startled, she dropped the mask of formality. " But James, I know you to be innocent of the King's death. It is all but a mile and more from Holyrood house to Kirk o' Field, with two guarded gateways to pass. How could you have fired the charge and yet be found in your bed when the explosion roused us? "

Bothwell bowed. " I thank you, Madam, both for your reasoning and your confidence. Yet as your servant I demand the opportunity of making my innocence known to all the world. It would not be seemly for you to be counselled by a murderer."

She winced at his bluntness. " That is true."

" And furthermore," Bothwell went on, in the same harsh and angry voice, " while I stand under such an accusation, it is not meet that I should have charge of your son, the Prince of Scotland——"

" There is no man I would sooner trust."

" But for your honour's sake," Bothwell persisted, " it would be better that tradition should now be served. I ask to be allowed to hand over my charge to the Earl of Mar."

" Very well." She spoke with decision. " I will see it is done. Also that the Lord Justice calls a Court to clear you of the charges brought against you."

" I thank your Grace," said Bothwell. Then dropping his voice for the first time, he added: " Since subjects may not judge their Queen, my trial will serve to establish your innocence as well as mine."

" I am content that it should," she said.

As agreed, she commanded that the Prince should be placed in the care of the Earl of Mar, at Stirling Castle. But Mar was displeased to learn that in order to fulfil his hereditary task he must give up the command of Edinburgh Castle. His wife persuaded him that he had Bothwell to thank for it, which was true enough, but not out of malice, as she, the sister of James Murray who had produced the libellous placards, inevitably supposed.

Mary then wrote to inform Lennox that Bothwell would be required to stand his trial before the Lord Justice of Scotland, and commanded him to bring all his evidence to Court. Lennox, thus directly challenged, was disconcerted to find how little evidence he could produce. But since the heralds were already proclaiming the date of the trial from the Market Crosses of Edinburgh, Glasgow, Dumbarton and Perth, and demanding the attendance of the Earl of Lennox for the prosecution, it was imperative that he should not let this deter him. Raising three thousand men for his personal defence, he marched them as far as Linlithgow, where the Queen's officers reminded him that the number of attendants permitted to either party in a Court of Justice was six, though the others might remain at Linlithgow to await his return. But Lennox, who had heard that Bothwell, after the fashion set by Moray on another occasion, was filling Edinburgh with his own supporters, decided that the omens were unfavourable, pleaded illness, requesting a postponement, and returned to Glasgow.

But the wheels of the law were already turning. The Earl of Argyll, as Lord Justice, was not, as it became the fashion to suppose, a supporter of Bothwell, and was to sit with four assessors who were neither Hepburns nor allied with them. At least half of the jury were either already Bothwell's enemies or soon to become so. The parties concerned were summoned to the Tolbooth for noon on the 12th of April, 1567 and the trial was over by seven o'clock that night, less because of prejudice in favour of the accused than the complete absence of any evidence against him whatever.

Bothwell appeared in person, to stand frowning darkly

in the dock, in spite of the exhortations of anxious kinsmen, while the thin, dusty voice of the Clerk of the Court broke against his thunderous silence.

"James Hepburn, Earl of Bothwell, I charge you of being art and part in the cruel, odious, treasonable and abominable slaughter of the late, the right excellent, right high and mighty prince, the King's Grace, dearest spouse for the time to our sovereign lady the Queen's Majesty, under silence of night in his own lodging beside the Kirk o' Field, he taking his night's rest. My lord of Bothwell, how say you? Are you guilty or not guilty of the charge against you?"

"Not guilty."

A buzz of excitement broke out in the Court and was angrily suppressed by the Lord Justice.

"Matthew, Earl of Lennox . . . Matthew, Earl of Lennox . . ." The voices went echoing about the farthest corners of the grim building, but without response. At last one of Lennox's men stood up to read a long complaint and demand a postponement of the trial which would give the prosecutor the statutory forty days to collect evidence. But this inconsistency in a man who had been importuning the Queen for weeks could scarcely be allowed to pass.

"Your master," the Lord Justice pointed out, "cannot both entreat the Queen's Grace to take immediate action and when such action is taken demand postponement for forty days. Request disallowed. Let the trial proceed."

From the first it became clear that no direct evidence connected Bothwell with the crime. He gave an account of his actions on the Sunday which was contemptuously comprehensive. He had been in attendance on the Queen's Grace except for the time she spent in the Chapel Royal at the nuptial Mass for her servant Sebastian and his bride. He had taken dinner at Court, gone to see his mother at Morham, returning in time to escort the Queen's Grace first to the Bishop of Argyll's supper for the retiring ambassador of Savoy and then to the King's lodging at Kirk o' Field.

With the rest of those in attendance, he had escorted her back to Holyroodhouse as the city clocks were striking eleven, to dance at the masked ball with which the wedding celebrations were to conclude. Shortly before midnight he was consulted by the Captain of the Queen's Guard.

" His name, my lord? " asked the Lord Justice.

" John Stewart of Traquair."

Bothwell's impatience became more evident as he described how he and Traquair had refused to allow the Queen to return to Kirk o' Field that night in view of certain information which had reached them. Instead, he himself had taken his servants to investigate. Finding everything quiet at Kirk o' Field, he returned as he had come.

" You did not think to demand entry, my lord? "

" Since the King had already retired, being scarcely recovered from his sickness, I thought it best to let him take his rest until the morning," said Bothwell blandly. " I then returned to Holyroodhouse by the Netherbow port and the Palace gate, as they can vouch who challenged me. When the crack was heard, I was in my bed. You may ask of them that roused me."

Against the rock of such an alibi all the concentrated malice of the defamatory placards, the vicious slander of the whispering campaign against him, must break in vain. The jury withdrew and debated long and earnestly. But in the absence of either prosecutor or adequate evidence they inevitably acquitted the prisoner of being either art or part in the slaughter of the King. After the verdict had been given and the official proceedings were at an end, the representative of the Earl of Lennox rose and addressed Bothwell.

" I have to congratulate you, my lord, on the day's outcome. May I be so bold as to hope that you will take no revenge on me for the part I have been obliged to take against your lordship? "

Bothwell grinned. " Have no fear, my friend. I bear no grudges." His spurs chimed sharply on the stone as he turned, swinging his shoulders a little, to leave the Tolbooth, a free man, with honour vindicated.

The Earl of Moray was not present at the trial, though he had returned to Edinburgh by the end of March, to prepare for the next stage in the drama. He was, to Bothwell's surprise, most friendly, when, after their first encounter at a meeting of the Council, he drew Bothwell aside and took the incautious Borderer ostensibly into his confidence. Moray declared himself to be most anxious as to the future of the Queen, once more widowed in a land which needed a strong man to rule it. He could think of none she esteemed as highly as her trusty Lieutenant, nor one as likely to rule Scotland without fear or favour. Had the idea, he wondered, ever occurred to Bothwell?

" My lord, I am a married man," said Bothwell curtly. " And divorce is unlikely to please my lord of Huntly."

Moray smiled sourly. " By all accounts you have little pleasure from your lady," he said at last. " And—" his face indicated violent mental conflict—" Huntly might see the marriage ended more willingly if I offered to return some of the Huntly acres that came my way on his father's forfeiture. Eh? "

Bothwell's eyebrows rose. If Moray were prepared to surrender any of his precious possessions he must be genuinely anxious for the Queen to marry again. And when he offered personally to approach Huntly on the matter, Bothwell allowed the idea of becoming the Queen's consort to drift for the first time through his mind. Consort first, he might one day be King. The word's brief ring moved him strangely.

Moray watched him, contemptuously noting that James Hepburn had less skill than most as a dissembler. He could see the ruinous thought take root in his victim's mind as if through a pane of clear glass. He was sure of him now. Like Samson, blinded in Gaza, Bothwell's very strength would presently be turned against him, bringing ruin, not only on himself, but also on the Queen. But Bothwell was not yet convinced. As a soldier, he preferred to reckon his strength against that of his opponents before undertaking an engagement.

" In such a purpose," he said slowly, " how many would support me ? "

" Discover that for yourself," said Moray blandly. " Entertain a sufficient number of the nobility, state your cause and see how many will pledge support for it."

Bothwell gave him a quick, appreciative grin. " I will," he said.

Moray concealed his satisfaction. Now, at last, all was in train. Bothwell must break both himself and the Queen against the jealousy of those who saw him preferred before them. He himself would presently ask leave to go abroad. It was always best to be elsewhere when trouble came to the boil. He had business in France, but he would travel through England. Much of the Scottish news would be of interest to his good friend Cecil.

Four days after his vindication, Bothwell bore the Sceptre before the Queen at the Riding of Parliament. Here, at his request, the Court's findings were made public, and the subject officially closed. Anonymous placarding was prohibited under severe penalties, religious toleration commanded, and disputes over former church lands terminated by ratifying the titles to their present holders. This last provision, though sensible enough, was unlikely to diminish Lethington's resentment against Bothwell, who had now become, on the rebound from disgrace, the most powerful man in the kingdom. Had John Knox been present, he might have cawed a warning. Woe indeed unto James Hepburn when all men praised him . . .

Bothwell did not take such praise at its face value, but decided, with characteristic forthrightness, to put it to the test. On the Saturday evening, after Parliament had risen and the Queen had gone to Seton, he invited all the principal lords and churchmen left in Edinburgh to dine with him in his quarters at Holyroodhouse. This, as he anticipated, they were all happy to do.

When the excellent meal was over, but the wine still circulating, he rose to explain his purpose, wasting, as was his habit, little time in circumlocution. In his hands was a document to which, as he explained, he would presently welcome their signatures. Meanwhile he would read it aloud. The first paragraph recalled his recent trial and vindication, his family's long history of loyalty to the Crown. The second passed on to the Queen's present lonely state and suggested that he, " James, Earl of Bothwell, Lord of Hailes, Crichton and Liddesdale, Great Admiral of Scotland and Lieutenant of all the Marches," would be the most suitable husband for her Grace, provided that his family record and personal qualities should move her Majesty so far as to humble herself (preferring one of her native-born subjects before all foreign princes) to accept him. Finally, the signatories were required to pledge their support for the marriage in every possible way, holding its adversaries as their adversaries and spending life and goods in its defence.

It was a daring, but not an outrageous suggestion for the restoration of order to a distracted kingdom, made by the Queen's most able, though not the most aristocratic subject. It would not have been by any means the first time that royal marriages had been obliged to wait on the divorce of one of the contracting parties. After a good dinner, at least, it seemed a most reasonable arrangement. Eight bishops signed as requested, with nine earls—including Huntly, Argyll, and Morton—and eleven barons—including Herries, Boyd, and Seton, the Queen's host. The one man who did not like the look of it—Lord Eglinton—slipped unobtrusively away.

Bothwell saw his guests to the door in a glow of good fellowship and hope. He was unaware either of the malice or the subtlety of those against him, and somewhat naïvely believed that those who had sworn to support him to the uttermost could be relied on to keep their word.

CHAPTER TWENTY

THE next day Bothwell set out for Seton, accompanied by Lethington, who meant to make sure that the enterprise went forward. Unfortunately, on arrival he was required to quell the beginnings of a mutiny among the royal guards who accosted him in the presence of the Queen to demand payment of their wages, overlooked during the recent troubles. A man who prided himself on his efficiency could scarcely have made a worse beginning. The incident ruffled him, and Lethington's veiled amusement goaded him still further, so that he now demanded with impatience the private audience for which he had come.

The Queen agreed to it uneasily, for the last time he had come to her with such solemn urgency had been on the night of the tragedy at Kirk o' Field. What new disaster threatened her now?

Bothwell thought he knew women. But he was, as she herself had once called him, a vainglorious man. He blundered now in consequence. It did not occur to him that the shadow of Kirk o' Field lay so darkly across the memory of Castle Drummond that passionate love alone could exorcise it. Her voice was strained as she invited him to make his purpose known.

To Bothwell the occasion seemed to merit a formal approach. " Madam," he began elaborately, " it has been a cause of distress to your loyal subjects that you should once again be destitute of a husband——"

She looked at him in bewilderment, answering formality with formality, unable to believe in such ineptitude. " And so, my lord? "

" And so we have taken counsel together, the evidence of which I have here."

She had not noticed that he was carrying a formidable parchment, until now, when he beat it against his knee. " And what was the outcome of your deliberations, my lord? " she asked uncertainly.

" The lords whose signatures appear, Madam, have agreed to further my suit with your Grace."

Still she did not understand. " And what, then, is your suit? "

" That your Grace will do me the honour of becoming my wife," he said, blunt at last.

Her sudden anger took them both by surprise. The idea that he should presume to offer her, not the expression of his personal devotion, but the chilly approval of her assembled nobles for what should be the most exclusive decision in the world, suffused her pale face with furious colour. To woo her would have been in itself no presumption. As she clenched her fists on the black velvet of her gown she realised how gladly she would have welcomed his adoration. Instead, he offered her this—this huckstering decision reached by her subjects as to which should now be her custodian. Anger choked her. She could scarcely speak.

" No doubt, my lord," she said at last, " you tossed a coin to decide who should undertake the task? "

Too late, Bothwell saw the danger-signals. " No, Madam," he said hastily. " All were agreed that the honour should be mine."

" Then you may return to them that sent you," she flared, " and tell them their Queen's answer. It is no. And no, and no, my lord. Am I a bale of merchandise to be sold at the market cross? Or a pedigree mare to be offered to the highest bidder? "

" Of these things there has been no question, Madam," retorted Bothwell, angry too. But she went on as if he had not spoken.

"You are not settling the future of a serving-maid now, my lord. You have presumed to dictate to your sovereign. Believe me, I will not forget it. You may go. Go, I tell you," she cried aloud.

He went, as badly shaken as an incautious hound which has thrust its muzzle into a wasps' nest. But he was already pondering his next step. For the rebuff had kindled the ardour he had considered unnecessary, in the first instance, to admit. Somewhat to his surprise, he now found that what he had looked on as a matter of expediency had become an enterprise on which all his heart and will were set. The Queen's stinging rebuke had only confirmed him in his purpose. He had set about matters in the wrong way, that was all. It did not matter. There were other means.

Next day the Queen left Seton for Stirling to visit the Prince. With her rode Huntly, Lethington, and James Melville, whose ambition still prompted him to personal attendance on the Queen, while his brother Andrew was content to perform the less spectacular duties of an officer in her household. They were escorted by the troop of horsemen, about thirty in number, whose wage claim had so recently been met.

The visit was not a success. Constraint was evident in the manner of the Earl of Mar, and he was reluctant to permit the Queen to see the Prince except in his presence. Uneasily she remembered the relationship between his Countess and the instigator of the anonymous placarding of Bothwell, and left Stirling, both unhappy and perplexed, on the 23rd of April. On the way she had one of the fainting fits which so often came on her in times of stress, and was obliged to break her journey at Linlithgow. But next day she set off again for Edinburgh. Her cavalcade, within six miles of the city, had slowed down to file across a narrow bridge when a party of horsemen, outnumbering the royal escort several times over, appeared as unexpectedly as if dragons' teeth had been sown on the surrounding fields. The Queen had scarcely recognised the weathered, unsmiling faces of some of Bothwell's Borderers, when Bothwell himself appeared, bonnet in hand, by her side. Leaning forward, he took her horse's bridle.

" You will do me the honour, Madam," he said curtly, " of accompanying me to Dunbar."

The Queen's fingers tightened on her riding-switch, barely checking the impulse to slam it down across his wrist. " And if I will not? "

" I shall insist," Bothwell said. His manner was carefully respectful, but the boldness of his grin made it clear that he did not mean to be denied. " I have news of a rising against you, and am come with these men to your aid."

" If there is a rising, I must warn the Provost of Edinburgh," she said, uncertain whether to believe him.

" Do so by all means, Madam. But you will still be safer at Dunbar."

He rode beside her, bareheaded, all the way. Behind them, the royal escort was surrounded by Bothwell's Borderers. The Queen could hear Mary Seton expostulating with those who restrained her, and James Melville protesting against such an outrage. But of Huntly and Lethington she heard nothing. She could only guess that Huntly had reckoned the odds against them and Lethington shrugged his shoulders over a situation he could not mend. But how strange it was to be riding to Dunbar again, in such changed circumstances. And the way seemed longer, this time, than she remembered it. It was midnight when the chains of the drawbridge roared round the winch and the great doors yawned back to receive them.

Uncertainly, she looked round the strange gathering in the torchlit courtyard. How many would obey her if she commanded a rescue? Lethington's narrow face showed gratification, she fancied, rather than rage, Huntly was staring speculatively round his former prison, and James Melville looked exhausted rather than dismayed. Only Mary Seton's indignation was evident, as Bothwell, in outrageous good humour, set about playing the host. The royal visit, he implied, was an honour eagerly anticipated.

"Allow me, Madam, to assist you from the saddle. You must be weary after so long a ride."

It was true enough. She was so tired that she was compelled to accept the help he offered, though for the brief moment of contact, she held herself rigid in his arms. But when he let her go, she reeled on her feet, her voice failing in her throat as she tried to summon Seton to her aid.

"Her Grace is unwell . . ." She could hear Seton's indignant protest. "Let me go to her."

"Leave her Grace to me." Bothwell's voice seemed to come from an infinite distance. Then he stooped and picked her up like a tired child, strode with her across the courtyard, through the doorway, and up the turnpike stair. She was too weary to protest, too heartsick to assert her royal dignity as he bore her towards the apartment which, it appeared, had already been prepared for her. Mazily she realised that the fire on the hearth must have been kindled hours before their arrival, noticed that the many candles had burned half-way to their sockets. She was unexpectedly aware, too, of warmth and rest and safety, where she had refused to believe that such things could be found.

Twice married to weaklings, Mary had for years been called on to sustain when she should have been sustained. So now, overwhelmed by the strength she had never known before, all her senses cried aloud for her to yield. The conflict between pride and desire was so sharp that she lay as if dead against his shoulder. Then, as her eyelids flickered, he swung round, taking her weight easily on one arm as he shot the bolt home with his free hand against his agitated pursuers. The Queen's ladies might minister to their mistress in due course. This, he realised with mounting triumph, was his hour. And yet, as her brown eyes opened, the expression in them would have daunted most men. For the time being

pride had overwhelmed desire, and her voice was sharp with
rage.

" Set me down, my lord."

He had at first intended to debate the matter on the
morrow. But now he found her defiance irresistible. He
knew, beyond the possibility of doubt, that he could make her
yield. Queen or commoner, the omens were the same. But as
he silenced her protest by kissing her on the lips she wrenched a
hand free and struck him across the face, the sound of the open-
handed blow sharp as a snapping stick.

He threw back his head and roared with laughter, encircling
her with his long arms as she sought desperately to thrust him
from her, elbows braced and palms flat against his chest. When
that failed, she beat against him with her fists till the jewelled
buttons of his doublet bruised her. She was a tall woman,
so tall that their shoulders were level as he accepted her blows
unflinchingly, tasting blood as his upper lip was driven
against his teeth.

Her resistance delighted him, for he was always happiest in
conflict. The cold passivity of his wife had humiliated him,
the terrified excitement of such girls as Anna Throndsen had
enticed him, the bold skill of the foreign whores who had plied
their trade with him had served their elemental purpose. But
this was different from anything he had yet known, far more
disturbing than he could have guessed, even after her first
response at Castle Drummond. Her ferocious opposition not
only promised equal fervour, but roused in him an unfamiliar
anguish far transcending the brief needs of the flesh he knew
so well, shadowing forth the longings of the spirit which he had
denied.

Her blows were slackening as he bore her towards the
great bed with the dusty hangings from which the spiders' webs
had not been disturbed by the servants who had hastily
prepared it for their master's guest. Her hands were sore now,
her breathing unsteady as anger yielded to the passion she

dared not own. She felt his weight upon her, turned her lips frantically away.

"James . . . this is mortal sin . . ."

"Then I shall never seek heaven," he said between his teeth. The firelight revealed the outline of his taut, lean limbs as he wrenched impatiently at the alien stuffs that separated their bodies, so that they met at last in all the awful innocence of Eden, flesh to flesh, in a reconciliation so absolute that they seemed merged beyond recall. Drowning in light, exalted beyond imagination, she dreaded the inexorable return of individual awareness as if, in recognising the instant of her life's completion, she had also seen beyond it to its doom.

But sleep lay like lead upon her eyelids, lapped her limbs in delicious lassitude. Resisting it, she knew the passing sweetness to be already hollow as the jade green concavity of a breaking wave. Soon it would escape her, to dissolve into the past in a smother of reproaches and regrets, leaving her among the jealousies and antagonisms of an alien world, harsh as a pebbled beach, the substance of past beauty sucked from her in the grudging disillusionment of the undertow.

He lay beside her, already asleep, candlelight golden on his bare shoulder, one arm flung wide, the other still curved absently about her. Raising herself on one elbow, she was amazed by the change in his face. She had known him grave and gay, commanding and attentive, austere, passionate and angry. But she had never, until then, known him vulnerable. As he slept, a mask seemed to have fallen, leaving him as confiding as one of the little creatures that turned to her for protection. As she touched his cheek with a questioning finger, he drowsily kissed her palm, his lips curling into a smile that might have belonged to the morning of the world. She had meant to blow out the candle, but she did not, because she could not bear to lose sight of him, in the darkness. Then her arm began to ache, and she let herself slip down beside him. In spite of herself, she slept.

Hours later, his voice roused her, hoarse and discontented. " Faugh, how I hate the stench of a guttering candle! "

She woke with a start, to find the morning grey about them and James angrily stubbing out the acridly smelling wick-end in its dwindling pool of wax. Then he flung a few clothes about him, his face haggard in the merciless light, the fire dead on the hearth.

" Do not leave me, James." Her voice was high and desolate. If he went, what now remained?

He came to her at once, masterful again, but yawning before he kissed her. His eyes were blank. " Much must be done, sweetheart, before our plans can go forward as they should. I must be free to marry——"

" Yes . . ." she said softly.

He gave her his familiar, impish grin. " You will not dismiss me, this morning, for such presumption? "

She flung her arms wide. " No, James. Instead, I will make you so great that no man will think it so."

" I wonder? " he said dryly. " But if it be the Queen's wish, I shall not care who questions it. Now I will send your women to you."

But Mary Seton was weeping so bitterly that for once it was the Queen who sought to comfort her. " He is the greatest soldier in the kingdom, Seton."

" Yes, Madam."

" He has served me more faithfully than all the rest."

" Yes, Madam."

" And he was cleared of art or part in the late King's death by the highest Court in Scotland."

" Yes . . . Madam."

" Oh, Seton, Seton," she cried at last, " do not stand there like an accusing conscience. In the presence of my lord of Bothwell I am alive. When he is absent, I care not whether I live or die."

Then Mary Seton flung herself on her knees before her mistress, hiding her tear-streaked face in the Queen's lap.

" Oh, dearest Madam, if that be the way of it, then there is indeed no other choice. I will serve you both to the uttermost. But, alas, since he is also a married man, I fear no good will come of it."

" You are wrong, Seton," the Queen whispered dreamily.

" Heaven grant it, sweet Madam," Mary Seton sighed.

Proceedings for Bothwell's divorce began at once, in both Catholic and Protestant Courts. There was nothing irregular, from the Catholic view-point, in Bothwell's appeal for the annulment of a marriage belatedly discovered to be within the prohibited degrees. Or so the prelates consulted by the Queen agreeably informed her. What they did not disclose, and had perhaps forgotten, was that a dispensation had been obtained at the time of the marriage, and was still in existence. But the Lady Jean informed her husband of this fact just when the case seemed likely to go through without question. She had no wish to lose both her title and her property, and would only free him on the grounds of adultery, which would rid her of a defaulting husband but permit her to keep his gifts.

Bothwell shrugged and let it go at that. Lady Jean should have her pound of flesh. When she cited the little sewing-maid with whom he had consoled himself for her frigidity he did not dispute the charge. He had other causes of anxiety.

For he had now learned that the guests who had sworn to support his marriage with the Queen by every means in their power were already joining the opposition party now being formed at Stirling, where Mar mounted guard over the Prince, that invaluable hostage whom Bothwell had so casually surrendered. Morton, Argyll, and Glencairn were at Stirling already, and Lethington, no doubt, was merely biding his time. From France Moray was reputed to be in touch with their plans. The sooner he and the Queen were safely married the better, Bothwell thought wrathfully. For their marriage offered the only chance of riding out the storm now almost upon them.

But first the Queen must return to her capital, so

that the whole world might see her both free and well. On the 6th of May, therefore, he escorted her back to Edinburgh, riding with her at the head of a contingent of Borderers, formidable but unarmed, up the West Bow to the Castle, where he proposed she should remain till her people had been given time to accept her changed circumstances.

As they rode through the city the citizens of Edinburgh stood silent, less hostile than bewildered. There were no demonstrations, either of loyalty or revolt, but by the middle of May, Bothwell considered it wise to return with the Queen to Holyroodhouse. For James Balfour had recently demanded the command of Edinburgh Castle so pointedly that he had not cared to refuse it. It would be unfortunate if Balfour felt obliged to go to the Queen and explain why Bothwell had made no search at Kirk o' Field on the night of the explosion. It might even make her change her mind about the marriage.

The divorce, however, had now been hustled through the Courts. The Archbishop of St. Andrews and the supporting bishops of the old faith whom the Queen consulted gave her the ruling which she obviously desired. Once Bothwell's marriage had been annulled, they declared, she might consider herself free to marry him. It did not affect the case that the Lady Jean had asked for a divorce on the grounds of adultery. From their point of view, a marriage contracted within the prohibited degrees should never have existed. But the divorce granted by the appropriate Protestant Court, was on the grounds Lady Jean had chosen.

And so, one way or another, James Hepburn was free. The opposition of the ministers of the new faith to his re-marriage, therefore, took both the Queen and her intended husband completely by surprise. When Mr. Craig, minister of St. Giles, indomitably refused to cry their banns it seemed that all was lost. For Bothwell, she knew, would never consent to be married by the Roman rite, even if its priests would have been willing to perform it.

"Master Knox has done his work well. He hated me always," Mary cried. "Now he has persuaded the ministers to disobey me."

"The ministers," Bothwell said gloomily, "would not hesitate which to obey, if you seemed to give one command and God another."

"But what are we to do? They would die, I believe, sooner than yield. Have you ever encountered such obstinacy?"

"Often," said Bothwell wryly. "Your church has made martyrs of many such obstinate men. If Mr. Craig will not marry us, we must seek till we find a minister who will."

"I shall restore to you your family titles of Duke of Orkney and Lord of Shetland," said Mary. "They cannot then complain. I shall be marrying the greatest nobleman in Scotland."

"Do not be too sure, sweetheart," said Bothwell. "But at least the Protestant Bishop of Orkney will scarcely refuse to marry us."

And so it was arranged. By the 14th of May the wedding contract was ready. The signatures of the Queen and the newly created Duke of Orkney were witnessed by six oddly assorted noblemen, among them Huntly, Lindsay and Lethington. The ceremony took place at dawn on Thursday, 15th May. As on the former occasion, Mary wore the black outer robe of mourning over the white and gold splendour of her bridal gown. Among those present were the Archbishop of St. Andrews, the Bishops of Ross and Dunblane, and such distinguished laymen as Sutherland, Fleming, Livingstone and Glamis. Afterwards the Queen and the Duke entertained their guests to dinner, but after the gorgeous entertainments of recent years, the banquet, shorn of the traditional largesse and entertainment, seemed surprisingly austere.

The truth was that Mary was now uncomfortably short of money, and Bothwell had warned her that, in view of the discontent expressed by the ministers and aggravated by the hostile muster at Stirling, the royal guard must be supplemented by at least five hundred horsemen and two hundred men-at-arms. Mary recognised the need for reinforcements but questioned some of his other measures.

"I do not like that shifty fellow Balfour, James," she complained, two days after their marriage. She had dismissed her ladies, and was alone with Bothwell in their bedchamber, where she had been making ready to ride with him to Leith.

"No more do I," said Bothwell ruefully.

She swung round on her dressing-stool, the mirror glinting in her hand. "Then why did you take the command of Edinburgh from honest James Cochrane and give it to Balfour instead?" she asked in amazement.

"I had no choice, just then."

She frowned. "I do not understand."

Bothwell chewed the edge of his moustache and pondered. Then he decided to speak out. He did not care for blackmail, and now that they were safely married, he believed that Balfour could do him no further harm with the Queen. But just in case he tried, she had better know the truth.

"Balfour reminded me that if I did not give him the command he could explain why I did not search the cellars of Kirk o' Field that Sunday night," he said. "No, do not look as if you had seen the devil. I laid no hand on the young fool. But when I was advised to return to Holyroodhouse and leave justice in other hands, I saw no reason to do otherwise. Heavens above, Mary, what squeamishness is this? Darnley would have murdered us all. Why should he not be hoist with his own petard?"

But she was sobbing wildly, tears streaming between her fingers. Honestly amazed, he sought to comfort her. "Why, sweetheart, what is this? I believed you loved me."

"I do—heaven help me," she sobbed despairingly. "I love you so sorely that this news is like to break my heart. Oh, Mother of God, what shall I do? I thought you spoke the truth when——"

"So I did," Bothwell protested. "I tell you again I never touched the treacherous——"

"Yet you could have saved him——"

"Did you expect it?" Bothwell said impatiently. "Or did you look for me to tell you what had befallen, knowing well that I stood to lose you once that conscience of yours was roused?"

She beat her forehead with her clenched fists. "When they told me I would be marrying my husband's murderer I defied them. I believed you. But now . . . but now . . . Saints in heaven, what shall I do? Had I a knife," she cried, her distraught voice rising to a scream, "I would kill myself!"

"Be quiet," he commanded her roughly. "Are you crazy, to proclaim such things to the whole world? I did nothing but leave others free to punish him as he richly deserved."

But she was not to be comforted. "One who permits a murder to be done is himself a murderer," she maintained in anguish. "Had I known——"

Unabashed, Bothwell grinned. "It was for that very reason, sweetheart, that I did not tell you. But enough of this. Do you wish those now listening at the door to report a lover's quarrel?" he added more softly. "What's done's done, so best forget it. Dry your eyes and ride with me to Leith."

Wretchedly, she obeyed, her face too pale for a newly married bride, so that those already apprehensive watched her and shook their heads. From that day the dread of retribution grew upon her, and with it, perversely, her love of the man for whom she so despairingly prayed.

And yet, during the next few weeks, they shared some happy times, snatching them, as it were, under the long faces of their enemies. They rode together about the summer countryside, attended water pageants on the Forth, shot at the butts, and walked together in the Palace gardens, arm-in-arm. Little bits of byplay were hopefully reported by those who wished them well, as when the Queen, taking her husband to task for persistently appearing bareheaded in her presence, snatched his cap and herself clapped it on his head.

They did not neglect the work of government. Their Council met regularly, with the Queen and the Duke in constant attendance. Acts were passed for the reform of the currency, the establishment of better order on the Border, the maintenance of the Reformed religion. The new Duke of Orkney wrote statesmanlike letters to the King of France, the Scottish Ambassador in Paris, Cecil, and the Queen of England. He showed a grasp of essentials, a tolerant attitude towards religious differences, and a most jealous devotion to the Queen's person. Sometimes, as Mary watched him presiding gravely over a debate, she smiled secretly to herself, glowing with pride. Were her prayers being answered? Would heaven permit them to be happy, in spite of all things? Sometimes she ventured to believe that her troubles were over.

But Bothwell, disillusioned now as to the value of fair promises, knew better. For his enemies were obviously preparing to strike, and memories of the last attack on Holyroodhouse made him unwilling to stand a siege there. Apart from Edinburgh Castle, whose custodian he had no wish to trust, the nearest stronghold in reliable hands was Borthwick, twelve miles from Edinburgh. By the beginning of June the situation was serious enough for him to feel obliged to escort the Queen there at a moment's notice, leaving her in Lord Borthwick's keeping while he rode on to rouse the Borders for her defence.

Promptly as he had acted, his enemies were only a few hours behind him. Borthwick was attacked soon after his departure, and Mary only escaped capture by changing into the breeches and leather jack of a man-at-arms and riding after her husband. Together, they reached Dunbar for the last time, to be greeted by the news that in the Queen's absence the confederate lords had entered Edinburgh and called

its citizens to arms in the cause of the infant Prince. Such
insolence infuriated the Queen.

"Do you hear that, James? We must ride back and drive
them out forthwith! Why do you shake your head? We did
it once before. The people will rally to us again——"

"I am a soldier, sweetheart," Bothwell said. "Before
I begin a battle, I reckon the odds against me. We would do
better to let this bonfire burn itself out. Other people may
also have difficulty in finding wages for idle soldiers——"

"Then let us give ours occupation," she retorted. "This
is unlike you, James. You, who take fire for a cause——"

"I must first be sure of the men I lead. Wait till the
Borderers join us."

She sighed. But she would have waited, had not
James Balfour's message jolted Bothwell unwillingly into
action against his judgment. For Balfour, now convinced
that the confederate lords might well defeat the Queen, had
adjusted his obligations accordingly. His despatch to Bothwell
warned him with apparent friendliness that unless the royal
forces regained control of Edinburgh immediately he would be
obliged to surrender the Castle to the confederate lords. To
prevent such a disaster, Bothwell reluctantly agreed to attack
the capital at once.

He had collected an army of sorts at Dunbar, and Mary,
at least, was confident that loyalists would join them by the
thousand as they marched on Edinburgh. They spent a night
on the way at Seton House, among many happier memories,
and the next morning Bothwell halted his forces on the
northern slopes of Carberry Hill, beyond which the formidable
army of the confederate lords prepared to block their entrance
to the capital.

Mary joined her husband as he rode slowly along the
lines of men and guns he had disposed after careful calculation
of the terrain and the opposing formations. She was in high
spirits, and still dressed in the short red skirt and bodice she
had borrowed from a soldier's wife at Dunbar, delighting the

donor by her gay promise to wear them to victory. As usual, the emergency had exhilarated her. But the look on Bothwell's face chilled her elation like frost.

" What's amiss, James? "

He gave her his crooked grin. " I have done my best, sweetheart. But I fear our enemies have done better."

" We are outnumbered? "

" Not by so much. But our men do not like the look of the banners flying yonder."

" Why not? "

" They have no stomach for an encounter with men pledged to avenge the Prince's cause against his father's murderers——"

Though she had herself accused him, she denied such an accusation with fury when her rebellious subjects echoed it. " How dare they pretend to such a cause? Surely our men will not endure it? But what ails them, James? I can see nothing wrong."

" Were you a soldier, my love, you would feel it," he told her wryly. " They have no stomach for this battle."

" You cannot mean that we should surrender? "

" We cannot afford to be defeated," he said curtly. " If we could contrive a delay, we might have the chance of leavening this lump with more courageous stuff."

She considered the unwelcome idea, frowning. Then the sight of a small party which had detached itself from the main body of their enemies and was riding deliberately towards them offered a distraction.

" It may be that some such thought is in their minds also. This looks like the offer of a parley, James. Who is it? The sun is in my eyes. It looks like—but yes, it is Du Croc. What can the French Ambassador want with us save to offer terms? "

" At least it will do no harm to listen," Bothwell agreed. " He has always acted in your interest. I will go forward to greet him——"

He returned with the French Ambassador, and Du Croc,

in a state of considerable agitation, knelt to kiss the Queen's hands.

" Madam," he said anxiously, " your lords protest themselves to be your most humble and affectionate servants——"

" Sir," Mary interrupted indignantly, " they show it very ill."

" You mean," said Bothwell, " that I alone am the object of their hatred ? "

" My lord," said Du Croc unhappily, " that, alas, is what I mean."

Bothwell nodded, almost indifferently. He drew himself up to his full height, thrusting his thumbs through his belt. " Then let me alone receive their assault, while the Queen goes free. I am willing, sir, to save bloodshed by encountering in my own person any man of valour and good family who will stand out with me between the armies and fight the issue to the death."

" My lord, I will convey your challenge to the lords," said Du Croc, with evident approval. But Mary seized her husband by the arm.

" James, you shall not do it," she said fiercely. " I forbid it, do you hear ? I forbid it utterly."

Discouraged, Du Croc halted.

" Give the lords my message," Bothwell roared. Then, as the Frenchmen trotted off, he turned impetuously to the Queen, once more his swashbuckling self as the prospect of dangerous action delighted him. " Dear heart, there is no other remedy. I can trust myself, but not these fellows. Look at them ! They have no more spirit than a flock of sheep. You must let me fight——"

" No, James." Her voice was anguished.

" It is my right, after all. Have I not brought all these troubles on you ? "

" I do not care," she cried defiantly. " The very thought of such a combat kills me with fear. If you died, James, why should I care to live ? "

He looked at her with an unexpected smile of utter gentleness. " Now, at last, I believe you love me."

She could only stare at him, speechless.

" It is strange," he said, his voice for once humble, " that you should."

She laughed unsteadily. " Is it? We are so like, and yet so unlike, you and I. It does not matter. You are so dear to me that I cannot bear to think of you fighting out there, alone, for me. Perhaps they will refuse your challenge. If they do not, I will forbid the combat." She drew herself to her full height. " I am the Queen."

" I do not know," he said, harsh again now, " what else we are to do. I tell you, these men of ours will run from the first charge."

She frowned, standing silent beside him, her eyes blank with dismay as she stared at the ranks of shifty-eyed men. " There is one other way," she said at last. " Listen, James. If the lords undertake to show me the loyal duty and obedience due to their Queen, I will yield myself to them, on condition that you and your men go free."

" But that is madness! " he said violently. " You cannot trust such traitors. Have they not broken the word they pledged to me ? "

" They would not dare break an oath to their sovereign lady," she said quickly. " And what else, indeed, can we do? If you remain and we are beaten, they will kill you. But if you go now, you can presently bring every Queen's man in Scotland to my aid."

" I tell you it is madness," he repeated. " They seek my death above all else. And that I have offered them, at a price. To your proposal they will never agree."

" We shall see," she insisted, almost gay again. " Here comes Kirkcaldy of Grange. I am glad of that, for he is an honest man. James, I command you as your sovereign lady, implore you as your most loving wife, to let me have my way. It is the only hope——"

" I do not like it——"

" No more do I. But for the present it must serve. Leave this to me. I shall speak as a Queen to her subjects." She smiled at him, in an anguish of tenderness. Then, as she turned from him to Kirkcaldy of Grange, regality came down on her again. Her voice was clear and strong as she offered her ultimatum.

" Laird of Grange," she said, " can you assure me, on your honour as a gentleman, and that of all the lords assembled with you, that if in my desire to save Scottish lives, I come to you, you will receive me and hold me in all honour as your Queen ? "

Kirkcaldy of Grange was an experienced and successful soldier. But he was no lover of warfare between Scots. His candid eyes were relieved as well as speculative as he glanced from the Queen to her husband, silent behind her. He answered promptly.

" I swear it, Madam."

" And will you also save the life of my husband, the Duke ? "

" No, Madam," said Grange decisively, " we are minded to kill him if we can."

" But if I come to you, will you permit that he, and all those with him, may depart ? "

For the first time Grange hesitated. His instructions had been only to get the Queen out of Bothwell's hands. Was the price she asked too high ?

" I will come on no other condition."

" Then, Madam," said Grange hastily, " the Duke and those with him shall go free."

" Then send someone back to your army. You must first make that condition clear."

As he turned to instruct one of the men who had ridden with him the Queen moved to where Bothwell was standing, expressionless, a few paces away. In silence she walked, before them all, into his arms.

" My dearest lord," she said, " I bid you farewell for but a little while. Once you are back at Dunbar you will be safe and able to work for my deliverance. Think of me always as your most loving wife. And I—I shall be the braver for my thoughts of you. Go now, my most dear lord. Before—before my heart fails me——"

He kissed her on the lips. " I will go. But I had rather die." Then, as if he could endure the leave-taking no longer, he swung away from her to vault across his horse, jerking out a command for his men to follow him.

Mary stood for a long time, staring after the column of white dust, the head of which indicated his whereabouts. Only when she could no longer hear his horse's hoof-beats did she turn to walk, tearless and resolute, towards Kirkcaldy of Grange and his waiting men.

CHAPTER TWENTY-ONE

HAD it been a nightmare, she would have wakened at last. But from such nightmarish reality there seemed to be no waking. In a state of mind bordering on madness, Mary paced up and down the comfortless attic chamber in the Provost's lodging, high above the High Street of Edinburgh. How right James had been to warn her against the promises of traitors. Anxiety for him tormented her with self-reproach. If they could so deceive their sovereign lady, were they likely to keep their promise that their enemy should go free?

She was only remotely aware, now, of the hostile roar from the crowds in the High Street below. The people of Edinburgh, hastening to their stair-heads at the sound of the returning troops, had seen her haled back from Carberry, not as a Queen attended by her nobles, but as a prisoner among her captors, weary and bedraggled in all ill-fitting bodice and short, scarlet skirt, mocked by the soldiers who bore before her the banner of revolt on which her pictured son knelt to pray for heaven's vengeance on his father's murderers. First one and then another had joined in the outcry, till their way was lined with a derisive mob of hostile hooligans, pointing their fingers, shaking their fists, whistling above the clamour as she rode past between Morton and Athol, her head high, while tears streamed down her face, hearing the tumult about her as the distant roar of an estranging sea.

Desperation had dried her eyes, as if in the breath of a furnace, when they forced her up the stairs and into the stifling little chamber, left her there alone and turned the key in the lock. At first she beat her fists on the door till the pain checked her, crying aloud to those who had treated her as a common criminal that they had sworn to show her the homage due to their Queen. Then she ran to the window. Surely her people would not see her imprisoned? Had she not always sought their welfare? She threw herself against the casement, thrusting her arms between the bars which had prevented so many prisoners from throwing themselves headlong to their death.

" Good people of Edinburgh——" she began.

The howl of execration that drowned her words was fierce as the yell of a hunting pack. The shocking sound appalled her. Could these be the same people who had called down heaven's blessing on her only a few short months ago? Now their hatred rose at her in a solid, jag-toothed roar.

" Murderess . . ."

" Wanton . . ."

" Whore . . ."

The words were cruel as blows. She had no means of knowing that the outcry was being sustained by men hired to rave against her whenever their neighbours' frenzy showed signs of dying down. It was even less subtle, but just as effective as the vilification of Bothwell had been.

" Stane her . . ."

" Droon her . . ."

" Burn the whore . . ."

In her raging desolation a lifetime's regal habit yielded to
the contagion of the frenzy below. As she was driven beyond
control she tore at her hair till it fell wildly about her face,
rent the constricting bodice so that she could get her breath
to hurl their insults back at the sea of bobbing pink faces with
darkly opening, vilely roaring mouths.

" Heretics . . ." She spat at them, shaking her fists.
" Traitors . . . you shall all burn for this . . ."

Her contorted face was so swollen with weeping as to be
almost unrecognisable, her wild gestures so unrestrained that
here and there sober citizens on the edge of the crowd shook
their heads and turned away from the sight of a gentle creature
driven out of her mind. Talk of attempting a rescue was so
persistent that her captors felt it would not be safe to keep her
in Edinburgh. Her imprisonment had been long since decreed,
even its whereabouts decided. Moray's mother had assured
him before he left Scotland that it would give her the greatest
pleasure to have the Queen she professed to consider a usurper
under lock and key in Lochleven Castle. Since Sir Robert's
death, she had remained its chatelaine, for her family, Sir
William, George Douglas, and the rest, were easy going and
disinclined to invite a lashing from her bitter tongue.

After a dreadful, comfortless night, alone in the attic prison
chamber in the Provost's lodging, Mary was next morning
exhausted enough to welcome the smoothly spoken deputation,
headed by Lethington, who assured her that her detention
had merely been intended to protect her from the fury of
the people, of which she could not have been unaware.
That evening, they promised, they would conduct her to
Holyroodhouse, where she should at once resume her royal
state.

Yet again, she believed them. The memory of the outcry
against her still made her shudder, and at Holyroodhouse,
they assured her, her own servants would be waiting. She
made no protest when she was taken out of the Provost's

lodging by a back stair and escorted by roundabout ways to the Palace where her servants ran into the forecourt to receive her, weeping as they knelt, covering their faces with their hands. She watched them with weary detachment. For once her own appearance scarcely interested her.

" Sweet Madam," Seton sobbed, " we shall soon set all to rights. Your own people shall bath and tend you. Alas, it is high time that your hair received my care." Laughing hysterically, she tried to make light of her mistress's shocking state. " Fresh clothes shall be laid out and your bed prepared . . ."

" Give me paper and writing materials," the Queen commanded as soon as they had changed her clothes and dressed her hair. " I must tell the Duke that I am safe and well."

" Surely, Madam, that can wait till the morning? "

" I will write now."

Her hand was shaking so that she could scarcely mark the paper at first. But she persisted. For now he had been two days without news of her.

" My dearest Heart," she wrote, " I pray you to forgive me because I have not written at once. But truly, things were not as I supposed. Your judgment was surer than mine. Would to heaven I had heeded it. But now that all seems somewhat mended, I will rejoin you as soon as I may. Continue in your utmost efforts, I pray you, to rouse our defenders, and believe that I care not where we be in the whole world if we are but together. Love me always as I——"

The last words scrawled into incoherence as the quill slipped from her fingers. Mary Seton caught her as she swayed. " Come to bed, dearest Madam," Seton implored. " Let all else wait till you have slept awhile."

But once more sleep was to be denied her. A violent summons on the main door brought her terrified French servants hurrying to say that two of the rebel lords had ridden into the forecourt with spare horses and men-at-arms. They

demanded that the Queen should receive the lords of Ruthven
and Lindsay immediately.

" Her Grace can see no one," Mary Seton protested.
" She is quite worn out and will shortly retire for the night."

But Lindsay, with young Ruthven, son of her old enemy,
had followed the servants into the Queen's presence unbidden,
and now shouldered them aside. They had been given the
task of conveying the Queen to Lochleven because they were
the most effective bullies among her enemies, and Lindsay
lost no more time in setting about his task.

" The Queen must prepare to accompany us forthwith,"
he announced.

Outraged and incredulous, Mary Seton stepped between
him and her mistress. " Sir, it would disgrace you to speak
so to a simple gentlewoman. How dare you thus address the
Queen's Grace ? "

Lindsay laughed unpleasantly. " You shall learn in due
course. Keep a civil tongue in your head meanwhile, or we
shall leave you behind."

" You shall not part me from her Grace," said Mary
Seton fiercely.

" Then prepare her to proceed without delay."

" But whither, at this hour ? You can see for yourself that
she is broken with weariness."

" For her own protection, she must leave Edinburgh,"
said Ruthven roughly. " The people are ready to stone
her."

" And we shall leave as midnight chaps from the kirk
tower," added Lindsay, losing patience. " If you women
are not ready, I swear by heaven above that I will truss you
both like fowls for market and tie you each across a horse's
back."

The Queen rose slowly from her writing-table, slipping
her unfinished letter out of sight under the score of a French
song. It was evident that resistance was futile. Her enemies
might even be speaking the truth when they warned her of

danger from the Edinburgh mob. "Bring me my hooded russet mantle, Seton," she said quietly. "Will you now retire, sirs, so that we may prepare for this journey? We will not keep you waiting long."

But Lindsay, standing with feet astride and folded arms in front of the Queen's hearth, grinned as he shook his head. "You will make greater haste if we are at hand to urge you."

She was obliged to leave them in possession of the presence chamber while she retired to the bedchamber beyond. But as Seton brought out her plainest riding dress and mantle, she contrived to whisper to the French lady-in-waiting who had been summoned to put on her riding-boots.

"When we have gone, Estelle, take the letter I have written to my lord Duke. It is under the song that Bastian set to music in honour of our marriage. See it is despatched. And send someone trustworthy to James Balfour at the Castle. Command him, on his allegiance, to hold out against the traitors——"

"Madam, I fear that if you do not hasten, these brutal fellows will invade your very bedchamber," warned Mary Seton.

"I am ready. Give me your arm, Seton. Bid farewell to my household, Estelle, and tell them to be in good heart. It cannot be long before the Duke leads every true man in Scotland to my rescue."

"Oh, Madam, Madam," wailed the distracted French-woman unbelievingly, "what is to become of us all?"

The Queen shook her head at her. "Be brave, Estelle. We shall yet be merry together, as in the old days. If you are in distress, go to the French Ambassador's lodging. M. Du Croc will care for you."

But the sound of terror-stricken weeping followed her all the way down the stairs. Then she and Mary Seton paced silently past the impatient Lindsay and his scowling companion and prepared to mount the horses which were waiting for them in the courtyard, just visible in the afterglow that thinned the midsummer night.

Their departure had been well timed. Next morning the Palace was ransacked by the Queen's enemies, each after his own fashion and regardless of the outcry from her servants. Lethington, quiet and deadly, came first, going meticulously from room to room, in search of any confidential papers which would help his party to justify their actions before a world which still took the divine right by which sovereigns ruled as a matter of course. After him came others who were noisier and less fastidious in their search for plate, jewels and costly materials with which to finance their rebellion. On the same day Morton peremptorily dismissed all the Queen's French servants, and Glencairn, whose puritanical aversion from the adoration of images was only equalled by John Knox's revulsion from women in authority, saw no reason to prevent his soldiers from looting the Chapel Royal.

Two days later Morton entertained Lethington to dinner at Douglas House. His guest's narrow face indicated a secret satisfaction, and he bore an object draped in the cloak which he insisted on retaining, in spite of the warmth of the weather, while the servants remained in the room.

" Have you taken the rheum, man ? " wondered Morton, as meat was set before them and a discreet allowance of wine produced.

" I have taken something a deal worse," said Lethington complacently.

" It'll not be catching, though ? " said Morton anxiously.

Mr. Secretary Lethington wiped his lips delicately with a lace-edged napkin. " Some folk may catch their death on't," he said agreeably. And in spite of his host's alarm, it was not till the servants had left the room that he was prepared to make his meaning clear. Even when he laid on the table between them a small coffer, daintily silver-gilt, with crowned capital F's elegantly displayed among the scroll work, Morton had no idea of its significance. It was a pretty thing, of evident

French workmanship, but much less valuable than many of the objects they had already acquired from Holyroodhouse. And Lethington, enjoying the evidence of his subtlety, exasperatingly took his time before making any explanation.

" What's in it? " asked Morton bluntly.

At last Lethington produced a key. " I learned the way of this from my sweet wife," he explained. " Though if she guessed the use I had for it she might have been less willing to disclose the secret."

Very deliberately, he turned the key to and fro in the lock, lifted the domed lid of the silk-lined coffer, and beckoned Morton to look within.

" Letters! In the Queen's hand! " Greedily, Morton clutched a fistful, while Lethington sat back, a thin smile just twitching the corners of his mouth as he watched his host leaf the papers through. Now and then he swore incredulously. Then he sighed. " No names are mentioned."

" Some folk are hard to please," said Lethington. " All else is there."

" Aye," said Morton grudgingly. His small, piggish eyes narrowed as he surveyed his guest. " Strange to have here the very words we need to ruin them . . ."

" Is it not? " Lethington agreed blandly.

Morton cleared his throat. " This coffer now, these letters—" He hesitated. " Those verses, and all the rest, will they be just as you came upon them? "

Lethington's expression changed. Behind his smiling calm flickered for an instant an emotion as startling as a glimpse through a briefly opened furnace door. It was a little over a year since the Queen had humiliated him by her preference for that contemptible foreigner, David Rizzio, and made him look a fool before the Queen of England. He would have pleasure in settling these scores now, both with the Queen and the man to whom she had given his lands at Haddington. But he did not answer Morton's question at once, and when he did, it was in his own ambiguous fashion.

"It is strange how little is needed, when a writer has wrought in haste, and on what paper came to hand, to make the matter somewhat clearer than it at first appeared . . ."

"Say no more, my friend, say no more," Morton chuckled. "Mebbe I'd better not know what I could never have guessed." He smirked admiringly at the papers in his hand. "Nay, never in this world. But if these letters and verses were intended, as we believe, for the felon Bothwell, how is it that he did not receive them?"

"Need it be admitted that he did not?" murmured Lethington, stroking his thin beard. "Have we not laid hands on one Dalgleish, his servant? Now we need only use sufficient persuasion to make him confess that he was sent to retrieve this coffer which had been left behind in Edinburgh by his master when he fled."

"Just so, just so," Morton agreed admiringly. "The fellow can afterwards be hanged before he can contradict himself. True, the missives lack heading and subscription. But caution would explain that. Ihmhm. And the marriage contract, bearing the Queen's signature and Bothwell's. Man, what good fortune, to come upon that also!"

"Aye, was it not?" said Lethington dryly.

Morton gave him a shrewd glance, his little pig's eyes glinting. "We have enough here to convince the Pope himself both of the part she played in Darnley's murder and her infatuation for yon ugly devil——"

"But your conscience would no doubt be easier if I did not explain too clearly how these papers came together?"

"Aye, it would," said Morton hastily.

"Then I will suggest only that when you have cause to write letters dealing with matters of life and death you neither use odd scraps of paper nor leave too great spaces above and below the lines."

"I'll mind that," Morton said soberly. "But what now?"

Deliberate as a chess player, Lethington pondered the next

move. " It would be best," he said at last, " that this discovery——"

As he tapped the little coffer Morton guffawed.

"—should rest no longer than need be on our word alone.
I suggest you summon as many lords as are now in Edinburgh
to hear the tale of its capture and see it broken into because
you have not the key."

" Ihmhm . . ."

" Thereafter, the documents should be listed and held in
safe keeping, to be displayed as need arises. What news is
there from Moray? "

" He sends us, from Normandy, his blessing, urges the
greatest expedition, and quotes more scripture than the
messenger could mind, since he preferred to put nothing on
paper."

" He'll wait till the cat has jumped, as ever," said Lethington sourly.

" He's feared she'll best us yet. What's to do to stop her? "

" We must compel her to resign the crown in favour of the
Prince, with Moray regent," said Lethington. " He will not
support us for less."

" Man, she'll never do that! "

" She will, one way or another," said Lethington. " We'll
see what Robert Melville can achieve with fair words once he
returns from England. If fair words fail, then we'll use others."

" Will the people remain steadfast against her? "

" We'll set John Knox to keep their conscience on the boil.
If need be, we have these . . ." Lethington tapped the coffer
lightly.

Grinning, Morton rubbed his hands together. " She'll not
best us this time."

" She should not," Lethington agreed.

In the island fortress of Lochleven, the Queen so obstinately
refused to touch bite or sup that after two weeks Lady Douglas
became alarmed lest her prisoner should die. For that would
not suit her son, the Earl of Moray. She was also uneasily

aware that she might be held responsible for goading her to
extremes, for she had assured the heartbroken Queen that she
need not look for the respect due to her title, since she had no
right to it. King James, said Lady Douglas, had married her
in secret, and their son was Scotland's rightful king. She did
not expect to be believed, since everyone, unfortunately,
knew that her royal lover had married her off to Sir Robert
Douglas before her son was born. But the fiction of regality at
least gave her the excuse to treat Mary with such vindictive-
ness that even her Douglas sons protested, and when Robert
Melville was rowed out to the island she was thankful for the
arrival of someone likely to improve her prisoner's spirits.

"She's been wearying for your coming, Sir Robert," she
assured the ambassador, "though I'm sure I've done what I
can."

"Indeed, I am sure you have," said Sir Robert agreeably.

"The first bite she's taken since she came here was after
the news of your coming."

"Tch, tch," said Sir Robert. He was the most worldly
of the Melville brothers, with the assured manners of the
professional diplomat, and he obviously anticipated little
difficulty in persuading the Queen to accept the course of
action he had come to propose. But as he knelt to greet her he
was genuinely shocked by the sight of her haggard misery,
and promised that comforts and clothing for her small household should be sent from Holyroodhouse.

"I am here, Madam, to help you, above all else. What
would you wish me to do?"

Mary surveyed him uncertainly. All her life she had
instinctively believed everyone, save only when it had become
clear, as in the case of her mother-in-law, Catherine de Medici,
that she was implacably hostile. It was hard, now, to have to
pick and choose whom she might trust. She had done what she
could to receive her ambassador with proper formality, seated
under her canopy of state, embroidered with the coat of arms
she had herself worked in happier days, completed by her

enigmatic motto: "*En ma fin est mon commencement.*" Her dark
eyes were larger than ever for the shadows under them, her
lips almost colourless as she whispered:

"Will you bear a letter from me to my dear lord, the Duke
of Orkney?"

He sighed and shook his head. "Alas, Madam, I may
not."

"But you can give me news of him?"

"None you would care to hear."

"He is not—dead?"

"He has been outlawed, Madam. There is a price of a
thousand crowns upon his head——"

"Only a thousand?" Her laugh zigzagged along the edge
of hysteria. "How affronted he will be. But he is raising
an army——"

"Madam," said Sir Robert gravely, "since he was outlawed
no man will follow him——"

"So much," she said fiercely, "for their bond to assist
him, with their life and lands——"

"Madam," Sir Robert sighed, "few men will venture
either in a cause as lost as his."

"Lost? Not while I live!"

Sir Robert looked down at his well-tended finger-nails and
changed the subject. "As your Grace is aware, I have recently
returned from the Court of her English Majesty——"

"Ah, yes," Mary said quickly, "that reminds me. I had
a ring from my good sister Queen Elizabeth some years
since. It is of no great value, but she vowed that if I were ever
in trouble I might command her assistance by returning it.
Will you find it, among my other jewels, and bring it here?"

"Madam, I dare not," said Sir Robert. "Nor should
such a token be needful. The Queen of England is deeply
shocked by your misfortunes. She assured me she would do
her utmost to see all set to rights. Provided only——"

"Ah, yes." The Queen smiled bleakly. "Provided
what, Sir Robert?"

" Provided, Madam, that you will have no more to do with the Duke of Orkney, and consent to have your marriage set aside."

She sprang up indignantly, twisting a fine kerchief to a rag between her hands. " You may tell the Queen of England that such a condition is intolerable. I am not accustomed to play the traitor, and I will not abandon my husband to regain my freedom. No, not to save my head. Tell the Queen of England, Sir Robert, that both my love and duty bind me still to him. Tell her also that I hope to bear his child. Would she have it born a bastard? "

Sir Robert shook his head in judicious sympathy, averting his eyes from her distress. For some minutes she continued to pace about the room, then flung herself, exhausted, back into her chair. " Is there yet more? " she demanded.

" Yes, Madam. Her Majesty of England further requests that you will permit your son, the Prince, to be placed in her care, to be educated in England at her personal charge."

Mary looked at him with sudden, uncertain hope. The old ambition had not died in her. Was her cousin Elizabeth, after all, perhaps better disposed towards her claim than she had dared suppose? Then she spread her hands wide in a gesture of helplessness.

" But how is he to be conveyed to England? He is as much a captive as I am myself."

" Queen Elizabeth has offered to send a sufficient force to free him from his present bondage, or so I understand from my brother James, who has seen Sir Nicholas Throckmorton, her special envoy."

She shook her head reluctantly. " These wretches would sooner murder the child than give him up."

" That may be so, Madam," Sir Robert agreed. " But, as I understand them, there is one thing you can do which will beyond all doubt ensure his safety." He paused. After the tortuous habit of his calling, he had at last reached the object of his interview. " If you will agree to lay down your crown in favour of the Prince your son, I believe that neither you nor he need have further cause for anxiety."

But, once again, he had misunderstood her temper.

"Resign my crown?" she cried. "Never will I agree to such a thing! Never, I tell you, while I have life and breath to defend my royal state, into which I was born."

"I beg you, Madam, to consider a little——"

"Not for one instant, sir!"

"That is your final word?"

"It is. You may take your leave."

She was puzzled, after he had gone and her temper had had time to cool, by his insistence on her abdication. She had always found him sufficiently devoted to her interests. Even now, he had urged her voluntary resignation of the crown as if it were the lesser of two evils. He was, she guessed bitterly, taking care to keep on good terms with her enemies. But, as he took his leave, he had been sincerely sorrowful. And because she had always liked the Melvilles, in spite of the knowledge that James was the close associate of her brother Moray, she wondered why. It was not long before she knew.

This time the courtesies were absent. She was aware of angry voices below only a few moments before the entrance of Lord Lindsay, in a towering rage, as he wrenched his arm free from the restraint of Sir William Douglas, who had followed him, unannounced, into her presence chamber. As Lindsay struggled for breath, crimson-faced, Sir William spoke briefly.

"Madam, I have some knowledge of what my brother-in-law proposes, and I wish to ask your forgiveness for being unable to prevent such a scene from taking place under my roof."

Bewildered, Mary looked from one angry man to the other. Then Ruthven entered, followed by George Douglas, with Sir Robert Melville hovering uneasily in the background.

"I am here, Madam, by the command of the Council," said Lindsay roughly, " to invite you to sign the deeds I have brought." He thrust them towards her across the table. " Read them first if you wish. But sign them you shall."

" With your Grace's permission," said Sir William, in a choked voice, " I will go. I ask you only to remember, Madam, that I have played no part in this affair."

The Queen bowed her head, then picked up the papers Lindsay had offered. As she read, she drew herself up to her full, commanding height, her eyes wide with incredulous rage.

" What farce is this, my lord? You ask me to sign a declaration that I, ' being in infirm health and worn out with the cares of government, take purpose voluntarily to resign my crown and office to my dearest son, James, Prince of Scotland? ' How can you suppose that I would ever do so? "

" Read on, Madam," said Lindsay grimly.

She turned to the second paper. " I am further to agree to constitute my ' trusty brother, James, Earl of Moray, Regent for the Prince——' "

" There is yet more."

The third decree appointed a provisional council of regency, pending Moray's return, to carry on the government. Violently she flung the papers down.

" I would sooner die than sign them! "

" If you do not sign them, Madam, you shall die indeed," said Lindsay fiercely.

She looked at him in dismay. " What, am I to set my hand to a deliberate falsehood? Shall I relinquish the office God has given me to my son, who is but a year old and cannot reign, so that my brother of Moray shall reign in his name? "

" Madam," said Lindsay, " I have not come here to dispute these deeds, but to ensure that you sign them. If you will not, then by God's death, I will sign them with your heart's blood and cast your body to the fishes."

Here young George Douglas's indignation, which Melville had been trying to restrain, exploded into words.

" By heaven above, my lord, you shall not speak so to the Queen's Grace! "

Lindsay swung round with a snarl. " Yea, by God's truth I will so speak, and act, too, if she does not what is required."

Mary put a hand to her head. She believed that Lindsay was ready to do what he threatened, in spite of Douglas's protest, regardless of the terrified outcry of her ladies, huddled together at the far end of the chamber. Sir Robert Melville, it seemed, thought so too. Hurriedly, he intervened.

" I beseech you, Madam, to do what he demands," he murmured. " The Lords of the Council are adamant on the matter. They will denounce you otherwise, for connivance with the Duke of Orkney in the King's murder. They have evidence in your own handwriting, it seems, which will convict you both of it."

" That cannot be," she cried despairingly, sickened by the stench of the quintessence of malice. What new treachery was this? The stiflingly crowded chamber seemed to tilt and darken round her. She was weak and sick from lack of food and queasy with pregnancy. But Lindsay jabbed a quill into the ink-pot they had brought, and thrust it, dripping, towards her.

" Sign," he insisted, between clenched teeth.

" I am not yet twenty-five," she cried, in one last desperate appeal. " I cannot be compelled to renounce my birthright before I am of full age. I have not the right to do so . . ."

Lindsay laughed harshly. " I care not. But if you do not sign, I swear you will never see another birthday. I will cut your living flesh in collops with this sword."

She heard steel grate on steel as he half drew his weapon from its scabbard, she felt Ruthven's breath hot on her neck as he closed in behind her. Even Robert Melville's eyes were cold as stone. The fear of such a death, unshriven, caught her by the throat. Abandoned among these wolves, she had no choice. Her fingers were so clumsy with shock that she scarcely felt the quill as she stooped over the table and signed.

After that, everything was blurred. She was aware of Lindsay's grunt of triumph, Robert Melville's lukewarm consolation, the sobbing fury of young George Douglas. Then the world seemed to explode in a roaring tide of darkness. Mary Seton ran forward to catch her as she fell.

She took weeks to recover from the miscarriage which prostrated her with despair, weakness and loss of blood. The news of her infant son's coronation, on the 29th of July, scarcely reached her consciousness. She hoped only to die. But, little by little, Mary Seton's whispered entreaties brought her back to life, and her own courage responded to the challenge of the great wrong which had been done her.

" Sweet Madam," Mary Seton would whisper, as the Queen lay, tearless and wakeful, through the endless nights, " remember that no undertaking given under duress and in fear of death is binding. Remember also that you are not yet of age. When you are free again, you can renounce your signature . . ."

Once she was free again . . .

Mary began to respond to the picture that Seton's words conjured up. Once she was free again, she would defy all her enemies and summon James, her own dearest lord, to her side. Together, what could they not accomplish? Never again would she be so foolish as to allow herself to be parted from him, however fair their enemies' words might be. He had been outlawed: she would re-instate him. They had devised proofs against him: together they would deny them. Once she was free again . . . once she was free . . .

" There's my sweet lady," whispered Seton, as she saw hope begin to kindle behind those lifeless eyes.

At first, her efforts to escape were unsuccessful. A promising plot, devised by George Douglas for her departure, disguised as a laundress, in the boat which plied to and fro between the castle and the mainland, was frustrated by Lady Douglas and

George dismissed from the island. But once Mary had begun to hope, she was not to be discouraged. The first necessity was to give the impression that she was becoming reconciled to her imprisonment. Then her gaolers' vigilance might be relaxed. To this end, she busied herself with her embroidery again, ate the food which was set before her, demanded extra clothes and small comforts for herself and her ladies as an indication that she had accepted her fate.

News from the outside world reached her only occasionally, distorted by the sympathies of those who brought it as the reflections of the surrounding mountains were distorted by the breezes that blew this way or that across the waters of the loch. She knew that Moray had been invested with the title of the Lord Regent in the Parliament Hall in the third week of August, though his supporters did not risk summoning Parliament to hear the declaration which had been extorted by Lindsay from the Queen at Lochleven read aloud.

It was not a popular appointment. In many towns the citizens refused to hear the heralds' proclamation, even stoned them from the market cross. But Moray was indifferent. He gave orders for Mary's royal seals to be called in and broken up, also for new coinage to be issued in her son's name. He offered James Balfour a full pardon for his share in the Kirk o' Field tragedy, five thousand pounds, the Priory of Pitten-weem and a pension for his son, in exchange for the surrender of the Castle of Edinburgh and an undertaking to keep his mouth shut as to the events at Kirk o' Field.

He next set about the capture of Bothwell, who was still raging about the country, trying, with savagely frustrating failure, to unify the widespread but haphazard support for the Queen under his command. For the poison of the recent placarding had done its work, and many who would otherwise have followed him were too jealous of his influence with the Queen to subordinate their own claims to lead her cause to victory. By the end of September, Kirkcaldy of Grange and a company of his hereditary enemies had first hounded him out

of Scotland, then followed him to Orkney, till finally the storm
which saved his battered ship from capture drove it helplessly
on to the Norwegian coast, where he and his ship's company
were taken to be pirates and imprisoned for trial.

Even the establishment of his true identity only involved
him in further trouble. For one of those able to confirm it
was the very Anna Throndsen who now sued him for breach of
promise and unpaid debts. He was finally removed, in close
custody, to Denmark. Moray was disappointed, for imprisonment offered only a poor second best to the execution for which
he had hoped. Stone-dead, for him, had no fellow. But at
least Bothwell, in a Danish prison, would be unable to defend
either himself or the Queen from the charges he now proposed
to bring against them. For Scottish opinion, he considered,
now required further instruction.

He called his first Parliament in December, and there
announced the capture, five days after the Queen's surrender
at Carberry, of Bothwell's tailor, Geordie Dalgleish, with a
small silver casket in his possession. Under torture, he had
admitted that he had been sent to recover it from Bothwell's
quarters in Edinburgh Castle, then in the custody of Sir
James Balfour. No further testimony, unfortunately, could be
obtained, since Dalgleish had been summarily executed for
complicity in his master's crimes.

In the casket, Moray announced, were a number of letters,
verses, and other documents, either written or subscribed
by the Queen in her own hand, which made her connivance in
Bothwell's murder of her husband so plain that nobody in his
senses could seek her restoration. The uproar produced by
the news was such that he did not consider it safe to display
the original documents so clamorously demanded. Copies,
he promised, would be made, which they could all study for
themselves. Meanwhile, men with hands on their swords
glared at each other across Parliament Hall, while others
shrugged and asked what could have been expected after
such an upbringing. But though some protested her innocence

with rage, almost with tears, Moray reflected with satisfaction that he had broken the heart of the royal resistance.

So autumn and winter went by. Then spring came at last to Lochleven, and with it came a longing for freedom which was almost too much for the Queen to bear. One evening towards the end of April she was walking by the shore, watching the cormorants dive into the pearly water, when a commotion among the bushes roused her. She was interested rather than afraid. Death itself, she sometimes thought nowadays, would only be another sort of liberation. But at the sight of the sturdy, fair-haired boy in his early teens, she smiled.

" Madam," gasped Willie Douglas, almost inarticulate between shyness and excitement, " I ken fine yon plan for escaping didna gang as it should. But would ye be minded, mebbe, to try again? "

CHAPTER TWENTY-TWO

HER leaden mood splintered into a spray of stars. Escape had become, and was to remain for the rest of her life, a passionate and supreme necessity. Often, as she fretted in her island prison, she realised how truly James had spoken for them both. She, too, had the uttermost horror of imprisonment. Once she was free again, all things would be possible.

" I'm always minded to try again, Willie," she said quickly. The boy was no stranger. One of the family's dependants of uncertain origin, treated sometimes as odd-job boy and sometimes as a grandson of the house, he had already executed several small commissions for her with intelligence and despatch. " Whose is the plan? "

" Mine, Madam." Willie's voice was hoarse with pride and excitement. " And it's a gude yin."

" Is it? " She smiled at him in the way that had already made so many men ready to die for her. " What must I do? "

Willie nodded approval. Here was a lady who wasted no time on foolish objections. " Come doon to the courtyard," he said, " as soon as they ding the bell for supper in the hall above. Wait till I come wi' the keys o' the water gate. Sir William aye lays them on the table beside him, and I can easy pick them up in my napkin when I serve his wine. Wait by the gate——"

" To-night? "

" Aye. When ye're safe oot I'll lock the gate ahint us. Then I'll row ye across. George keeps watch frae the far shore——"

" How many will the boat take, Willie? "

" How mony hae ye a mind to bring? " said Willie warily.

" Mary Seton must go. And Janet Kennedy."

" Aye. But nae mair. I'll see to't the nicht, then."

He plunged back into the bushes, while the Queen, wondering if she had dreamed the entire interview, waited for Mary Seton, who had paused to take a pebble from her shoe. Anxiously Seton listened to Willie's plan. Its simplicity troubled her.

" But that is what is best," said the Queen earnestly. " Let us walk on now, Seton, for fear that the sentry marks us lingering. Pretend to be admiring the morning light on Ben Lomond or the ruins of the Culdee monastery yonder, on St. Serf's Inch. May it be for the last time! "

" Amen to that," said Seton fervently. " But we had best start a new panel of tapestry this morning. Our chatelaine will not guess how little idea you have of completing it."

Laughing, the Queen agreed. On their return they made a great parade of begging certain silks from Lady Douglas, also of drawing the design and preparing the canvas for a sufficiently ambitious project to keep them busy for months. Mary was thankful for a task exacting enough to prevent her excitement from betraying her. And as she and Mary Seton

busied themselves with charcoal and canvas, they were able
to discuss more interesting matters than the work before them.

Secrecy was essential, for Lady Douglas had sent two of
her younger daughters to wait on the Queen and bring back
news of all that went on about her. But Mary had begun to
find conspiracy much more amusing than the charades with
which she and her ladies had once entertained themselves,
and so, as the girls settled themselves down to sorting silks
on the far side of the chamber, she enjoyed eluding their
vigilance.

" Seton," she said, in the clear voice that all could hear,
" I wonder if we shall have enough crimson silk for the ladies'
mantles on this canvas? " Then, lowering her voice, she added
softly: " have you told Janet Kennedy what is afoot? "

" If there is not enough, Madam, some can wear blue,"
Mary Seton answered in the same way. " She knows, and will
be ready."

" The huntsman's pose is ill chosen," said Mary presently.
" How are we to persuade these Douglas girls to leave us at
supper-time? "

" Will you re-draw the huntsman, then, Madam? I have
told them that those below are to have venison, while we have
only broth."

Her mistress's answering laugh made her ladies look up,
smiling at the joke they had not heard because they were happy
to hear her laugh after so much sorrow.

" Give me the charcoal then, Seton. Hush, we must be
more careful, or they will guess." Mary put her hand to her
head, then went on gravely. " I will take supper early this
evening. My head aches," she added more loudly. " I should
perhaps retire sooner than usual."

" I will see to it, Madam," said Mary Seton meekly.
" Would you wish to rest now? "

" I could not bear it," said the Queen frankly. " Let us
proceed with the design. I dare not risk being idle."

The royal apartments were on the second floor of the castle

keep, which was only large enough to have one good-sized room on each level, linked by the usual spiral of stone stairs. Above the presence chamber were the bedchambers for the Queen and her ladies, while the Douglas family occupied the two floors below. In order to reach the courtyard, therefore, the Queen would have to pass down the stairs at the end of the hall in which the family sat at supper, hidden from them only by the curtain which sheltered those at table from the draught.

As the slow hours passed, the Queen's apparent interest in the new piece of tapestry grew feverish. She drew and re-drew the design, planned a new colour scheme, and called her ladies to admire it. The Douglas girls yawned. They had seen enough of embroidery, during the months they had waited on the captive Queen, to last them for the rest of their lives. So when only bowls of broth were sent up for supper they exchanged glances, then sidled off towards the stairs, up which the savoury smell of roast meat drifted from the floor below.

At last the bell in the courtyard was struck to summon the household to supper. The soldiers locked the gates, handed the keys to Sir William, and went off duty. No special precautions were thought necessary during the evening meal. They were, after all, islanded from the rest of the world. But on this occasion, as the two Douglas girls hurried down the stairs to make sure of their supper, the Queen, with Mary Seton and Janet Kennedy, rose from their places. Casually, the Queen said: " I believe it will ease my head to stroll round the courtyard, Seton."

" Here is your mantle, Madam," said Janet Kennedy.

" You and Seton shall attend me."

Sedately they moved to the head of the stairs. Then they paused in dismay. " Seton," the Queen whispered, " these heedless girls have drawn aside the curtain across the end of the hall. We should be seen by everyone if we passed by."

Mary Seton turned to beckon the little girl who had for some weeks past attached herself to the Queen's household, running

errands and doing small jobs for the prisoners. Like Willie
Douglas, she was an unofficial member of the Lochleven
household, and those at supper would not be surprised to see
her flit across the hall.

"Run down ahead of us, Kirsty," Mary Seton commanded, "and draw the curtain across below. Her Grace
does not care to be stared at as she goes by."

Kirsty was delighted to throw down the tangled skein
of silk she was unravelling, and the hubbub of conversation
at the supper-table masked the soft clash of curtain rings.
In a moment the Queen and her ladies had slipped by. Once
at the foot of the final flight they had no fear of being observed,
and almost at once Willie came down, as if to fetch something
from the kitchen. At the sight of them he threw his napkin
down and ran wildly for the gate. Unlocking it, he pushed the
Queen and her ladies through before him, then stared blankly
at the child who had slid her hand into the Queen's.

"Sweet heavens," gasped Mary Seton, "what shall we
do with her? She cannot go back now. If she gave the
alarm——"

"Get in," said Willie gloomily. "It's to be hoped she
doesna sink the boat."

"Give me one oar, Willie, and take the other," cried the
Queen. "There are many boats here. They may follow us."

"Huh," said Willie contemptuously, "I've got the bungs
here." He nudged them with his foot. "They'll sink."

Grinning, he shook his head at the Queen's offer of assistance. Then he dipped the oars gently into the pearly waters
of the loch, which faithfully mirrored the surrounding peaks in
the utter stillness of the early summer evening, till its surface
was suddenly broken by a splashing plop.

"Saints in heaven, what was that?" cried Janet Kennedy.

"They are firing at us!" cried the Queen. "We must make
greater haste. Willie, I command you, as your sovereign, to
give me an oar. With two rowing we shall be the sooner
out of range."

" It was but the keys, Madam," said Willie, grinning. " I thocht they'd be safe at the bottom of the loch."

They laughed then, almost hysterical with triumph, their voices carrying far across the water, as Willie's vigorous strokes took them steadily forward. Heads appeared above the sentry walk behind the castle wall. The alarm bell clanged. Biting his lip, Willie hauled at the oars.

" Can ye see ony folk on the shore ? " he gasped anxiously.

They shaded their eyes from the westering sunlight. " There's a man by the water's edge . . . and horsemen in the distance," cried Mary Seton.

" Then wave to them, Madam," cried Willie, wrenching at the oars.

The clumsy boat rocked dangerously as the Queen stood up to wave the white veil she had snatched from her head. Willie had to rest on his oars to steady it, his face awed as he watched her joy. Laughing and crying at once, she was babbling a strange mixture of thanksgiving, supplication and sheer delight in French, Latin and Scots. Willie had been taught that Latin prayers were idolatrous, and he could no more understand them than he could understand the dawn chorus of the birds. But he knew happiness when he heard it. For her, like the birds, the long night had gone.

" They are galloping to the shore to meet us," cried Janet Kennedy.

" They have thrown their bonnets high," said Mary Seton.

" They have horses waiting for us——"

" George Douglas is wading out——"

" Row faster, Willie," cried the Queen.

" Sit doon, Madam," Willie yelled. " Ye'll coup the boat! "

But they were in shallow water now. George Douglas, waist-deep, gripped the gunwale as Willie shipped his oars. Borne ashore between them, the Queen found herself surrounded by kneeling men who wept as they kissed her hands.

She spread her arms wide in a gesture that sought to

embrace the whole world. " My friends . . ." she said brokenly, " my dear, good friends . . ."

" Madam," said Lord Seton gruffly, " the sooner we are away from here the better. Horses are ready."

" Oh, but how good it will be to ride again," she cried. " My lord, you will see that Willie is not forgotten? I owe everything to his ingenuity. And the little maiden also——"

" They shall ride behind two of my men," Lord Seton promised. " Permit me, Madam, to assist you to the saddle. Now then, up and away . . ."

They reached Niddry Castle that night, for Mary could not rest till she had put the Forth between her and her former gaolers. Dusty, exhausted, and jubilant, they escorted her to the best chair by the hearth in the great hall. But her first question took them all aback.

" And how fares my dear Lord, the Duke of Orkney? "

They turned to each other, ill at ease, uncertain, their hesitation chilling her delight like dew. Heads were shaken, throats cleared. At last someone mumbled that the Laird of Riccarton should know more than they.

" The Laird of Riccarton? Then send for him forthwith."

" He is here, Madam."

As they stood aside she went to meet Sir Alexander down the hall, her attention all for him, as if the rest were shadows. " Welcome, Sir Alexander," she cried, both hands outstretched. " What have they done to my lord? "

" Madam," said Sir Alexander, " they have done him no harm. As yet——"

" Then what harm threatens him? "

" He is a prisoner in Denmark, Madam, sent from Bergen to Copenhagen after his shipwreck. King Frederick will not surrender him to anyone; no, not to my lord of Moray, who demands his head so that he may set it on a pike at Kirk o' Field, nor to the Queen of England, who offers him a trial to clear his name. Nor to——" He broke off in confusion, seeking to conceal the last words by clearing his throat.

"To whom?" Mary demanded. "Who else seeks to harm him? Sir Alexander, remember that he is my husband. I demand the truth."

"It seems, Madam," said Sir Alexander unhappily, "that some years since he encountered a certain lady when he was in Denmark in your royal mother's service. She followed him home to Scotland——"

"Is that all?" said Mary defiantly. "I knew of that folly long since." She faced him so boldly that she might have been telling the truth. "But why recall it now?"

"Because, Madam," said Sir Alexander, "through the strangest misfortune, this very Anna Throndsen was in Bergen at the time of the Duke's shipwreck, when his identity was questioned. She vouched for it, but only in order to demand his imprisonment for false promises of marriage and the return of money owed."

"She shall have it, to the last bawbee," said the Queen scornfully. "But my lord she shall not have. How much will set him free?"

Sir Alexander shook his head. "Her cause was but a pretext on which to hold him. It is to be feared that King Frederick is now too well aware of the Duke's importance to surrender him, even to you."

"I will see to that," said Mary regally, "as soon as I regain my throne. Meanwhile, Sir Alexander, you shall go at once to Denmark——"

"Most gladly, Madam."

"Tell my dearest lord of my escape. Assure him that I will demand his release from King Frederick in the moment of victory. Bear him meanwhile my most loving greetings and assure him many times that I shall not rest till his freedom completes my own. For I know . . ."

Her voice faded, her eyes grew remote. Once more she seemed to be hearing Bothwell's harsh voice, looking into his ice-blue eyes in the firelit parlour at Coldingham. "For I know," she repeated, her voice suddenly anguished, "that he has the uttermost horror of imprisonment. You will mind above all, Sir Alexander, to say how steadfastly I will work for his liberation? "

" I will mind it indeed, Madam."

" You are also to demand the surrender of the castle of Dunbar, which the rebels now hold, in his name and mine."

" It shall be done, Madam." Sir Alexander knelt briefly to kiss her hand, then clashed importantly out of the hall. As the clamour of newly arrived supporters rose about her, the ordinary world reasserted its claims.

Next morning she was escorted to Hamilton House by Lord Claud Hamilton, son of the Duke of Chatelherault and representative of the ambitious house which now stood so near to the throne. Behind them streamed a medley of supporters, some mounted and others on foot, drawn from all parts of Scotland and armed with every variety of weapons, from cross-bows to muskets, their wild enthusiasm masking, for the time being, their complete lack of a leader whose authority would be accepted by all.

For the Earl of Argyll was barely on speaking terms with the Hamiltons, who had already annoyed the leaders of many other contingents by constituting themselves the Queen's supreme champions, and the Queen herself, still wildly excited by her freedom, was too delighted by the assurances of loyalty she had already received to realise how many rivalries must threaten it. As she welcomed the Earls of Cassilis, Eglinton and Rothes; the lords of Somerville, Livingstone, Ross, Herries, Fleming and Borthwick, she only knew that they were returning to their allegiance, and greeted them like prodigal sons, caring little what their record had been or what faith they professed. She received two of the Melville brothers with special pleasure.

" Why, Sir Robert, it does my heart good to see you. Sometimes I thought my brother of Moray and his friends had cajoled you away."

For once Sir Robert looked shamefaced. " They did their

best, Madam. But I have returned gladly to your service, bringing what resources I could. Three horses and their equipment were all that remained in the stables at Holyroodhouse, but I have them here. Also the ring for which your Grace asked in vain at Lochleven——"

She put it triumphantly on her finger. It was not in her nature to bear a grudge. "Well done, Sir Robert. You have made ample amends. And welcome also, Sir Andrew. You were ever my friend. But what of your brother, James?"

"He is not with us, Madam," said Sir Andrew unhappily.

Mary sighed. "I did not expect it. But it is a sore thing to see families torn apart by my service. When I am on my throne once more it will be my task to heal these wounds. Sir Robert, I mean to inform my Council that my consent to the demission of my authority, the coronation of my son, and the regency of my brother Moray, was extorted from me under the threat of immediate death, while I was yet under age. You will endorse the truth of this?"

"I will, Madam," said Sir Robert. "Did I not see it done?"

And so the emergency Council which met at Hamilton House duly declared that the steps taken to deprive their sovereign lady of her crown and make the Earl of Moray Regent were both treasonable and void. A bond for her defence and restoration was signed by nine bishops, eight earls and eighteen lords; with a dozen abbots or priors and a hundred barons and lesser gentlemen. The thunder of their wrath against Moray and his confederates warmed Mary's heart. But the thought of bloodshed between Scots sickened her.

"Before you take the vengeance you propose, my lords," she said, "I would have my brother of Moray offered the chance of coming to terms. I ask only that he will recognise my authority and leave me free to reign with the husband of my choice."

But Lord Claud Hamilton was at once on his feet. "Madam, with all obedience, I declare that in my view any clemency of ours will but be taken for weakness. Unless we can now utterly crush your enemies, this will all be to do again."

Moray was at Glasgow, less than ten miles from the Queen's headquarters, when the news of her escape reached him, spreading such consternation among his supporters that many of them were prepared to compromise, even to surrender. But Moray knew that he had gone too far to retreat. " It would be certain ruin," he declared, echoing his enemies unawares. " Any signs of conciliation would be interpreted as weakness. Our only chance is to strike now, before Huntly can rouse the north. But I will not refuse the Queen's offer outright," he added. " While we appear to consider it, my messengers will have time to summon the reinforcements we shall need to defeat her."

And so, while Mary sought to curb the brash zeal of the Hamiltons, Moray summoned such allies as Morton, Lennox and Glencairn, and instructed the veteran soldier, Kirkcaldy of Grange to make all the dispositions for the battle by which his cause must stand or fall.

But Mary was still hoping to avoid a direct conflict. Lord Fleming held Dumbarton for her, and she believed that if she could take shelter there with her army, it should be possible to hold out till Bothwell was free to return. For, as Argyll wrangled with Lord Claud Hamilton, she was beginning to realise that the command of her army was in no certain hands. She was further encouraged to postpone hostilities by Queen Elizabeth's message of congratulation on her escape. If Mary would leave the decision to her, the English Queen promised, she would presently compel the Scottish rebels to recognise their rightful Queen's authority.

To Moray, therefore, it was evident that an immediate victory was essential. He had already experienced the English Queen's impatience with failure. And so, when Mary had persuaded the Hamiltons to move towards Dumbarton, he placed his own force between them and their objective, on the north side of the Clyde, which her army must cross.

As it became obvious that they would, after all, have to fight, the disputed leadership of the Queen's forces came to a head in a violent quarrel between Argyll and the Hamiltons, unexpectedly settled by Argyll's collapse after a seizure. Lord Claud Hamilton, now in command, jogged blandly towards Langside at the head of the royal army, unaware that Kirkcaldy of Grange had already anticipated his route, ambushing the narrow lane between cottage gardens down which his men must pass to reach the nearest ford. The royal vanguard was well in the trap when Grange gave the signal for such a demoralising crossfire that they were already in confusion when Morton, leading the main rebel body, which had crossed further down, crashed full on their flank. Now the lack of leadership began to take its ruinous toll. Men shouted themselves hoarse, performed prodigies of valour in half a dozen directions, only to lose track of friend and enemy in the all-eclipsing dust.

The Queen and her ladies, watching the crossing from a vantage point well to the rear, were at first unaware of the possibility of disaster and watched their troops defile as if to take part in a summer's day spectacle, to be followed by accolades and garlands. Mary herself was the first to realise, as the rattle of musketry, the clash of steel and the clouds of dust rolled up towards them from the lane in which her army had been engulfed, that something had gone wrong.

" Oh, Seton," she cried, beating her hands together, " if we had but the Duke here to-day! He would not charge about shouting, like these Hamiltons. Look, look, Lord Claud has led them straight into a trap! Oh, but they will rally. They must. Blessed Mother of God, if I could but fight like a man! "

" They will rally indeed, Madam," cried Janet Kennedy.

But they did not. The sinister swirl which indicated the first break in the royal ranks grew into a turmoil as riderless horses, and horseless fugitives were spewed out in a blood-stained stream. The issue hung in the balance for less than an hour. When Moray led the final charge, the morning, which had begun so brightly, seemed to darken as Mary saw her shattered army disintegrate before her unbelieving eyes.

Behind her, the lords in attendance stood appalled. Lord Herries was swearing softly, Lord Livingstone's face was ashen, while Lord Fleming shook his fists in helpless rage at the impossibility of conveying the Queen to the promised safety of Dumbarton's fortress. As they watched, confusion became a rout. Mary swung round, her face stony as if at the sight of Medusa, her voice broken with despair.

" My lords . . . can it . . . be all over ? "

" Maybe, for a while," Lord Livingstone growled. " And yet, worse defeats have been turned into victory at last."

Sickened by the rapid alternation of high hope and blackest misery, Mary cried: " Do not seek to humour me like a child, my lord. I am a fugitive in my own land. They will hunt me like a forest creature, the hounds' teeth bared for my throat. Have your pistols ready, my friends, for I swear by all in heaven above that I will not be taken alive and haled back to Lochleven."

" Come with me, your Grace," said Lord Herries urgently. " I can promise you the safety of the same glens in Galloway that sheltered the great Bruce. Scotland will surely rally to you as it did to him."

" I will come," the Queen cried, her voice wild as that of a curlew overhead.

" Madam, we also will ride with you," cried Mary Seton and Janet Kennedy, almost in the same breath.

" Into the wilderness ? "

" To the world's end."

" Make haste then, ladies," urged Lord Herries. But at the Queen's signal, horses were already being led forward, while George and Willie Douglas ran to untether their beasts, and the lords in attendance shouted for their grooms. Then, with a curt: "follow me, Madam," Lord Herries led the little party at a gallop towards the distant refuge of the rolling western hills.

It was a headlong journey, for they knew they must be pursued. Yet after the first daylight dash, they dared travel only by night, sleeping by day in their cloaks among the heather, thankful for a few oatmeal bannocks and a draught of sour milk at a cottage door. At any other time, Mary would have been delighted by the wild beauty of the western glens, and found the early summer nights in the saddle no hardship. But now, even the sight of Earlston Castle, the remotest of Bothwell's Border strongholds, reduced her to tears.

"We could take shelter there. You would sleep sounder, Madam, within stone walls," Lord Herries suggested.

Speechless, she shook her head. To make free with his possessions, now that all her hopes had been blighted, would be more than she could bear.

At Kenmure Castle, they were received by the Laird of Lochinvar, and next day they rode on to Kirkgunzeon. On the 15th of May, they reached the Herries headquarters at Terreagles, near Dumfries. There Mary might have remained, Lord Herries assured her, as long as she wished. But when she heard that fugitives from Langside had reached Dundrennan Abbey, she insisted on riding on. Perhaps the last news from the battlefield, she insisted, might be better than the first.

Instead, it was worse. Archbishop Hamilton and his weary companions told her that the disaster had been complete. Among the casualties were the names of so many of the men who had rejoiced with her in the great hall of Niddry Castle over her new freedom, that she could not check her tears. Lord Seton, gravely wounded, was a prisoner; Robert and Andrew Melville were both prisoners. She grew almost as pale, while she listened, as if her own blood were being drained from her by the wounds of her good friends.

As the mist seeps over the Border hills, the old melancholy

came upon her like a shroud, their voices reaching her, it seemed, from a great distance. She sat there silent, twisting the ring given her by Queen Elizabeth. It was a curious piece of workmanship. A diamond heart, made of two stones, was held between two hands of gold. Its whimsy was that the ring might be parted and sent from one friend to another at need. But in her weariness, Mary could not find the trick of unscrewing it, though she persisted, obsessed by the fancy that success might be an omen. If only she knew whether she dared trust Elizabeth . . .

" We shall do well enough here in the west," Lord Herries was saying.

" Supplies and reinforcements will without doubt be sent to us from France," added his son.

But Mary sat among them like a ghost, her face blank, her fingers ceaselessly fretting at the Queen of England's ring. At last they realised her to be beyond their consolation. Like a sleepwalker she rose and allowed herself to be escorted to her chamber.

Left behind, the lords looked at each other in dismay. Could her misfortunes have affected her reason? Each avoided his companions' eyes as he remembered her father's collapse, twenty-five years before, after the defeat of Solway Moss.

" Her Grace is but wearied to death," said Lord Herries defiantly, voicing their fears even as he denied them. " She will be very different in the morning."

But even he was astonished by the change in her next day. She had spent the night at the home of his Maxwell kinsfolk nearby, from which she emerged to attend the Council meeting she had summoned in the Abbey. She was even paler, if possible, than the night before, but she bore herself as proudly as if she were in the presence of the entire nobility of her kingdom, instead of a few fugitives and a huddle of frightened monks in a forsaken abbey at the end of the world. As she took her place at the head of the table in the improvised

Council Chamber at the Guest House, her gracious gesture seemed to acknowledge the homage of all the three Estates of her realm, in their fairest silks and velvets, assembled in Parliament Hall. But her first words swept formality aside.

"My friends," she said, leaning a little forward, as if to take them all into her confidence, while her sudden smile broke their hearts with its courage, "My mind is made up. I shall go to England."

They could not believe it. Nor could they realise the impossibility of dissuading her from her purpose. They fell on their knees before her; they urged, implored, and insisted that she should change her mind. She still smiled; but they found it as impossible to change her purpose as it had been to comfort her father.

"It is all arranged," she told them. "When I found the trick of the ring again, I knew what I must do."

"The ring?" They were bewildered.

"The Queen of England's ring," she told them patiently. "It is a token of her friendship. If ever I needed her assistance, I was to send her one half and retain the other. My lords, early this morning I discovered how to take the ring apart. It was like a sign from heaven. At once I despatched a messenger to my dearest sister, with news of my distress and a request for safe conduct into her royal presence——"

She broke off, her lips trembling. James, who loved all heroic gestures, would have understood, and the knowledge that they did not made her long for him so sharply that she could have cried aloud.

"Madam," groaned Lord Herries, "this is madness. I beseech you, if you must leave Scotland, to go to France."

She shook her head violently. "No, not to France."

To go to France would be but to step out of one nightmare into another. How could she, who had been Queen, return as a subject, submit to the whiplash tongue of the mother-in-law who had never been able to hide her dislike of the young wife whom her eldest son had adored? It would be different if she went to England. Had not her royal cousin Elizabeth sent her warmest congratulations on her escape, and promised to see that her rebellious subjects returned to their obedience?

" I beseech you, Madam," urged Archbishop Hamilton, " not to trust the word of such a woman as Elizabeth of England."

" My lord," she rebuked him, " she is also my sister Queen."

" You are not to be turned from this course by any words of ours? " said Lord Livingstone.

" No, my lord. How shall I remain in Scotland, where I know not whom to trust? "

Their stricken faces reproached her, but in her desolation she was scarcely aware of what she had said. In the hollow silence which followed they could hear the young lambs bleating on the hillside beyond the Abbey's bounds.

" If you are bent on this course," said Lord Herries at last, " will you permit me to write to the Deputy-Governor of Carlisle asking permission for you to cross the Border and assurance of your safety in England? "

" Write, my lord, by all means," she said graciously.

But she would not wait for the return of the messenger. It was as if her ordeal at Lochleven had so turned her against her brother and his confederates that she would take any risk rather than that of being recaptured. And before her still, wavering like a mirage in sunlight, rose the distant prospect of the English crown, to which, as far back as she could remember, she had been taught that she had a better right than her cousin Elizabeth. Admittedly, the Queen of England could scarcely be expected to take that crown from her own head and offer it to her exiled guest. But surely she would cherish that exile as her successor? It would scarcely suit her Majesty of England, to put her motives at their lowest, to see a precedent established for subjects to de-throne their rulers with impunity. The last thought made her smile, for an instant, as wryly as James had ever done. They still argued, but they could not turn her.

At last Lord Herries said in despair: " Madam, since we

cannot persuade you to remain with us, we can at least prepare to share your journey."

" I will not have you make such a sacrifice," she said. But the immediate assent of those about her brought the quick tears again to her eyes.

" We are no more to be turned from our purpose than you from yours, Madam," said Lord Herries. And once again those present echoed him. " We need only decide the best way of setting about it. It is still possible, I believe, to take ship from the Abbey Burnfoot, though their trade is but a shadow of that in the old days."

So it was arranged. But Mary was puzzled by the sense of unreality which came upon her once the decision had been fairly taken. Could she have died, after all, at Langside? Was it only her unsubstantial ghost which heard Mass for the last time in Scotland before riding down the grassy track to the Abbey Burnfoot? She found it quite impossible to keep her mind on what awaited her. Instead, her thoughts doubled back into the past, like conies sheltering vainly from the march of harvesting sickles, so that their arrival on the bleak shore took her sharply by surprise.

The waves of the incoming tide sent the grey-black cobbles rattling against each other like dead men's bones, and the grey swell of the sea was fretted with greyer squalls. Men were bringing the clumsy fishing-boat to the weed-hung jetty as they arrived, and the little party went at once aboard. With Lord Herries and Lord Fleming came Lord and Lady Livingstone, Lord Boyd, Mary Seton and Janet Kennedy, with George and Willie Douglas close behind. But the Archbishop of St. Andrews had decided not to desert his responsibilities in Scotland, such as they still were. And yet, at the very last moment, he plunged into the sea after the departing boat, to clutch the gunwale and implore the Queen to return.

" Madam, if you are lost to Scotland, all we hope for, here and hereafter, must be at an end."

Out of her anaesthetising dream she surveyed his anxious,

ignoble face as he stumbled among the cobbles, resisting the undertow. When she sought for words with which to reassure him, the motto she had so often embroidered on cloth of state or coat-of-arms came to her mind. The high hopes she had brought to Scotland might be in ruins, the man she loved an exile, those she had trusted untrue. But it was typical of her to believe, even now, in the desperate expedient. It had so often succeeded, against what had seemed impossible odds. She refused to believe it would fail now. Might it not be at the very point where one kingdom rejected her that her conquest of another began? The thought blazed like wildfire across the despairing darkness of her mind as she shook her head at the archbishop.

" Say rather, ' *In my End is my Beginning,*' my lord."

She was smiling, transfigured as by a sense of the bitterness of death surmounted, as she turned her face towards the alien sea.

EPILOGUE

February, 1587

EPILOGUE

KNOCK, knock, knock. . . .
The bitter darkness of the winter night still held the countryside. But already the prophecies of cockcrow splintered it with stars of light as the Queen's exhausted ladies roused her for the last time.

"You must dress me as for a festival," she had commanded them the night before. "We will essay the gown of black brocaded satin, with the train, presently. It will need letting out a little, I believe. The petticoats of crimson velvet should serve, however. With them I shall wear the crimson sleeves. The white lawn of my coif must be freshly wired and the veil made fast. Set aside my shoes of Spanish leather, the watchet hose clocked with silver, and underclothes conforming. My other garments, saving these only, I will distribute among you when my Will is made."

They tried to remember her least instructions as they struggled with frozen fingers to light every candle they possessed. The little flames could at first scarcely thrust aside the darkness, but while they toiled about their mistress the eastern sky grew livid as the face of a corpse. As eight o'clock approached each sound on the stairs or from the passage below checked their hearts with fear.

Only their Queen's composure shamed their fumbling hands and streaming eyes as she returned from her devotions to complete the letter to the young King of France which she had largely written the night before. This morning her fingers were so stiff that Janet Kennedy had to fold them about the quill, and her hand moved laboriously across the parchment as she commended all her faithful servants to his care and concluded without a tremor:

" The morning of my death, this Wednesday, 8th February, Marie R."

She laid the quill down beside the letter and turned towards her attendants. The ladies of her bedchamber had gladly admitted her physician with the cup of mulled wine and fingers of toast he had prescribed. But what were they to do with all the lesser folk now crowding after him through the doorway: her butler, pantler, valet, apothecary and all the kitchen servants who would not be denied? The Queen herself beckoned them forwards, each kneeling as she stooped to say farewell. Then, as the last of the kitchen lads sobbingly raised her hand to his lips, she checked their lamentations with a gesture.

" My friends, I have finished with the world. Let us kneel and pray together for the last time."

When they rose, the High Sheriff was standing silently behind them, his white wand of office shaking in his hand, his distaste for his task obvious.

" Madam, the Lords have sent for you."

Behind him loomed the impassive figures of Sir Amyas Paulet and the Earl of Kent, ready to overcome any attempt at resistance. But their authority was not required. As the Queen stepped forward, her little dog, unseen, at her heels, the chamber door closed on those servants who had been forbidden to accompany her. She had been allowed to choose half-a-dozen, among them Janet Kennedy, who had been with her through all her troubles, and Sir Andrew Melville, detained from his duties during the last dreadful days, who now fell on his knees before her as she was supported down the stairs by two of Paulet's servants. Tears were streaming down his face as she greeted him.

" Madam," he said brokenly, " this is the sorest duty that has ever been laid upon me, save only that of carrying such news back to Scotland."

For the first time that day the Queen's composure faltered.

To comfort him she must speak from her very heart. Laying her hands on his shoulders, she stooped and kissed him.

"Weep not, Melville, my good and faithful servant," she said gently. "Rejoice rather that to-day thou shalt see the end of Mary Stuart's troubles. I am Catholic, thou Protestant, yet there is one Christ for us all . . ."

"Madam, my officers must do their duty," said Sir Amyas Paulet.

"Then let us go."

She laid her hand on Sir Andrew Melville's arm, and forced herself to take step after painful step, aware of irrelevant images drifting across the mind she sought to keep steadfastly turned heavenwards, as of tiny puff-ball clouds that briefly shadowed the face of the sun. From time to time her lips moved silently.

"*In te, Domine, speravi* . . ."

She heard the high, excited laughter of the four little girls who had raced behind her through the splendours of the royal palace at St. Germain-en-Laye, the grating voice of Catherine de Medici as she reproved the exuberance of "notre petite reinette d'Ecosse . . ."

She saw John Knox's angry, sick eagle eyes; Lethington's crooked smile as he watched his monkey take a sweetmeat in its tiny fingers; Darnley's face blotched with measles; Bothwell stooping to lift her palfrey's hoof, his hair the very russet of last year's bracken in the Perthshire glen; the puckered crimson of her new-born son's face as he lay in the crook of her arm . . .

These things were past. So Henry had said when the Prince was born. Then let them go, she had replied. Now all were gone. All, or nearly all. . . . But they should not have torn down her cloth of state, the royal arms of Scotland ablaze with scarlet and gold.

"*In my End is my Beginning* . . ."

But who could ever have guessed how strange that end would be? When the English lawyers declared it proven beyond all reasonable doubt that she had conspired to bring about the Queen of England's death she had denied it passionately. How could she have plotted the death of the Queen of England when she, Mary Stuart, was England's only rightful Queen? Every Catholic believed it. The death of Elizabeth Tudor, excommunicate heretic, would have been quite another matter. Had not His Holiness assured the faithful that his anathema conferred special merit on such a deed? She herself would die, not as a criminal, but as a martyr. She must remember that. Only that. A martyr for the holy Catholic faith . . .

" *In my End* . . ."

The ushers swung back the doors of the great hall. Within, she saw the black-draped scaffold, the brooding, bare-armed executioners, the axe, the block. Beyond them, silent and motionless, stood the men who had convicted her. And the impact of their hostility was like a blow between the eyes.

She paused, to get her breath indeed, but also to impose her dedicated will on her shrinking body's horror, so that she might make the ultimate surrender now demanded. And in that instant the dregs of vanity and petulance, all bitterness, anger and fear, were reduced to ashes by such a conflagration of sheer spirit that only love and courage remained. Exalted far beyond controversy, her acceptance of the death imposed on her transfigured it into the liberation for which she had so long prayed, laboured and conspired in vain.

" *In manus tuas, Domine* . . ."

The procession moved slowly forward into the great hall.

SOME BOOKS CONSULTED

BAIN, J.: Calendar of the State Papers relating to Mary, Queen of Scots. H.M. Register House, Edinburgh.

COULTON, G. G.: Five Centuries of Religion. Vol. 4. Cambridge University Press.

COWAN: Mary, Queen of Scots. Samson Low.

GOODALL, W.: Examination of the Letters of Mary, Queen of Scots. 2 Vols. Ruddiman.

GORE-BROWNE, R.: Lord Bothwell. Collins.

HENDERSON, T. F.: The Casket Letters. A. & C. Black.

Inventaires de la Royne d'Escosse. Bannantyne Club.

J.F.N.: Mary Stuart and the Casket Letters. Edmonston and Douglas.

MACGIBBON, D., AND ROSS, T.: Castellated and Domestic Architecture of Scotland. 4 Vols. Douglas.

MACKENZIE, A. M.: The Scotland of Queen Mary. Maclehose.

MACMILLAN, W.: The Worship of the Scottish Reformed Church. Clarke.

MAHON, MAJ.-GEN. R. H.: The Tragedy of Kirk o' Field. Cambridge University Press.

MUIR, E.: John Knox. Cape.

NAU, C.: History of Mary Stewart. Paterson.

NEALE, J. E.: Queen Elizabeth. Cape.

PARRY, SIR E.: The Persecution of Mary Stewart. Cassell.

PITCAIRN: Criminal Trials in Scotland.

SKELTON: Maitland of Lethington. 2 Vols. Blackwood.

STEUART, F. (editor): Memoirs of Sir James Melville of Halhill. Routledge.

STRICKLAND, A.: Letters of Mary, Queen of Scots. 2 Vols. Cockburn.

STRICKLAND, A.: Queens of Scotland. Vols. 3–7. Blackwood.

TYTLER, R. F.: History of Scotland. Vols. 6 and 7. Tait.

ZWEIG, S.: The Queen of Scots. Cassell.